Delightful . . . Heart-Pounding . . .
Sexy . . . Unforgettable . . .

Savor "romance at its finest" (*New York Times*
bestselling author Liz Carlyle) in these
acclaimed novels from Meredith Duran!

LUCK BE A LADY
RT Book Reviews Top Pick

"Flawless novel. . . . These intelligent, multilayered characters embody the best aspects of this wonderfully indulgent
series."

—*Publishers Weekly*, starred review

"Well-paced, simmering with sexual tension and peopled
with memorable characters, this is a love story to be savored."
—*RT Book Reviews*

LADY BE GOOD
RT Book Reviews Top Pick

"*Lady Be Good* has extraordinary characters plus enthralling
developments."

—*Single Titles*

"Romance, passion, heartbreak, excitement, suspense, and
a stellar resolution . . . *Lady Be Good* packs an emotional
wallop!"

—*Fresh Fiction*

MEREDITH DURAN

A LADY'S CODE OF MISCONDUCT

Delhi

Pocket Books
An Imprint of Simon & Schuster, Inc.
1230 Avenue of the Americas
New York, NY 10020

This book is a work of fiction. Any references to historical events, real people, or real places are used fictitiously. Other names, characters, places, and events are products of the author's imagination, and any resemblance to actual events or places or persons, living or dead, is entirely coincidental.

First Pocket Books paperback edition March 2017

POCKET and colophon are registered trademarks of Simon & Schuster, Inc.

For information about special discounts for bulk purchases, please contact Simon & Schuster Special Sales at 1-866-506-1949 or business@simonandschuster.com.

The Simon & Schuster Speakers Bureau can bring authors to your live event. For more information or to book an event, contact the Simon & Schuster Speakers Bureau at 1-866-248-3049 or visit our website at www.simonspeakers.com.

Manufactured in the United States of America

10 9 8 7 6 5 4 3 2 1

ISBN 978-1-5011-3902-4
ISBN 978-1-5011-3903-1 (ebook)

To Joyce Littell, a teacher who not only revitalized my love of school but told me I would certainly grow up to be a writer. In dedicating this book to you, I at last fulfill the secret vow I made on the final day of the sixth grade. It's long overdue.

ACKNOWLEDGMENTS

Thanks to Lauren McKenna, Elana Cohen, Melissa Gramstad, Marla Daniels, and everyone else who makes Pocket feel like home; to Holly Root, S. J. Kincaid, and Janine Ballard for advice, feedback, and encouragement; to my husband, Matt, for his creativity, humor, empathy, and general perfection; and to family and friends for humoring me through another round of fevered research, late-night writing binges, and random digressions on parliamentary politics which you all graciously pretended to find fascinating.

A
LADY'S
CODE
OF
MISCONDUCT

CHAPTER ONE

February 1860

The first sensation was light. Red, the color of hellfire.

Then . . . weight. Weight compressing and lifting. Squeezing and relaxing.

Breathing. Air. *Nose-throat-chest.* A body—flesh, his own, his mind anchored within it.

He flexed his fingers.

"Look!" The soft voice startled him. It came from nearby. "Did you see that? His hand . . ."

Girlish voice. Recognition sifted through him, thinning the murk. He felt himself settling more deeply into this body. Pillow cradling his skull. His toes, trapped by smothering weight. *Blanket.* The air scratched in his nostrils. Smell of . . . soap.

"Open your eyes," whispered the girl.

His eyes! Yes, he could open them.

The light was scalding. So bright! He could not bear it.

"Go fetch your mother." A new voice, hoarse, masculine. "Go!"

Hurried footsteps. Floorboards groaning. Slam of a door.

A vise closed on his fingers, crushing them. "Crispin. Open your eyes. Now."

He knew this voice. It was the voice of command, of expectations. It was the voice of disappointment, but he had always tried to answer it, to prove himself worthy.

He forced open his eyes, braving the glare.

His father gazed down at him. Face deeply lined. Rheumy eyes, shining strangely.

A tear plummeted, splashing Crispin's chin.

Later. Much later. Or only minutes. Surfacing from deep sucking darkness. Exhausted, bone weary, so hot.

The light had gone. Square stamps of darkness filled the windows. A low fire revealed the contours of the room. A man, gray-haired, with pitted cheeks, slept nearby in a settee, his limbs contorted, slumped at an angle that guaranteed a backache tomorrow. The woman beside him, who nestled into his shoulder—her eyes were open, fastened on Crispin's.

She blinked rapidly, then eased straight. "Can you hear me?"

What an odd question. He cleared his throat. Searched for his voice. "Yes, Mother."

She reached for her husband's arm, squeezing silently until he started awake, rubbed his eyes, saw what she had seen.

The wrongness registered on Crispin then. This bedroom—he knew it. It belonged in his parents' London townhouse. But a Gainsborough now hung in place of the still life. The carpet was the wrong shade. And his parents . . .

They looked shrunken. Hollow-cheeked, aged.

He pushed upright. His head exploded.

Time skipped then. He was flat on his back, gasping. His parents were hovering over him, caught in the middle of an argument.

"—call the doctor back at once," said his mother. "Let *him* decide."

"No. I am going to wake him."

Crispin took a strained breath. "What happened?" he asked.

Their relief was almost comical—wide-eyed, gaping. But they both fell silent. Some charged look passed between them. His mother laid her hand over his.

"You've been ill," she said.

That much was clear. He tried to remember . . . anything. But recent days felt hazy. The tour through Italy? No, there had been much more after that. Studies with the German tutor? They felt very distant. He was missing something. But he felt sure he should be in Cambridge, cramming for the exam. "Why am I here?"

The question had a peculiar effect. His mother's grip slipped away. She retreated a pace from the bed. "Oh, Crispin." Her voice was clogged with tears.

"A fine question," his father bit out. "Should we pretend to be strangers, then? Your goddamned stubbornness—"

"Stop it," his mother choked.

Strangers? Crispin's bafflement redoubled, pulsing in time to the ache in his head. The agony was . . . exquisite.

He felt for the source of it, moving gingerly, groping

across his own skull. *What on earth?* A patch of hair had been denuded. It was growing back short and bristly. The stubble covered a thick gash, as though he'd been axed.

"What happened?" He heard fear in his own voice now, but for God's sake—"How long have I been here?"

"Five days," his father said. "But we can see you off by morning if that is your preference."

"Stop it!" His mother loosed a sob. "I won't have it—"

The door banged open. In came his sister. God above! She had brought a young woman with her, a stranger— here, to his sickbed!

"Awake again!" With a dazzling smile, Charlotte drew the other girl forward. "I promised you, didn't I? Look, Jane! I promised you."

Charlotte was beaming, oblivious to her own lunacy in showing off her invalid brother like an animal at the zoo.

At least the other girl looked properly mortified. She stared at Crispin mutely, her great brown eyes seeming to plead with him, perhaps to save her from his family's madness.

Crispin cast an amazed glance at his parents, waiting for them to scold Charlotte, to escort this stranger out.

But they said nothing. They looked grim, resigned. Indeed, his father's expression was all too familiar—the tense, dour face of a man disappointed too often to be surprised by it. "We should give them a moment of privacy," he muttered to Crispin's mother, and then pushed and prodded the others toward the door.

Surely they were not serious! "Wait," he said—but the door closed, leaving him alone with the stranger, who looked as miserable as he felt.

A strange fragment of laughter fell out of him. It made the girl flinch, for which he felt a flicker of regret, but really, what else was there to do but laugh? He had woken into a nightmare. The room changed, his parents changed. Only the main themes remained constant: their disapproval and disappointment. His inability to please them.

At least his brother hadn't appeared to condemn him. "Madam," he began awkwardly, but she interrupted him.

"Listen," she said. "I know you must be confused. But I promise you, I can explain."

He stared at her. She spoke as though they knew each other. He had never seen her before in his life. She did not look like the kind of fashionable, flashy beauty that Charlotte usually befriended. Her prettiness was quiet, easily overlooked. Her dark eyes held mossy hints of green and gold. The muted lilac and jet of her walking dress, the modest neckline and minimal trimming, could have passed for half mourning.

Yet she had offered to explain, and he would gladly take that offer. Besides, the resolute set of her square jaw, the levelness of her gaze, and her cool voice seemed . . . steadying. An air of authority surrounded her.

"Go ahead, then," he said.

"Everyone thought you would die."

Shock lashed through him. "How charming," he said—aiming for dryness, failing with a cough.

"Your injuries were grave." She sounded insistent, as though he had argued with her. "And you were . . . asleep . . . for five days. Nobody could help you. The doctors told your family not to hope."

Her pause seemed to suggest that he would find this sufficient. "And? Go on."

She opened her mouth, then seemed to falter. Her gaze broke from his to wander the room, a certain desperate haste to her survey, as though she were looking for something better to discuss.

But when she met his eyes again, she took a deep breath and said in a resigned tone, "And so I thought it a perfect solution. Besides, the archbishop had heard the rumors—he knew you weren't expected to live."

The *archbishop*? She was babbling. He felt exhausted again and leaned back into the pillows to close his eyes. *This is a dream,* he told himself. *A nightmare, that's all.*

"Mr. Burke." Her voice came from very close now. It shook. "Please. We can undo it. You mustn't believe I meant to cross you!"

He opened his eyes and she flinched.

Why, this girl was *afraid* of him.

He struggled to hide how disturbed he was. He knew his family often believed the worst of him, but until now, he had not imagined the world did so as well. "Who are you?"

"Who am I? I'm . . . Are you joking?"

"My sense of humor is not so poor as that," he said. "Who are you? How do you know me?"

The color drained from her face. "I . . ." Her lips opened and closed. "I'm Jane," she said unsteadily. "And you . . ." Her indrawn breath sounded ragged. "You, Crispin, are my husband."

CHAPTER TWO

Three months earlier

*B*ullies like her cousin had an animal instinct, a gift for sensing rebellion. Archibald had stolen Jane's needlepoint six days ago. She had woken to find her embroidery frame empty, all the threads neatly sliced. Ten months of work, gone.

Jane could guess what had happened. Archie had got some new toy from the inventor, a marching monkey with bladed claws. After Archie set the monkey loose in the drawing room and left scratch marks on the furniture, Aunt Mary had furiously told him to put the machine to work on his own things.

Instead, he'd picked Jane's.

Archie had the hobbies of a child raised by wolves—dangerous toys, mean pranks. But he was twenty-two years old, only ten months younger than Jane, and he wasn't stupid. He would have paused to look at the embroidery after his monkey tore it free. He would have recognized the chance for a new lark.

For six days, then, Jane had waited for Archie's

ambush. But he bided his time until tonight, when company gathered at Marylebigh.

It was a frosty November evening, and a fire leapt in the great Jacobean hearth of the drawing room. Jane's aunt sat nearby it with the Countess of Elborough and Archibald, while Uncle Philip gathered at a short remove with his political cronies—Lord Elborough and Crispin Burke, a Member of Parliament like her uncle.

Jane, as usual, took the window seat in the corner. Her late mother would have scolded her for sitting so far apart from the others, and for ignoring their conversation in favor of a patch of canvas she was stitching without design or care. Her parents had expected her to listen carefully, to think deeply, and to offer her opinions with poised confidence.

But her aunt and uncle, who had become her guardians after her parents' death, took a different view. In company, they expected Jane to hold her tongue and look shy. She was the golden goose, after all, whose inheritance funded this household. Treasures were not paraded brazenly before those who might covet them. Eligible gentlemen, in particular, were not invited to Marylebigh—save Crispin Burke, of course, but he did not signify. For all his breeding, he was no gentleman.

Jane did not mind the window seat. It made an ideal spot from which to eavesdrop on her uncle. He was arguing with Mr. Burke, in a rare show of discord. It seemed like a gift from the heavens, really, for this was the last chance Jane would have to witness such quarrels. By tomorrow, she intended to be in London, free at last.

But her escape had to be secret. She was biding her time this evening, giving nobody cause to notice her.

"The French aren't building their battle fleet for show," Uncle Philip said hotly. Mr. Burke had been needling him about his support for the prime minister, who wanted to spend a fortune to reinforce Britain's coastal defenses. "Besides, it's a damned embarrassment, the state of our naval bases. A child could penetrate them."

"Goodness," said Mr. Burke. He was a tall, dark man, unjustly attractive, who spoke and moved and shredded men's ideas with a languid, careless confidence that was probably inherited—his father was a viscount, his maternal grandfather a duke. "A child could do it?" He cast a dubious glance toward Archie, her uncle's heir, who was picking his nails with a distracted smirk. "Not any child, surely."

Her uncle scowled. "You were with me on this," he said. "I *will* have your support in committee."

Burke adjusted his posture, a lazy roll of his shoulders as he retrieved his port. "You'll have it. But not because I lie awake at night riven with dread over a French invasion. Half a million pounds are earmarked for the improvements, and your friend the inventor will win the bid. Very well." He lifted his glass. "To profit—your personal deity."

Jane inwardly snorted. Had her uncle prayed to profit, then Jane herself would have been treated as a goddess, not kept in the corner and ignored.

Her uncle was flushing. "Marlowe is *your* friend as well, I believe."

"No." Burke drank. "My friends at present are a small and select company: those who can help with the penal bill."

Uncle Philip twisted his mouth. "Marlowe has offered to help fund that campaign, too. He owns half the newspaper editors in the north—"

"I do not want him involved."

"So the *party* is to finance the whole of it? That's a pretty idea—"

Burke's glass slammed down, and the entire room froze. Jane was suddenly aware of how much taller he was than her uncle—or, for that matter, any other man in the room. Archibald had yet to look up from his nails, but Lord Elborough shrank into himself and pretended to be invisible.

"Listen well," Burke said in a cold, clear voice. "The *party* will pay whatever it takes. The *party* will do what I say. As will the men we've purchased from the opposition. They are bought and sold; the deal is done. That bill *will* be carried."

Bought and sold! Burke spoke of men like cattle at the market. He was not only ruthless, but amoral to boot.

Her uncle's jaw worked, chewing over his next words for a long, red-faced moment. "It will carry," he said roughly. "But by God, Burke, it will take a *decade* to see the profits from that bill that will come in a *year* from the defense works."

"Happy news, then: you'll have no worries for your retirement."

"I was never worried," her uncle retorted.

A curious smile curved Burke's full lips. "No, of course not," he said smoothly—and then his cold, dark glance flicked to Jane's, startling her so badly that she flinched.

For the briefest moment, he, too, looked startled. Then his eyes narrowed, shrewd and probing.

She looked quickly back to her needlepoint, cursing herself for having been caught listening. That was not her role. Her conspicuous inattention, her obvious disinterest, were what made the others so loose lipped around her.

From the corner of her eye, she saw Archibald stand. He looked around, scrubbing his head like a man risen dazedly from a nap, then went bounding from the room.

Satisfaction purled through her. He was going for the embroidery. She *knew* it.

"At any rate," Burke went on, "the profits are all yours. The penal bill will bring down the government. That is my only concern."

The Earl of Elborough spoke at last, his voice timid. "But if Palmerston steps down, then what becomes of his plan for the defense works?"

Her uncle snorted. "Didn't you know? Burke here means to step in as prime minister. He will see it through."

God save the country, Jane thought. Such ruthlessness, wedded to such power—she shuddered to imagine it.

"And he will remember his friends," her uncle added in a low, ominous voice. "*Assuming* one makes that list."

"The list will be very predictable," Burke said with a shrug. "It will include any man who helped to carry the penal bill."

"I was always in favor of the penal bill," her uncle said. "I helped draft the bloody thing, didn't I? I only wish you would spare a few thoughts for how to *pay* for your ambitions."

"That's *your* job," Burke drawled.

"Look here!" Archibald cried as he came back into the room. "I have a surprise for you all." He took center stage in front of the fire as he lifted a folded bundle of cloth. "A great entertainment."

Jane hid a dark smile. Though the room did not know it, her embroidery was about to deliver them a fitting farewell.

"Oh dear," said Aunt Mary. She was blond, very thin, patrician looking; she had mastered the eternally amused demeanor of a woman bred to privilege, though her family was no better born than her husband's. "We were doing very well without your help, Archibald."

"But this is art," Archie sneered, and unfurled the embroidery—struggling a little to hold it out wide. It had taken ten months, after all.

Lady Elborough gasped. Somebody coughed. Aunt Mary, turning a peculiar shade of green, tried a titter. "Good heavens," she said. "What on earth *is* that?"

"Jane's fancywork," Archibald said.

"Always sewing," Aunt Mary said nervously. "Our little angel of the house."

Lady Elborough rose and slowly approached the piece. Jane found her troubled expression quite fascinating. The others were doing so well to gaze upon the work blandly.

Nobody dared look at Jane, of course.

Save Crispin Burke. His sardonic gaze delved through the shadows, finding hers and holding.

She fluttered her lashes and ducked her head, as though abashed.

When she dared to peek up through her lashes, he was still watching. He offered her a slow-growing smile, somehow unkind.

To her own annoyance, Jane felt herself flush. She picked up her needlework again. The nice thing about

being a wraith was that nobody expected her to account
for herself. That would, after all, require her to have a
brain, which everybody very much hoped she did not.

"But I don't understand," said Lady Elborough, bewildered. "This is . . . Is this *you*, Mr. Mason? Here, in
the middle?"

Jane stabbed her needle through the canvas. *Obviously*
it was her uncle. His brown beard was unmistakable.

"Oh, I think not," her uncle said gruffly. "Why, surely
it is a likeness of our savior! See the blood in his palms?"

"Yes . . ." Lady Elborough did not sound convinced.
"But if this is Jesus Christ, then who is this . . . dark man
at his elbow?"

"That's Burke!" Archibald crowed. "See? You can tell
by the ruby on his finger!"

"Archie," hissed Aunt Mary.

Lady Elborough was squinting. "Does he have *horns*?"

"Oh no," said Uncle Philip hastily. "Why, I believe
that is simply an illusion caused by the . . . the smoke
rising behind their two figures."

"But what do the flames mean, surrounding them?"
Lady Elborough's words pitched higher now, tighter.
"And why are they standing on all those poor children?"

"Jane." Her uncle's voice lashed like a whip. "Will
you explain this bizarre piece, please, lest Lady Elborough misinterpret it?"

No better proof of victory than being summoned to
speak! Jane laid aside her embroidery frame and rose,
locking her hands at her waist and gazing meekly at the
carpet. "Of course, Uncle. It is a tribute to your great
political work."

"Politics! Is that quite the proper subject for fancywork?" asked Lord Elborough.

"Her needlework is very poor," Aunt Mary said hurriedly. "Her parents neglected her education—"

"Give me that!" Her uncle snatched the piece from Archibald and chucked it into the fire. The bulge-eyed glare he turned on her promised retribution.

Jane pulled a shocked face. "I'm so sorry. I never thought— The fire, you see, was meant to represent the struggle for justice, in the ancient Greek tradition."

Silence fell, thick with disbelief.

"She is slow," Aunt Mary muttered to Lady Elborough, who nodded, her expression collapsing into pity.

A choked sound came from Mr. Burke. The fire was licking over the canvas, finding poor purchase, smoking as it singed the silk floss. Burke rose in one lithe, powerful movement, as if on springs. "Excuse me," he managed, and coughed as he strode out.

"Go to your room," snapped Aunt Mary to Jane. "Look through your magazines for some pleasant pattern to copy, or you will not sew at all."

"Yes, Aunt."

As Jane hurried out, she heard her aunt say, "Archibald, fetch down that monkey," which made Jane swallow a laugh. Truly, her aunt must be desperate for a distraction to call down such trouble willingly. "We are great friends with Mr. Marlowe, you know, the inventor. He has made the most cunning device . . ."

In the hallway, Burke stood leaning against the wall, his face hidden in his forearm, his shoulders jerking.

Good. Jane hoped he choked on the smoke. She picked up her skirts and walked faster toward the stairs. Illusion of horns, ha! Burke was the devil. Her uncle supplied the money for Burke's political career. (*Her* money.) Burke supplied the breeding and connections that her uncle required for his own campaigns. Monsters, both of them.

Her heel squeaked on the first step. Burke obviously heard it, for he called after her. "Miss Mason."

She laid a hand on the banister and continued to climb, pretending to be deaf.

"Jane Mason," came his low purr, much closer. "Where do you think you're going?"

His question startled her into halting. In all the years he had consorted with her uncle, paying calls at Marylebigh in the off-season to plan for the parliamentary sessions ahead, he had never addressed her so intimately.

He'd never addressed her at all, in fact, save when formalities called for it. That he should break form tonight, of all nights, seemed alarming.

She took a deep breath and turned, careful to hunch a little, to keep her chin tucked. She knew how her uncle's cronies viewed her: a dusty bauble, deliberately kept on the shelf, lest her fortune be transferred to a husband. Cloistered, buried alive in the countryside. She was twenty-three, and she had never had a season.

"Yes, Mr. Burke?" she whispered.

He looked up at her from the base of the stairs, a position that should have given her the advantage, allowing her to feel as though she looked down her nose.

But he was tall, lean, broad shouldered. He managed to loom even when standing a foot beneath her. And the wicked smile on his face shifted his angular features to their best advantage, emphasizing the Viking broadness of his cheekbones, the masculine squareness of his jaw. His dark eyes glittered unusually. He looked . . .

Amused. He had been laughing, not coughing!

"You're clever," he said. "I didn't realize that."

What a pity. Her only aim had been to amuse herself. "Thank you," she said in a deliberately confused tone. "I'm so clumsy with a needle. How mortifying that everyone should know it!"

His hair was black and glossy; from this high vantage, it looked thick enough to grab in great handfuls. She'd like to try it, and yank *very* hard. What an unfeeling monster he was with this penal reform bill he'd drafted! "Yes, you should take care," he agreed. "Who knows what else you've proved clumsy with?"

She took a step backward. That sounded like a threat.

"Fine advice," she said breathlessly. "I'm ever so grateful for it."

"Are you?" His full lips tipped to a peculiar angle, not quite a smile. "Then here's more advice: go to bed early tonight."

Her heart jumped. There was no way he could know. She'd been so careful! "Why do you say so?"

As his smile faded, she had the impression of a mask falling over him, though his handsome face never revealed anything useful. "Sleep profits a young woman's beauty," he said, his mockery light but clear. "And every girl wishes to be a beautiful bride."

She clenched her teeth. "But I am not engaged, Mr. Burke."

"Oh?" He lifted one dark brow. "Your uncle tells a different story. And Archibald, just now—was he not beaming with pleasure over his future wife's work?"

They could not force her to marry Archie.

She would not give them a chance.

She managed a wide smile. "Then perhaps I am

wrong," she said. "My uncle does know best. And I will take your advice, Mr. Burke. Good evening to you."

She turned and continued up the stairs, ears straining for the sound of his retreat. But she heard no footsteps. He remained where he was, watching her until she crested the staircase. Her skin prickled; she shivered, but did not look back.

A driving rain was churning the garden into mud. The woods beyond huddled like dark monsters, limbs whipping, leaves hissing. Jane sprinted toward them.

Six years she had waited, prayed, deliberated, stewed. For six years she had kept meekly obedient, in penance for those first months in which she'd known no better, and had spoken her mind without fear.

Six years was long enough to fool anyone. Her family had forgotten she was capable of rebellion. They would not check on her for hours yet.

Only once she reached the country lane did Jane slow down. Her heart was drumming, her mouth full of rainwater. She spat her mouthful into the road. *Not ladylike.* Ha! She'd never been a lady. Never allowed to go into society. She would follow her own code.

Thunder cracked in the distance; lightning lit the roiling clouds. The night was wild, and it sang to her. *Free, yes, at last!* A warm cloak and wool-lined boots were all she carried. Money wasn't required—or wouldn't be, soon enough. She was, after all, the golden goose. Once married, once properly roasted, the goose would lay golden coins. Like magic, all she needed was a husband.

By the terms of her father's will, her inheritance would then come under her control.

The trickiest part had been finding a man desperate enough to elope with her. Jonathan Pine, her uncle's elderly stable master, had told her he would meet her at the Cross Keys pub tonight. Four miles' walk to the tavern. As long as she made it by ten o'clock, they would catch the last coach toward London.

The mud sucked at Jane's boots like a hungry mouth. She slogged faster, head down, breath burning in her throat. The wind yanked off her hood and shoved her backward. She pushed on, step by step, her sodden skirts heavy as stones.

First, her uncle had stolen her father's political career. He'd stepped into Papa's seat after the cholera had killed her parents.

Now he meant to steal her father's fortune. Not content with embezzling, he would wed her to Archibald, and have access to the whole.

Alas, Uncle Philip. You made one mistake: you forgot I had a brain.

Perhaps the clock was broken. Perhaps Mr. Pine had grown confused, and thought to meet at eleven instead of ten. There was still a way. Once he arrived, he could hire horses—

"He's not coming."

The smooth words came from behind her. Jane felt a horrible surprise, followed by a bolt of acidic nausea. Of course it would be Crispin Burke who caught her.

She kept her eyes on the old clock in the corner. The tavern was crowded, ruddy workmen slumped in exhaustion at the wooden tables around her. These same men—miners, farmers, decent men all—were made of nobler stuff than anyone at Marylebigh. They would find the energy to protest, should they see a young lady dragged screaming from the taproom.

"I tried to warn you." Burke's voice remained calm, low pitched. "I'll do so again: don't make a scene."

She turned. Burke was straddling the bench on the other side of her table, a tankard of ale cupped in his hands. How had she missed his entrance, much less his passage to the bar? Nobody overlooked Burke. When he strode in, great dark coat flapping, the world itself paused. He was beautiful, the rippling waves of his dark hair and the strong bones of his face framing black eyes that shone with a dangerous intelligence. Beautiful as a cobra.

"Why should I not cause a scene?" she asked flatly. "Sparing you is no concern of mine."

His gaze was dark, cold, and steady. "Then spare yourself. It won't work."

"Oh," she said, struggling to keep her voice light, scathing, when it wanted to shake. She could not go back! "My uncle's dog threatens to bite! Careful, sir. You will not want to injure the golden goose."

One corner of his mouth lifted—the barest intimation of a smile. "Goose, indeed. If you wished to run away, you should have waited until your uncle went to town."

Wait? She had already waited six years. If she waited any longer, she would . . . why, she would lose her mind. A woman could not pretend to be brainless forever without the charade becoming truth. Her wits were rotting by the hour.

But of course a man like Burke could not imagine

what that was like. To live, day after day, as a shadow—
to speak and be ignored, as though one's words made no
sound. To protest and be patted on the head, as though
one's concerns were a child's. Her uncle had not burned
the embroidery in an outrage, Jane thought suddenly,
but in the righteous grip of moral duty. His niece's role
was to be used, not to think or speak or feel. And so,
in the very act of communicating an opinion, she had
committed the egregious offense of insisting on her hu-
manity.

Burke glimpsed none of this. He barely knew her, for
all that he was a regular visitor to Marylebigh. Nobody
bothered to know her.

"You will have to tie me up and drag me back," she
said. "And I will make sure there are witnesses. Your political career will not profit from it."

"Goodness. All for Mr. Pine?" He took a long swallow
of his beer. "A heated passion, was it? Let me guess. He
pledged his devotion while shoveling manure. Vowed
to see to your comfort while mucking out a box stall."

She refused to look away from him, though his dark
eyes mocked her.

"How fierce you look," Burke murmured. "If this is
the face you showed your lover, it's no wonder he chose
to jilt you."

She and Mr. Pine had never been lovers. Their agreement had been practical: an arthritic stable master with
failing eyesight required money for retirement. An heiress kept prisoner by her family required a husband to
access her funds. Voilà: the perfect match.

A terrible thought struck her. "What did you do to
him?" She leaned forward. "If you have hurt Mr. Pine, I
will make you regret it."

He leaned forward, too. "*Will* you, now?" he asked in a warm and interested voice.

She clenched her jaw. He imagined her powerless—an heiress whose money was controlled by her guardian, and who knew nobody that her uncle did not introduce to her.

But he did not know everything. Sometimes, watching her family speak so cruelly of others, plot so mercilessly to exploit the world, Jane felt an intimation of that same wickedness in herself. Only *she* would use it for noble ends. Given a chance, granted access to her own money, she would punish those who amused themselves by making others' lives harder. "Justice finds a way," she said. "Even if it takes time."

Mr. Burke's smile displayed white, even teeth. He'd been raised in luxury, but he had the lounging, easy posture of a man bred to street brawls. "The mouse grows claws."

"You mistake me," she said. "I have always had them."

His glance flickered briefly. At least she was surprising him. "I did nothing to Pine. Your uncle made him an offer, which he accepted of his own free will. By now, if he is wise, he will be on the road to somewhere far, far away. Wherever five hundred pounds will take him."

Liar. "Five hundred pounds is nothing next to what I offered."

Mr. Burke drummed his fingers atop the scarred wood table. The ruby cabochon on his middle finger glittered violently. "Cowards take what they can get."

She drew a strangled breath and looked away, her gaze fixing on the fire, which grew blurry through the haze of rising tears. It had taken a great deal of persuasion to talk Mr. Pine into agreeing to her plan. A comfortable retirement in some warm, dry climate—absolute freedom to do as he wished. The prospect had finally won out over his fear of her uncle.

But she could well imagine that when he was confronted by the Masons, Mr. Pine's dreams of a pretty cottage in Cornwall had collapsed under terror.

How smug her uncle must feel right now! She was only surprised that he had not sent Archie to rout her. Burke was too lofty for such errands. He was a star in the House of Commons, whose aristocratic connections gave him the upper hand over her uncle, despite her uncle's access to her wealth.

"You make a fine messenger boy," she said. "And here I mistook you for a man with a spine."

"Your uncle did not send me."

Startled, she frowned at him. The firelight painted his skin golden and played across the chiseled planes of his face. Rarely had she allowed herself to study him at length. But sometimes, to her distress, she had dreamed of him anyway.

In those dreams he was a different person, kinder, gentler. She always woke disturbed. Beauty had a horrible power. It did not conceal faults so much as it persuaded the viewer to ignore them, and to disregard the instinct that screamed *danger*.

"If my uncle didn't send you, why are you here?"

Burke shrugged. "Mason intends to leave you stewing for a time. And then he will send Archibald to fetch you."

She digested this bitterness. "Teaching me a lesson, is he?"

"You've been quite foolish." Burke's tone was gentle. "Archibald will come alone, you see. I cannot say, Miss

Mason, what might transpire between you on the road home. But upon your arrival at Marylebigh, I feel certain that the Elboroughs will discover you together. Returning at midnight, in a state of disrepair, your gown perhaps ripped, with no chaperone . . ."

She could not breathe.

"It could be covered up," he continued with dreadful patience, "if only the Elboroughs did not witness it. Your uncle will be alarmed and mortified. He will insist that his son does his duty by you. The Elboroughs will approve, and carry the tale of your engagement far and wide—as well as the cause for it. You will not be allowed to refuse this time."

"I will not marry Archibald." She had said so time and again. "No one can force me."

"No one could have done," Burke agreed. "But you made it possible. You arranged your own disgrace tonight." He paused. "You and Jonathan Pine. How convenient! Mr. Pine certainly earned his payment."

She recoiled so sharply that the bench tipped. As it slammed back against the flagstones, the noise drew attention from rough men nearby. Mr. Burke appeared unalarmed by their scowls. He lifted his tankard to them, his smile easy.

She battled a temptation to speak to the onlookers—to beg for their help. But nobody could help her. Her uncle was the most powerful man in the county, his influence built from the funds he steadily siphoned from her inheritance—and the cleverness and power of his friends.

"I wish you joy of your marriage, Miss Mason."

As Burke rose, she leapt up. "Wait! I don't—" She could not marry Archie. She would not live the rest of her life beneath her uncle's thumb. "Please, you must help me." Burke was allied with her uncle for a reason. Born high but a second son, he had no fortune of his own. "I offered Pine five thousand pounds. I will offer you the same if you help me to escape."

Burke turned back, considering her from head to toe. The thoroughness of his inspection made her aware of her dishevelment. She had walked four miles in the rain and mud; her skirts were stained, her hair straggling.

Burke was right: the guests at Marylebigh would leap to the worst conclusion if they witnessed her returning alone, in Archibald's company.

"I do not want your money," he said.

"Ten thousand, then."

He smiled faintly. "Perhaps there is something else you might do for me. We might, as they say, become *friends*."

She had a vague notion of what friendship meant to a man like Burke. It had nothing to do with affection and everything to do with conspiracies.

"I have nothing to offer but money," she said.

"Not true." Burke sat back down, and so did she. "You know everything that goes on in your uncle's household. They speak freely around you."

Jane hesitated. Did they not speak freely around *him*? She knew Burke had been quarreling more and more with her uncle—it was the debate over the mutiny that had first put them at odds. Philip was a warmonger, whereas Burke preferred subtler methods of intimidation. Still, she had imagined their alliance unbreakable. "You want me to . . . spy for you?"

"I want you to use your brain," he said coolly. "You don't wish to marry Archibald? Then what you need is a friend—one who might do you favors, in return for those that you do him."

She felt a wave of revulsion. Was this how Burke conducted his career? Like a spider in the dark, weaving webs of shameful debts? At least her uncle's motives were straightforward, his politics dictated by what would enrich him.

But she'd long guessed Burke to be a more poisonous species. He had a cool temper, a clever mind, endless charm. He used people and then, elegantly, destroyed them. He never forgot a name or face or a slight against him. She had heard him quote, verbatim, conversations she had long forgotten, and pinpoint weaknesses in opponents that no honorable man would admit to knowing.

"You would do anything," she said unsteadily, "to become prime minister. Wouldn't you?"

He would overtake her uncle one day, and eat him alive. That Uncle Philip did not foresee the danger to himself amazed her.

Burke laughed, a low and beautiful sound that made her swallow. "Certainly," he said. "Far worse things than this, to be sure. And more useful things, too. For whatever reason, I'm feeling benevolent tonight."

"How fortunate for me," she said, full of sarcasm.

His sigh sounded impatient. "I'll spare you the midnight ruination. In return, you will listen for a single name and tell me whatever you hear spoken of it. Are we agreed?"

That did seem a simple trade. But Jane knew better than to trust such simplicity. Whosoever name it was, it would lead her down a twisted path. "Oh," she said softly, bitterly, "to be free of all of you!"

Burke snorted. "You are not on a stage, darling. Spare me the melodrama. If freedom is your aim, then do what you must. Otherwise, I'm off."

She took a deep breath. What choice did she have? "Yes," she said. "Tell me the name."

Crispin considered his unwilling companion. "Would you really have married Pine?" he asked.

Jane Mason sat across from him, clutching the hand strap as his carriage lurched down the flooding road. Crispin half expected her to refuse to answer. But her ordeal tonight, of hope dashed and defeat postponed, seemed to have left her too tired to assemble her usual restraint.

"Of course," she said. She gave him a brief, wondering look from beneath the shadows of her hood. The damp had undone her carefully pinned coiffure; curls rioted freely at her temples and brow. She shed pins as regularly as trees shed leaves; he was holding one in his hand right now, turning it over and over as he studied her.

"What did you imagine?" she asked. "That I'd arranged the whole business for the pleasure of jilting a seventy-year-old?"

Her bluntness amused him. "Seventy? You certainly were desperate."

"Or practical," she said. "In a marriage of pure convenience, an elderly groom is far preferable to one bound to live fifty years."

His laughter startled him. This made three times tonight that his view of Jane Mason had twisted to reveal new angles. She made such a convincing show of drifting ghostlike through Marylebigh that one would never guess her soft-spoken demeanor concealed such a sharp tongue.

"And?" he asked, for he was genuinely curious now. It was so rare to find himself mistaken about a person's mettle. "After the marriage, what then?"

She shrugged. "I would have provided him with a handsome settlement so he could live out his days in the style he desired."

"But you would not have lived with him."

She narrowed her eyes. "Convenience, sir, works both ways. Mr. Pine would have gone his way, and I mine."

For a woman so cloistered and coddled, she seemed quite confident that she would have faced no difficulties in setting off alone. "And where would you have gone?"

But he had reached the end of her generosity. She turned her face toward the window, the stony set of her profile warning him not to prod her.

She'd formulated some plan for herself. What could it be? Mason occasionally intercepted the letters she wrote to newspapers, earnest pleas to care for the poor, to reform the educational system, all manner of women's concerns. Perhaps, then, she dreamed of a house in Bloomsbury, charity work, a life of noblesse oblige.

Or perhaps, for all Crispin knew, she hungered for Parisian bohemianism. He no longer trusted his instincts about her; until this evening, he had discounted her entirely. In company, she always kept to a script of murmured neutralities that communicated both her polite attention and her overarching disinterest in the conversation.

Today, however . . . He'd been amazed when he'd overheard Philip Mason discussing his ward's midnight assignation. Only Mason's rage—which, unlike his muffled words, had translated clearly through the door—had convinced Crispin that he was hearing correctly.

He'd not intended to interfere with Mason's plan. After all, Jane's money was what made Philip such a useful ally. But tonight, in the drawing room, she had caught his attention. She'd been listening too closely to his brawl with Mason. Later, as Archibald had produced Jane's embroidery, Crispin had glanced over at her again. *The golden goose*, she had called herself earlier—he had wondered then if she referenced the less kind nickname her uncle used for her, *the brown goose*, his tired joke about her dull wit and homely airs.

But in the drawing room, caught off guard by her cousin's prank, Jane Mason had forgotten to restrain herself. The malicious delight on her face had been Crispin's first inkling, in all the time he'd known her, that she restrained herself at all. Indeed, that single moment had revealed more of Jane Mason than years of casual acquaintance. In one glance, Crispin had realized not only the strength of the passions underlying her wan mask but the ferocious strength of will that she had wielded in order to present such a bland front to the world.

Astonishing. His entire life had been a firsthand lesson in how badly others could misjudge a person. Yet he'd still overlooked her.

No longer. A woman capable of such restraint and anger was far more interesting to him than any commonplace beauty. *Brown goose*, indeed. The brown goose could prove very useful, and Philip Mason's carelessness had given Crispin the single opportunity he needed to place her in his power.

"You don't trust my uncle," she said abruptly.

"Oh, are we talking again?" He crossed his legs. "Excellent. So tell me, where did you intend to go, once you had your fortune in your hands?"

"Has he given you cause for mistrust, or do you suspect people as a general policy?"

"You first," he said.

"I intended to move to New York." She shrugged. "Unmarried women have far more freedom in America. It's only the married ones who have to behave. Your turn."

So she didn't want to behave. Was this a recent desire? She'd certainly done a brilliant job of playing the pushover. "I trust no one," he said. "Especially my friends."

"I expect that's wise, since friendship with you suggests something very troubling about their characters."

The smile he gave her appeared to make her uneasy. She shrank back a little into the deep cushions on her bench.

Interesting effect. He let his smile widen further, and watched her gaze drop from his and her chest rise on a sudden deep breath.

Well, wasn't this delightful? The goose was attracted to him. Very useful to know. Indeed, the more sharp angles he uncovered in her, the more intrigued he felt. She wasn't actually as plain as Philip Mason hoped. Her skin was clear, her hazel eyes large and brilliant, and even the untamed spirals of her dark hair had a certain winsome charm, now that he could read them as metonyms for her frustrated desires.

"You have a dark view of my character," he said. What a terribly uncomfortable quandary for her, to want him and loathe him at once. He wondered if the struggle kept her awake at night.

She licked her lips, and he felt a stirring of animal interest. The idea of touching her, of tempting her into surrendering to a wholly reluctant attraction, beckoned him. Why not? His family—and several others besides—already believed him well versed in worse.

"I don't think you much care about my opinion of you," she said.

"That's true." Others' opinions were so often wrong that to set store by them was idiocy. But living up to those baseless opinions—ah, now, that could make a fine game. "More to the point, your view is quite correct. I'm not a good man, Miss Mason. I do not deserve your approval."

A line appeared between her dark brows. She studied him a moment, in which he let his own gaze dip to her lips, which were pink and prettily shaped.

She averted her face. "You have no shame."

"None. Why would I? It's a useless quality, and deadly to one's ambitions."

"I think ambitions can coexist with decency," she said quietly.

"Indeed? Pray tell, what have *you* aspired to, Miss Mason?"

She clearly registered his mockery, for she refused to look at him now. He let the moment draw out, gauging his next dose of it with an eye to how it would best serve to disarm her.

"Oh, forgive me," he said apologetically. "I suppose

you are thinking of your needlepoint. That tapestry, by the way, was very clever. But ugly. I recommend you stick to flowers."

"It was needlepoint, Mr. Burke. Tapestries are woven, you see, and I find it far more satisfying to stab than to weave."

"Needlepoint!" He was amazed. "Good God, that must have taken you . . ." He could not begin to guess how long.

"Ten months," she said. "It was so *difficult* to abandon the social whirl."

Her sarcasm was cutting. Mason did not allow her to set foot outside the estate. To Crispin's knowledge, she had been cloistered at Marylebigh since her parents' death.

"Well," he said. "No wonder I haven't seen you recently."

"Oh, the needlepoint wasn't to blame for that." She offered him a brilliant smile. "I strive to avoid you."

Was that meant to wound him? He laughed. "Amazing. And yet you still made time for your little letters to the newspapers."

Shock widened her eyes. She mastered it quickly, but not before he had the satisfaction of glimpsing it.

"Goodness," he said. "Didn't you know? Mason quite enjoys them. But you can't blame him for your failure to be published." A lie. The editors, being an unprincipled lot, knew that discarding the letters would earn a handy fee from her uncle. "At any rate, it seems your talents lie elsewhere. Do keep looking, sweetheart."

Her pause seemed promising, filled with self-doubt. But then she startled him by saying in a low voice,

"Maybe I have no brain for politics, then. But I mean to keep trying anyway."

Her resolve made him feel irritated and weary all at once. "Without any conviction of talent? That sounds like a great waste of time."

"I don't think so." She met his eyes, her expression solemn. "I do find my thoughts worth sharing, sir. I think the fault must lie with the listeners. But even if I were a fool . . . it would still be worth the effort to think."

Where had this woman come from? Her voice was made of steel and her dignity, unbreakable.

"You've been having a good deal of fun," he said slowly, "haven't you? Convincing the world that you're a mouse."

"I haven't yet had a chance to convince the world of anything." She did not so much as blink. "You may notice that I spend all year here. If my ideas are small-minded, then they reflect my experience. But that must change—now, soon. So bear in mind, Mr. Burke, that whatever *friendship* I have offered you, it will expire within the year. One way or another, I will escape my uncle's household."

She meant what she said. But she underestimated her uncle's dependence on her wealth.

The feeling that flickered through him was so unfamiliar and ridiculous that it took a moment to register. He opened his mouth, then made himself close it. Her safety was not his concern.

"Anyway," she went on, "you must think the whole thing laughable. I am cared for, am I not? Provided with every luxury my heart can desire, all the ink and paper and silk floss I could ask for. But you've never been powerless, Mr. Burke. Or discounted in every regard that makes one *human*. So you must trust me when I say that comfort can be a prison."

He clenched his teeth. "Very moving," he said, intending sarcasm, but his voice came out roughly. He cleared his throat and scowled out the window.

"I did not mean to move you," she said. "I suspect it impossible, in fact. But I wonder. Would you really do *anything* to be prime minister?"

A curious wariness came over him—the same kind of edged alertness he felt when sparring with the opposition on the floor of the Commons. A presentiment of an oncoming trap, a rhetorical gambit that might skewer him.

The sensation irked him. She was surprisingly intelligent, but naïve and overconfident to boot. "Are you concerned for your safety, Miss Mason? Be at ease. Nobody ever won the office for doing away with an annoying woman."

"So you *would* murder someone, if it came to it?"

He turned to stare at her. "Do you think me such a pathetic politician that murder would be necessary?"

"That is not a denial."

She was goading him in the hope of rousing his indignation. But she had no idea that he'd been provoked a thousand times with these sordid insinuations. He had been punished for crimes that he'd never imagined, much less committed. And he had borne it all from people who'd had cause to know him far better than *she*.

She wanted him to defend himself. Instead, he laughed.

He watched her shrink into herself. Now she imagined herself sitting across from a monster. Very well, let her believe so. She was also sitting across from the future prime minister, which meant that he'd given her a fine story to tell her grandchildren. History remembered the villains even better than the saints.

Besides, even if nobody ever looked at him differently than she was looking at him right now—so pale, so appalled—he wouldn't give a damn. Power made a fine panacea for any number of old aches. It would be revenge and pleasure and comfort rolled up in one.

They were nearly to the gate. Crispin pounded on the roof to signal the coachman to halt. "We'll go on foot from here," he said. "There's a tunnel that runs in through the woods. You will go straight to your rooms, and let them discover you there, sleeping. You never left tonight. Do you understand?"

"Yes," she muttered.

He helped her out of the carriage, into the damp, cold night. The wind had died, and the air was filled with the sound of dripping, the fragrance of green and growing things yet to be slain by winter. The water caught on the tall grasses reflected the light of the moon.

When they neared the door concealed in a bank of earth, he caught her wrist. She turned questioningly, and he saw the transformation she had undertaken during their brief walk. Her very posture had changed, her shoulders caving in, her head seeming to weigh more heavily on her long, slim neck. She was folding her true self away from sight.

But he had seen her clearly now. He would not forget what he had glimpsed.

She misunderstood his reason for halting. "I will listen for the name."

"No," he said. "Not that." He silently cursed himself,

then shook his head—no, this was not sentimental. She could be a valuable asset to him. Keeping her safe was his wisest, most self-serving course. "Your uncle will not let you go."

She snorted. "I know that."

"No, I don't think you do. He is deeply in debt. He—"

"He just bought a new coach," she said.

"With Marlowe's money," he snapped. "And if something goes awry with the proposed defense works, the inventor will abandon him, and your money will be his only hope. Until now, he has simply embezzled from you, Jane. But if you find a way to remove your wealth entirely . . ." He took a deep breath. Listen to him, prattling warnings like some love-struck suitor! "Miss Mason, you do realize that if you die, your estate passes to your closest living relative?"

Her expression did not change; it merely seemed to tighten, so shadows now appeared beneath her wide cheekbones. "Yes," she said after a moment, her voice flat. "I am aware of that."

What marvelous control she had! His respect did not even feel grudging. "So your best path," he said, "is to agree to marry Archibald. Insist on a long engagement, with the condition that you be allowed a season in town. And once in London, find a better husband, and elope with him quickly."

In the moonlight, her eyes were dark pools, opaque yet watchful. Her hand closed over his, small and startlingly soft.

"Careful," she said softly. "You begin to sound like a true friend. That was not your intention."

No. It had not been. He felt a stir of discomfort, too

deep and unreachable to analyze, but strong enough to make him wish to push it away, or twist it into some more palatable emotion.

"Of course, you won't manage it," he said. "Need no one and trust no one, Miss Mason. If you follow that law, you may survive."

"Is that your own law, Mr. Burke?"

He did not like the goading note in her voice. "Make it yours," he bit out. "Otherwise, someone will come along to smash you like china."

To his amazement, she suddenly laughed. "In fact, I think it already *was* my law. Trust nobody, need nobody—yes, that's a fine way to describe it. But do I truly strike you as fragile, even after tonight? I thought you were more perceptive. What a pity!"

He did not know whence she'd procured her confidence, but it was falsely founded. It would blind her to future dangers.

"Forgive me," he said sarcastically. "You're made of steel. Go ahead and prove it, darling."

He pulled his hand free of hers and tipped up her chin. As he leaned down, her calm fractured; she tried to jerk away.

He gripped her arms ungently to hold her in place. The kiss was a lesson: she had no hope against a stronger opponent.

She smelled of lavender and soap, and her mouth was warm . . . She tried to clamp it shut. He bit her lower lip, then used her indrawn breath to push inside. Her tongue was startled, clumsy. Her shock tasted like barley and hops—some drink at the tavern.

She quivered, a full-bodied tremor, as though in an icy wind. Resentment, hatred, could feel so much like bashfulness. He stroked deeper. Had anyone ever kissed her before? Her rigid grip on his shoulders, an impotent attempt to push him away, suddenly relaxed. For one moment, he felt the curiosity in her lips—fragile, groping, as easily ruined as encouraged.

Then she sagged, becoming a boneless burden in his arms. He was kissing clay.

He eased back, his triumph oddly hollow. He cupped her cheek, stroking to goad her. Her skin was impossibly soft.

Her cheeks felt hot. She was blushing. But she lifted her chin and stared him in the eyes. "Do you feel like a villain?" she asked. "Or do you require more?"

He flinched.

Had this been a lesson to her? Or was it merely an example of commonplace evil? "I . . ." His throat closed on unthinkable words. *I am sorry.*

For what? He owed her nothing.

He turned her by the shoulders to face the doorway. "Go," he said roughly.

But she twisted out of his grip and turned back to him, reaching up to seize hold of his face. Surprise made him recoil. "What—"

She went on her tiptoes and smashed her mouth against his.

Astonishment felt so novel. It held him still as she rubbed her mouth against his. She bit his lip, then pushed her tongue into his mouth. Echoing what he had done to her. She mimicked his kiss so expertly that she turned it into mockery. A mockery of *him*.

He wrested free.

"Forgive me," she said breathlessly. "I just wanted to see how villainy was done. Child's play, it seems!"

He groped for a reply but found none. He felt . . . unnerved.

She turned and disappeared into the tunnel. For three long beats, he stared after her, until the whisper of insects, the hiss of the wind, and the pattering of fresh rain called him back to himself.

He turned away, frowning.

He did not like what he did not understand.

CHAPTER THREE

Seven weeks later—January 1860

The ballroom hushed. The violinists lifted their bows. Jane's cousin settled his meaty hand at her waist and squinted, his pale blue eyes watering in the blaze of the chandeliers overhead. Archibald was not bad looking. His blond hair was thick, his jaw strong. No doubt many of the debutantes would swallow a sigh for his sake.

"Don't make a hash of it," he muttered.

And thus came the first words he had spoken to her since their engagement. How her heart fluttered!

Jane offered him a bland smile. She didn't intend to make a hash *just* yet. They had come to London for the opening of Parliament, but would stay on through the season. Aunt Mary would not contemplate a wedding anywhere but St. George's, the most fashionable church in town, and then, too, at the height of the social whirl. That gave Jane three months in which to find some meek-mannered man to elope with.

The strings launched into a rollicking waltz. Her fiancé swung her into movement, and a polite scattering of applause followed their sweep down the floor. In love, a newly engaged girl might relish such attention. Jane struggled not to cringe.

As the first bars of music concluded, other couples joined them on the floor. But in a political crowd like this one, many guests had no interest in dancing. Their attention lay in the hissed gossip of their companions, the looks of their enemies across the room, and in Crispin Burke and Jane's uncle, who stood together near the stand of ferns that screened off the orchestra. Like magnets, the two men were dragging half the room toward them. It might have been happenstance that so many guests found themselves nearby. But if one squinted, one could make out a rudimentary queue. Guests were lining up to pay obeisance.

Vultures. Jane's father would have been appalled. Papa had come to politics in midlife, after making an extraordinary fortune in manufacturing. Ideals had driven him. He'd met his constituents in town squares, on street corners, in the shops and factories where they worked. But after his death, when her uncle had stepped into his seat, ordinary constituents had ceased to matter.

This bill that her uncle and Burke meant to introduce at the next Friday session was a fine example of that inhumanity. The legislation would eliminate the ticket-of-leave system, which allowed petty criminals to receive early parole. In the new era, thieving boys and inveterate drunkards would be condemned to rot in prison alongside murderers. The government newspapers were aflame with indignation. But other newspapers were in her uncle's pockets. *Their* editorials warned of a growing wave of crime, families slaughtered by criminals released early. Support was growing for Burke's bill. If it carried, some said it would topple the government.

Mr. Burke might become prime minister, after all.

Archibald's palm had begun to sweat. He prided himself on his waltz, but he was not sparing any effort on Jane. When she stumbled over his sluggish feet, he snapped at her to pay attention.

He wanted this marriage no more than she did. Jane might have felt an inkling of sympathy for him—they were caught in the same trap—if only he hadn't made it clear that he felt entitled to her money and furious that she came attached to it.

That was Uncle Philip's fault, really. He always insisted that he'd never been repaid properly for his investment in her father's first factory. He felt cheated of her father's wealth, and had taught his son to feel the same.

When the waltz ended, Archie released her and stalked off without a backward glance. Like clockwork, Aunt Mary swept up to seize her arm. Jane's submission to marriage had come with a condition: that she be allowed to experience a London season. But nobody was letting her out of their sight. Sneaking away would be a challenge, much less finding a willing dupe who needed money desperately enough to risk her uncle's wrath.

Three months—she would manage it somehow. She *must.*

The next hour dragged by at a tedious limp. Aunt Mary politely rebuffed any gentleman who approached Jane to dance. Jane herself held on to a polite smile until her cheeks trembled and her lips felt numb. Her aunt's acquaintances rarely spoke to her, instead scrutinizing her like horseflesh before manufacturing weak compliments to Mary about her "fine eyes." Her olive skin and curling hair, they probably felt gracious in ignoring.

The whole time, Jane remained acutely aware of Burke. Wherever the crowd proved thickest, whichever spot held the focus of most eyes, and whichever corner of the room positively fluttered with women preening themselves, there he stood. He would want to speak to her tonight. Her last letter seemed to have alarmed him in some way, for his answering reply had demanded an interview with her.

Her uncle came over to join them. Jane listened with half an ear to his low conversation with her aunt—some gossip about the inventor; he had built a castle like Udolpho's. Her aunt made an appropriately scandalized noise.

The ballroom was growing hotter, a sweaty racket of shrieks and laughter and the frenetic swells of the orchestra. The *valseurs* waltzed now as though trying to throw themselves off a cliff. Jewels glittered violently in the candlelight. In the center of this bright chaos, Crispin Burke made a tall, long-limbed shadow, conspicuous for the leisurely menace that he radiated.

She did not realize she was staring at him until he glanced over and caught her eye. His expression did not so much as flicker, but that brief, cool, deliberate glance felt like a summons. As though to confirm it, he promptly disentangled himself from his interlocutors— not pulling away so much as becoming, all at once, an indifferent wall of coldness to them, the slight smile on his face dying.

Jane watched two heavyset men in rich suits and jew- eled stickpins falter in their enthusiasm, then take their leave of him. With another brief, instructional glance at Jane, Burke turned and walked out of the room.

Jane said quickly to her aunt, "I must—the retiring room—"

"Oh, I'll come with you," said Aunt Mary.

"Do you imagine she'll get lost?" one of Aunt Mary's friends cackled. "Or is the company so base that you fear for her safety?"

Aunt Mary flushed. "Don't be silly," she snapped, but she let go of Jane's arm. "Run along, then. And come back at once."

By the time Jane caught up with Mr. Burke in the shadowy rear hallway, he was no longer alone. A beautiful blonde was hanging on his arm, pleading with him in low, urgent tones. The woman's ruby silk gown rippled in the torchlight; she was swaying into Mr. Burke, whispering to him like a lover.

Jane took a step backward. Burke looked up, his dark eyes spearing through the darkness to lock with hers. *Wait*, he mouthed.

"Crispin," the woman said. "After all we've been through . . ."

Jane stepped behind a statue, a clumsy copy of some Roman emperor, conscious of embarrassment and— much worse—base curiosity.

She recognized that woman from her aunt's remarks earlier in the ballroom. One of the great society beauties, the Duchess of Farnsworth.

"Yes, a storied history," came Mr. Burke's calm reply. "Not quite fit for children's ears, though, is it?"

"You can't hold that against me," the duchess said

hoarsely. "He needs an heir. I could not keep him waiting forever."

"Of course not." Burke's voice dropped, growing almost too soft for Jane to make out. "I wish you all the joy, madam. What a fine mother you'll make."

The duchess swore—a manly curse. Jane felt unwillingly impressed. "Don't be a fool. This is our opportunity! We can meet freely now. He is satisfied."

"Not quite," said Burke. "Your husband wishes you in the country for the season."

Some wordless exclamation. "You can't mean you *spoke* with him—"

"We reached an understanding."

A brief, charged silence. Then: "And when have you ever cared for what *he* thinks? After what he did to you! Why should *he* be allowed to—"

"Because I need his vote."

"His *vote*!"

"Forgive me. Was I meant to place you above politics?"

A sharp smacking sound made Jane flinch.

After a brief pause, Mr. Burke said, "Feel better, Laura?"

"Not at all." The words were choked by loathing. "I'd like to see you bleed."

"Consult the duke. Perhaps a shared goal will draw you close."

Jane realized she was hugging herself. Burke's words, so full of dry scorn, seemed to burn.

Silk rustled; the woman stalked past Jane's hiding place, no less lovely in a fury.

After a few moments, Mr. Burke came into view. A red mark was fading from his jaw, but he looked, otherwise, perfectly unruffled. His full, well-sculpted lips did not smile, precisely, but they held the impression of sardonic good humor. "Swooning, Miss Mason?"

She wished he were not so tall. Then the Duchess of Farnsworth might have blackened his eye. "It would take more to make me swoon. First, I would have to feel surprised."

"Ah, good! A native cynic." He extended his elbow, and with a resentful grimace she stepped past him, cutting a brisk pace down the hall.

He spoke from behind her, his amusement plain. "Do you think depravity proves contagious?"

She tried the doorknob to her uncle's study. Locked, of course. Her uncle zealously cultivated each of his guests, but he did not trust any of them. "So you admit to being depraved."

"I wouldn't waste the effort to argue it."

The next door opened into the morning room. She stepped inside, and Burke followed, closing the door.

He leaned his weight against the door, no doubt entirely mindful of the threat he offered by blocking the exit. Six feet of muscle. She backed away from him. In this cozy little room—flowered wallpaper, soft chintz upholstery, lace doilies cluttering every surface—he seemed as out of place as a panther.

"So," he said. "You managed to get yourself to London. Does it live up to your hopes?"

So they would pretend to be friendly. Very well, she could do that. "I cannot tell yet," she said with a shrug. "My aunt will not let me out of her sight. She refused to drive through the park yesterday for fear that ruffians might kidnap us. And she says the weather is too cold for sightseeing."

"Oh, come, now, Miss Mason." His tone was indulgent.

"A schemer like you? Surely you could invent some reason to leave the house."

A *schemer*. The idea reverberated unpleasantly. She had been raised by honest, upstanding parents. Her mother had held truth to be a sacred charge; it was Mama who'd first insisted that Jane's father look into conditions at the very manufactories that had made him rich. *Profit*, she'd said, *has no bearing on the question of what is right*. It was her moral certainty that Papa had absorbed, and that had driven him into his political career.

But that career had been cut short. At seventeen, Jane had been thrust into a new world in which honesty was considered intolerable cheek. Slapped one too many times for talking back, she had learned to hold her tongue. She had learned how to scheme.

"Yes," she said now, flatly. "Your friend Mr. Mason has taught me many things."

"And Archibald?" asked Mr. Burke. "Have you undergone a sea change, and sworn your love to him?"

"Of course not."

He straightened. "Then we have much to discuss." He locked the door, then pocketed the key.

"That's not necessary!"

He lifted a brow as he faced her. "Do you want to be caught with me? Imagine how that might play out." He held up the key, a silent offer: he would unlock the door, if she liked.

She could not imagine what her uncle would do if he caught them closeted together. He would probably invent a dungeon for her. "Fine," she said shortly. "Leave it locked."

He surprised her by handing her the key, then strode

across the carpet, yanking shut the curtains and enclosing them in darkness.

She crossed her arms, the key icy against her elbow. "Is *that* necessary?"

"One never knows who might be watching."

Did he often discover people spying through windows on him? What a terrifying world he lived in!

"Now," came his voice, low and silken, "tell me more of your news. What did the letter say, precisely?"

"I didn't read it."

The gas lamps hissed; light rose as Burke turned the valve. He stopped too soon. A dull, hellish glow suffused the room, barely sufficient to see by. But it illuminated the irritation on his face. "You didn't read it." His tone was withering.

"I could hardly read over his shoulder! I only know that it concerned Elland."

"You will need to get your hands on it, then."

She squinted at him. "I cannot do that."

"You can."

"I *won't* do it."

He considered her a moment, then issued a sigh, somehow disappointed, scolding—a schoolmaster with a lackluster pupil. "Miss Mason. I thought you a girl of some wit. What leads you to imagine you have any right to refuse?"

"*Some* wit! Why, you do know how to turn a girl's head. But you should really think before you speak, sir." Suddenly, in some perverse way, she was enjoying herself. It had been a very long time since she had spoken without fear of giving offense. "I have every right to refuse you, and more to the point, you have every cause to coddle me. If I told my uncle you had asked me to spy on him, your friendship might undergo a decline."

A brief pause opened, in which he considered her narrowly. Then he prowled close, moving so quickly that she had no chance to avoid his touch: he hooked her chin with one finger and yanked up her face.

For all the unpleasantries of her recent life, she was not accustomed to being handled like livestock. She jerked free. He caught her again, ungently now, gripping her jaw to hold her in place.

"Careful," he said. "I don't like to argue."

Alarm shot through her. She had known him for an unprincipled wretch. But she had never imagined he would pose a danger to her person. "You assault women, do you?"

His lips twitched, an attempt at a smile that did not take. He released her and retreated a pace, shoving his hands into his pockets in a silent concession.

Now she was angry again, livid at his temerity. "How good to know you have *some* standards. Corrupt, amoral, with no cause save your own advancement— but you won't abuse a woman. Yes, what a fine recipe for a politician!"

"You know what it requires to be a politician, do you?"

"I knew the finest politician who ever lived," she said. "A man of true ideals, who thought foremost of the needs of the poorest—who put his fortune into helping those who needed it most, rather than enriching his friends—"

"Ah yes, the saintly magnate," he said in a cutting voice. "It's easy to be noble with a million pounds at one's disposal."

"My father would have been noble in the gutter," she

retorted. "He *believed* in his efforts. He *lived* his ideals. He educated me as he would have a son—he funded schools, he gave food to the poor, he treated *everyone* with respect—"

"How lovely," he said in a flat tone. "I'm certain his workers quite cherished that respect while scraping together the pennies he paid them."

She flinched. That was not fair. "His factory men were well paid—"

"Oh? Would you thrive on their salaries?"

"You know nothing about him!"

"His bank accounts spoke for themselves," he said. "And I've no objection to feeding the poor, Miss Mason, provided I am well stocked myself. But we second sons, we workaday men—lacking a fortune, we must rely on our wits. Ideals, you see, do not fund our grand plans."

"Grand plans?" Her scoff burned. "Plans to make sure that the miserable suffer further? Your penal bill—"

"That bill," he said, "will save lives. It will keep dangerous criminals off the streets and away from neighborhoods that *you* will never live in. You are sheltered, Miss Mason, so I will forgive you for failing to see how that bill might benefit the same deserving poor whom you weep for in your silk-covered bed."

"I don't weep for them, sir." She *planned*. Her father had drawn up a dozen proposals for how to best use his fortune for the improvement of the needy. Once she came into possession of that money, she would see his plans through, and invent more besides. "I do nothing so useless. The penal bill is a travesty. You would acknowledge that in an instant if it didn't serve your purposes."

"Yes, so I would. Just as I have fought against a dozen proposals that you also would have condemned, precisely because they did *not* serve my purposes. You had no complaints in those instances, I'm certain." His smile looked cold. "But I do believe in removing criminals from the street. Which is convenient."

She scowled. "You may launch any defense you like—"

"I need that letter copied."

Oh, why bother arguing with him? He was rotted through. "Hire someone. I don't answer to your bidding."

"You have free access to Mason's study. It would take months for a hireling to manage that."

"You're still young, Mr. Burke. Or . . . close to it." He could not be much above thirty. "I'm quite sure you have the time to wait."

"But do *you* have the time?"

She hesitated. There was a trap here. "I have three months, in fact."

Burke sat down. His clear retreat eased the pressure in her chest, made her feel she could draw a free and full breath. When he gestured to the seat opposite him, she warily took it.

"You told me," he said, "that comfort could be a prison. Do you recall?"

She nodded.

"That isn't comfort," he said. "What you have at Marylebigh. It is a . . . smothering. They imagine you brainless. Your words make no sound to them."

He was too perceptive. It made her feel peculiarly exposed, almost humiliated. "So?"

"It's a strange kind of torture," he said quietly. "To be caged by the lowest expectations. A humiliation of the soul."

She took a sharp breath. He could not read her mind. It was only a coincidence. But the look on his face . . . it was pity. As though he had suddenly decided to be human.

"Do we have time for this?" She did not want him to pretend to be humane. His heart was as black as her uncle's, and she wouldn't forget it. He would not cozen her into doing his work for him.

"No," he said calmly. "You don't. Three months? A trifle. You made a mistake by allowing the Masons to announce your engagement. No gentleman will look twice at you now that you've been publicly claimed. You won't find a husband in a ballroom, Jane. And you say they won't let you wander elsewhere."

Her nails were cutting into her palms. "And how was I meant to prevent the announcement?"

"That is what friends are for," he said. "I might have helped. But you failed to ask."

The last thing she wished was to cast herself deeper into his web! "It makes no difference. I'll find a way. I don't want a man bred to this world anyway." She knew how Burke's circle of friends looked upon her uncle— and her, too. Her fortune was dirty, the product of honest labor. "I want a husband who's grateful to wed me, not one who condescends to it."

"Good sense," Burke murmured. "But then, commoners pose a different problem. MPs, peers of the realm—such men can procure a special license to wed. Ordinary folk must register their intentions publicly, and wait to be granted permission. That leaves a window of opportunity for your uncle to discover your plans. A very large window, in fact."

She had thought of all this. "We'll run away first."

"And risk being caught? Besides, you cannot be married in a parish to which you don't belong. It will take three weeks of waiting, wherever you go."

"Or a—on a ship," she said. "A British captain can marry subjects at sea."

"You won't have any money," he said gently. "And you don't mean to marry a gentleman. So who will buy your passage? Three months to find a man, woo him, persuade him to take an expensive gamble, with an uncle whose name is well known and feared besides?"

"Enough." She could not listen to this. "I will do what I must." Somehow she would make it work.

"Better," he said, "to find a way to marry instantly— by special license, or something even quicker."

"Perhaps *you* can marry me," she bit out. "MP that you are."

His gaze narrowed on her. "You joke. But I could do a great deal with your money. Why, I might even afford to have *ideals*."

Horror iced through her. He was the last man on earth she would marry. "Not in a thousand years, Mr. Burke."

He offered her a dark smile. "How flattering. And yet you made free with my mouth two months ago."

How shameless he was to speak of it. "I was only returning the favor," she said. "To teach you a lesson."

"Oh?" He leaned forward, his voice turning silken. "And what lesson was that? For it seems I didn't learn it." Very slowly, he reached across the space between them and cupped her face. His thumb traced her cheekbone.

Awareness prickled over her skin. He had not risen

from his seat. He posed no immediate threat. That was the only reason she did not leap away.

But the rhythm of his caress . . . the intent look in his eyes . . . it was hypnotic, oddly riveting.

"Perhaps you should teach me that lesson again," he whispered. "I promise to prove a better student."

The notion punctured his spell. She leaned away, out of reach. "Go learn from Lady Farnsworth."

He sat back, his face darkening. "I need that letter."

"I'm sorry for it."

He blew out a breath, raked his hand through his hair. "Six years," he said. "That is how long you've been at Marylebigh. I expect I am the first person, in all that time, to see you for what you are. To recognize that you are capable. Is that so?"

The remark struck her like a fist. What a pathetic ruin her life had become. "Am I meant to be *grateful* to you?"

"No," he said. "But by God, I hope I am right about you. I know a man," he said curtly. "Ordained, to my amazement. But of very flexible morals. He has been known to produce marriage lines when required."

Astonishment prickled through her. He could not be suggesting . . . "Go on."

"Some of these marriages did take place, but too late. Others never happened at all. But this man's records document them, regardless. Pick a name, pick a date: it often proves very useful in matters of inheritance."

"A . . . forger of marriage records?"

"Indeed. Although he prefers to be addressed as his grace the archbishop."

An *archbishop*? "Does he also provide the groom?"

His laugh was husky. "That falls to you, I'm afraid. But with this gentleman's aid, you can be sure that no court in the land will dispute the validity of your union. A prince, a pauper, the czar of Russia—take your pick, so long as you feel sure the groom will not object. All the archbishop requires is a name. You'll be able to present the marriage to your uncle as a fait accompli."

Her heart was drumming now. "And in exchange, all I must do is copy you the letter?"

"A small favor," he said. "Nothing much, between friends."

One week later

Night was falling rapidly, a sallow fog choking out the last trace of sunset. Crispin stepped out of the church into the narrow street. The air was salted, thick with the odors of rotting fish and brackish mudflats. The cottages here sank into their foundations, pockmarked and crumbling, with broken shutters that swung in the wind.

It was not too late to turn back from this idiocy.

Behind him, the door slammed. The reverend had not enjoyed their discussion.

Crispin stared into the darkness down the road. He should not be here. Someone else, someone who could afford it, who would want the praise, who would revel in it—some pampered, celebrated idiot should be here right now.

Yet Crispin started down the pavement.

There was no name for this street. Evidently parts of London existed that even the mapmakers shunned.

Something else to fix, once the power was his. But he was in the right place. The letter copied by Jane Mason, the record at the General Register, the reverend's remarks—they all fit together. The puzzle was finally resolving, and it made him livid.

He was livid, too, at himself: this was not *his* problem. His temper had probably spilled out on the reverend. So be it. This was not his bloody concern.

Yet he was walking.

A movement flickered from a window ahead. When he squinted, he saw nobody. The flutter of a torn curtain, perhaps.

Curious, this sensation in his stomach. He had not felt his own nerves for some time. Bribery, intimidation, threats, betrayals—he dealt them expertly, then slept peacefully through the night. He made men weep by reciting the secrets that they'd imagined well hidden; he watched from a cold remove as they begged him to think of their livelihoods, their families. *I will lose my seat. I made promises to constituents! My good name will be ruined. I'll lose contracts; I'll be bankrupted. Think of my daughters. My own borough will turn against me!*

But that was politics. Men entered the game willingly. It was not Crispin's fault if they failed to play well. He never felt a moment's anxiety over breaking an opponent, whatever it took. There were no rules. Not at the top. His conscience, his nerves, did not bother him.

But now, walking down this darkened road, he felt . . . uneasy, and deeply, implacably angry. If he was correct—and in minutes, he would know for certain— then at last, for the first time, he might get to experience that most Christian of virtues: righteous indignation.

Perhaps he would even act on it. Perhaps, for once, he would play the hero rather than the villain.

He snorted at the thought. Once he was prime minister, *then* he would entertain the notion of heroism. But he had mapped a clear plan for himself, a climb both direct and brutal. Without money—without a fortune like Jane Mason's sainted father's—it took brutality to scale the peak. Once atop it, he might once again pause to consider how others saw him. They would be looking up at him then, rather than down on him. Perhaps, at last, they might take a different view and see him clearly.

Until then, what point? *Climb, climb.* This business tonight was a distraction. It would not lead him upward. It was useless.

Still, he kept walking.

How satisfied it would make that naïve, self-righteous girl, her great luminous eyes alight with such easy-won certainty, to know that there were atrocities even *he* could not abide.

Tonight, then—tonight alone, he would make an exception. Tomorrow, he would hand the proof off to the authorities and set to climbing again, with no further distractions.

At last, he came to the door he'd been told to look for, the red paint peeling. His brief, hard rap did not merit an immediate response. He knocked again and then turned to survey the street.

The silence felt unnatural, thick and somehow staged. In any other neighborhood, one would catch the spill of conversations, of cooking pots knocking together, of children's quarrels and cries. He took a long, steadying breath.

He knocked again, harder yet.

Was this a prank, then? Lure the nob into the seedy underbelly of the city and watch him piss himself for a laugh?

If so, he would not give onlookers the satisfaction of watching him wait. One more minute, and then he would walk back to the Great Northern Railway station, where civilization yet resided.

But as he turned to go, the door creaked open. He could see nothing of the interior, but a gruff voice said, "Come inside and pull shut the door."

Enough with the games. "Your name," he demanded—but received no reply, only the sound of footsteps retreating into darkness.

He laid a hand to the doorknob. No one in the entirety of the world knew where he was at this moment— no one but whoever waited within.

Another man would have come with company. But while Crispin was counted a man with many friends, he had no friend whom he would have asked for help in this matter. No one he could trust.

A noise sounded behind him. He nearly jumped, but it was only an alley kitten, mewling.

Need no one, trust no one. At the tender age of twelve, Crispin had coined this motto. During the rare holidays in which no school friend had offered to host him, his silent chant had carried him through his strained interviews with his father, often as he squeezed the tender web of flesh between his thumb and forefinger so the pain would anchor his focus. The same chant had drowned out the sound of his mother's weeping in the night, and left him unmoved by his brother's contempt.

His family's grief could not affect him, their disappointment and blame could not touch him, because he did not need them. Nor could their lack of faith wound him, for he trusted no one to look on him kindly.

He had forgotten this code for a time. Now he lived by it. Yet if his instincts and suspicions were right—and in a moment, if he stepped inside, he might finally know—then he had never anticipated this kind of evil. He had been caught off guard. He could have no part in this.

His chest tightened. *Doing the right thing.* What a thought!

But if he left now, the truth might never be uncovered.

Need no one, trust no one. A man who needed and trusted no one was a man with nothing to lose, and therefore a man with no cause for fear.

What was the worst that could happen inside? He would be killed. No one would mourn. Someone else would become prime minister after Palmerston. But the failure would not touch him. He would be dead.

He chambered his pistol and shoved open the door, stepping inside.

Someone knocked the door shut. Total blackness. "Well?" he snapped.

A fist smashed into his face. Knocked him to the ground. Rough scrape of wood, footsteps hard behind him.

He shoved to his knees. The gun barked in his hand. A raw cry came from somewhere in the darkness. He spat blood and stepped backward, reaching for the doorknob, but it was no longer there.

The second blow knocked him back down.

Some distant part of his brain found the humor in it: *The arrogant bastard finally gets what he deserves.*

The third blow made him see stars.

The fourth was the last he felt.

"Jane? Jane! I am *speaking* to you!"

Jane startled. Her aunt was glaring down the table at her. "I beg your pardon, ma'am."

"You are pleased, are you not?"

Jane cast a sidelong look toward Archie, who was glowering at his plate as though the Scotch eggs had insulted him. Whatever the tidings, he did not like them. "Very pleased," she said. Where was her uncle? He had yet to come to the table, though it was his wont to finish his breakfast long before them.

"That gives us only four weeks, of course." Aunt Mary tapped a nail against the rim of her teacup, her eyes narrowing. "They say Madame Fouchet is not taking new clients. But for the right price, I expect she'll change her mind."

"Madame . . . Fouchet?" Should she know this name?

"Yes, the modiste." Aunt Mary twisted her mouth. "Haven't you heard a word? There has been a new opening at St. George's, the last Sunday of February."

Archibald's grim expression made sense now. "But—but surely, February . . ." Jane swallowed down a wave of panicked nausea. Her aunt had wanted a grand society event. "Many people will still be in the country at that time."

"Yes." Aunt Mary's nail was tapping steadily now, a stern and determined rhythm. "A pity. But I have spoken with your uncle, and he agrees: there is no point in waiting on the flightier fringes of the beau monde. The political lights will be in attendance, and that's all that matters."

They had seen through her. They knew she was plotting to find a substitute groom. They were not willing to risk waiting until the height of the season.

Jane took a hard breath. Her throat felt cramped, as though a noose were closing around it. Four weeks. That was no time at all, particularly when she was guarded more closely than the crown jewels. "But—I don't—"

"Oh, but you will," Archie muttered into his coffee. "And so will I."

The look they exchanged then felt peculiarly intimate. In their perfect misery, they were at last in accord.

"Naturally you feel bashful," Aunt Mary said briskly. "Maidenly shyness, very fitting. I've written to Lady Elborough to see if she can put in a word with Madame Fouchet, but if that fails—"

The door crashed open. Her uncle entered, pale and staggering, his cravat askew.

"By God," he rasped, and tossed a letter at his wife. "Look at this."

Aunt Mary unfolded the page and began to read. The contents caused her lips to whiten. "Is this . . . Is it public yet?"

"Morning edition," her uncle said.

"What's going on?" Archie asked.

"None of your concern," snapped Uncle Philip. He fell into a seat, but shoved away his plate. "What in God's name are we to do?"

In a single regard, her uncle and aunt did remind

Jane of her parents. They trusted each other and con-spired together, an intimate confederacy of two. Jane folded her napkin, preparing to be dismissed, but when she made to rise, her uncle snapped, "And where do you think *you're* going?"

Startled, she sank back into her seat—finding herself now the object of everyone's regard.

She cleared her throat, unnerved. She was far more accustomed to being ignored. Gone were the days of her youth, when her presence at the table, her thought-ful and confident contributions to debate, had not only been welcomed but expected. This household's table was but an extension of the political battlefield, in which she had no place.

But suddenly the atmosphere had transformed. A chilling idea came to her: suddenly *she* was enlisted in the battle.

"We are going to move up the date," her uncle said slowly, never removing his eyes from her.

Her aunt made an unhappy noise. "But four weeks is already—"

"Four days would be too long," he said through his teeth. "Do you not grasp the news? With Burke dead, there will be blood in the water. We must solidify our defenses, *now*. We need the money in our hands."

Jane covered her mouth. "Mr. Burke is—"

"Dead?" finished Archie. "How? When?"

"Soon enough," her uncle said. "On his deathbed, skull broken." He shoved back from the table, rose, and nodded tightly as he looked between Jane and his son. "It will take a special license. I will find a way to pro-cure one."

"But that's impossible," Aunt Mary cried. Her clear

distress had nothing to do with Burke and everything to do with her visions of an ostentatious wedding. "Archie is no MP—"

"Anything is possible," her uncle said bitterly, "given the connections and the funds. And we won't be short on *those* anymore." His brief glance to Jane sent a new shock through her: he looked her over as one might a chair or a ladder, something to be used, without the brain or soul to look back.

"I will go make arrangements," he said, and pivoted to leave.

"Wait!" Jane was on her feet, speaking desperately, without forethought or care. "I won't agree to this! I can't—I—" She dragged in a breath. *Think.* "I insist on a church wedding!"

Her uncle's laugh was horrible. "You *insist*, do you?" He took a pace toward her, and she was deeply grateful for the table that separated them. "I think you mean you *wish*. And what you *wish* is not my concern."

"My father," she blurted. "My father would have wanted a proper wedding in a church—"

"What your father did," he said with icy precision, "was always quite different than what *I* would have done. But rest assured that I know my duty, and I will do it, regardless of your girlish fancies. You will marry my son, and you will never want for anything. You will live in comfort for the rest of your life. Whether or not you find cause to complain of it is your own concern, Jane. But I doubt your *father* would fault me for seeing to your welfare, or for deeming you a fitting bride for my son."

"He would!" She could not hold back the words now.

What was there to lose? "My father would give me the choice. My father would not want a loveless marriage for me. He would never have permitted—"

"Your father stole this family's chance!" he roared.

She shrank back.

"Without my five hundred pounds," her uncle snarled, "there never would have been a factory. Without my introductions, he never would have come to know the men who invested in the rest. And yet when it came time to repayment—what did I receive? A paltry five thousand? Do not speak to me again of your *father*, Jane. What you mistake for fine ideals was no more than calculating self-interest. But I have put it aside. For your sake, I have found a way to right that wrong, and to keep you in comfort besides. Be grateful for that." He paused, glaring at her. "There were worse alternatives."

He turned on his heel and stalked out.

A long moment passed, Jane frozen, Aunt Mary staring into space.

Archie loosed a noisy breath, then picked up a Scotch egg and shoved the whole of it into his mouth. "So," he said as he rose, still chewing. "Four days? I'll be at my club until then."

The door banged shut again. Jane collapsed into a chair.

"Dying," Aunt Mary said softly. She picked up the letter, held it between thumb and forefinger as she studied it. "Of all men. So young, so robust. Who would have guessed?"

Jane felt almost too exhausted to stir her thoughts toward Mr. Burke. But after a moment, they gathered around him of their own accord. He'd been a villain, an amoral rogue. Yet it was impossible, almost revolting, to imagine him killed. His vitality had all but filled a room. Had it only been turned toward good, he might have done so much.

But he'd been wicked. The desolation that leached through her expanded to encompass him. What hope for heaven was there for Mr. Burke? For a man who'd corrupted even an archbishop?

An archbishop.

"I suppose we must pay a call," Aunt Mary said. "Not today, of course. But tomorrow, on his family. As a matter of form."

Jane realized she was gripping her knife like a weapon. Very carefully, she laid it down. "Yes." Her voice came out as a rasp. "Yes, I think that would be very decent." Slowly she eased to her feet. "I would like to go with you, if you don't mind. I have known him for so long."

"Of course."

"And now, if you'll excuse me?"

"Yes." Aunt Mary scrubbed a hand over her eyes. "All right. Well . . . I suppose I must . . ."

Jane stepped into the hallway. She felt dizzy. Dazed. She could not mean to do this.

But she'd already meant to do it. Was it more sinful to gull a dead man than to bribe and buy a living one? Let the philosophers decide.

Lifting her skirts, she bounded up the stairs into her room. Her hands fumbled on her lockbox. The key stuck before turning.

There it was—the archbishop's name, written in Burke's slashing hand. His voice rang clearly through her mind:

*A prince, a pauper, the czar of Russia—take your pick,
so long as you feel sure the groom will not object.*

A dead man could not object. A dead man would not
even care.

What had he told her? "If freedom is your aim," she
whispered, "then do what you must."

On a harsh breath, she went to the writing desk and
took up her pen.

CHAPTER FOUR

Present day—February 1860

You're in shock," Charlotte said kindly. "It's entirely natural. But he will recover his memories, Jane. I promise you that."

Jane gave a halting nod. They sat together in the back parlor, crowded on every side by pots of scarlet roses from Lady Sibley's hothouse. Jane had opened a window, but the damp breeze only seemed to excite the flowers. Their dark, rich perfume was clogging her lungs. When she shifted in her seat, velvety petals brushed her face, stroked her cheek. She felt nauseated, penned in. *Trapped.*

Alive and awake! For almost a day now, Mr. Burke had been napping and then waking. *Waking!* In her desperate gamble, Jane had never foreseen this turn. Every doctor whom Viscount Sibley had summoned—from the Queen's own physicians to the crème de la crème of Edinburgh and Paris—had instructed the family to abandon hope. But they had been mistaken. He would live.

"It's a miracle," Charlotte said softly.

A log split in the hearth, releasing a shower of sparks that caused them both to jump. The difference was that Charlotte laughed, an exultant and giddy sound, while Jane swallowed a curse.

She had never felt more dark hearted. Burke's recovery had brought joy to a family that showed nothing but kindness to her. But even for their sake, she could not be happy.

He had lost some of his memories. How many? And how permanently? Last night, he had not seemed to believe her. *My wife*, he'd repeated flatly. And then he'd demanded to speak with his father again.

Jane had gone to her bedroom. What else was there to do? She had drawn the blankets to her chin and listened as new doctors arrived, tramping up the stairs to inspect Mr. Burke. They had stood in the hallway for hours, conferring in low murmurs. But nobody had come to accuse her. She had finally fallen asleep near dawn and been tossed by paranoid dreams until, at half ten, Charlotte had come to wake her.

It was three thirty in the afternoon now. Nobody had yet called her a fraud. But the day was young.

What would she do if Burke's memories returned by nightfall? It would take time to finalize the transfer of her wealth. Until she had access to her inheritance, she could not run. Not without finding herself worse off than she had been at Marylebigh—alone and penniless besides.

But if Crispin Burke were to suddenly remember that he had no wife . . .

"Mama does not know this," Charlotte said in a hushed voice as she poured the tea, "and I pray you won't tell her. But . . . Jane, I had ceased to go to church."

Jane nodded, and then—when Charlotte's expectant silence continued—she produced a surprised noise. "Oh dear. And now?"

"Today I slipped out and walked to Matins." Charlotte held out a steaming cup. "I felt His presence again, Jane! And I wept in thanks, and felt so ashamed that I had lost faith even for a moment!"

The tea was exactly as Jane liked it: lightly sugared, with two teaspoons of milk. She had lived in this house for four days now, for lack of anywhere else to go. Her uncle had been so enraged when she'd produced the marriage lines that she had feared for her safety.

No frightened girl could have hoped for better protectors than the Sibleys. Amid their grief and shock, they had nevertheless managed to comfort her, telling her not to worry about anything. Her only concern must be her husband, they said.

They had left her alone for long hours at Burke's sickbed. Those hours had felt like purgatory. From the first, her exhilaration at having escaped her uncle was mixed with guilt over the lie she had told.

The forgery would hurt nobody, she'd reminded herself. Mr. Burke possessed no fortune. She would inherit nothing from him when he died.

But quickly it had become clear that Burke possessed a fortune more rare than her own. He had a warm and loving family that, in the face of their helplessness to aid him, instead turned their affections on the woman they considered his wife.

She hated lying to them.

But what choice did she have? Sitting at Burke's bedside, Jane had listened, three times, as her uncle forced his way into the house. He demanded her return. He accused Crispin of kidnap and seduction. The last time, he'd brought the police.

Charlotte had come to her then, and they had sat trembling, hands locked together, as her uncle raged in the entry hall. Viscount Sibley had allowed him no farther inside.

Sibley's voice had never lifted. But his rich, confident baritone had demolished her uncle's accusations. *My son's marriage was witnessed by one of the highest officials in the land. You challenge the honor not only of the Church but of a Member of Parliament. And you try my patience as well. Tell me, Constable—what are the penalties for harassment? And what would your supervisors think of your support for it?*

The police had left then. Mason had soon followed.

Charlotte's thoughts trailed hers. "I'd like to see your uncle accuse Crispin to his face," she said with relish. "I expect he'll learn to hold his tongue very quickly. One word from Cris ought to do it!"

"Yes," Jane said weakly. She could see it in her mind's eye—Mr. Burke's dark and merciless look, the cruel humor of his slow smile. The cold pleasure of a predator on spotting new prey.

Only it wasn't Mason he'd be hunting.

A drop of tea splashed hot against her knuckles. Her hands were shaking. Very carefully, she returned her teacup to the saucer.

She needn't panic. Nearby Southampton was full of ships, docking and departing at every hour. All she needed to do was to complete the paperwork that would finalize her access to the trust. Her husband's signature was also required. Now that Burke was awake, she could insist on it. But she must time the request carefully, lest it make her look venal.

A bitter taste filled her mouth. *But I am venal. I have gulled this lovely family in order to secure my freedom.*

What a pity he'd not been parented by brutes!

How such decent people had produced Crispin Burke, she could not begin to guess. But their love was the noble counterpoint to his own dark nature. She hated to exploit it.

Yet there was no other choice.

The trip across the room cost him his breath. Crispin collapsed onto the chair, panting. *You nearly died.* For the first time since waking, he believed it. His head was spinning. Almost two days had passed since he'd woken to this strange new world. It felt like aeons. He could not comprehend half of what he'd been told about himself.

It was the cheval mirror that had drawn him out of bed. His breath recovered, he gathered the strength to stand and turn his chair toward it.

The glass showed a man in his thirties, well removed from boyhood. Crispin sank back into his seat, skin prickling. He touched his chin. The man in the mirror did the same.

This was *his* face, subtly changed. Lines fanned from the corners of his eyes. His skin looked sun burnished, the texture of it slightly roughened. His beard came in faster and thicker; he'd been shaved this morning, and already sported stubble. His lips, in repose, settled into a hard cast, unwittingly foreboding. He looked . . . fearsome.

Fitting for a powerful politician. A man, his father claimed, who all but controlled the Commons.

Controlled the Commons! Crispin sat back, amazed anew. He had always been ambitious, but the last he remembered, his world had been crumbling around him. The love of his life had rebuffed him; Laura's family had decided a second son would not do for her, and engaged her instead to the Duke of Farnsworth. Crispin had managed to pass the entrance exam to the diplomatic corps, but he'd not been selected after all. He'd gone then to his father, who refused to use his connections to make inquiries. "The corps is a grueling route," he'd told Crispin. "Atticus has said he will find you a position in the City. Short hours and a fine salary—just your line."

He'd assumed, as always, that Crispin's aim had outstripped his abilities. And that Atticus, the golden child, would provide a solution.

The mirror showed Crispin's darkening expression. It seemed he had made a success of himself despite everyone's expectations to the contrary. But today, when delivering that news—that Crispin was an accomplished leader, the man who *controlled* the bloody Commons— even *today*, his father had managed to sound dubious. "Your methods, well . . ." His mouth had pinched. "They are not always honorable. Indeed, I fear they may have provoked someone to try to kill you."

Crispin stared at his now frowning reflection. What sort of man would have made such violent enemies?

No. London was a dangerous city. And how typical of his father to assume that he might have done something to incite his own misfortune!

A knock came softly at the door. "Mr. Burke? You called for me?"

A political career was not his only accomplishment. He had married—not high, but handsomely. "One of the great fortunes of our time," his father had called it.

On a deep breath, he turned in his seat. "Come."

The door creaked open. Crispin's bride hovered in the doorway, as though reluctant to approach. "You are dressed."

Soft, cool voice. An impression of surprise. The doctors had counseled bed rest for him.

But he was done sleeping. This room had been forecast to house his corpse. He would not stay in it any longer than necessary. Nor did he mean to linger beneath his parents' roof. It had not been a comfortable home since his childhood.

He braced himself, then slowly rose, resisting the violent trembling of his limbs, the dizziness, the strain of muscles that still seemed to be sleeping.

"Well done," murmured the woman.

Generous of her. But his intention had been to bow. He would not manage it. His heart was already thundering, and his knees wobbled.

With a silent curse, he dropped back into his seat before he could fall.

"As spry as a toddler," he said—aiming for wry, landing instead on embittered.

She took a step inside, her skirts whispering along the floor. A thick braid of dark hair wrapped like a crown around her oval face. She had large, watchful eyes, a wide and neatly shaped mouth. Lovely, really. But the opposite of Laura. Dark complexioned, tall. "You must be patient," she said.

"Patience is not my strong suit."

Her gaze fell. "Yes, I know."

A wave of amazement lapped over him—another in an endless series, regular as the tide. She *would* know. For she was his wife, whom he had courted and married.

She did not appear to be particularly . . . affectionate. She had the posture of a woman bracing herself: shoulders squared, hands locked together at her waist.

He remembered her curious manner at his sickbed two nights ago. His recall was hazy; he could not remember her exact words. But he'd had a clear impression of her fear. And she had not come to see him since then. What kind of marriage had they made?

A furtive one, by all accounts. He had eloped with Jane Mason using a special license vouchsafed to him by the archbishop. They had kept the marriage secret—perhaps would have continued to do so, had he not been felled by random cutthroats.

He wanted to know the reason for it. "Will you sit?"

She moved elegantly, her step light and gliding. Today's gown, like the one before it, was high necked and unadorned, a dull gray silk that ate the light. It was the choice of a woman who wished to go unnoticed. It could not conceal the swell of her bosom, though, or the narrowness of her waist.

The plump curves of her arms suggested that she was generously molded all around. A man's hands would feel full of her. Crispin would have enjoyed filling his hands with her; he felt certain of that. But he could not remember doing so.

She settled onto the very edge of the wing chair opposite, gripping the arms as though in preparation for a quick leap away.

He could not remember mistreating a woman. But

none of them had ever looked at him as this one did—aslant, so warily.

He did not like it. He had hoped for . . . an ally, he supposed. His relationship with his family had always been strained, but a wife, he had hoped, would make a natural confederate.

He searched himself for a remark that might set her at ease. But he had no idea how to address her.

"Forgive me," he said, "but what shall I call you?" Some husbands addressed their wives intimately. But her manner toward him . . . "Shall I call you Mrs. Burke?"

She flinched. "Jane. Jane will do."

"Jane," he said with relief. So perhaps there had been affection between them, after all. "Jane, I imagine this must be as strange for you as for me. If you have any questions, I will gladly answer them."

She spoke instantly. "Exactly how much have you forgotten?"

Crispin's father had asked the same. But the tenor of that conversation, his father's weighted silences and watchful looks, had felt so familiar that Crispin had not hesitated before answering. No matter what he had forgotten, he still knew exactly how every conversation between them was meant to go. Being ambushed by criminals was only a new variation on the old pattern in which Crispin failed to live up to his brother's example, failed to exemplify dignity and self-possession.

This time, he'd gone so far as to lose his own memories, and nearly his life.

Yes, he knew how to speak to the resigned skepticism in his father's look. How much had he forgotten? "Not enough," he'd replied.

But with his wife, he stumbled on the impulse to

glibness. He studied her now, with a thoroughness that his shock had not permitted during their first conversation at his sickbed.

What had drawn them together? Not her fortune, despite what his father claimed. Money had never been Crispin's aim. Despite himself, he'd imbibed enough of the family's self-importance to dismiss wealth as a goal far beneath him.

Power, then? Power often required money, and a man who controlled the Commons would certainly covet it. But Crispin knew himself. He would not have made a marriage solely for bloodless advantage.

Passion, maybe. Yes, he could imagine it. She was not dressed to her best advantage, but her husband had been ill—not an occasion for vanity. She wore her dark hair slicked viciously against her skull, twisted into submission in that painfully tight but practical braid. The hairstyle emphasized the perfect oval of her face, the straight, thick lines of her dark brows. It also tugged up the corners of her eyes, which were . . . lovely. Large and penetrating, shades of bark brown stippled with amber and mossy green. He stared into them until her gaze dropped again, and a slight flush pinked her cheeks.

Her nose was too bony and pronounced for classic beauty. But it lent her an air of hauteur, which paired well with the penetrating quality of her eyes. She was intelligent, he sensed. He would not have wed her otherwise.

He crafted his tone as an apology. "I'm not certain of precisely where my memories falter. After speaking with my father, it seems I am missing roughly five years. I have no memory of my campaign for the seat, or my friendship with your uncle, or . . ." *You.*

She seemed to hear that unspoken word, for her mouth flattened. "Yes," she said. "You and my uncle were great friends."

"Don't lose heart," he said gently. "The memories will come back."

A pulse beat in the hollow of her throat. "Are you certain?"

None of the doctors had guaranteed it. But for her sake, he lied. "Of course. It may take some time, but there is no question."

"How long, do you think?"

How tense she sounded. How miserable. "I'm afraid no one knows." For a brief moment, he imagined never knowing. Never understanding what had led him into politics, or from the brink of failure to success.

You have hopes for the prime ministership, I believe, his father had said. Had anyone else claimed so, Crispin would have thought it a poor joke.

Prime minister! "The memories will come back," he said roughly. He would know how he had achieved so much, or else it would forever remain a myth to him, unreal, no source of pride. "Perhaps you will help me remember."

Her face was deeply expressive, but he did not yet remember how to read the emotions that flickered through her eyes. At last, her expression softened, and she leaned forward to touch his wrist—a light, shy touch, more like a question. "It must be very difficult for you," she said haltingly. "To wake up to . . . so much."

Her sympathy made something ease in his chest. Surely this was its own form of remembering? He would not take solace from the touch of a stranger.

He turned his hand so their fingers linked together,

and his sense of rightness strengthened. "You mustn't worry, Jane." It was his duty to care for her, to comfort her. They were married, after all. "It will be deuced awkward for a time. But we will find a way to get through it together."

Her fingers twitched within his. "You're kind," she said in an odd tone—as though it were a revelation.

Surely he was misinterpreting. Surely, after a lifetime of enduring his family's disappointment, he had not managed to find a wife who felt the same.

"We, you and I . . . we are fond of each other," he said—stilted, trying to conceal his great need for reassurance. "Are we not?"

She bit her lip, then lowered her gaze to where their hands joined. After a moment, the silence began to feel awkward.

Was she timid? They had not been married long. A new bride might be shy, certainly. And in a situation like this, God above, who could blame her?

But if this strange new reality was indeed a triumph—controlling the Commons! An ambition for the prime ministership!—then *she* was a crucial part of it. And claiming that triumph as his own, making it feel *real* to him, could begin here, now, by reestablishing whatever connection bound them together.

So he lifted her hand to his lips and kissed it.

She jumped. Startling like a bird, her fingers flexing. But she did not pull her hand away. Her skin smelled like lavender. At length, her hand relaxed within his, which he took as an invitation to kiss it again.

Her breath hitched. Color came into her cheeks. She liked his touch.

Craved it, perhaps.

He had a sudden vivid image of kissing his way up her arm, of golden limbs bare in a hazy afternoon light. Fantasy or memory? Surely the latter.

"I cannot imagine I married for convenience," he said, increasingly confident. Some elements of a character never changed, regardless of the circumstances. He had never been a man to take the easy path.

"Of course not," she said slowly. "We were . . . very fond of each other."

Fond, were they? He wondered if that was a maidenly synonym for *lust*. Well, then. He fought back a smile. Shyness, indeed. He knew how to coax a lady from her shell.

Very gently, he cupped her cheek. Her skin was so astonishingly smooth. As though no one, nothing, had ever touched it. As he stroked her cheek, her blush rose again, enchanting him. "Jane," he said. "Look at me."

Her face lifted, but her eyes remained downcast; she had the look of an Italian Madonna meditating on sacred mysteries.

"How difficult this must have been for you," he murmured. His bride had a full lower lip, the lip of a voluptuary; she was nibbling on it, and he could not say he blamed her. He felt certain he had done the same in the past. "You risked your family's wrath to wed me—and then, suddenly, I wake a stranger to you. You must feel very alone."

Her sigh was the only response she offered.

"But I am still here," he pressed on, "and I mean to honor my vows to you, and to show you the same respect and affection that you enjoyed from me before." Indeed, perhaps she was the key to remembering. Surely familiarity would stir recollection.

Her lashes lifted, revealing an opaque, brilliant gaze, unreadable. "I do so appreciate that, Crispin. But for now, you must concentrate on healing."

He shook his head. The headache, the weakness, the nausea—he could endure those. Healing would happen on its own. Far more pressing was this great curiosity unfolding inside him. From a heartbroken failure to a powerful politician married to a woman who blushed like a child, with great changeable eyes the color of autumn . . .

"You know me better than my family does," he said. He felt sure of that. His family's view of him would forever remain clouded by the boy he'd been, a prankster and dreamer whose carelessness ultimately had shattered their lives. He had abandoned all hope of changing that. But he would not have guarded himself with his wife. "Tell me—what kind of man am I now? I'm an MP—how did that come to pass?"

She took a deep breath and sat back, removing herself from his reach. "My uncle sponsored you. There was a borough in Cornwall for contest. You came to him, I believe."

Cornwall. Apart from a few trips in his childhood, he could not remember having spent time there. "And we . . . what is our platform?"

"You shift allegiances as it suits you. At present, you have a solid block of support from the Conservative-leaning radicals."

For a moment he felt certain he hadn't heard correctly. The Burkes had always kept to the liberal edges of the Whigs. "I—has my family abandoned reform?"

Her smile looked thin. "Not your family, no."

"I broke with them? Why?"

"Why?" Her laugh was faint and humorless. "I cannot say *why*. But I know that you and my uncle worked to bring down Prime Minister Palmerston two years ago. There was an uprising in India, you see. Many felt that Palmerston did not grasp the urgency of the crisis. He felt sure that the Russians had fomented it and that the uprising would come to an end quickly. He sent troops to Ireland that might have been sent to India. My uncle did not like that; he wanted a full-scale war. You . . . well, you quarreled. I believe you were sympathetic to Disraeli's views, that it was not a mutiny so much as a national revolt, one sparked by our mishandling of the Indian princedoms, our violations of native customs. But my uncle was . . ." She shrugged. "At any rate, both of you wanted Palmerston out of office. The mutiny offered a way to do it."

He gripped his temples, massaging hard. God in heaven. "An uprising." What else had he forgotten? "Palmerston." He was as stupid as a three-year-old child right now. How in God's name would he come to grips with all of this? "So Palmerston is out?"

"He was. Lord Derby briefly came into power. But in the last election, Palmerston came back. Your aim is to unseat him and to take the prime ministership for your own."

Good God. Now she had said it, too. His father was not mistaken. He felt breathless—torn between wonder and panic. Did he truly have a chance at that office?

"To what purpose?" he asked. "What is my aim?" Not warmongering, surely. He could not believe that.

"Power," she said.

But that was no answer. "Power to do *what*?"

Her smile was odd. "Some would say that power is an end to itself."

"Not I." He must have had some scheme, some deep plan to account for his actions.

"I'm . . . You did not confide in me that way," she said after a moment.

The notion startled him. In whom had he confided, then? Her uncle, he supposed.

"I regret not doing so." He fought to keep the frustration from his voice. "I suppose I never foresaw waking to discover my mind so blank. I . . ." God above, he would need to educate himself very quickly if he meant to keep hold of what he'd earned. "I will need copies of my speeches, all my files—the records of last year's session, all the blue books—and a meeting with your uncle, of course. That should come first—"

"You can't." For the first time, he saw panic in her face. "He did not approve of our marriage. He is no longer a friend to you, Crispin."

Bloody brilliant. He blew out a breath. "I must keep a secretary."

"My uncle always said you did not."

He stared. "What kind of man—much less an MP— keeps no secretary?"

Again, a curious hesitation. "A man concerned for discretion, I suppose."

This was absurd. He realized he was cupping the wound on his head and forced his hand back to his lap. He would not indulge in weakness. There was no time for it. "Will you guide me, then, Jane? For—" He let slip an unhappy laugh. What a turn—he did not even remember the names of his friends. "I'm not sure who else to ask." Not his family. He remembered enough to know that. His political rise had no doubt astonished them more than his near death.

"Of—of course," she stammered. A blush darkened her face; she turned toward the door. "Is that the dinner bell?"

He could not hear the gong, but the grandfather clock showed the right hour. "Yes, I suppose so."

It was no wonder if she startled again when he took her hand to slowly, haltingly walk her downstairs. After all, the man she had married no longer remembered her—how to touch her, how to please her, how to make her glow. He would simply have to learn it all over again.

That, at least, would not be an unpleasant task.

CHAPTER FIVE

$\mathcal{G}$ood comes even of great evil," said Lady Sibley
from the foot of the table. "To have all my
children assembled here again, after so long . . ." She
reached for the pearls at her throat, twisting the strand
into a knot. She had her son's dark eyes, but not his talent for concealing emotion; for a moment, it seemed
that she might weep.

Beside Jane, Crispin Burke lifted his water glass. The
doctors had forbidden him anything stronger. "Hear,
hear, Mother."

"Oh yes," Charlotte said warmly from across the
table. She sat next to her husband, Sir Richard. Together, they made a matched pair, blond and round
cheeked, smiling genially as they joined in the toast.

The rest of the table was oddly subdued. Viscount
Sibley, his leonine white mane tamed by pomade,
kept his craggy face blank. His heir, Atticus, Baron
Randol—a shorter and heavier version of Crispin—
seemed to swallow a protest along with his wine.
Meanwhile, Lady Randol, a slim redhead decked out

in glittering sapphires, gave a quick, covert squeeze to Atticus's arm—more in warning, Jane thought, than in comfort.

As the first course, a julienne soup, was laid, Atticus broke the silence. "One of those doctors has loose lips. The news was all over Westminster today. You can expect a steady stream of ruffians at your door, Mother, starting at three o'clock tomorrow. Or earlier," he added with disgust. "Crispin's friends do not stand on ceremony."

"Then they will be turned away with thanks for their well-wishes," Lady Sibley said. "Politics can wait while he mends."

"I'll receive them," said Crispin. "But not here. I assume I must keep a residence of my own? And Jane, of course, will be eager to establish the household."

Soup splattered into Jane's lap. Carefully, she returned her spoon to the bowl. Live *alone* with him?

"So soon?" Lady Sibley looked aghast. "Crispin, really. You have every comfort here—and staff who've known you since childhood! I can't trust that majordomo of yours."

"The sooner I catch up, the sooner I can return to my routine."

"But you don't remember your routine," Charlotte said.

"A great blessing," muttered Atticus.

"Pray tell," Crispin purred, "what does that mean?"

"Not tonight," bit out Lord Sibley. "If you please, Crispin."

Jane hid a frown. It was Atticus, currently glowering, who had made the first jab. But nobody else seemed to remark on the injustice, save perhaps Charlotte, who shifted in her seat.

"In fact," Crispin said, "I would welcome news of my routine, provided Atticus can manage an objective view of it."

Lady Sibley's laugh sounded strained. "Why, Atticus is a scientist," she said. "If he is not capable of objectivity, then I despair for his experiments!"

"I believe experiments are easier to analyze than people," Charlotte said lightly, but Atticus cut her off.

"Oh, I'm quite objective. Conspiracies for breakfast, bribery for lunch, and backstabbing over dinner, Crispin. That's about the whole of it."

Charlotte sat straight and looked ripe to object, but Crispin forestalled her. "Dear me. That seems an uncharitable way to view a representative of government."

Atticus snorted. "You *have* forgotten, haven't you? You represent nobody but yourself. You're a muck who runs with the wolves."

The viscountess slammed down her wineglass. "I will not endure slang at my table!"

As though slang were the main complaint here! Jane looked around the table, amazed. Atticus was still glaring. One would think his brother had just slunk home from some ill-advised lark rather than risen from his sickbed.

The servants cleared the bowls, most of them still full. Now came lamb cutlets, their fragrance so rich and savory that Jane paused to breathe it in.

Charlotte noticed. "Cook is a marvel, isn't he? I've warned my brothers that I mean to steal him one day. That is the only inheritance I demand!"

"Cheerful thought," said Atticus. "Have you any other plans dependent on our parents' demise?"

Charlotte flinched, and her husband, jaw tense, fixed Atticus with a stony look.

Lady Sibley cleared her throat. "It seems to me that we must hold a proper celebration to return Crispin to society. A ball, I think—"

"Us?" Atticus straightened in his seat. "This family?"

"It's quite all right," Crispin said flatly. "No celebration required."

"Then to announce your marriage, certainly." Lady Sibley's voice, steel sheathed in silk, matched the smile she turned first on Crispin and then on her elder son. "Surely no one can object to that."

I can, Jane thought with horror. But how? On what grounds?

She had never planned to continue this masquerade for longer than a week. That was all the time the doctors had given Crispin to live. But now, she saw with sudden crushing clarity, she was locked into the role.

If the truth came out, the loss of her fortune would be the least concern. People went to prison for forgery and fraud.

"I am not certain we wish to advertise an elopement," said Atticus.

"I think it a fine idea," Charlotte said brightly.

Atticus turned to the viscount. "Father? What say you?"

Lord Sibley lowered his silverware, looking between his sons with a grave, assessing squint. "No," he said finally. "I can see no cause for objection."

"There you have it," Lady Sibley exclaimed. "Only we must time it carefully. I want nobody to have the excuse of another commitment."

"The end of this month is still quite thin," said Atticus's wife—and then, catching her husband's look, cast her gaze downward to her wineglass and drank deeply.

"Mason," said Atticus through his teeth, "has been prating to all and sundry that his niece was seized by force. Better to send them abroad for a time, don't you say? Until the gossip dies down."

"Abroad?" Crispin's voice was bland. "When Parliament is sitting?"

"You can't mean to retake your seat. Not in your condition! You'd be quite overtaxed."

"And I suppose your concern has nothing to do with your opposition to the bill I've authored," Crispin drawled. "I saw your very interesting editorial in today's *Times*."

Atticus flushed. "And I suppose that same editorial is the reason you know you authored a bill at all!" He looked incredulously around the table. "Am I the only one who sees the madness in this? He remembers nothing! Imagine what people will think! They'll talk of lunacy—our family name will be smeared—"

"Amnesia is not lunacy," Lady Sibley said sharply. "It's a known condition, Atticus, with no bearing on one's sanity."

Charlotte nodded vigorously. Lord Sibley, meanwhile, appeared immersed in a censorious study of his lamb cutlet.

"Oh?" Atticus sat back. "Had we thought Crispin *sane* beforehand? For he eloped with a perfect stranger—"

Crispin's hand came over Jane's, startling her. For the first time, she noticed the absence of his ruby cabochon ring. His hand looked bare without it, but somehow more graceful. His fingers were long and thick, but well shaped, strong looking.

Who was this man? His altered manner made her feel increasingly flustered and uncertain of herself.

"I will thank you," he said in a low and dangerous tone, "to speak kindly, or not at all, of my *wife*."

The viscount looked up. "Well said."

This mild remonstrance made Atticus flinch. "Very well. My apologies, Mrs. Burke. But . . . do let us speak of that bill, then! It is a travesty—a black mark on this family's proud legacy of reform. It has nothing to do with sound law, and you know it. Nothing to do with justice, and everything to do with fattening his friends' pockets!"

"I will not discuss politics at the table," their mother said stonily.

Thus were Atticus's aspersions against his brother recast as *political debate*. Jane felt disoriented. Before Crispin had awakened, she had gathered a picture of the Burkes: Lady Sibley was high-strung, her flightiness steadied by her husband's gruff, taciturn dignity. Atticus's filial loyalty, Charlotte's concern for everyone's comfort, had painted an enchanting picture for Jane.

Now a different angle revealed itself. Crispin had a role in this family as well. He had been cast as the black sheep, the younger son gone rotten, whose faults only emphasized the virtues of the heir.

But . . . that was right. Crispin *was* rotten. Jane stared at her plate. She could not judge Atticus for maligning his brother.

But couldn't he reserve his complaints for some later date? Did it not bother him that his brother had nearly just died?

"Atticus is correct in one point," Lady Sibley said. "Crispin, I hope you will take care in whom you trust with the details of your . . . indisposition. Certain of your friends may abuse the knowledge. Meanwhile, we will do our part—*all* of us"—she fixed a gimlet eye on Atticus—"to show how delighted we are with Crispin's recovery, and his marriage besides. A ball will serve that aim nicely."

Atticus snorted. "How is that?"

"Why, by displaying the true love and affection between Crispin and Jane."

Everybody turned to look at them—Charlotte and Lady Sibley smiling, Atticus squinting dubiously.

Viscount Sibley's expression was guarded.

Crispin made some small noise in his throat, scorn or amusement, perhaps both. "What do you imagine, Atticus? That my heart is too black for love?"

Jane found herself the focus of Atticus's probing gaze. Paired with his similarity to Crispin, the cold shrewdness of his look made her pulse trip. It reminded her too vividly of the man hiding beneath Crispin's amnesia, the merciless and vengeful intelligence that he would turn on her once he knew what she'd done.

"Tell me, Jane," said Atticus. "How *did* you fall in love?"

Crispin had not let go of her hand. His grip tightened now, as though to lend her strength.

How idiotic to feel comforted. She had made him her greatest enemy; he simply didn't know it yet. But Atticus's look was so mocking, so cold. Crispin, too, could wield this look with suffocating intensity—but now she knew where he had learned it. His contemptuous brother had taught it to him.

"Well?" prompted Atticus. "Do share how the mouse caught the cat."

"*Atticus*," hissed his wife.

"You must forgive my brother," Crispin said smoothly to Jane. "He never had any manners, but he did once know how to pretend to them."

"Quite right," Charlotte put in—ever the peacemaker, mindful of fairness. But Atticus snorted.

"Forgive me, I'd imagined all women enjoyed recounting love stories. Of course, if the lady doesn't have one . . ."

"Don't be foolish, Atticus." Viscount Sibley spoke gruffly, but his dark eyes were no less penetrating than his son's. "Give her a moment."

It was no less a challenge, although subtler.

Meanwhile, Crispin's grip had gone rigid. His family's criticism, their skepticism, wounded him, even if he fought not to show it.

It made no sense! Nothing hurt Crispin Burke. He was immune to tender feeling.

Or so he *had* been. But not, it seemed, now.

"We . . . certainly did not expect to fall in love." Oh, heavens, she was going to lie for him. For *him*! "But as you know, Crispin is—was—a close friend of my uncle's. He often came to Marylebigh to pay his respects." Lord Sibley had turned back to his plate, but Atticus was nearly sneering. She felt a hot wave of dislike for him. She had wondered how such a family created a man like Crispin Burke. Atticus clearly had a hand in it! "I suppose, over long nights of conversations, anything may happen. Why, the star of London politics might even come to love a *mouse*."

"Oh, well done," said Charlotte warmly, as a muscle ticked in Atticus's jaw.

"You understand I intended no offense with that term," he said. "It was . . . metaphorical only."

"It was a clumsy metaphor, then," snapped the viscount. He'd rarely spoken tonight, Jane realized, save to reprimand or support Atticus—as though his eldest son were the only one in view.

Crispin lifted Jane's hand to his mouth. With his lips against her knuckles, he murmured, "No mouse, I think, but a lioness."

Startled, she felt a peculiar sensation wash through her. The heat of his breath, the softness of his lips . . .

She had never seen him wear such a smile, a *true* smile. He was impossibly handsome.

And in ten minutes, for all she knew, he might remember everything and ring for the police.

Well, and if he did, she would produce the license, and tell the authorities how Crispin Burke had conspired with an archbishop to create a forgery. She would have company in her march to prison.

The thought did not calm her, precisely. She pulled her hand from his and retrieved her wineglass, drinking the rest straight down.

CHAPTER SIX

Crispin fumbled for a match, struck it with shaking hands. As the wick caught, his bedchamber came into view. Long dark carpet. Looming shadows of heavy furniture crowding the walls. A squat bookshelf in one corner, shoved beneath the window.

He carried the candle over to the shelf, pulled out a book at random. *Gulliver's Travels*. He remembered reading this as a boy. But now, in his current predicament, it held no appeal. He knew well what it was like to be dropped into a strange universe in which one no longer seemed to fit.

He replaced the book. His legs felt steadier, at least. He turned back toward the bed.

He did not think he would be able to sleep again. That dream . . .

He'd been kissing a woman. Naked, entwined with her. But it hadn't been his wife. He'd driven his fingers through blond hair, tightened his grip when teeth closed on his shoulder. The woman's laughter had been low and husky, somehow . . . malicious.

And in his lust, he had felt the same. Such a savage, inhuman feeling, as he'd thrust into her—

It had been *Laura*.

A corner stabbed into his thigh. He'd lost his balance, lurched backward against the bookshelf. He braced himself against it, waiting for the dizziness to pass.

What a foul fantasy. It could not have been a memory. He refused to believe so. Laura had never said such vulgar things to him—speaking to him of her hatred, her misery. And he had never bedded her. Nor had he ever, in his life, bedded *any* woman with such cold-blooded, cruel feelings brewing in his chest.

He swallowed. Cast a glance toward the washstand. No pitcher. The bellpull was . . . somewhere. He slowly made his way toward it, caught his balance on it before he tugged. Then sat on the bed to wait.

A clock ticked nearby. His clock, his house, a gloriously grand Georgian townhome that had astonished and delighted him only this morning, when he'd arrived to take possession again. Marble staircase, handsomely carpeted rooms, brocaded furniture. Silk wallpaper and embroidered swags. Even his wife, not given to exclamations, had gaped at the luxury of their new abode.

Only now did it occur to him to wonder how he afforded it. MPs did not receive salaries. His small trust from his late uncle had barely covered his bachelor's flat while a student.

After a few minutes, when he still heard no footsteps in the hall, he forced himself up again. The staff was in shambles. They had not been prepared to receive him this morning. Half of them absent, including Crispin's valet. So much for loyalty! The butler had stammered apologies. His wife had promised to take it in hand.

He stepped into the hallway. The balcony was lit in a dim warm light, the sconces along the walls turned to their lowest. He started for the stairs—then halted again, as the world seemed to turn around him.

Where was he?

He clutched the railing and turned back to look the way he had come.

The balconied hallway showed two doors in front of him, and a third to the left, where the hallway turned sharply.

He did not know which door he had emerged from.

For the first time—since awakening, since entering into a year he did not remember, a life he could not explain—he found himself truly afraid.

Amnesia is not lunacy, his mother had claimed.

But finding oneself lost after ten steps? What else could one call that?

He glanced again toward the stairs, which vanished downward into darkness. The kitchen would have water. But would he manage to find his way back again?

His heart was pounding. *Exertion*, he told himself. *Not panic.* He considered the three doors again, wrestling with himself. Only a child—a babe in leading strings—would be unable to retrace his own steps.

He gritted his teeth and chose the door directly in front of him. It opened soundlessly. Too dark to make out the features. The carpet felt right.

He passed through the dressing room. There stood the bed, the curtains drawn back. All right, he'd done it. His thirst had died. He could ring for water in the morning.

When he sat, a sound soft came from nearby.

This wasn't his bed.

As his eyes adjusted, he made out the figure of his sleeping wife, her hair snaking along the pillow in a long, thick braid, the beribboned end an inch from his hand.

Her face came into focus. Dark brows knitted tightly, a horizontal wrinkle scoring the bridge of her nose.

Her dreams weren't pleasant, either.

His pulse was starting to slow. He struggled to keep his breathing silent. If she woke and found him sitting here staring at her, he'd not blame her for shrieking. She was nervous around him, despite her best efforts to seem otherwise. It would take time to persuade her that he meant to do right by her, that the failure of his damnable brain would not undo her happiness. He owed her that.

He knew in his gut that he owed her a great deal more.

After Laura had spurned him, he'd vowed not to love again. He was sick of disappointing people. He would not give another person a chance to disapprove.

But this woman had somehow changed his mind. With such a fortune, she might have married almost anyone, but she had chosen *him*.

He could not recall what he had done to win her. But he felt a great swelling gratitude as he gazed at her now. Whatever he'd done, she had found it praiseworthy. She had chosen him.

The ticking of a clock pressed again on his ears. Where was it coming from? He looked around, did not see it. But was there any lonelier sound, in the barren stretch of night, than this reminder of time slipping away?

So much he had forgotten. So much he had lost. He did not know what to make of his disorientation in the hallway. Could an MP afford such weaknesses? Atticus was right: men would dismiss him as a lunatic if they knew what ailed him. He had woken up to miracles, accomplishments beyond anything he'd ever dreamed. Would he manage now to lose them one by one?

His wife murmured in her sleep, tossed to one side. Her sharp movements carried her braid onto his hand.

Slowly, he turned his palm. Ran his finger, very lightly, over the ends of her hair.

It was not soft, like Laura's had been. Curls required stronger mettle. But as he stroked it, one of those curls wrapped around his thumb.

It was an embrace as light as air. But it calmed him, somehow.

He released his breath, slowly, slowly. A wave of fatigue washed over him. He should go back to his room, if he could find it.

Her brow was relaxed now. She was smiling in her sleep.

They were married. Surely she would have no objection if he were to lie here for just a few minutes, and breathe in the scent of her skin, and let himself rest.

She was not alone in the bed.

The realization came slowly as Jane's eyes opened. Weak light, the first hint of dawn, was filtering through the lace curtains. A warm arm wrapped around her waist. A head lay pillowed against her nape, someone's breath brushing her skin.

She went rigid.

He thinks himself your husband. You cannot object.

But her heart did not heed logic. It started to hammer.

She swallowed, forcing herself to remain motionless. His embrace was not . . . unpleasant. Indeed, she felt better rested than she had in weeks.

In years, in fact.

For the first time in memory, she could remember no nightmares.

Her nose was tickling. Breath held, she eased her hand from beneath the pillow to rub away the itch.

The man beside her did not waken, but adjusted his posture, rolling onto his back.

She inched away, meaning to sneak out of bed. The fire had gone out in the night. The staff, what remained of it, had not listened to her instructions.

As she sat up, the mattress shifted, and Crispin's lashes flickered.

She froze, waiting to see if he'd waken.

A strange thing, to discover a man in one's bed. Strange to see him stripped of the masculine defenses. In the night, his beard had come in, his hard jaw shadowed now with stubble. The whiskers drew attention to the shape of his mouth, the sensitive bow of his upper lip, the fullness of the lower. A vertical seam divided his lower lip in half. A lover would use her fingertip to trace that seam, Jane felt sure.

What a thought! And yet . . . here was how his lovers must know him: tousled, his black hair in glossy, rumpled waves around his face. In her imagination, his face was always so cold, beautiful in the way of a marble statue, bloodless and sneering. But in sleep, he looked younger, warmer, his black lashes fanning over his high cheekbones, extravagantly long, like a child's.

His nightshirt was of fine lawn, almost transparent. His shoulders were broad, well muscled. His chest . . .

she had not known men had nipples! The statues never
included them. But they were flat and small, set well
apart, and beneath them his belly made a flat, chiseled
plane, segmented into bands of muscle that moved as
he stretched.

Stretched! She glanced up and found him watching her.

She recoiled from the bed so quickly that she tripped
and fell.

Husky laughter preceded his appearance over the
edge of the bed. He leaned on his elbows, grinning
down at her. "Are you all right?"

She scrambled to her feet, feeling like an utter idiot.
A wife would not leap away from her husband! "I didn't
expect— You startled me."

"I crept in during the night." There was no apology
in his voice, but he pulled a face, as though to com-
miserate with her about the oddness of his choice. "You
looked so peaceful. I hoped it might be catching."

She could not think of any objection a wife would
have to that, either. "Oh."

He sat up, scrubbing a hand through his hair, which
had the effect of pulling the shirt more tightly against
his body. The muscles in his upper arm bunched. His
waist was narrow and lean, and with his posture so contorted, the edge of his shirt lifted to reveal his navel, and
a narrow line of dark hair that led downward . . .

He dropped his hand, and she swallowed.

Some new light entered his narrow gaze. A look of
speculative interest. The corners of his mouth curved,
lending it a flavor of good humor.

She felt flushed. "Water?" she croaked, and turned
toward the dresser, retrieving the pitcher with hands
that only shook a little.

"Please," he said from behind her. "I woke past midnight, parched as a desert. But the servants had neglected to spare me a drop."

"You may have to hire replacements." She carried a glass to him, then poured herself one as well. This was safer ground, the brisk work of household management, a wifely duty that required no . . . bed sharing. "Your butler—Cusworth, was it? Or Custer?"

He made an amused noise. "Your guess is as good as mine."

She smiled despite herself. "I think it was Cusworth. At any rate, he said that several of them had taken advantage of your absence to go on holiday, visit their families in the country. Some of them may not return."

"You have a free hand to do the hiring," he said. "And in everything else as well, of course."

Everything! That was generous. Which reminded her . . . "Of course, finding good help on short notice will not be easy. A handsome salary would help a great deal." She sat down on the edge of the bed, taking a sip of cold water as she formulated her next words. "Perhaps you might summon your family's solicitor. He will need your signature for the trust to be released."

"A fine idea." His tone was distracted. He was watching her hand around the cup—or no, she realized, his attention was fixed at a point somewhat higher . . .

She looked down at herself and realized her gown had come untied. The tops of her breasts were visible.

She slapped a hand to her chest and sloshed water into her lap in the process.

He laughed again, but his laugh was soft, husky, no malice or mockery in it. "Jane," he said, and his hand came onto her knee, giving her a start. She stared at his knuckles, square and dark, and her heart tripped.

She cleared her throat, made herself look at him. His expression was . . . warm, rueful, amused.

"You needn't be nervous," he said. "I won't . . . jump on you. That wasn't my intention in sleeping here."

Some knot inside her relaxed. Perhaps it relaxed too far. As his hand smoothed over her knee, she felt a peculiar melting sensation in the pit of her stomach. "It . . . wasn't? Of course it wasn't," she said quickly, lest he mistake her tone for disappointment.

"No. Although the temptation is . . ." Once again, his gaze dipped to her neckline, roving with unguarded admiration over her bosom before lifting again. He held her gaze frankly then—unapologetic, unashamed. She felt dizzy.

He desired her. He was showing her so plainly. But there was nothing . . . cold in it, or unkind.

And so, to her amazement, it was impossible to take offense. Or even to bridle.

"I would like nothing better," he murmured, "than to take up where we left off. Before I was injured, I mean."

"Oh." She battled a hysterical laugh. "No, I don't think that would be wise."

"I agree," he said solemnly. "It would not be fair to you, when you must see me as . . . so altered. Though . . ." He offered her a quick, crooked grin. "I understand quite well how I looked at *you*."

How wrong he was. She could not offer more than a helpless smile.

"You are beautiful," he said earnestly, sitting up a little, drawing closer. "Surely I told you this a thousand times. But your hair, in the light . . ." To her amazement, he threaded his hand through the tangled nest of curls at her temple, stroking it as though he took no notice of the snarls. Her braid must be half demolished; it never survived the night intact.

"It's glorious," he said. "Wild and violent, with a life of its own."

"Violent?" She cleared her throat. Nobody had ever praised her hair; curls might be fashionable, but only the well-behaved kind created with heating tongs. Nevertheless, she might have hoped for a better attempt than *that*. "Well. I suppose 'violent' might be one word for it—"

"A force of nature," he cut in, smiling. "A powerful force." He smoothed lightly down the length of her braid. "And to think you tame it every day." As he toyed with the end of her braid, he tugged ever so slightly, and a startling shiver of pleasure rippled through her. "What a pity that is," he said. "It would make a fine crown. A halo, announcing your inner mettle."

Nonsense. What was she doing, letting herself be seduced by this babble? She drew back a little, and he, noticing, took his hands back into his lap.

That small consideration struck her by force.

This was not the man who had forced kisses on her.

She did not know who this man was.

"You don't know my inner mettle." Her words were clipped. He did not *know* her. His honeyed words were empty; she would not be cozened by them. "You don't know me at all."

His hand came over hers. Touching her again, stroking the back of her hand lightly, persuasively, as one might soothe a nervous animal. "True," he said. "Perhaps . . . I'm the luckiest of men. To be allowed to discover my bride twice; to have the chance to fall in love all over again."

Stop saying such things. You don't mean them.

But when she opened her mouth, nothing came out.

The Crispin Burke she had known would not have meant such things. But the way this man was gazing on her . . .

Perhaps he did mean them. Or he was a man who *could* mean such things; who could say them without embarrassment, and hope them to be true.

Oh, God.

He leaned closer to her. Why, his eyes were not black after all. They were the darkest blue, the shade of a moonless night sky. "May I kiss you, Jane?"

No. That would be a very bad idea. Her gaze fell to his lips, that secret seam that she had never before noticed. His breath felt warm against her mouth. "I don't think . . ."

His lips touched hers. The slightest brush. A whisper. His fingertips landed lightly on her face, bracketing her cheek, his thumb beneath her jaw nudging her face ever so slightly upward, so their mouths came together squarely. Soft touches. A soft kiss. A request, tentative, hopeful.

Here was a kiss. That other one, at Marylebigh—that had only been a facsimile. *Here* was the lesson worth learning.

No. The other man was still in there somewhere. She opened her mouth to him, daring that other man to appear. To show his true and forceful nature.

But he ignored the invitation. He broke free of her lips to kiss his way across her cheek. His fingertips, gentle, warm, guided her once more, tilting her face to an angle that offered him her throat. She shuddered as his mouth found her pulse. He lingered there, his lips making a study of her heartbeat.

His hand passed like a ghost over her braid, her shoulder, her upper arm. His palm cupped her elbow as though it were precious, a breakable thing.

He inhaled, long and deep. "The smell of you," he murmured. "My God, Jane. I swear . . . I remember it."

Everything in her contracted. Everything warm, melting—it froze.

He eased back. "What is it? What did I say?"

"You remember?" she said roughly.

His expression darkened. "Ah. No. I'm sorry," he said gently. "It was . . . I'm sorry, Jane; it was a stupid thing to say."

Her pulse began to slow. "No," she said, relief making her generous. "It was . . . lovely."

He offered her a hesitant smile—one that sought forgiveness. She reached for his hand without thinking and squeezed it. His smile widened; suddenly they were beaming at each other.

What on earth was she *doing*?

The door banged open. They sprang apart like guilty schoolchildren as a mobcapped maid bustled inside, firewood in her arms.

"Oh!" The maid turned red as she dropped a curtsey. "Begging your pardon!"

CHAPTER SEVEN

Crispin had walked through the house nine times this morning. Nine times, he'd passed through every room. With his eyes closed, he could now envision its layout. He sat in the drawing room, whose sash windows overlooked the street. The pocket doors to the right opened into the dining room. The door to the left led to the hallway, his study, and the stairs. Up those stairs to the immediate right lay his bedroom; the door next to it was his wife's apartment.

How in hell, then, had he got lost again half an hour ago?

"Burke? Are you . . . quite well?"

No. He was not well. His brain felt . . . gelded. Why in God's name could he not remember? How much longer would this intolerable state endure?

He opened his eyes. Samuel Noyes was the fifth of his friends whom he had received today. Perhaps his last. He knew that it would behoove him to familiarize himself with as many allies as possible before he returned to Westminster, but his patience was wearing thin.

It was peculiar how many of these "friends" of his were known to him from his school days. They were the same lads whom he'd avoided on the playing field for their tendency to cheat. Crispin supposed the decent ones would be hesitating to impose themselves so soon after his recovery—to say nothing of his nuptials. A newlywed deserved privacy.

"Go on," he said.

Noyes nodded. He was not one of the younger set; he had been a politician when Crispin was still learning to read, and spoke with casual authority. "The second reading will finish quickly," he said. "The Cabinet hasn't got much fight left. Assuming it passes committee, we must think ahead to the Lords. Auburn and Chad mean to work against it, of course, but if you still feel certain of Farnsworth's support . . ." He paused, his cocked white brow making a question of it.

Farnsworth? The Duke of Farnsworth, Laura's husband?

The feeling of the dream came over him again, slick and cold and dark. "Did I tell you I had his support?"

Noyes mistook the question as rhetorical and smirked. "Well, there you have it, then. And once it passes—why, the sky's our limit. *Your* limit, to be precise. Particularly now that you find yourself so handsomely equipped." His white brows waggled. "Ha! You might have shared that plan, old boy. Proper mess you've made! Mason's lost his wits, all but foaming at the mouth. What inspired you to steal off with the girl? May I ask?"

Each of his callers this morning had expressed similar astonishment about Crispin's marriage, and asked to know the cause. Crispin had told the first that love knew no logic—a remark that the other man had taken for a hilarious joke. "You, in *love*?"

So he contented himself now with a shrug.

Silence and honesty made surprisingly effective masks for ignorance. None of his visitors seemed to have noticed his infirmity. His blunders, they took for jokes; his taciturn replies, for some subtle strategy of intimidation. When he'd bluntly told the Earl of Elborough that he did not remember their last meeting, Elborough had gone quite pale, as though Crispin's remark were intended as an insult. More curiously yet, Elborough had then *apologized* for presuming the meeting was memorable.

As the silence extended now, Noyes, too, looked discomfited. "Don't mistake me," he said in a subdued voice. "We'll handle Mason. Trying to bullyrag you— the cheek!"

And now an elder statesman was placating him. Crispin's growing headache was counterbalanced by amazement. It was true: he *was* powerful.

But the renewed wonder brought anxiety along with it, sharp as a spur. If he did not remember soon, he would lose everything he'd gained. *Remember, damn it!*

"I'll speak to him today," Noyes went on. "And if he continues to yap, we'll muzzle him."

He could not let that remark pass unchallenged. "Have a care. That's my wife's uncle you're discussing."

Noyes's eyes rounded in astonishment—an unfortunate effect. With his tuft of white hair, his sloping brow, and his recessed chin, he already had the bulge-eyed look of a pug. "Why—er, quite so. My apologies."

With a flustered air, he patted his jacket, then carefully extracted two cigars. He fitted one to his lips before holding out the other.

Crispin shook his head. "I don't smoke."

"What's that? Since when?"

Another point noted. Apparently he'd taken up tobacco. "Full of surprises, I am."

Truer words were never spoken. Each of the associates he'd received this morning had offered a peculiar glimpse into the man he'd been. Evidently he'd altered legislation at his wealthiest voters' instructions. He'd gambled for high stakes and demanded prompt payment; Elborough had begged him for an extension on his vowels. He also appeared to be the natural choice when pressure was wanted. A fellow MP had visited to request he "teach" a green backbencher to "fall in line."

Once he remembered, he would no doubt understand the cause for all of this. But the tidings had left Crispin nauseated. The doctors warned him to expect this—along with dizziness, headache, and confusion. These were the inevitable companions to convalescence from a head injury.

Losing one's way in familiar places—the doctors had not warned him of *that*. That was a secret best kept from everyone.

Noyes was tucking away his cigars with the doting care of a father for his infants. "Well," he said. "No matter. It's a relief to see you back in the game. And Mason will see reason eventually. Victory has a way of sweetening a man's temper."

Crispin glanced toward the clock on the mantel. "Was that all to discuss, then?" The room was swimming oddly at the corners of his vision.

"Oh. Quite." Stiffly, Noyes rose. "Yes, I suppose you'll have a dozen other appointments. Say, when can we expect you back on the floor?"

There lay the rub. The nausea and headaches, he could manage. But with no memory of the issues at hand, no recognition of his friends and allies, how on earth would he manage it? Perhaps charm and luck could carry him through . . . But then there was the matter of this damnable disorientation. In memory, Crispin had not set foot in Westminster since his childhood, when he'd gone with his family to watch his father take his seat.

It was too easy to envision the spectacle he'd make, should he get lost there. Taking the wrong door from the Central Hall, stumbling into the Peers Court. Or losing his way from his seat to the water closet. Good God, the place was a maze.

He took a hard breath to channel his frustration. "The doctors' orders were strict. But I'll certainly be there for the third reading." His memories would return by then, surely.

Noyes looked unsatisfied. Crispin added deliberately, "Unless you feel unable to handle it without me?"

"Oh! No." Noyes grimaced. "But some of these northerners are still threatening to kick up a fuss. Not saying you should cross the doctors, but if you can find a chance to speak to Lambert and Culver, I'd be grateful. Stubborn asses."

"Yes, of course." *Lambert and Culver*, he repeated silently. *Lambert and Culver*. God above, he needed a secretary. Why on earth hadn't he kept one? His wife claimed he had wanted discretion. One of his visitors earlier had made a jape about his "paranoia." But it would take an uncommon dark secret to make a politician forgo an assistant. And the contents of Crispin's desk, so far, had not yielded anything so interesting.

A silence had opened. Noyes was lingering, waiting for Crispin to walk him out.

But Crispin's exhaustion felt leaden. If he stood up now, he felt certain he would topple.

Worse, he might not be able to find the way to the door.

"Keep me informed," he said, his tone dismissive.

Noyes, flushing in surprise, nodded and hurried out.

Someone was pounding at the front door.

Crispin looked up from his desk, bleary-eyed. The scattered remnants of a late dinner sat on the table by the fire. No one had come to retrieve them.

The sight of the clock startled him. It was nearly midnight? The day had dragged, the hours ground down by fatigue. He hadn't napped, though. Children napped. Men did not.

He forced his attention back to the blue book in front of him. Atticus would have needed no more than a week to wade through the records from the last session of Parliament. Crispin feared he would not be done for a month. He'd never had the knack for prolonged, studious focus. His attention wandered.

But tomorrow would bring new visitors, and while he would not know their names, he could damned well learn about the issues they would discuss. He would finish reading just this one report before he slept. So perhaps he would get no sleep at all. *So be it.* He would read and reread this report until it stuck. He had no bloody choice.

The knocking came again. Something frenzied in it now.

Frowning, he listened for Cusworth. Or a footman. Or a scullery maid, for all he cared—someone needed to answer the bloody door.

He caught the smell of a souring glass of milk, abandoned on his dinner tray.

The stench suddenly seemed unbearable. Milk! Drinking *milk* like an infant! Tomorrow he would have a brandy. The doctors could go hang.

Still knocking. Was nobody going to answer? If a caller arrived so late, was it not considered urgent to discover his purpose?

Very well, *he* would answer the door. He pushed to his feet—and the floor lurched. He staggered and caught himself against the desk.

Blue books thudded onto the carpet. Loose papers began to slide after them. He lunged to catch them.

Mistake.

Nausea rolled through him. He held still, stretched flat across the desktop, one brass-capped corner digging into his belly. He was gasping, the dying rasps of an old man.

Pathetic.

A muffled shout came from without—the visitor yelling for entry.

A harsh sound slipped from him. The staff was pathetic. *He* was pathetic. They were all of them bloody pathetic and useless.

Gritting his teeth, he stood. The floor rolled beneath him like the deck of a ship. He gritted his teeth and slowly made his way toward the door.

The doorjamb tilted around him. He leaned into it

for a moment, cursing silently, then stepped into the hall.

The wallpaper was dark flocked velvet, the floral patterning soft beneath his palm. Like a blinded invalid, Crispin let the wall support him as he inched his way into the entry hall.

The sight of the empty foyer—the stairs so conspicuously vacant, the frantic pounding at the door so completely counterbalanced by the stillness inside his house—inflamed him. His frustration sharpened into resolve. He was going to sack every servant in his employ. He would start again from bloody scratch.

"I know you're in there!"

And who in God's name could *this* be? Who would come pounding on his door, screaming, after eleven o'clock?

Perhaps the bastard who'd tried to kill him. Yes, wouldn't that be delightful? Because someone *had* tried to kill him. He'd nearly been victim to murder, at the hands of a phantom or a nun for all he knew, because his memory was a gaping dark hole. Why, perhaps he'd even smiled this very morning at the villain who'd half killed him. Who could say? Not he! He was worse than an idiot—he did not even know what he didn't know. He was a bloody witless disaster—

He took a large breath. *Enough.*

Carefully, lest he lose his balance again, he unlocked and pulled open the door.

The man standing on the threshold was a stranger. Of course he was! What else was new?

Brown beard, squinting eyes, medium height. Dark suit expertly tailored. Glossy coach waiting on the curb below, driver hunching in the light rain.

"Done hiding, are you?" the man sneered, and shoved past Crispin, almost knocking him over. Crispin caught his balance on the doorframe, swallowed a curse, before turning to face the man.

His visitor had fallen into the hunched posture of a boxer: chin down, shoulders cocked, fists displayed. "I never thought you a fool," the man snarled. Spit collected in the corners of his mouth, flecking his beard as he continued: "Disloyalty, I might have expected. But sheer idiocy, I never foresaw! Well done, Burke!"

The floor rolled again. Light rain misted his back. Crispin shut the door and leaned against it for balance. "Mind your tongue." He borrowed his father's iciest tones. "Or I will put you back outside."

"Mind my tongue!" The man clawed his hands through his hair, dislodging his top hat, which fell to his feet and was promptly crushed as he stepped onto it, turning in a tight circle. "That's a fine idea! You think I will be *civil*? I will crush you, Burke! Don't think I won't! Or—" The man pivoted toward him. "Or you will undo this," he said fiercely. "We will let bygones be bygones. It's not too late. Any man might make a mistake—"

"Hello, Uncle."

Jane was descending the stairs. The man stiffened, his jaw squaring as he glared at her.

Uncle. *Ah.* This rabid animal was Jane's former guardian, Philip Mason. No wonder she did not care to speak of him.

"You ungrateful, conniving little bitch," Mason said.

"My, such eloquence!" Any other woman would have remained at a safe distance, but Jane, fearless, walked straight toward him. "No wonder you depended on

Crispin to make your speeches for you." Her smile looked cold.

Mason lunged for her.

Crispin's vision hazed. One moment he was leaning against the door; the next, his arm had closed around Mason's throat. He hauled the bastard backward and threw him up against the door.

Come into his house at midnight and attack his wife? "Careful," he said, very low.

The whites of Mason's eyes showed. "You're mad. Mad! If I fall, you fall with me. Do you truly imagine otherwise? You have no secrets that I do not know. If you walk away from this friendship, I will—"

"Threats from the weak are more amusing than jokes." Jane spoke clearly from behind Crispin, who adjusted his body to ensure Mason could not reach for her. "Is that not one of your favorite sayings? And without my money . . . why, how amusing you've become!"

Mason's nostrils flared. "By God, I will make you—"

"Enough." Crispin's patience was done. "You are finished here. Come near my wife again, and I will end you."

Mason's eyes narrowed. "You will regret this very soon, I think."

Had he felt, a minute ago, disoriented and drained? Crispin laughed. He seized Mason by the arm, hauled open the door, and threw him into the rain.

The door slammed.

"Thank you," said his wife, her voice suddenly tremulous.

Crispin turned to her. She looked . . . shaken. "What is it?" he said. "He didn't scare you?"

"No, of course not." The denial was automatic, absent. "You—you don't remember, do you?"

Bloody hell. His laugh now felt black, scraping. "How many times will you ask? Do you not think I would *tell* you if I remembered?"

She flinched. "I . . . of course . . . it's only, you seemed . . ."

The world was spinning again. But he would not reach for support, not in front of her. "Only *what?*" he snapped.

She answered in a whisper. "You seemed so like him, for a moment."

Like him? Like *himself*, did she mean? Why in God's name did she sound so gloomy about the prospect? "I would bloody hope so! Isn't that the damned—"

The world went dark.

"Crispin? Crispin!"

His eyes opened. He was sprawled on the floor, his wife kneeling over him, patting his cheek like an anxious nursemaid.

"I'll send for the doctor," she said.

"No." He shoved away from her, ignoring her proffered hand as he lurched inelegantly to his feet. "You will not." Doctors could do nothing for him. They could only cluck and frown and make predictions as vague and useless as a fortune-teller's. *You may recover your mind. You may not.* He was sick of it.

His wife, usually so calm and cool-eyed, was all but fluttering around him. "But surely—"

"Leave me." He did not mean to speak so harshly. But by God, he did not want her to witness such weakness. What must she think? Her husband had turned into a lunatic—worse, a lunatic *child*, coddled with glasses of milk, unable to walk properly, unable to keep his bloody balance. "Just go."

"I . . ." She folded her hands together at her lips. "May I at least help you up the—"

"*Go!*"

Oh, well done. Shouting at his own wife, driving her to lift her skirts and flee as though from a predator. Or from her uncle.

Who had been, apparently, Crispin's *friend*.

Bravo! He'd clearly made some fine choices in these last few years. No wonder somebody had tried to murder him.

He sagged back against the door, disgust like acid in his throat.

This could not continue.

He was half tempted to strike his own skull, hard, again and again. To strike until his brain resettled into its proper position and gave him his life back.

Instead, after a long minute, he pushed off the door and made his way toward the stairs.

Crispin Burke had subscribed to every newspaper published within fifty miles of London—including those whose editors deplored him. This made him a much more widely read man than her uncle. Jane had intercepted a maid yesterday and saved a stack from the fire; she sat now at the little table by the window in her bedroom, picking through the old issues, trying to work up an interest in what normally fascinated her most: the world, laid out and parsed in neatly numbered pages and intelligent, erudite prose.

But her mind kept wandering to the apartment next door. He had come upstairs at last. Quite a ruckus he'd made, opening and slamming every other door in the hallway, including the door to her sitting room, before entering his own. She'd been waiting, worrying despite herself, fretting as she donned her night rail and combed her fingers through her hair. It was not her place to over-rule him and summon a doctor. She was not, after all, truly his wife. But if she had been . . .

He'd be in bed, no matter what he wanted. A medical professional would be standing over him and giving him what for, too. There was no call for him to push him-self, to work without pause until midnight. And then, to tackle her uncle—

Well. At the time, she'd been terrified, because the ruthless face he'd shown Uncle Philip seemed to belong to the other Crispin, the man she hoped never again to meet.

Now, relieved of that fear, she belatedly felt deeply grateful. Crispin was ailing, but for her sake, he had summoned some deep reserve of strength and put on a cold and terrifying show. Even her uncle would not be stupid enough to come harass her again.

She closed the newspaper. Perhaps she *should* sum-mon a doctor.

A thump came from nearby. She jumped to her feet. Had he fallen again?

She hurried to the door that separated their bed-rooms, opening it before she could doubt herself.

His room was empty.

Something clanked, sharp and metallic. She turned slowly, following the noise as it came again.

Her bedroom was paneled in blond oak, a feminine match for the dark walnut in Crispin's. The noise seemed to be coming from within the wall. She laid her hand to the smooth-grained panel and felt it *move* slightly.

Why, it was a door—a cunning door, with a hidden

handhold in the carved panel frame. Breath held, she slid it open.

Steam billowed out at her. A hidden chamber! The room was lined in vividly glazed tiles, aquamarine and terra-cotta and scarlet. Exposed copper taps ran along the wall, emptying into a long, deep copper tub in which lounged—

Crispin Burke, utterly naked.

She froze. Crispin was facing away from her, his dark head tipped back against the rim of the tub. A large mirror affixed to the wall in front of him showed her foggy reflection, her hair a wild loose cloud, her expression stupefied. She could see his face as well: eyes closed, face slack. Alarm flickered, then died: his bare chest was rising and falling in a steady rhythm.

His bare chest. Broad, powerfully developed. Water glistened on the bunched brawn of his upper arms. His shoulders were thickly hewn, sturdy. His neck—damp, strong, and corded—lay at an angle that emphasized his Adam's apple.

He shifted, and she saw the water lick at his navel. The mirror was not long enough to capture anything below his waist. A pity.

Good heavens! Shocked at herself, she stepped backward.

His eyes opened. As their gazes locked in the mirror, a current passed through her, hot and startling.

His hair was wet. It clung to his sharp cheekbones. A drop of water snaked down his jaw.

She fumbled frantically for the door.

"Wait." He sat up, water sloshing. Rivulets ran down the rippled planes of his back. He did not look away from her in the mirror. "Jane."

The sound of her name snagged her like a hook. Mouth dry, she faced him. The air held some dark mélange of spices, a peculiar soap.

"Your hair," he said, very low.

He was staring at her as though at a marvel.

A peculiar tremor went through her. "I . . ." She touched her hair, this bane of her youth. The damp was causing her curls to frizz. *You shouldn't look at it so.* Not with admiration—not at such an untamable mess.

Who had taught her to feel so?

The world, of course.

"So much of it," he murmured. "My God. I had no idea. And your skin . . ."

Her skin? She took after her mother's Italian ancestors, who had lived under a stronger sun. "I'm no English rose."

His dark gaze moved down her. "You're golden."

That low, rough word stroked some secret pleasurable place in her. She felt light-headed, disoriented. That strange, seductive scent, spices like drugs. The humid air collected on her skin, making her wool robe feel muffling, itchy. She felt . . . crowded, though he had not moved. His broad bare shoulders, his large hands gripping the sides of the tub . . . He was an animal presence that filled the room, making it difficult to breathe.

She crossed her arms and looked at the tiled floor. *Step out*, she told herself, but the tiles caught her attention. Each was unique, an intricate geometric design inlaid with colored stones.

"A Turkish bath." His voice had shifted, smoothed. "Impressive, no?"

She cast him the briefest glance. Were they really going to have a discussion? For all that the tub concealed the most interesting half of him, he was still naked! "Yes, I . . ." She had never heard of such a thing. "It's lovely."

"And expensive." And now, once again, she heard the old Crispin in him, that cynical edge that made her feel uncertain, unsettled. "It makes one wonder, doesn't it?"

She hesitated, daring to find his gaze in the mirror again. "Wonder what?"

He lifted one solid, gleaming shoulder. "How I afforded it."

She blinked. She certainly had theories—corruption, bribery, blackmail, cheating—but none that would speak well of him.

Happily, he did not seem to expect an answer. "Did I wake you?" he asked. "I didn't mean to open your door."

She crossed her arms again. "Did you want to speak with me?"

"No." A peculiar smile twisted his lips. "I seem to have a new talent for . . . losing myself."

"What do you mean?"

"Just as it sounds. I'm encouraged that you haven't noticed. But in places I don't know—places not known to me from childhood, like my parents' house—I become . . ." He gave an impatient tug of his mouth. "Turned around."

Her pulse hitched. That was, indeed, very odd. "But not all the time." Then she *would* have noticed.

"It comes and goes. For several hours, I'll be fine. And then, suddenly . . ." He drew a circle in the air with his finger. "The world seems rearranged."

"Have you told the doctors?"

He lapsed into a short, brooding silence. "They warned me," he said, "of every possible ailment under the sun. They said I might see double at times. That I might lose my vision temporarily from the headaches. But they never mentioned this. I don't think it's . . . a common consequence." He shook his head, then blew out a breath. "I'm sorry," he said more stiltedly. "For earlier. I should not have spoken so harshly to you."

She hesitated. "Are you—when you fell, I thought— I mean, I feared . . .'

He closed his eyes. She noticed the shadows beneath them, the hollowness beneath his cheekbones.

A droplet of water lingered on his philtrum. It slowly coasted downward, slipping over his full lips, then plummeting off his chin.

Irritated with herself, she stepped hard on the insole of her foot. "Are you in pain?" she asked bluntly.

His pause felt as thick as the steamy air. "Pain," he said absently. "Curious how hard it is to speak of it. I remember nothing of my life—nothing of this room, this house. Nothing of my work." His eyes opened, meeting hers in the mirror. "Or my wife. But pain—*pain* is what shames me." His smile looked sharp, almost mocking. "Yes, that makes sense, doesn't it? I'm a fine specimen, all right."

That seemed unfair, deeply unfair to him. His suffering was not of his own making. And how bizarre and impossible it must be, to find himself in such a position! Softly she said, "Any man in your shoes—"

"I'm well enough, Jane." He spoke gently. "I only wished to apologize. I won't keep you any longer."

His dismissal could not be clearer. Flushing, she turned to leave—but then spied, from the corner of her eye, his grimace as he reached for the pitcher beside the tub.

"I should ring for someone," she blurted. "To help you."

His laugh was curt. "Good luck with that."

The staff required a severe scolding. She made a note

to deliver one tomorrow. She felt angry on his behalf. It was not right that he should have nobody to help him.

She could help him.

Her pulse hitched. She spoke quickly, before better sense could change her mind. "I'll do it."

"No," he said, but she had already seized the pitcher. "Jane. I can make do on my—"

"Lie back." She spoke briskly, as any paid servant might do, impersonal and sexless, attending to duty without feeling or care.

He twisted—wincing as he did so—to scowl at her. "I am well able—"

"Lie back," she said stridently. *Too* stridently. He visibly startled.

But then a curious smile tipped the corner of his mouth. "Very well," he said, and lay back again.

She tested the water in the pitcher with her finger. It was lukewarm, not the source of the steam settling now around her. But it would serve. She poured it over his head, and it called forth suds that suggested he had already soaped his hair thoroughly. "Rinsing, then?"

"Yes."

Very easy. She poured another stream, gently combing her fingers through his hair to clean it. His hair was thick, impossibly soft compared to hers. She kept her eyes firmly trained on it, although her position now, kneeling behind him, gave her a clear view to the parts of him that the tub had formerly concealed. But eyes could be disciplined. She would not look. She would focus only on—

She gasped, and sloshed half the pitcher into his face.

"I'm so sorry!" she cried, setting down the pitcher as he sputtered and wiped his face clean.

But after a moment, his sputter resolved into laughter. "Quite all right," he said.

"I only . . ." She took a hard breath. "I didn't know . . ."

The thickness of his hair had concealed, until now, the shaven patch where some criminal's weapon had landed. The wound had not entirely healed—the gash was deep, a depression in his skull.

"Yes," he said at length. "Someone tried to kill me."

"I hadn't realized . . ." *That the injury was so serious.* She swallowed the words. Of course it had been serious. It had injured his very brain.

"I take solace," he said, "from the knowledge of how frustrated they must be. At least I'm not alone in my foul temper."

She sensed some discordant note buried in his levity. A hint that he was shaken, for all that he tried to conceal it.

"A fine lesson for them," she said softly. "Nobody defeats Crispin Burke."

The remark was not clever, but it made him relax again, his shoulders loosening visibly.

What fascinating, almost leonine languor. She watched her hand settle on the stretch of muscle between the base of his neck and the cap of his shoulder. Hot, smooth skin. She could feel his muscle flex.

Swallowing, she retrieved the pitcher and continued rinsing his hair. With his every minute movement, his taut skin revealed the workings of his body, of bulked, leashed power. Suds slipped down his throat, chased past his collarbone, and slipped over his chest. She aimed the pitcher to follow them. But it seemed cowardly, really, to keep herself at such a distance. She laid the pitcher aside and took up a sponge and a bar of soap from the far rim of the tub, using them to wipe his throat and chest.

Don't look. But her gaze escaped her. It jumped down his belly—remembered decorum long enough to skip his pelvis—and landed on his sculptured thighs. *Good heavens.* His legs were long, his knees square, his calves elegantly muscled.

Her fingertips, distracted, brushed the skin above his navel, and his belly flinched. The sensation plucked a weird echo from her own belly.

Why was her hand there? She yanked the sponge back up his chest. She was finished; his hair was clean.

But when her mouth opened, what came out was: "Your back?"

Water shifted as he obligingly sat forward.

The breath went from her. Was this how men were shaped beneath their clothes? A great wingspan, thick and powerful shoulders whittling into a lean, hard waist.

No, no, no. Some inward alarm announced the imminent collapse of her brain, her restraint, her modesty, her virtue. Her hands felt possessed by the devil, twitching with curiosity as she smoothed them across his shoulder blades. *Stop. Stop at once.*

She cast down the sponge with a wet slap. "That will do." She sounded wheezy.

He lay back again, tipping his chin so he was looking up into her face, so close above his own. The angle was so novel that it caught her, held her in place for a brief moment's study. His cheekbones were broad and wide. His lips full and plush. His jaw was adamantine, chiseled. His eyes were slumberous and heavy lidded yet somehow intent, focused and fully aware.

In that long, breathless moment, their gazes did not

hold so much as mingle, communicating some message that her brain could not decipher but that caused her body to grow heavy, her lips to part, her breath to shorten.

"Thank you," he murmured, barely making sound.

Her grip convulsively tightened around the soap. Soap! She was still holding the soap. "The soap," she muttered. She handed it to him.

His hand closed over hers. He drew her wrist to his mouth and pressed his lips against it.

A squeak came from her. *She* had made that noise.

His lips felt hot. He spoke against her skin. "Your hair," he said, "is a glory. Promise me you will never pin it up again."

The brush of his mouth sent static sparks along her skin. She felt flushed, shivering, light-headed. "I don't . . . It would be a scandal."

He turned her wrist ever so slightly, finding her pulse with his tongue. Her breath caught. She heard him breathe in deeply. "Then unpin it just for me," he whispered.

For a sweet wild second, she saw it—a vision so vivid it seemed like memory: this man, this Crispin, treasuring her . . . admiring, protecting, cherishing her just as she was. Running his hands over her hair and kissing his way down her throat, every morning and night, forever.

She snatched her hand free. "Your—the soap is gone from your hair," she said stupidly. "I—good luck."

Good luck? What an idiot she was!

Face burning, she walked out.

CHAPTER EIGHT

"Everything seems to be in order," Mr. Gaultier said. He picked through the papers once more, mumbling unintelligibly beneath his breath. He was the perfect age for a solicitor—somewhere around sixty, with a bald head, glinting spectacles, and a neat, dapper appearance that spoke of modest but discerning self-regard.

Nevertheless, Jane held her breath until she caught him muttering the words *marriage certificate*. Only then did she relax. The archbishop's forgery continued to fool everybody.

Indeed, *was* it a forgery? The thought struck her with a jolt. If a prince of the Church declared one married, and the government's official records agreed, then by what technicality could the marriage be called false?

The groom's objection might do it. But if the groom did not know to object, and the archbishop continued to hold his tongue . . .

As though God had heard her secret thoughts and decided to punish her for sacrilege, the solicitor rifled back to the certificate and picked it up to hold to the light. "Remarkable," he said, squinting.

Some noise escaped her. She sensed Crispin's curious look. "How so?" he asked.

"Oh, to have been married by an archbishop is remarkable enough—a great honor," Mr. Gaultier said with an unctuous smile. "But for his grace, there must have been a sweet poetry to it, to revisit the humbler and more joyful offices of the clergy, so soon before his passing."

"His *passing*?" Jane croaked.

Mr. Gaultier lowered the paper, looking startled. "Oh dear. Had you not heard? Yes, I'm afraid so. Ten days ago. Apoplexy, I believe."

Crispin, turning toward her, lifted a brow in silent inquiry. No doubt she wore a very curious expression. With the archbishop gone, and the certificate filed . . .

Until now, she had been afraid of discovery, and so fixated on the pressing issue of how to get her hands on the money, that it had never struck her to wonder whether she would require a *divorce*.

"May his soul rest in peace," she whispered.

"Amen," Crispin said. "So that settles it, Mr. Gaultier, am I right?"

"Quite right," the solicitor said briskly. "By the terms of the will, half of the stocks and funds will be transferred into both your names, with the remainder held in a trust exclusively for your wife, in case of . . ." He cleared his throat. "Unforeseen circumstances."

"In case I prove a blackguard," Crispin said amiably.

"Those specific terms were not employed." But after a beat, Gaultier offered a dry smile. "Nevertheless, the late Mr. Mason clearly had a care for all eventualities."

He slipped the papers into his leather case. "I'll make arrangements with your family's man at the Bank of England, who will see to the other paperwork."

"How long will it take?" Jane blurted. For she was losing her mind. Even sitting beside Crispin seemed peculiarly provocative. Every time she glanced at him, she remembered the look of his bare broad shoulders . . . the feel of his lips against her wrist.

"Oh, no more than a day or two. The only formality remaining is to procure the signature of the executor."

Jane's nails cut into the upholstery of her seat.

"The executor?" Crispin spoke pleasantly, blessedly ignorant of the death knell that had just sounded for her hopes.

"Yes, of the estate. Just a formality, of course. I believe he would be . . ." Gaultier pulled out the papers again, flicking over the topmost page. "Ah. Your wife's uncle." He offered Jane a perfunctory smile of acknowledgment as he slotted the stack back into his case.

She felt sick. "And if he refuses to sign?"

"Refuses?" Mr. Gautier, caught rising, settled back into his seat with a frown. "Why, that would be highly irregular. I cannot imagine why he should do so."

Crispin spoke. "Our marriage took him by surprise. He may feel some dudgeon over that."

Some dudgeon. Jane shot Crispin a look. A more masterful understatement she'd never heard.

"I see." Mr. Gaultier rolled his lips together, looking thoughtful. "Well, the terms of the inheritance were quite clear. Her guardian's consent was not required for her marriage." He nodded to Jane. "It seems your father had a high opinion of your judgment, madam."

"He did," she said softly. Would that he'd had a lower

opinion of his brother! But Papa could never have foreseen how Uncle Philip would comport himself after acquiring a taste of power and wealth.

She'd long since abandoned trying to square her
uncle with the man she'd known as a child. So what if
he'd dandled her on his knee and chucked her chin? In
retrospect, such memories were not even charming. No
matter how old she'd grown, he'd never stopped treating
her like a witless doll.

"Well, if he refuses to sign, I will pay a call to explain
how little he stands to gain from such shenanigans," Mr.
Gaultier said. "Once he understands so, I expect he'll do
his duty."

"In the meantime," she said, "he cannot access the
accounts, I hope."

"He was never able to touch them," Mr. Gaultier assured her. "The interest, yes, but only for your mainte-
nance. The principal was never available to him."

"You may want to make certain of that."

Again, the solicitor worked to hide his surprise. "I
see. Well, I will go directly to the bank, Mrs. Burke. Rest
assured I will review all the particulars."

"Thank you," Crispin said. He stood, walking toward the pocket doors and opening them into the dining room for some reason Jane could not guess. When
he turned back, he swayed.

Realization dawned. *I have a new talent for losing myself*, he'd told her.

She rose, eager to make a distraction for him. "Mr.
Gaultier, you've been too kind. May I walk you out?"

The solicitor, looking only mildly puzzled by this un-
orthodox offer from a lady, allowed her to lead him into
the entry hall.

But there, by the front door, his manner suddenly changed. When she offered a polite handshake, he held on to her fingers, gripping with startling force.

"I knew your father somewhat," he said. He glanced furtively beyond her. "For his sake, I wish you to know you may always count me as a friend."

Bewildered, she pulled her hand free. "I . . . thank you, Mr. Gaultier. I had no idea you knew my father."

"I admired him, I should say. I went twice to watch him speak when he was campaigning for his seat. You were there, I believe. And your mother."

A smile overtook her. "Yes, we were always there." Her parents had raised her to believe that politics were as much a woman's concern as a man's, for neither sex was spared their effect.

"He was a very fine speaker, ma'am. A great thinker, a natural leader of men. Though his greatness lifted him high, he never once forgot nor tried to conceal his origins. He understood the people, their true needs, and wished only to serve them."

Jane felt flushed with pleasure now. "Yes, that was him exactly!" Earnest, idealistic, committed. "He was a man of very strong principles."

"And morals," Mr. Gaultier muttered, with another cautious glance behind her, as though fearful of being overheard. "He would have gone high, I feel certain of it. But I fear that Westminster no longer rewards such honesty. It is cunning, rather than moral fiber, which makes a man's career nowadays."

Realization prickled through her. He was warning her in some way. "I'm sorry to hear that."

"I am a man of integrity myself. I would never speak ill of any client. But I have served two generations of

Burkes." His look now was adamant, speaking volumes more than his words. "And I am honored to serve you, ma'am. I will make sure that your uncle cannot touch your accounts—and that *no one* may interfere with that trust that was vouchsafed to you, and you alone."

He was warning her against Crispin.

"I see." If she had been as naïve as Mr. Gaultier imagined—and if Crispin had not taken a knock to the head—this warning would have proved more than useful. Why, it might have saved a gullible bride from ruin.

Why, then, did she feel a flicker of resentment on Crispin's behalf?

"You are very kind, Mr. Gaultier." Of course he was. "I am most grateful to you."

When Jane retraced her steps to the drawing room, she found Crispin sitting again, bent over the documents that the solicitor had left for him. His color looked healthy, and he no longer seemed disoriented.

"We are wealthy," he said.

She leaned against the doorjamb, loosing a small breath. Every time she left him, she half expected him to revert to his old self while her back was turned.

Curiously, every time she came back and discovered him unchanged, her relief seemed stronger. Why? Her fear had not diminished. If anything, the more time that passed, the greater the likelihood that his mind would finish healing—and the greater cause he'd have for wrath. She was well in it now, sleeping in a bed with him, nodding to his callers in the hallway when they addressed her as *Mrs. Burke*.

I like him. Dear heaven, that did not even capture

it. More than liking him, she felt . . . intrigued by him. Drawn to know more, to discover what had wrought such a terrible change in him during the time he could not remember.

For an hour or more last night, she had lain awake in her bedroom, riveted by the silence coming from his, wondering if he thought of her, too. Stupid, stupid.

"Very wealthy," he said insistently. He held up the documents.

"I know." She felt restless, cross with herself. He was not her mystery to solve. This marriage was a sham. With the paperwork finalized, she should be canvassing the newspapers for shipping schedules, plotting the last leg of her great escape.

But what if he never remembered? What cause to hurry away then? She could linger, satisfy her curiosity about him . . .

Dolt! Curiosity killed the cat.

A curio cabinet stood in one corner, its mahogany shutters left open to display treasures. Jane walked over to it. Arguing with herself was pointless. She had no money until her uncle signed the paperwork, so there was no choice but to remain here a little while longer.

The curio collection was peculiarly curated. A rusted fishhook filled one cupboard, a chunk of amber in the next. She picked up the stone, holding it to the light. A fly was caught in the golden, bubbled depths. "Before he went into politics," she said, "my father was a great businessman and investor. A magnate, really." As a result, she was very wealthy—and so, too, would be her husband. "But he intended to spend most of that fortune in his lifetime. He'd plotted out a whole host of programs, social improvements for the poor, which he never had the chance to implement."

"I didn't know that," Crispin said from behind her. "How admirable."

This poor fly. She felt sorry for it—trapped for infinity, suspended in limbo. "He left detailed records of his plans. My uncle paid them no attention. But I mean to see them through."

"That would make a fine tribute to him."

She replaced the amber and faced him. "Perhaps. But that's not how I intend it. I *believe* in those plans, you see."

He frowned a little, no doubt hearing the edge in her voice. It was aimed at the man he had been, whose politics had stood against everything her father—and she—believed. "I imagine you'll do a great deal of good."

She noted his choice of pronoun. He did not include himself in this prediction. Perhaps he was not entirely different from his other self, after all. She must keep that firmly in mind. "I think it a moral duty," she said. "If one inherits the privilege of wealth, or of education or good family, one must use that privilege wisely. Men speak of progress like a machine, an engine that rolls forward without human direction, pulling everyone with it. But that isn't true. If you read the newspapers"—the critical, adventurous, daring newspapers, not the conservative rags that her uncle favored—"it's easy to see that many get left behind. Many, in fact, get crushed."

"You're in an argument," he said quietly. "With whom, I wonder?"

She took a deep breath. Why not risk it? What, precisely, did she have to lose? "With you."

He blinked. "My . . . family has always had a sense of our obligations, I hope. Perhaps we aren't visionaries, but we do lend our weight to reform. Why, my father was instrumental in defeating the Pittites in '32."

Yes, Viscount Sibley was no friend of her uncle's. He also staunchly opposed his son's penal bill. "But you no longer see eye to eye with your father."

His mouth tightened. He looked into his lap, at the papers he held. "These aren't your bank accounts," he said quietly. "These are mine."

A startled silence opened. She felt suddenly foolish. She had been speechifying at him, warning him that her wealth was not to be squandered. But he'd been discussing his own fortune.

And anyway, he was right; her quarrel was not with him, precisely.

She made the concession of sitting down across from him. He handed over the documents.

Nearly forty thousand pounds in the first account. In the next, a more modest sum of three thousand—more than most men would earn in a lifetime, to be sure. The third held seven thousand, give or take.

It was no match against her million, but it made a fine start. "You may be counted a magnate yourself one day."

He did not smile. "Note the dates of deposit."

A quick glance showed them all to have been made in the last five years.

"Tell me, Jane. How does an MP come into such money?"

She realized now that she had misread him. He was not pleased by his newfound fortune. He was brooding. And that dark voice made him sound, once again, like himself: like the real Crispin Burke, who had amassed these funds through every method but honesty.

She kept her own manner neutral. "I believe, like many MPs, you sat on the board of various companies."

He lifted a black brow. "None of them appear to have marked my absence," he said. "So it can't be said that I contributed much. And do companies pay their directors so handsomely? If that is so, I wonder that any of them turn a profit."

She took a long breath. He was a very handsome man. She had always noted it, albeit reluctantly, with resentment for the poor decisions of Mother Nature. But now, his exquisitely chiseled cheekbones, the hardness of his jaw so perfectly counterbalanced by the lush fullness of his lips—the entire stunning assemblage that constituted his beauty—seemed . . . more real, somehow. Harder to ignore. For his expression was unguarded, honest and vulnerable in its uncertainty.

He looked *touchable*. Moreover, he looked like a man who wanted touching, and who would have welcomed her comforting denials.

Her fingers curled tightly, trapping temptation. And after a long moment, he offered her a lopsided smile. "Well. Silence *does* speak louder than words. Am I rotten, then, Jane?"

"I would not call you rotten." It was not kindness, she told herself, that led her to lie—it was expediency, a leaf from the old Crispin's book. She was not his true wife. It was not her job to do his work for him, to give him the true picture of who he'd been.

But he didn't believe her. She could tell from his face. "Do you know," he said slowly, "when I woke . . ."

His unhappiness should not move her. But . . . it was

the *other* Crispin whom she resented. This man, who-ever he was, had shown himself thoughtful, considerate, gentle. He respected her wishes. He apologized when he erred. He kissed her so softly . . .

He asked for her opinions, and never sneered at her replies.

"Go on," she said unsteadily. *God save me.* "When you woke?"

He set a fist against his lips. The bareness of his ring finger struck her again. How much handsomer he looked without his sneers and gaudy jewelry. "I was glad," he said. "I was . . . *relieved.* To know I had come so far, that I had made something of myself after all. I don't know how much I told you of my childhood, of my family . . ."

A decent woman would stop him from speaking. En-ticing him to confide in her was akin to doing a violence to him, for in his right mind, he would never offer in-timacies.

But what if this is his right mind? a small and danger-ous voice whispered. *What if this is the true Crispin?*

She found herself leaning closer. "You told me very little."

"Perhaps that was wise." He paused. "There is little in it to compliment me."

In his childhood? She thought of his mother's lov-ing concern for him, his sister's clear adoration. "I don't believe that."

He shrugged. "I was born impatient, I think. Care-less, given to hijinks, ungifted at schoolwork, unable to focus on anything for too long." His fist fell; with his thumb, he began to crack his knuckles, one by one, methodically. "But I had charm. I could endear myself;

I could make people laugh. That was never quite . . . enough, though. I think my parents hoped for another Atticus—who, as you may have noticed, is a wondrous disciplined sort." A strange smile flickered over his lips. "A fine thing that he was born first. Only . . . perhaps, if I had been the youngest . . ." He flattened his fist against the arm of the chair, stretching his fingers, relaxing them. Then, abruptly: "Did I wear a ring on this hand?"

She followed his gaze. A faint band of paleness marked the ruby's absence now. "Yes. A cabochon, a ruby."

He flinched as though she had struck him. Then, before she could speak, he shoved to his feet and stalked across the room to the liquor cabinet.

"Whisky," came his voice, savagely cheerful. "Just the thing. And you, dear wife? Will you partake?"

It was the other Crispin's voice. But for the first time, she did not quail to hear it. She was building a feel for this Crispin; she could sense that his displeasure was self-directed. What had sparked his temper? "No, thank you." With a pointed glance to the grandfather clock— it was unseemly early for a man to tipple—she said, "I wonder if the doctors would approve of —"

"Oh, this is medicine," he drawled, and slugged down a healthy dram before turning to consider her. "Your ring, Jane? Where is it?"

She glanced down at her bare hand. "I . . ." He meant her wedding ring, of course. "We married in haste. There was no chance to procure one."

"Well, then." He set the glass down. "We must rectify that." His smile looked sharp. "God knows I have the money."

She hesitated. It would be wrong, so wrong, to encourage this charade.

"The jeweler's will be open by now," he went on. "Let's slip out before the visitors come knocking." He laid down his glass and smiled at her.

Why, she did not give a fig for what that other Crispin would think. She wanted to know *this* one. Her curiosity felt like an elemental drive, ferocious as hunger or thirst. She wanted to know why news of the ruby ring had upset him. She wanted to spend the morning with him.

She was a fool. She was setting herself up for a great punishment, a deadly fall.

But as she rose, she could not keep from smiling back at him.

"Do none of them please you?"

Jane turned away from the window. "No, they're all lovely." Crispin had brought her to a shop on Regent Street which was cunningly modeled to resemble the interior of a jewelry box. The walls were covered in blush velvet swags, the ceiling mirrored. Diamonds the size of a child's fist glittered in the glass cabinets. The air was softly perfumed.

She felt a little light-headed. Smothered, really. But the rings lying on the counter, cushioned by a swath of apricot velvet, were very fine. She stepped forward hesitantly, conscious of the carefully bland smile of the jeweler. He had recognized Crispin when they entered. "All my mother's jewelry comes from Howell and James," Crispin had told her. But she wondered if he had forgotten his own purchases. Mr. Howell's greeting sounded too familiar, too eager, and when Crispin introduced her as his wife, he made the briefest pause before modulating his tone to a more subdued geniality.

She knew Mr. Burke had kept lovers—not even courtesans, but married women. She had seen the proof with her own eyes. So what if Mr. Howell had mistaken her for one of them? She should be flattered to be placed in company with the beautiful Duchess of Farnsworth.

In fact, she should not care at all. She was not Crispin's wife.

"Perhaps I don't need a ring," she said. These were rich, ornate, breathtakingly lovely pieces—delicate, twisting gold bands cleverly inset with precious stones. She would have to abandon the ring when she fled, for she was no thief. He would find it afterward, transformed into a token of betrayal. What an injustice to do to such beauty. Why had she agreed to come?

"Nonsense," he said. "What wife does not need a wedding ring?"

"A clumsy one." She manufactured a laugh. "I have never worn a ring, or a pair of earrings, or a bracelet"—for she had seen him eyeing those as well—"that I haven't managed to lose by night's end."

"Splendid news for Mr. Howell," Crispin said with a smile. "We'll be visiting him regularly."

She sighed. "Mr. Burke . . ."

He took her hand and placed it on the glass counter. "Behold the fairest hand in England," he told the jeweler. "In your expert opinion, sir, which ring would do it justice?"

If Mr. Howell's study of her hand appeared mildly

skeptical, Jane could not blame him. She had spent years wielding a needle, and not always carefully. The rhythmic, repetitive act of sewing had sometimes been a comfort to her, removing her mind from her predicament, lulling her thoughts into a numbed slumber. But in her blackest moods, she had sometimes not bothered to mind her aim.

The fingers of her left hand bore numerous small scars. Sometimes a little pain—a reminder, in its own curious way, that her body, at least, remained in her control—had helped to counterbalance the larger pain of her helplessness.

"Well," he said, and cleared his throat. "You are quite right, Mr. Burke, to flatter your wife's hand. It is a rare combination, shapely and graceful. I think it would be a pity not to highlight such beauty." He reached, naturally, for the most ornately jeweled ring—the most expensive, too, Jane did not doubt.

"I prefer that one." She laid the forefinger of her free hand on the glass counter, to indicate a gold band that Mr. Howell had not pulled out for them.

"That band is very popular, madam." Mr. Howell made this sound like an indictment.

"It's quite plain," Crispin said hesitantly.

"Yes, indeed, Mr. Burke," said the jeweler. "It is intended for those with a care for . . . economy. I fear it would not best express the rare and extraordinary nature of your sentiments."

Hogwash. "And here I thought that a love expressed through jewelry was the flimsiest kind," Jane said lightly. "I will take that ring, sir, and none other."

With a sigh, Mr. Howell bent to retrieve it. "Have you a matching ring for a gentleman?" asked Crispin.

Here was the first sign that he had forgotten more than his recent experience. "Gentlemen do not wear wedding rings," Jane said gently.

"Is there a rule against it?" He stretched out his fingers, displaying the paler band of skin that testified to his missing ruby. "I would like," he said more quietly, "to cover that up."

That ring held no sweet memories for him. She wanted desperately to know why he had worn it.

"I do believe I have a broader band in gold." Mr. Howell held out the ring to Jane, but Crispin took it. "If you will give me one moment, I'll check in the storeroom."

"Very good."

Jane turned away to the window again as Mr. Howell went rummaging. It was one o'clock, and in sharp contrast to the muffled serenity of the shop, the street outside was choked with traffic. Matched grays trotted past, hauling a glossy carriage whose black lacquer reflected the stucco terrace building in which Jane stood. Horsemen, buggies, pedestrians in lace-fringed gowns, footmen staggering beneath packages, young boys hawking penknives, vendors waving prints, a grand dowager in bombazine with a poodle on a leash . . . The entire world was parading down Regent Street. Jane squinted across the road. As she and Crispin had stepped out of the carriage earlier, a man crouched on the curb had been playing an odd tune through a quill dipped in a tin bucket of water. He had now gathered an audience of bored-looking dandies in top hats and paletots.

"Does something catch your eye?" came Crispin's voice at her ear.

"All of it," she said honestly. "I've seen nothing of London." Her aunt and uncle's surveillance had been total, and then . . .

Then Mr. Burke had been attacked.

How distant it all seemed now! Sitting rigidly in his parents' drawing room, Jane had been terrified to speak up. The archbishop's work had been quick. The marriage record looked authentic. But her palm had sweated so fiercely around the paper that she had feared she might smudge the lines.

How shocked his family had been to see that paper.

How furious, hers.

"Surely you've been to London before," said Crispin. "This can't be your first season."

He'd forgotten, of course. She looked at him. "The Masons kept me in the country. An heiress is not easy to keep unmarried, you know."

Amazement widened his eyes. How unguarded this Crispin was; how generous with his shows of emotion. What had the other Crispin been trying so hard to hide?

She was beginning to have suspicions. She remembered his elder brother's rudeness, and Crispin's own strained confession. *My parents hoped for another Atticus* . . . Mr. Burke had stopped bothering to court approval. Instead, he'd welcomed condemnation.

This Crispin was braver. He had not let his own history harden him yet.

He was still holding the ring. She smiled at him. "I don't think that one will fit you."

"Ah." He smiled back at her, a wide and lovely smile that caused her heart to trip.

She would miss this man when Mr. Burke came back. *May he never come back.*

Was that very sinful to wish? Was she a villain to do so?

"Give me your hand," he said. When he put the ring over her fingertip, he glanced up through his lashes. "I suspect this moment properly requires some poetic remark."

She laughed. "Typically it comes from the minister."

But she'd misjudged; he was quite serious. A muscle ticked in his jaw. "I can't remember asking you to marry me," he said. "It's . . . ludicrous."

Yes, she *was* a villain. She'd seen firsthand how his infirmity pained him. How could she be grateful for it? "It's all right, Crispin."

"Listen to me," he said, his gaze steady. "I doubt almost everything, Jane. I find more evidence every day that my memories won't be pleasant. But I know I did one thing well. I did very well in marrying you."

Her lips parted. If it had been true, it would have been the loveliest praise ever offered her.

He gave a rueful tug of his mouth. "Well, I was never a poet," he said, and pushed the ring over her knuckle.

It felt cool and firm against her skin. Weighty, as a wedding ring should be.

"Here we are," said Mr. Howell, bustling back into the showroom. "See if this fits you, Mr. Burke."

The band was broad enough to conceal all evidence that he had once worn another. "Perfection," said Crispin. "Have the bill sent to . . ."

Jane opened her mouth to supply his address, but Mr. Howell stepped in smoothly. "Yes, of course. The regular arrangement, sir."

*   *   *

"Have I bought you other jewelry?" Crispin asked as they stepped back into the sunshine. "Enough to have a . . . regular arrangement?"

She thought of the jewels at the Duchess of Farnsworth's throat. "You have a mother and a sister, Crispin. I'm certain you never let their birthdays pass unremarked."

"Ah. Yes." He relaxed visibly, then took her arm, drawing her out of the way of an oncoming stampede of sashed and beribboned children. They stepped into a patch of shade provided by a baker's awning to wait for the coach.

Sunlight gleamed off her ring. She held out her hand, tilting it until the band glinted.

"Where next?" Crispin asked, startling her.

She tucked her hand into her pocket. There was no call to admire the symbol of her lies. "Was there some other errand to run?"

He grinned. "You wanted to see London. Where shall we start?"

Excitement leapt through her. "Do you mean it?"

"Of course," he said. "The day is yours, m'lady." He sketched a mock bow.

A thousand possibilities raced through her brain. At Marylebigh, she had made a study of *Baedeker's Guide to London*—the Crystal Palace, the zoo, the Tower, the British Museum.

But there was one place above all that she wished to go. Since her girlhood, she had desired to see it.

"I—"

A hand seized her arm.

"Here's a surprise," sneered Archibald.

Instantly Crispin was between them. She could not

tell what he did—one moment he had taken hold of Archibald's wrist, and the next, her cousin cried out and staggered backward, clutching his wounded hand.

"That's assault!" he shrilled. "I'll summon the police!"

"I'll summon them for you," Crispin said coldly.

In the distance, Jane spied her aunt, who had just stepped out of a milliner's shop. As their eyes met, Aunt Mary's lips curled as though she'd tasted a lemon.

Where was the coach? Jane's heart was thudding. There was nothing these two could do to her, but still—

"We won't sign your papers," Archibald spat. "If it's our fortune you were counting on, prepare yourself for the poorhouse. You're done for, Burke."

"*Your* fortune?" Jane forgot her trepidation. "You mean my *father's* fortune, which you failed to steal!"

Aunt Mary drew up. "Is this anything to discuss on the street?" she hissed. "Archibald, go fetch the coach. Jane—" Her eyes fell to the wedding ring on Jane's finger, and she scoffed. "Economizing already, I see. I hope you grow accustomed to it."

"Come," Crispin said, steering Jane toward the curb.

"And you—you've run mad," came Aunt Mary's voice from behind them. "Do you really imagine that my husband won't act? His secrets are your secrets, Burke. Don't think he'll fear to use them."

Crispin pivoted, fixing her aunt with a look that made Jane's blood run cold.

Mary took a step backward, her hand at her throat.

"C-Crispin?" Jane's lips felt frozen. She did not know if it was *Crispin* whom she was addressing any longer.

But his gentle touch on her shoulder answered that question. Mr. Burke hadn't yet returned. He silently urged her into the waiting coach, then rapped the ceiling to alert the driver to move onward.

Only once they were well under way did he speak. "Secrets," he said darkly. "What secrets did she mean?"

"The new residence marks a great step forward for us." Elizabeth Reid spoke haltingly, as though each word were a great and grave charge in itself, to be delivered with care. Her hair was snow white, her face deeply lined. She had the habit of squinting through her wire-rimmed spectacles, as if prepared, by nature, to doubt what she saw.

Crispin's wife, who sat across from Mrs. Reid, strained forward to hear better. Jane's face was flushed; since setting foot on the curb in front of the brownstone, she'd seemed wracked by some private, building emotion. "Bedford College," she had whispered, hushed and reverent, as though beholding a miracle.

The sight of her, in that moment, had taken his breath away. His wife schooled her passions so well that in those rare moments when they overwhelmed her, one found oneself startled, transfixed, by the vivid beauty of her face. Olive skin, smooth and poreless; eyes as bright and luminous as stars.

He was tired. Increasingly dizzy. But he would not rush her, nor show any sign of exhaustion. He would give her the day she deserved, because she, all unwittingly, had given him something he'd very much needed: a clear view, at last, of *his wife*, unguarded and enchanting and utterly irresistible. He would gladly bring her here every day simply to see that expression—and to satisfy his intense curiosity about what else might cause her to glow.

The building itself offered no clues. It was unprepossessing, three stories of plain brick—well situated in a shady green square at the heart of Bloomsbury, but hardly large enough, Crispin had thought, to lay claim to the collegiate title.

Once inside, though, he'd realized the cause for its modesty. A flock of students had passed by—every one in skirts, their lecture notes gripped in kidskin gloves.

In this college, the students were *women*.

"I think your father would have been very pleased," Mrs. Reid said. She paused to cough; the room was cramped and dark, choked with the smells of paper and leather and wood smoke. "You will not recall—you are too young—but we faced a great deal of opposition in the early days. Unitarians were not looked on so kindly then. Your father did us a great favor by lending his support."

"That is wonderful to hear, ma'am." His wife sounded transported. That husky note in her voice—what might he do to lure it out? Surely she did not reserve it only for schoolmistresses. "And I do remember how very much he believed in your mission. Why, he teased me that one day I might have the good fortune to enroll."

Mrs. Reid's laughter was cracked and phlegmy. "And why don't you, my dear?"

"Oh . . ." Jane's smile looked wistful. "I'm afraid it's too late."

"But what rubbish!" Mrs. Reid caught Crispin's eye. "We have several matrons enrolled in our courses. Perhaps your wife will join them. And if not—why, we're always in need of Lady Visitors, volunteers who chaperone our younger pupils."

Chaperone? Could anyone look at his wife and imagine

her as a chaperone? The full, pouting curve of her lower lip, the tender cove beneath it—the swell of her bosom, the sinuous curve of her waist—to imagine her as the face of virtuous rectitude felt like a travesty. A great wonder, wasted.

"I'd have no objection to it," he said.

Mrs. Reid gave him a benevolent smile, but Jane's looked far more uncertain. Surely she didn't doubt her own aptitude? It only took a minute in her presence to recognize she had a very fine mind. Among other things. Her hoops disguised the poetry of her hips, but on two rare and precious occasions, when he'd glimpsed her in a robe—

Irritated with himself, Crispin turned to look out the doorway. This was neither the time nor the place to lose control over himself. In a women's college, of all places—

A women's college! Amazing that he'd not known such things existed. Of course, a good deal of society still argued that a woman's only place was in the home. But with women now employed as telegraph clerks, at the post office, and for the newspapers, it seemed strange to him that Bedford College remained as small as it was.

"If there is anything else I can do," Jane said from behind him, "I hope you will let me know. My father . . . I'm quite certain he would have extended his support. His passing was so sudden . . . there was no time to make bequests."

"It has been a struggle of late," came Mrs. Reid's slow reply, "to keep a ready stable of lecturers. Most of them come from University College, you know, and we cannot match the salaries which their expertise might lead them to expect. And they find it a challenge, I believe, to adapt their materials to an audience that was not raised to the same scholastic standards as young men."

"I quite understand," said his wife. "I fear I cannot be of immediate help, but very soon, I hope within the month, I might be in a position to make a sizable donation—"

Crispin wheeled back. "Why not now? How much is required, Mrs. Reid? Think ambitiously, if you please; I mean to make it my wedding gift to my bride."

Jane turned toward him, the surprise in her face already all the repayment he could hope for.

"That is very kind of you," Mrs. Reid said—her speech abruptly brisk, her posture straighter, and her gaze hawkish. "I believe fifty pounds should make a fine start, Mr. Burke, but if you could find it in your heart to look ahead to next year, a hundred would—"

"Five hundred," he said with a wink to his gaping wife. "I am always thinking of the future."

"It's remarkable," Crispin murmured into her ear. They stood side by side at the back of the lecture hall, watching a dozen women bend their heads over their notes as a stentorian lecturer explained the meaning of the striations of rocks deep beneath the surface of the earth.

Jane drew a full, joyous breath. She felt too full, actually—overflowing with joy. "This was my mother's dream," she whispered. "She was Unitarian, like Mrs. Reid. My father had never thought such a thing possible. But she persuaded him. They had searched the Continent for the best tutors for me. But so many felt it a wasted effort to teach a girl. Would it not be marvelous to create a place that might prove otherwise? That's what she told him."

"Yet you don't wish to become a student yourself?"

She hesitated, then motioned him to follow her into the hall. Two young women nearby were arguing over Latin declensions. Ah, she could sit here and watch forever! How rare, how miraculous, to see a wild dream come true.

A bench by a large paned window offered a place to sit; sunlight spilled in squares across the glossy wooden floor. Jane took a seat and looked up at Crispin. "I'm twenty-three," she said.

The sunlight illuminated his navy eyes, picked out the crow's-feet that deepened as he smiled. "Hardly ancient, Jane."

"True. But sometimes I feel so."

He sat down beside her. "And why is that?"

"I feel . . ." She took a breath. Did she truly intend to ruin this atmosphere by speaking of her uncle? But Crispin was watching her with such patient attention. How long had it been since somebody had taken such interest in her thoughts? "As a girl, I felt very confident, very certain of myself." She managed a smile. "My parents ensured that. They encouraged me to speak my mind, to reason through my opinions, to offer them with confidence. But then . . ." She cleared her throat. "After they died, when I went to Marylebigh . . ."

His face darkened. "What did he do?"

She shrugged. "My uncle had a particular opinion of how women should be. And he imagined himself to be doing his duty by me. A woman is not to consider her opinions equal to a man's. And so he set out to fix what he thought my parents had broken." She pulled a face. "To be honest, it was not his treatment I minded so much as . . . the realization I had, from what little of the world I glimpsed through his guests and newspapers and novels, that *his* view was the common one. Not my parents'."

His hand came over hers. "The world is often wrong," he said steadily. "That is why men like your father make such a difference. What is broken *can* be fixed. But you were never broken, Jane. I hope you know that."

"No, of course not." She hesitated. "But I *do* feel ancient," she said slowly. "I feel as though I was worn down while at Marylebigh. That I stopped believing, hoping, that things could be different. And I fear . . ."

Her throat closed. Of all men, she meant to confide in *him*?

His grip tightened. He leaned close, so close that she caught the scent of the spiced soap she had stroked over him. His lips brushed her temple for the briefest moment before he eased back to look into her eyes again. "Go on," he said quietly.

"I fear I won't have my parents' strength," she said in a rush of breath. "To see their plans through. That instead of ignoring the sneers and braving through the wickedness, I will let it embitter me, and give up on the world, and tell myself there's no point to working for others when all I receive is contempt. And—and become useless and indulgent, and shut myself away like a hermit to count my coins and order books and write letters and never do anything worthwhile."

His lips twitched. And then—he laughed!

She sprang off the bench. "That is hardly—"

"But, Jane," he said, still smiling as he rose and caught her hand back despite her ill-tempered resistance. "I'm sorry, but that's absurd. Yes, I understand you're afraid. But you? Crumpling before sneers? You came down the stairs last night and had at your uncle like an avenging angel. Do you mean to say that there was a *moment* at Marylebigh when you thought your uncle was right thinking? I won't believe it. Surrender is not in you."

She blinked very rapidly. "I—" Her face felt warm. "You—" She liked very much this picture he painted. But . . . "You don't *know* me, Crispin."

His smile gentled. "And yet I already know enough to see you clearly. Or will you deny it?"

No. No, she would not. Her throat felt very full suddenly; the sunlight felt too bright. She blinked to clear her vision, breathing hard against a bizarre, fleeting impulse to tears.

"Besides," he went on. "If ever a moment comes when you lose faith, I'll be there to encourage you. What is marriage but a partnership? I won't let you go astray, Jane."

The very world seemed to lurch. Or her soul to strain out from her body. *A partnership.* Yes.

She took back her hand, wrapped her arms around herself for fear they would reach for him again.

She had the shipping schedules memorized. A valise sat in her wardrobe, containing the essential items she would need to flee in the night. If he remembered—she would go.

But until then, *oh,* what point in continuing this silent debate? She would stay. She would find out what he was made of, this man who kept surprising her.

When he offered his arm, she bit back a shy, pleased smile. He led her out from the college, into the sleepy green-shaded square. After the hectic furor of Regent

Street, Bloomsbury felt pastoral. Jane inhaled the grass-scented breeze, feeling light as air, positively giddy.

Her parents would have been so pleased today. They would even have been pleased to imagine her wed to the man who guided her down the pavement now—this man who had continued their work for the college and praised her mettle with a smile.

Over the treetops rose the famous pediment that topped the forecourt of the British Museum. A thrill went through her. She was in *London*. At last, it felt real. So many wonders at her fingertips—and perfect liberty to see them. The man at her side would find no objection to her curiosity, her hunger for experience. He had just proved it. Far from recoiling at women's education, he had made a sizable gift. He had promised to *encourage* her.

She tucked her hand more deeply into the crook of his arm, letting herself at last relish the feel of his muscled forearm, the closeness of their bodies. She could trust him with such intimacies. He would not press her for more unless she invited it, welcomed it. "That donation was very good of you. I will repay you every penny, I promise."

He cut her a glance, his mouth shifting to a teasing angle. "Is that how our marriage is to go? Tallied and budgeted, with ledger books beneath our pillows? I meant it as a gift, Jane. A women's college is a fine idea, and I hope it continues to flourish. Even if most of its students go on to dedicate themselves to hearth and home, their children will benefit for their mothers' educations."

Her mood dimmed a little. That was precisely the kind of logic that Mr. Burke would have used, if forced to support the college. *Very well, let the women have their little adventure. Perhaps it will prove useful for their sons.* "Their daughters may be the ones to profit most. Why, perhaps they will grow up thinking an education their right, and aim to earn their degrees. If women were professors, Bedford wouldn't suffer for want of lecturers."

"Are you arguing with me again?" he asked mildly. "Or rather, let us say 'him,' for the sake of clarity. Did *he*, this mysteriously enriched politician, express some objection to female education?"

"No, of course not," she said, startled. It was very disconcerting to hear him jape at . . . himself.

He came to a stop, facing her. The wind kicked up, ruffling the edges of his cravat, luring a few strands of dark hair across his eyes. "I can't tell when you're being honest, and when you're trying to shelter me," he said. "So I'll ask again: did I discourage you from it? Is that why you hesitated when Mrs. Reid invited you to take tuition?"

"The subject never came up," she said. "That is the perfect truth."

But he did not look satisfied. "And why, may I ask, did we not speak of it? Did we not share such things, you and I? What did we talk about, if not our passions?"

Why did he insist on probing so deeply? He was forcing her to invent lie upon lie, when she did not *want* to lie to him, not anymore.

She turned away, staring blindly at the entrance to the museum, now in clear view, well-dressed families loitering on the steps. *Say it.*

She didn't want to. This ring . . . she closed her hand, rubbing her thumb over the smooth surface. The way he looked at her, the romantic things he said . . .

She didn't want to discourage them. They unsettled her, they surprised her, they . . . *pleased* her.

Which was why she must say it. At once.

"It was not a love match." She cleared her throat. "I'm so sorry, Crispin. I know I misled you. But we married for convenience. Once we had control of my fortune—"

"Jane."

"—we intended to divide it and go separate ways," she said stubbornly. There. It was done. No more flattery for her, no more admiring looks and gentle courtesies.

His hand on her arm forced her to face him. "I don't believe you," he said.

She huffed out a breath. The man was impossible! "What cause have I to lie about *that*? It hardly flatters me."

He studied her a long moment, his expression troubled. "Perhaps you're not lying," he said at last. "I . . . am sorry to hear it, if so. But for all that I cannot remember our courtship . . . the memories are still there, Jane, only buried. And I feel them guiding me at times." He took a deep breath. "On my part, it was not convenience. I am certain of that."

He was half-right. He'd never thought to marry her at all.

A laugh escaped her, a wretched little sound. She lifted a hand to her eyes to shield her expression, for she would not be able to explain the misery in it.

"Jane," he said, taking her hand, pulling it away. "I didn't mean to upset you. Or challenge your word. If you married me for convenience, so be it. I'll simply have to persuade you that convenience isn't all we might share. We have all the time in the world to come to know each other—"

She laid her hand over his mouth. Then, glancing right and left to make sure no one was nearby, she pulled him behind a tree and kissed him.

He went rigid. Who could blame him? Her own wits seemed to take flight, so she watched herself from somewhere outside her body as she pressed her lips to his.

And then he made some noise in his throat and gripped her face in his palms, kissing her back, and she was embodied again, a creature of flesh, exhilarated and alive. The warm sunlight, the cool breeze, his lips, slightly rough, stroking her own. He opened her mouth with his and she went on her tiptoes in eager reply. Their tongues touched; a delicious thrill purled through her, strange, wild. She wrapped her arms around his shoulders—

"Shame!" came a sharp cry from nearby. They broke apart, Jane shrinking against the tree trunk, as an elderly woman shook her umbrella at them.

Crispin sketched the woman a mocking bow, then laughed as she hissed out, "Hussy." With a sniff, she yanked her small dog away from them and stalked off in the direction of the college.

Grinning, Crispin turned back to her. "If that's a Lady Visitor, you may have lost your chance at volunteering."

She pressed her palms to her cheeks, which burned with the violence of her blush. "Forgive me," she said breathlessly. "You must think me a trollop—"

"I think you perfect," he said with relish, and seized her arm, tugging her back onto the sidewalk in the direction of the museum. "I command you to remain exactly as you are, Mrs. Burke, and to shock each elderly lady whose path we might cross, from now until eternity."

Yes, yes—as long as he remained as *he* now was, she could gladly do so forever. She laughed, and the giddy sound of it awoke some small, sharp foreboding.

What are you doing? This can't last forever.

But in that moment before her madness, as she had looked on his earnest face so alight with concern for her, his beautiful lips shaping promises, she had forgotten everything but the desire to reward him for coming so close to the ideal he'd once lived to mock. She would not regret it now.

CHAPTER NINE

*J*ane did not flatter herself that she had anything to do with their rapport as they strolled through the museum, pausing to peer at displays of artifacts from ancient Greece and Egypt. Crispin's good humor was the key. But the novelty of embarrassing herself, and emerging unscathed—of being not criticized but *praised*—was heady indeed.

Here was a new lesson for her, then: it was possible to behave like an utter goose in front of a man, and then to take his arm again and stroll companionably onward, without feeling any awkwardness. It made her a little drunk, it seemed. She felt suddenly able to take other, smaller risks. To speak without thinking. To confide in him, as they admired sarcophagi, that she'd nursed a peculiar obsession with mummies as a girl, and had managed to squeeze herself so tightly inside a wooden box that she had got trapped there, necessitating a thorough greasing with butter in order to be removed.

"We would have been great friends, then," Crispin told her. "I once got my arm stuck in a banister railing.

I wasn't so lucky as to be rescued with butter, though. I reeked of tallow for days."

Speaking without thinking led to *acting* without thinking. They paused by a collection of peculiar masks, the sign beside which claimed they had been modeled from life. She found herself testing the truth of that statement by attempting to screw up her face. Was it anatomically possible?

"Almost there," Crispin said. "Bit wider." He hooked back the corners of his lips and bared his teeth.

Her giggling fit drove them out of the room, chased by a shushing guard.

She might gladly have stayed there with him until the museum forced them out at closing, but after two hours, he began to sway on his feet. With typical masculine pride, he denied his fatigue, so she, hiding a smile, pled exhaustion herself. On their way home, seated across from each other inside the carriage, she lapsed into a wondering, happy silence.

Somewhere in the past few years, she had stopped laughing. The only jokes she'd overheard were made at somebody else's expense, designed to produce a snicker, not genuine mirth. But it seemed she had more laughter left in her than she'd guessed. Once she had relaxed her guard and begun speaking without a care for how she might sound, jokes had tumbled out. And Crispin had enjoyed them. She was funny; she'd forgotten that.

She'd forgotten so many things. How many times today had she surprised herself? Every room of the museum seemed to stir a new memory of happier times. Adventures with her parents. Girlish interests she'd once pursued confidently, heedless of whether such hobbies were feminine, appropriate, becoming.

Once home, Crispin disappeared for an hour—to nap, she suspected—before rejoining her for a light supper. How domestic, how peculiarly companionable, to sit afterward in the drawing room, reading by the fire as Crispin worked at his desk. Imagine living in a house like this one, with a chivalrous husband, and freedom to do exactly as one pleased—visit any corner of London, sponsor any cause, write and read and sip tea at perfect liberty.

It was very close to the vision that she had chased on her midnight flight from Marylebigh. But in that long-cherished dream, she was in a strange country, and always alone. She had no companion to visit museums with her, nor to laugh away a stranger's disapproval when she embarrassed herself. No one to tell her she was perfect just as she was.

He doesn't know you.

But that rehearsed caution began to ring hollow. Who else in the world knew so much of her? Who knew of her plans for her father's fortune? Or that she had once hoped to matriculate at Bedford College? Who else could she have trusted with such facts, without fear of their scorn?

Nobody in the world.

She realized she had turned three pages without absorbing a word. *I am going mad.* To know something for a lie, and to begin to believe it anyway. To allow oneself to be caught up in a fantasy. That was not sanity, at any rate.

But she was done castigating herself. She had a plan of escape. Perhaps . . . she would not require it. But she was prepared.

Crispin rose and crossed the room. He poured himself a tumbler of brandy, and then splashed another finger into a second glass. "For you," he said, carrying it over to her.

Her father had always allowed her to take his brandy glass in hand, to inhale its harsh, complex fragrance. As she lifted hers, the first breath transported her to the atmosphere of her childhood: indulgence, approval, a certainty of safety so complete that fear had been only an empty word.

Until today, she had not thought she would ever manage to recapture such feelings. But the laughter still lived in her. So perhaps there was hope.

She returned the glass to the table.

"Won't you try it?" he asked.

"I was raised in a tradesman's family," she said with a smile, "so I will confess to a taste for coffee. But even I know that ladies don't drink brandy."

Crispin shrugged. "Who's nearby to judge?"

Her smile widened. "Too true." Besides, when had she ever desired to become a lady? A *lady* was the kind of woman praised by her uncle: taciturn, meek, obedient, and unimaginative. Jane had been raised to a different code of conduct—although, strictly speaking, hers had become a code of *mis*conduct in recent weeks.

Why reform now? She retrieved the glass, taking a healthy sip.

Good heavens. With her fist to her mouth, she choked. "That is . . . quite . . . I believe I understand why ladies don't drink brandy."

He laughed. "Small sips to start."

She returned the glass to the table. The firelight painted his face, causing a memory to twinge through her: his face cast in hellish tones by the firelight in the Cross Keys pub.

He *looked* different now. The playful light laid shadows beneath his high cheekbones and the curve of his full lower lip. But his dark eyes did not look devilish. In fact, he looked . . . troubled.

She closed her book. "Is all well?"

"I had several letters waiting in the post," he said. "Your uncle refuses to comply with his duties as the executor. Mr. Gaultier is taking him to court."

"I'm not surprised." More peculiarly, she was not even vexed. "We will win the suit, of course."

"Yes, but it may take several weeks."

That, too, should panic her. But she felt oddly serene. There was nothing to be done about it anyway. "What else?"

"The penal servitude bill. It went to committee today."

Her calm shattered. She felt shoved to the edge of a precipice—dizzy, breath knocked away. "Did you—did you read through it?"

Crispin nodded. His expression revealed nothing. It was closed, meditative, inward looking.

Tell me you don't approve of it.

She retrieved her drink. "And what did you think?"

"What are your thoughts?"

She choked again, though this sip had been quite small. Giving up on the brandy, she said, "*My* thoughts? On the bill?"

"Yes."

Nobody had asked for her political opinion in . . . years. "I think . . ." She had a brief flash of memory: a lively debate around the dinner table. Her parents and two guests, lecturers from the local university. *And you, Jane? Which do you consider to be the defining characteristic of humankind? Reason, or the immortal soul?*

She could no longer recall her answer. But she did remember the self-assurance with which she'd formulated her reply, her eager and unquestioning sense of entitlement: of course her opinion mattered.

"Do you want me to be honest?" she asked slowly.

"Wait." He took a long sip of his drink. "All right, yes."

"The bill is devoid of human feeling."

His brows arched. He laid down his glass. "Don't mince words," he said mildly.

"I would not know how."

He blinked, then gave her a slow, charmed smile, all the more startling for how prepared she'd been for irritation. All at once, she remembered their kiss this afternoon—the gentleness of his touch. The taste of his tongue. Her glance fell to his mouth.

His own gaze grew hooded. "We can adjourn this discussion," he murmured. "If you are in the mood for other . . . diversions."

"No." She cleared her throat. She would not squander the first opportunity in recent memory to speak her mind about politics.

"The bill," she said with effort, and he, interpreting her tone correctly, leaned back and cocked his head, "shows a want of compassion and an equal want of good economy. The ticket-of-leave system is not perfect, but the answer to its flaws is not to revoke it entirely. Why should a man who stole a loaf of bread be locked away for years on end? And if his absence robs his family of their main provider, how much more likely are they to turn to crime themselves, if the only other choice is starvation?"

Crispin gave a nod. "Elegantly argued," he said. "Yet from what I am told, a great many public personages are scheduled to speak, all in defense of the bill."

"They've been carefully selected," she shot back. "Besides, one would not find it difficult to locate supporters, more's the pity. For months, the newspapers have been drumming up alarm, telling the people that garroters are marauding through the streets. Your attack seemed to prove it. Of course public sentiment has been swayed. But the newspapers craft their headlines to sell papers, not facts. If crime has gone up in London, it has not gone up to such an extent that we should repeat the mistakes of the past. And in fact, as your father has pointed out in the Lords, there is no real proof that crime has increased. This bill panders to popular sentiment without reason or cause."

"Indeed." He gave his glass a quarter turn, an idle and distracted motion. "Now tell me what my objection would be."

"To . . . my arguments?"

"Quite."

She knew precisely what his objections would have been a month ago. He would have mocked her as a softhearted idealist, or, if that did not deter her, he would have demanded to know if *she* wished to live beside prisoners released on tickets-of-leave. *Never say you hadn't entertained the notion?* he would then purr. *That's right; it won't be you forced to share a street with criminals. But the deserving poor, the decent hardworking laborers who keep you in comfort—who cares for their happiness? Their safety means nothing, not when you might instead show how merciful and forgiving you are.*

He had been a masterful debater, that other Crispin.

This Crispin was still waiting, his brows lifted expectantly. She shifted in her seat. "You . . . feel that crime has risen thanks to the ticket-of-leave system."

"Yes, so I read. But the draft cites no proof. Nor can I see how petty thieves and swindlers might be converted into garroters simply by receipt of early release."

"I don't think you felt you needed proof," she said, flustered. "You've gathered great support for your effort, after all. Many people feel as you do."

"They *feel* so," he said. "Is that the kind of politician I am, then? A mere panderer?"

"No, not at all."

She winced and wanted to call back the words, for they opened a line to his next question, which he fired instantly:

"Then what was I? Please do explain, Jane. For I can find no sentiment in that bill that seems supportable by fact."

She took a deep breath. "Your aim is to become prime minister, Crispin. And Palmerston and his cabinet are staunchly opposed to this bill. If you manage to push it through, his government may topple. So this bill—I don't think you placed as much import on its content as on what it might do for your career."

She could not read his expression, but as he stared at her, the silence began to make her nervous. She was only speaking the truth. Did he not believe her? "Also," she heard herself say, "there's a great deal of profit in prisons."

"Profit?" He repeated it softly, as though the word tasted strange. "Profit, how?"

She hesitantly quoted her uncle: "A prisoner is a captive audience. He, or his loving family, will pay a great deal for the smallest comforts. Meanwhile, his labor comes free. Why, as a business, criminals are far more dependable than stocks, with a better return besides."

She heard his long breath. "And I suppose," he said flatly, "that I have friends who could use that free labor."

She bit her lip. "You have . . . many friends. I don't know all of them."

With a black smile, he sat back. "I thought that I had woken into a nightmare. Perhaps I was right. But what I failed to remember was that *I* was the monster."

"No." She shook her head. "*You* are not a monster." *You, the man with me now.*

He did not misunderstand her. "And the man you married? What of him, Jane?"

"He . . . ." What an impossible bind to be placed in! No newlywed wife would speak ill of her husband without inspiring questions about why she had wed him, convenient or no. "He made mistakes," she said. "It is . . . not easy to succeed in politics. Compromise can so quickly become corruption. But that doesn't mean there was any . . . deliberate evil in it."

Crispin's slow nod, his distracted look, belonged to a man in deep thought. "Then we must fix his mistakes," he said finally.

"We?"

"We. You know far more of politics than I do at present. You know your uncle's friends, who happen to be my own. And you have a political mind," he went on, his tone casual, as though this acknowledgment were not the most wondrous amazing remark he had made to her yet. "You say this bill has support—but together, perhaps, we can find a way to dismantle it."

"You wish to defeat *your own bill*?"

He saw the shock in her face, for he took a quick breath and sat forward. "Look here: I won't deny that I'm ambitious. That hasn't changed. To become prime minister would be . . ." He shook his head. "Exquisitely satisfying," he said softly. "For a number of reasons. To be recognized, so universally, for one's work—"

"It wasn't that." The words spilled from her. "It was power you wanted. Not admiration."

He gave her a long, level look. "I don't remember enough to argue. But what good is power unless used wisely? This bill . . ." His mouth twisted. "I don't know how I justified it—I only know what I feel *now*. What kind of legacy would this make? It would be no cause for pride. I cannot support it, Jane."

She felt her last defense, her sole remaining shred of caution, collapse. "You are changed."

"And I mean to prove that," he said quietly. "To you, and to myself. But I need a partner in this business. Someone I can trust to keep my secrets." He reached for her hand. "May I count on you?"

Some startled unhappy feeling twisted inside her. *Yes*, she wanted to say, *of course*. But he could not trust her entirely. She was lying to him.

In this matter, though . . . She squeezed his hand. "Yes."

His smile was quick and beautiful. "A toast, then: to bringing down this bill."

Their glasses clinked. She took the smallest sip of brandy, which still tasted as hot as a flame. Such faith in Crispin's face—no trace of wariness. As though he really did trust her completely. She cleared her throat. "'Need no one, trust no one.' That was your motto once."

"Was it?" Briefly he frowned. "Well, based on what

I've seen of my so-called friends, it seems a sound policy . . . with the single exception, of course, of you."

The brandy felt like acid in her throat. "I *will* help you." Her voice was thick. "I promise, I will do everything I can to help." That was the truth.

If her ferocity was too overstated, he did not remark on it. "We'll start with Atticus, I think."

Atticus! Cautiously she said, "I thought you two did not . . . get along."

"He thinks me an incompetent schemer," he said easily. "But for once, he may approve of my plans. Lambert and Culver are the key waverers, and Atticus went to school with Culver; he can lend a hand in the persuasion."

"It must be done with subtlety." She paused, thinking. "Privately done—not in a club where others might see and eavesdrop and talk afterward. And not at their homes, either; they would feel too comfortable there, and once they realized what you were proposing, they could manufacture some reason to take their leave. You'll want them as a captive audience—unable to stir until you've persuaded them."

He lifted a brow. "A dinner party?"

"Yes, that could work." She knew from firsthand experience at Marylebigh that many great matters of state were decided over a six-course meal.

"Lambert and Culver, then." Crispin counted the names on his fingers. "Their wives, and Atticus and Elise. You and I—eight of us, a fine number. What do you say? I know the staff's in shambles. Can we manage it?"

To defeat that dreadful bill? "Without doubt," Jane said. She would make certain of it.

He grinned at her. "My secret weapon," he said, and she flushed.

Atticus glanced up from his microscope. "This is your idea of a joke, I take it."

"Not in the least." Crispin glanced around again, still battling astonishment. When Atticus's butler had given him the address of the laboratory, Crispin imagined his brother holed up in some cramped, dark room full of rotting leaves.

Instead, Atticus had purchased a proper house, gutted the interior, and created a room as large as any exhibition hall in the British Museum. Large windows and skylights illuminated several gleaming counters, glass cases filled with specimens, and towering shelves filled with polished tools.

The expense must have been staggering. Atticus had no degree in botany; there would be no point to it, since he would one day inherit the estates and responsibilities of their father. But every scientific society of note welcomed him. And it seemed that the allowance he drew from their father funded the hobby as handsomely as it did his lifestyle in the mansion on Park Lane.

Crispin took a deep breath. He had come today with an eye to the future. He would not linger on old grudges. But after his school days at Harrow, he had never been offered a penny of their father's money. A trust from his mother's late brother had paid for his tuition and lodgings at Cambridge. He'd needed to count every penny.

Atticus was adjusting the glass slide that pinned a leaf beneath his microscope. Fussy, precise little movements.

The task would have annoyed Crispin unbearably, but Atticus looked calm, intent, and satisfied.

To be firstborn was not an unqualified blessing. Once he became the viscount, Atticus would no longer have time for such research.

"Do you ever regret," Crispin said, "that you could not become a scientist?"

Atticus looked up, scowling. "I *am* a man of science."

"Right." The air held a faint chemical smell that seemed to swim straight into Crispin's brain. With his luck, it would trigger a bout of dizziness, and he'd turn the wrong way for the door when it came time to leave. He glanced at it, trying to fix its location in his mind. He would rather stand here until midnight than risk his brother witnessing his confusion.

"Bedford College," he said lightly, "is in need of lecturers. I'm sure they would be honored to have you, if you offered."

Atticus scoffed. "The women's college? Waste of time."

Crispin scoffed back. "Your wife has never struck me as slow. Nor has our sister. Do you mean to call them brainless?"

Atticus's jaw worked as he turned the dial of his microscope. "Women have brains, I will not deny it. In nature, one finds the female sex is often the sharper witted. But civilization requires a different role. A woman's place is in the home, with her children."

Crispin thought of Jane's radical and intriguing notion, that women might one day be professors as well. But he doubted Atticus would find the idea as compelling as he did. "And would her children not profit from their mother's learning?" he said instead.

Atticus glanced up. "A reasonable point." He sounded mildly surprised that Crispin had managed as much. "Curious to hear it from *you*. Has that knock to your head made you a revolutionary?"

Crispin shrugged. "My wife is the one to thank. She takes an interest in the place."

"And what of you?"

"My interest lies in the matter of the penal bill."

"Mm." Atticus turned back to his microscope, his indifference patent, and Crispin's patience fractured.

"Might you pause a moment so we can discuss it?"

With a long-suffering sigh, Atticus straightened and wiped his hands clean on a rag. "Make it quick. I am speaking at the Linnean Society next week, and I haven't yet finished the analysis."

"This bill cannot pass," Crispin said. "It is a miscarriage of justice, a step backward. I want to defeat it."

Atticus took a seat on a nearby stool. There was none other, so Crispin remained standing. "Defeat the bill *you authored*, do you mean?"

"I do not remember writing it. I cannot account for why I did so. But—"

"I'll tell you why—it's your ticket to take down Palmerston," Atticus said. "The glorious prime ministership. Never say you lost your appetite for power along with your wits."

"I have my wits," Crispin said through his teeth. *No, no—easy, now.* He would not let Atticus provoke him. "The ticket-of-leave system ensures that petty criminals will not be left to rot alongside murderers. I cannot support its abolishment."

"I see." Atticus's smile was unreadable. "What changed your mind, may I ask?"

Crispin cast another quick glance toward the door. Yes, he still knew where it was.

"And there's the shifty look of a man preparing to lie," Atticus said.

Crispin allowed himself a small smile. "I have never required any thought to formulate a lie, and well you know it."

His brother blinked, then sat back a little, as though to see him better. "True enough—though I am amazed to hear you admit it."

As though Crispin had just confessed to blackest depravity!

He bit back a sigh. In the distribution at birth of familial talents, Atticus had inherited some mysterious ancestor's Puritan inflexibility. He had not an ounce of humor in him. "The bill relies on public hysteria. Even if there is an epidemic of violent crime, revoking the ticket-of-leave system will do nothing to better it. I will not take power by exploiting panic, Atticus. I mean to prevent it from going to a vote."

"Oh, but it will go." Atticus drummed his fingers lightly on the grain of the tabletop. "You assured that."

"Not in my memory."

"What matter? The rest of the world remembers. I saw Culver yesterday, by the way, driving down Pall Mall. Very fine pair of matched grays in the harness." Atticus's eyes narrowed. "High-flying for a man with pockets to let, eh? I hailed him, but he looked frightened as a hare and hurried onward. Guilty conscience, no doubt."

The tacit accusation of bribery rankled. But Crispin thought of the accounts in his name, so mysteriously fattened . . .

Well, he would not allow himself to be driven off course. "Culver put up a solid fight, according to Noyes. If you would speak to him now—"

"Noyes—there's another fine specimen of integrity," Atticus muttered. "The man would vote to hand our government to the Germans if they paid enough."

"Culver may still be swayed back to our side," Crispin said forcefully. "That is the main point."

"Our side!" Atticus slipped the specimen slide from the microscope, holding it up to the light with a squint. "You and I do not share a side, Crispin. I think we never did."

"But we might *now*. Do you hear me? I am offering an olive branch."

Atticus sat back, a peculiar smile on his lips. He did not look like a man in his prime. Too many indulgent meals had padded him out. His jaw was slack and soft, and the high color in his cheeks was not simply an effect of his mood. The signet ring on his finger looked too tight to be removed.

"It might be . . . very good," Crispin said hesitantly. "To forge a truce, Atticus. What point to remaining at odds with each other? We are brothers, and I . . ." *I could use a brother.* He had woken to a strange new world in which he seemed to have no friends. Apart from his wife, he could not tell whom to trust.

His wife. There was another gnawing concern. *Once we had control of my fortune,* she'd told him, *we intended to divide it and go separate ways.* He could not believe that he'd intended to use her so mercilessly—that her wit, her humor, her wild hair and lambent eyes, had somehow left him so unmoved.

But he had seen her, more than once now, studying

the newspapers, poring over the schedules of departing ships. She had never planned to remain with the man she'd married. Crispin was a different man now, but how to persuade her of it? He could be a partner to her. Defeating this bill was his best chance of showing her so.

And showing himself so, for that matter. He could be a man of true integrity.

Time, however, was running out.

"I would like to be a brother to you," Crispin said.

Atticus rolled his lips together into a tight, disciplined line. "Another change of heart, is it?"

"Yes." He pushed forward. "Your essays are greatly respected. You have great sway as a thinker. Working together will gain us a good deal of attention besides. We can defeat this bill together."

Atticus made a gruff noise. "Newspapers would have a field day with that."

"And we'd need that attention," Crispin said readily. "The public has only seen Mason's story till now. He has been feeding the editorialists with tall tales."

"And you?"

"What of me?"

Atticus tipped his head, an affectation copied straight from their father. "You can't imagine that the reformers will receive you with open arms. If you go against the bill, you'll be finished. No prime ministership for you."

Crispin's gut tightened. Was that so? Would he end up destroying everything he'd worked for?

"There is nothing so unusual in a man breaking with his party," he said uneasily. "It happens all the time."

"Certainly. But you're no ordinary man, Crispin. You've burned your bridges. You're a tyrant. And tyrants . . ." Atticus offered a cold smile. "Well, I know you were no hand at history as a boy, but surely even you recall what happened to Cromwell. Tyrants do not live to fight another day. When toppled, they generally lose their heads."

There was a malice in his brother's voice that he had never expected. He paused, oddly shaken. Had his methods been so brutal that there could be no rehabilitation for him?

"Would you be among that mob?" he asked. "Did something happen in these last few years that you found so unforgivable that you would wish me ill?"

His brother had not been prepared for plain speaking. With a frown, he looked down at his specimen slide, inched it straight with his forefinger. "Of course I do not wish you ill," he said gruffly, "save in matters directly bearing on the nation. What a buffle-headed question."

Crispin let out the breath he'd been holding. "I am glad to hear it," he said. "For, while we were never cut from the same cloth, I always looked up to you. I hope you know that."

Now Atticus's hand suddenly curled into a fist, the startled reflex of a man threatened. "Don't mock me."

"Mock you? I—" Crispin frowned. "Atticus, you have always been everything I could not be." As a boy, Atticus had spent his holidays holed up in the library. Crispin, in desperate want of a playmate, would cajole and wheedle him, but on the days when Atticus stubbornly refused to abandon his reading, Crispin would stomp off in a huff. It was not possible to sit so still, to concentrate on a single book, for so long! Atticus was pretending to do so to spite him, he'd thought.

But once he'd joined Atticus at Harrow, he'd realized his mistake. Many boys could concentrate for hours. The fault lay in *him*.

"I don't think," Atticus said, "you ever much wanted to follow in my footsteps. Let us not revise history, Crispin. You may have forgotten it, but I haven't."

"I haven't forgotten that much," Crispin muttered. He remembered very well his tutors' irritation with him. So unlike his brother. Such a disappointment. *Master Crispin shows no want of talent*, they told his father. *But he suffers a grievous want of discipline.*

In some subjects, he'd managed to prove he had a brain. He excelled in rhetoric, where one must think on one's feet and foresee all the possible twists to an argument. He pulled off dazzling marks in mathematics, which made intuitive sense. He thrived on the playing fields, where he was praised for his unwavering good sportsmanship even in his rare defeats.

But in quiet, contemplative, sustained efforts, he was hopeless. Atticus spoke Latin and Greek like an ancient native; Crispin could barely conjugate a sentence. He jumbled his history, unable to retain what he'd read.

Look at your brother, Crispin! So their father had urged him, time and again. *He does not give up after half an hour. You must* apply *yourself if you wish to achieve!*

"You were the ideal," Crispin said. But their minds had been fashioned differently. Atticus's mind was like a knife, amenable to slow, steady sharpening. Crispin's, on the other hand, had always felt like clay. Fresh and wet, it took any impression. But given a little time, it began to harden. He would *try* to discipline himself, *try* to pay attention. But once hardened, clay could not be imprinted.

"You did not bother to try," Atticus said.

"I stopped trying. That's true." Gradually, he had come to resent his brother. Their father might revere Atticus, but nobody at school did. He had few friends. Crispin had dozens. This was possible because people were like math: they had a logic to them, a patterned consistency. Once Crispin figured that out, it was easy to make a person feel good about himself, to keep him amused and entertained.

Crispin was popular. But popularity was not an achievement prized by their father—not in him, at least. *He* would need to earn his living. He needed practical skills. *No*, his father told him, *you cannot go on holiday with John Darby; you must catch up on your studies. Atticus, why have the Darbys not invited* you *home for the holidays? Their northern estates adjourn ours; that would prove a useful connection for you. Crispin, ask the Darby boy if he would not like Atticus to stay with him instead.*

Nobody had ever wanted Atticus for company. Who wished a guest who would spend every day in the library, ransacking bookshelves?

But while Atticus's serious disposition had never altered, he had grown, over the years, into a man of great learning. His opinion held weight in rarefied circles, among gentlemen scholars, members of the royal societies, men who traveled to study glaciers or chronicle exotic plants and rare breeds of bird life.

Meanwhile, Crispin had found a use for his own talents. Perhaps his brand of politicking had required bribery; he could not say. But he would not have burned bridges. He would not have been a tyrant. Would he have done?

"I will survive a turncoat showing," he said uneasily.

Perhaps he was mistaken. Perhaps he *had* been a monster, and he would now destroy his last chance at greatness.

But Jane did not see him as a monster. She knew him best now, and she had promised to help him. He would defeat this bill, and prove to her—and to Atticus and the world—what kind of man he was.

And then, if his bridges were indeed destroyed, he would build some bloody new ones.

He stepped forward, flattening his palms on the cool laboratory table. "All I ask is one evening. I am having a dinner for the men who held out longest against the bill, Culver included. He's your friend. You can persuade him."

Atticus hesitated. "Culver *was* my friend. But then you purchased him. Now he is *your* friend, Crispin, and your friends like me no better than you do."

Damn it. "Atticus, I am your brother," he snapped. "Whether or not we meet each week to play whist makes no bloody difference. We are blood, and I am asking you to help me fight for what *you* believe. You are a learned man, and your alliance with me will prove that I am serious. If I *am* such a tyrant as you say, then I will make them fall in line. But I must have a man beside me who is able to feed them the arguments *they* will use to then seed dissent among *their* followers. I'm certain Jane could do it, but if my friends are as rotten as you say, what hope they will listen to a woman?"

Atticus exhaled. "Well," he said, and then, "Well, your *wife* could even do it, could she? How flattered I am by your need for me."

Crispin gritted his teeth. "If you mean to take that as an insult, then you will insult me in the process. She is the daughter and niece of politicians, and she has a fine, educated mind—and a better grasp on Parliament than I do at present."

"That, I believe." But Atticus cracked a thin smile, and his shoulders seemed to loosen. "All right," he said. "Perhaps I will make an appearance. But I promise you, if you mean to ambush me—"

"I mean," Crispin said in exasperation, "to feed you dinner."

Jane stared at herself in the pier glass. She looked faintly green. It was not an effect of the gaslight.

What had she been thinking? She had never organized a dinner party, much less one intended to double as a campaign for the guests' hearts and minds. To be a political hostess, so Jane's aunt had often said with a long-suffering air, required years of training, a cool head tempered by deep experience. One must know how to steer the conversation, to keep every guest at his ease, and to ensure, above all, that when the conversation turned contentious, they found themselves, either from sated pleasure or sodden heads, unable to bolt from the table.

All that, with a poorly trained staff—half of whom had been hired in the last three days!

The door opened behind her. "Half an hour," Crispin said.

Jane took a deep breath. Much could be accomplished with a brave smile and brazen hope. She forced her lips to curve before she turned. "I'm . . ." The sight of him caused her to stammer. "R-ready."

She must have seen him formally dressed before. At

dinners at Marylebigh—and her uncle's ball. Perhaps an instinct for preservation had blinded her to his full beauty. But her eyes were open now. His black evening coat fit him like a second skin. It clung to the breadth of his shoulders and chest, and skimmed over his lean waist and narrow hips. Her hands curled, her desire physical: to sweep her hands down him. To feel his chest again, and the muscled plane of his belly.

"Jane . . ." He was looking her over, his admiration unmistakable. "Is this the gown you were deploring for a 'ready-made rag'? God in heaven, woman. Do you need spectacles?"

She managed a laugh. "It was the finest I could procure on half a week's notice. Aunt Mary always made sure to poke holes in my hem. I doubt your political friends would have liked their hostess looking so ragtag."

He came swiftly toward her, catching her hands. "You are a mistress of understatement." He turned her toward the mirror, his arms looping around her waist as he stepped up behind her.

He was half a head taller. His lips were very near to her ear. With an adjustment of an inch, they would touch her. That was all she could think.

"You look," he said, "like Caesar's wife."

"Oh dear. *That* didn't end well."

His laughter warmed her cheek, causing a shiver to rise. "You look regal."

Regal? She considered herself skeptically. Having never kept a lady's maid, she had resisted Crispin's suggestion to hire one. Her hair was simply dressed— but elegantly so, she hoped. With small, glass-tipped pins, she had looped a coronet of braids twice around her head. The paste jewels winked in the light, and echoed the glimmer of the rich apricot silk gown, sleeveless and low-cut. The skirts bloomed over her steel-hooped crinoline into scalloped tiers trimmed with glass beading.

He pressed his palm against her belly, drawing her back into his hard body, and she swallowed a breath.

"Sorry," he murmured into her ear. "Am I crushing your skirts?"

She shook her head. Their reflection in the mirror riveted her. His hand looked so large, spanning her waist, his fingers square and blunt. She laid her hand over his and felt his hot, dry skin. A fevered feeling yawned through her, an internal tremor.

Their gazes met in the glass—his brooding, contemplative. Slowly, he turned his face and gently set his teeth around her ear.

"Half an hour," he said softly. The flick of his tongue made her shudder; he turned her to face him. His thumb caught her chin, but she had already lifted her face. What was she doing? In this moment, she did not care. His breath brushed her chin. Very gently, he kissed the corner of her lips.

Her eyes drifted shut. In her daily life, she took her lips for granted. But as his own lips slowly learned hers, tracing the edges, stroking and rubbing, her mouth became . . . a wonder. A concentration of feeling, unbearably sensitive.

Their bodies pressed closer together. His mouth dragged once, twice, over hers. Then, with his lips, he pressed her mouth open.

The bottom dropped from her stomach. She swayed and his hard arm around her waist banded more tightly, keeping her against him. He smelled of cologne water. Her hands closed on the slick merino of his jacket. As their tongues tangled, she squeezed the muscled bulk of his shoulders. *Here, mine, now.*

He angled his head. His mouth tracked down her throat. Sensation purled in waves, slipping down her spine, along the backs of her knees. She threaded her fingers through his thick, fine hair, feeling the warm shape of his skull, the indentation—

Her eyes opened. She palmed the spot again, feeling sick. How had she forgotten it for a moment?

"Yes," he said, his voice hoarse. "Still rather impressive."

How close he had come to death! As she stroked his hair, she felt light-headed. A random attack, the police had concluded. A robbery gone wrong. The world could be so cruel.

Crispin eased away to study her. He was frowning a little; his eyes were the color of night, lashed thickly. "What is it?"

For days now, she had dreamed, prayed, that he would never regain his memory. *This* Crispin, this marvelous, delightful man, would be allowed to remain in the world forever.

But the other man had suffered terribly. And for the first time, she felt a powerful, startling anger on his behalf.

Mr. Burke had not deserved that. Nobody did! But especially not he—not when he'd had it in him to become *this* man, so delightful, so extraordinary—

But this man never would have existed had it not been for the attack. He would have remained a villain. For all she knew, he had done something to incite the assault. *You will listen for a name*, Mr. Burke had instructed her. *Tell me everything you hear of Elland.* Had his secrets caught up to him? She was enraged on behalf of a villain. Was she not?

Bewilderment made her step away from him. As the clock struck the quarter hour, she seized on the obvious excuse. "Someone might come early. We should be ready to receive them."

He took a large breath, then nodded. She retreated another pace, and without instruction, he brushed down her skirts with the palm of his hand, then turned a full circle himself, allowing her to check his appearance.

He wore a faint smile when he faced her again. "No damage done?"

"No." But damage had been done. The gash in his head proved it. Only a wicked woman would count that a blessing, and pray for him never to recover from it.

CHAPTER TEN

$\mathcal{D}$isaster took its time to unfold. Crispin's brother and sister-in-law arrived first, shown into the drawing room without ceremony by a footman hired only yesterday. When Atticus wheeled back to stare at him, Jane half anticipated some critique of his livery: procured in haste, it strained at his shoulders.

Instead, Atticus said, "Are we not to be announced in this household?"

The footman's startled gaze swung toward Jane, then fixed carefully in the middle distance. "Baron and Baroness Randol," he intoned—his booming volume better suited for a ballroom, or, for that matter, Westminster Cathedral.

Elise winced, then sent a strained smile to Jane.

"Oh, is *that* who you are?" Crispin's sarcasm was owed to nerves, of course, but they could not afford to start on this foot. "Come have a drink, Atticus, and try to knock some of that starch from your spine."

"How good to see you," Jane said to Elise, who, to her relief, looked amused. They shook hands but had no time to exchange intimacies, for now the Lamberts were being shown inside. With them came the crackling atmosphere of some unresolved argument. Lambert was scowling and taciturn, his wife frenetically cheerful.

On greeting Jane and Elise, Mrs. Lambert immediately flew into a high-pitched flurry of exclamations. She was very young and very pretty, a bright-eyed brunette in a yellow silk gown trimmed in exquisite ivory lace. She had an eye for finer things, it was clear, and if anybody doubted it, she immediately began to coo over each of the rare touches in the room.

"This vase!" she cried. "The enamelwork, so exquisite! You must tell me where you got it, Mrs. Burke."

Jane had no idea where the vase had come from. Nor would Crispin, she suspected. "A family piece," she said, "of my husband's."

"Oh, is it?" Elise asked idly.

"Naturally." A peculiar edge came into Mrs. Lambert's voice as she cast a glance toward her husband. "It is so *nice* to have a family with taste. Taste cannot be acquired; it must be bred, I think. Don't you agree, Lady Randol?"

"Quite," said Elise.

"With all these newcomers to society, I fear it is in increasingly short supply!"

With a murmur of agreement, Elise excused herself to speak with Atticus. Mr. and Mrs. Culver were now stepping into the room, but before Jane could go to them, Mrs. Lambert caught her wrist.

"Oh, I hope I didn't give offense," the woman said. "I had forgotten that your family—well . . ." She trailed off, fluttering her lashes. "I do hope you're enjoying

London, Mrs. Burke. I know it can be somewhat over-whelming for country folk."

Jane had studied up on the guests with Debrett's Peerage, so she knew that Mrs. Lambert's family held a minor baronetcy, while her husband's was distinguished only by its recent wealth. "So true," she said warmly. "But one does miss the rolling fields, the peace and quiet. Lord Randol's father has the most cunning home in Somerset—a castle, to be precise, but refitted with all the modern conveniences." She was lying through her teeth; she knew from her uncle that the Burkes had some ancient residence in Somerset, but for all she knew, it was in ruins. "Why, I believe the Queen visits regularly. Have you never been?"

Mrs. Lambert looked green. "I haven't had the pleasure. I always tell Lamb that he must accept these invitations, but he can't bear to pry himself away from Westminster!"

"Oh, but Lord Randol discusses nothing but politics himself. It would be no break from Westminster at all!" Jane manufactured a light laugh. "I *do* hope to see you there sometime." The bait thus set, she turned away to greet the Culvers.

"What a pleasure to meet you," Mrs. Culver said after Mr. Culver had detached himself to speak with the gentlemen. She was a handsome woman of middling age, her dark blond hair threaded with silver. "I confess, the entire town went into a tizzy when your marriage announcement was published. I will dine out for weeks on the strength of having met you!"

Such a remark might have served as a subtle insult, suggesting as it did that Jane's marriage had the buzz of a scandal. But she sensed no malice in the woman. "Oh goodness," she replied with a polite laugh. Who had published the announcement? Crispin's mother, no doubt. "How terrifying, to imagine myself the subject of discussion!"

"I am sure it is glowing." Mrs. Culver gave her hand a brief squeeze. "And what a time you've had, my dear! Such a shock it must have been, to have your newly-wed bliss so rudely interrupted. But Mr. Burke looks quite well now. What a relief! I know he has been sorely missed in Parliament."

"How good to hear. Yes, Mr. Burke has made a wonderful recovery."

They turned as one to consider Crispin. He was holding court across the room, speaking earnestly to Lambert, who looked very uneasy at having Atticus so close by—indeed, Lambert was making a subtle but distinct retreat, inch by inch, from the scope of Atticus's glowering regard.

Culver, meanwhile, looked wooden-faced. "Your husband," Jane said casually, "is an old friend of Lord Randol's, I think."

"So they are." Mrs. Culver spoke blandly. "But in recent days, it was Mr. Burke on whom my husband relied. I confess, my son does not understand that. But I tell him, 'Christopher'—Christopher one day hopes to be an MP himself—'Christopher, if you are ever so fortunate as to hold office, you will realize how new friends might change one's course.'"

Their eyes met. Jane kept hold of her steady smile. "And if the new course does not suit?"

Mrs. Culver's lashes flickered. "Friendship requires loyalty, I believe."

"Of course," Jane said. "But courses may twist. Friends may change their minds together."

The woman's pause was elegant, too brief to seem pointed. "What an interesting notion," she murmured. "I must remember to tell Christopher so. Until recently, he had a habit of learning politics from his father. I'm certain they would have much to discuss again, should such a twist come to pass."

Jane exhaled. This was very good, very encouraging. From the corner of her eye, she spotted Atticus's wife. "Have you greeted Lady Randol? No? Come, I know she was looking forward to seeing you."

By the time the gong was struck for dinner, Jane felt certain of three things, two of which she whispered into Crispin's ear as they led the guests into the dining room.

Mrs. Lambert was a snob with no care for politics. Her only aim tonight was to needle her husband into regret for whatever sin he had committed before arriving. Happily, his wretched looks showed that he valued her opinions. Wooed with namedropping and invitations, she would influence her husband to befriend whoever had the oldest and grandest country house.

The Culvers, on the other hand, were a political family at war with itself. The son had broken with his father over his support for Crispin. That sore spot could be prodded.

What Jane did not share with Crispin was her private conviction that Atticus was useless. For the past half hour, he had listened sullenly, grimaced regularly, and done a fine job of souring the atmosphere.

But Crispin sensed her restraint. "What else?" he whispered as a footman opened the door to the dining room for them.

"Nothing." She smiled at him. "Steady on."

He gave her a quick, flashing smile in reply. "Steady on," he agreed, and the guests spilled into the room behind them.

Murmurs of appreciation traveled the table as the guests took their seats. Jane had chosen to serve *à la russe*, freeing the table for a complicated arrangement of scarlet flowers and small ferns that spilled from graven silver bowls. Branches of candles marched across the table, and a multitiered epergne at the center offered a bounty of hothouse fruits, bright-skinned oranges, lemons, and ripe, fragrant pears. The extravagant chandelier overhead, the crystal beading of which shivered musically at the footfalls of the servants, cast a brilliant light over walls covered in Pompeii-red silk. The luxury and extravagance of the scene seemed to put everybody in a genial mood, and the first course, a savory mock turtle soup, was received with broad acclaim.

The pleasant idle talk about books and art exhibitions, the opera's upcoming productions, and the unusually wet weather lasted through the second course of salmon in Dutch sauce. But once the saddle of mutton was laid on the table, Crispin's brother seemed to come awake, saying flatly, without introduction or any attempt at politesse, "Now, this penal bill. Any man who means to support it is a fool or a blackguard."

Mr. Culver and Mr. Lambert both bolted upright in their seats.

"I say," Mr. Lambert spluttered. "That seems a bit— Burke, I expect you have something to say to that."

"My brother's diction suffers a want of style," Crispin said dryly. "But on the whole, I fear, I must agree."

"Agree?" Culver's glass thumped soundly to the table.

"I beg your pardon?" Jane caught his wife's eyes across the table. Mrs. Culver offered her a brief, crooked smile. "I—forgive me, Burke, but I'm certain I don't understand you. This bill flowed from your own pen, every line and syllable."

"I find that difficult to believe," Atticus drawled. "My brother was never a hand at composition. Extemporaneous speaking, now—quite a different matter. Perhaps it was dictated?"

A muscle ticked in Crispin's jaw. Jane felt quite ill-tempered herself. He had been promised his brother's support, and instead he was clawed and mocked at.

"Charm," Crispin said, "is not a family trait, I fear." Uneasy laughter traveled the table, and Atticus flushed. "But modesty, yes." He offered a mocking half smile, then continued over Culver's disbelieving snort. "My wife's uncle also had a hand in writing the bill—yes, I will gladly share the credit. His support is not philosophical—he takes great interest in the profit that might be extracted from prisons, which never fail to supply a steady pool of free labor."

"And your interest was purer," Culver said coldly. "Is that what you mean to claim now?"

"Not in the least." Crispin retrieved his wineglass, his wedding ring glinting as he took a long sip. "But as you know, I suffered a blow to the head recently. And to my deep and lasting regret, it appears to have awakened my conscience."

Mrs. Lambert tittered. Then, finding herself the object of her husband's censorious glare, she shrugged and said, "It's amusing."

"Isn't it?" Crispin's easy smile made her blush and fuss with her serviette. "And rather ludicrous, from a profiteer's perspective. The public good was never a lucrative undertaking. But having read the remarks made in committee, my eyes have opened to a new angle. The penal bill is a backward piece of legislation that will do nobody any good save the few who stand to make money from the suffering of the most wretched. I am no longer able to support it."

"This is extraordinary," Lambert said. "Why—it must be a joke. You *are* joking, Burke, are you not?"

"A man is allowed to change his mind, I believe." Crispin looked between Lambert and Culver. "And never more fortuitously than before, rather than after, his mistake becomes law. The bill is regressive. It will not deter crime. Indeed, it has a good chance of exacerbating that epidemic. I am withdrawing my support. I invite you both to join me in opposing it."

Lambert gaped like a fish in want of water.

"If this isn't a joke, then it's bound to be a scandal," Culver bit out.

Crispin shrugged. "Perhaps. But I will gladly weather a scandal for the sake of a legacy. Your son's son will live in the country that we create. Would he flinch from a scandal if it meant a better world for his heirs?"

Culver went pale. "I . . ."

"He would not," said his wife steadily.

Culver shot her a dark look before turning back to Crispin. "A fine time for your conscience to stir," he said. "You have spent months—every day since the last session—currying and browbeating and *buying* support for this bill." His wife gasped, and Lady Randol, too—for he had just bluntly accused Crispin of corruption.

"William," his wife murmured. "Take a moment—"

Mouth tightening, Culver jerked sharply to one

side—avoiding, no doubt, his wife's restraining touch beneath the table. "And now you mean to go volte-face? Ha! The scandal won't only touch *you*! Tell me, sir, how you plan to keep our people from appearing perfect laughingstocks? You, a recent victim of a brutal attack. *You*, deciding that criminals merit mercy? That will look very fine in the press, oh indeed. Why, the public will wonder if the assault did not disorder your brain!"

Jane flinched. That came perilously close to the truth. But Crispin looked unmoved. His mouth curved in a cold, humorless smile. "How amusing. And how naïve. The public wonders exactly what we wish them to wonder. Or did you imagine that the newspapers reported the truth?"

"I imagined," Culver said hotly, "that you meant what you said in December. Or has your *conscience* awakened on that matter as well?"

Crispin's jaw squared. He could not answer that, of course, for he did not remember.

Jane opened her mouth, but Atticus beat her to it. "Oh, this is rich," he drawled. "A fine place we've reached in our nation's great history, when conscience becomes a slur, and men cannot debate issues without ad hominem attacks. I'd expected better of you, Culver."

Culver recoiled. "Well, *I* expected—"

The door swung open. The footmen seemed briefly baffled by the untouched plates of mutton. But Jane now wished for nothing more than a swift conclusion to the meal so the men might withdraw to hash it out among themselves. She made a discreet gesture, and the servants quickly changed out the courses, laying down the platters of roasted pheasant alongside small bowls of compote of fruit.

"I had wondered," Culver said in a subdued voice, "at the company tonight. No offense to you, madam"—he gave a brief nod to Jane—"but I did think it a curious assembly. I imagined, in my naïveté, that a new bride might strive to reconcile feuding brothers. But I see now that this was an ambush."

Along the table, forks clattered inelegantly. Culver had just incinerated the tattered remnants of a polite fiction: that this dinner took place among friends.

"An ambush!" Jane said lightly. "Why, what a diverting analogy for a dinner party! I'm sure that all the ladies here will agree with you, sir. What is a hostess but the general of an army domestic? With the footmen our troops, and each course a new tactic."

"Quite right," said Lady Randol. "It is positively warlike, the dinner campaign."

Jane manufactured a beaming smile for her. "But instead of arrows and swords, we rely on butchers to slaughter little birds for our plates."

"This pheasant is very fine," Mrs. Culver said, adamantly ignoring her husband's sharp look.

"Isn't it?" Jane picked up her fork, spearing a bite of pheasant and chewing with an appreciative sound. "This new French chef," she said, catching Crispin's eye across the table, "knows just how to season the game."

The lines at the corners of his eyes deepened, though his smile did not quite reach his mouth. "A tribute to your wisdom, ma'am."

"But then, pheasant is no real challenge," Jane said. "We must make sure not to bore the Frenchman."

"Oh, there can be pleasure in skewering little creatures," Crispin said smoothly, and she offered a deliberate smile as she raised her wineglass to him.

Mr. Lambert, who had followed this exchange closely, now cleared his throat, a nervous little sound. "I say, Burke—I did have my own doubts about the bill, you might recall."

"That I do," Crispin said. Nobody would ever have guessed he was lying.

"But . . . what with the, eh, compromises I agreed to make . . ." Lambert gave a discreet tug of his cravat. "I can't quite see the way to, eh, revive my former view."

"I'm certain I can help you," Crispin said. "And my brother, of course, will also do his part."

"Oh, that's lovely!" exclaimed Mrs. Lambert. "Perhaps everybody can discuss it at his country home. This weekend, do you think?"

Culver lunged to his feet. "Remarkable!" His wife, red-faced, almost dropped her wineglass as she hurriedly stood. "Well, I will leave you all to arrange your second round of bribes. But I, gentlemen, am done being bullied."

With a jerky, grudging bow to Jane, he grabbed his wife's arm and stalked out.

As Jane finished undressing, a knock came at the door that separated her bedroom from Crispin's. He stepped inside, leaning against the doorjamb as he watched her remove her earrings.

"Lambert will vote against it," he said.

She shut the jewelry box and knotted the sash of her wrapper before sitting on the bed. "That is something, at least. Will Atticus call on Culver tomorrow?"

"He will. But it may not do any good." He rolled his shoulders, then touched the back of his head—feeling unconsciously, she thought, for his injury. "He's a proud man. Atticus says he was stubborn even in school." His hand dropped. "And he bitterly resented the pressure brought to bear on him with regard to this bill." His smile was dark and fleeting. "The pressure *I* brought, to be precise."

She hesitated. "Perhaps if you were to approach him, to apologize frankly . . ."

"Oh, quite." There was no humor in his short laugh. "'Dear Mr. Culver. It seems I strong-armed you, bribed you, perhaps even threatened you into bending. Apologies, old fellow. I take it all back. May I manipulate you again, this time for free?'"

She grimaced. "You could offer him something in return."

He came a few paces toward her, took hold of the bedpost, and tapped out a brisk tattoo with his wedding ring. *Click-clickety-click-click.* "Such as?"

She knew only the methods that her uncle favored. "A bribe? Another one, larger this time."

His tapping ceased. "I suppose I could," he said slowly. "But what would that make me?"

No different from the man he had been. Everything in her balked at encouraging that. If he fell into old routines, his mind might supply the old details.

But this matter was too important to indulge such fears. The bill was wretched. They had to defeat it— foremost for the sake of those who would be hurt grievously by its passage, but also . . . as an exorcism. For somehow, the bill had become like the ghost of the other Crispin, hovering over them like a great shadow.

"Offering a bribe . . . it would make you a politician," she said hesitantly. Not her father's type, but a commonplace one all the same. "Bribes fly in every corner of Westminster, I think."

"Among the corrupt, yes."

"Some would argue that corruption is required to prove effective." She could not believe she was, in effect, making the old Crispin's argument for him. But there was a simple, brutal truth in it. Otherwise Mr. Burke would never have wasted his time on such back-door dealings. "If you believe that justice requires the bill to be defeated, then why not pay a price for it? A lesser evil, to defray the greater one."

He sighed and looked away. Crossing to her dressing table, he picked up an ivory-handled brush, inspecting it before putting it down again. When he turned toward her, his jaw had tightened. "I hoped you might expect better of me."

Her words had cut him, somehow. Cautiously she said, "It has nothing to do with what *I* expect. This is how it's done, Crispin. Powerful men use their power—all the means at their disposal—to accomplish their visions. There's no . . ." She faltered briefly, appalled by her own words. Did she even believe this?

But many did. "From one view," she sighed, "there's no moral fault in using whatever means necessary to accomplish a good."

"From one view, certainly. And from *your* view?" He came to sit beside her. "The bill is bad policy. A miscarriage of justice." He studied her face. "But is it worth any price to defeat?"

"For the sake of countless strangers, who would suffer for its passage? Yes. I think so."

"And you would not think less of me," he said, still watching her, "if I dabbled in corruption to defeat it.

Instead of looking for another way, which might yet reveal itself."

She felt an inward twist of discomfort. He was not wrong to challenge her.

What a hypocrite she was! She saw herself clearly now. She wanted him to do the dark work, while her own hands remained clean. She wanted the comfort of being able to pass judgment from a safe, stainless distance.

"You would do so only in order to undo the corruption that preceded it," she said.

He gave her a crooked smile. "I believe there's an ancient proverb about that. Something about two wrongs . . ."

A breathless, frustrated laugh escaped her. "Here's a fine turn," she said. "You have woken up from your injury a moralist, and made *me* into the villain."

"Not a villain," he said instantly, and the warmth of his hand enclosed hers, his grip firm. "Perhaps you're right, and bribery is the only way forward." His gaze shifted, seeming to look beyond her now. "I'll think on it." He paused. "Do you sew?"

The tangent startled her. She followed his gaze to the sewing basket in the corner. Embroidery floss spilled in a tangle from the pile of crumpled canvas.

"Occasionally," she said. "Not recently."

He made a quick grimace. "It hasn't been an easy time, has it?"

"No." She looked at their joined hands. In some ways, it had been the most wondrous time of her life. "I never enjoyed sewing," she admitted. "It was only a . . . distraction. A kind of medicine to quiet my mind, when I thought I might run mad from holding my tongue and being told not to think."

Their eyes met. He offered a crooked smile. "I rely on you to think."

"Yes." And for all the fears and difficulties of recent weeks, she had not been so happy in years. It frightened her. "Perhaps, instead of a bribe, you might speak with Culver's son. See if *he* can sway his father."

He nodded. "I'll ask Atticus."

She pulled her hand free. "Atticus was hardly a boon to you tonight!"

"He's a bruiser," Crispin said amiably. "I never expected subtlety of him."

"He insulted you in the same breath that he bid you farewell." She still felt hot with anger, remembering it. *So much for that, Cris. Would say I'm disappointed, but I hadn't expected much anyway. If you're smart, you'll go tell a passel of lies to your cronies tonight, before Culver can speak to them. Oh, Mrs. Burke—our thanks for dinner.*

"He's not the easiest man," Crispin said. "But as bizarre as this all seemed to Lambert and Culver, it must seem doubly strange to him. We have been crossing swords for decades now. Since childhood."

"He expects you to reverse course again," she said tightly. To support the bill if he could not be guaranteed to defeat it.

He shrugged. "He has no cause to believe in me."

For a terrible second, she wished for the old Crispin. Just one brief moment, unsettling and wicked. Where was his anger, his resentment? "He's your *brother*," she said. "I know that family can be cruel. But that doesn't make it right. My uncle was wrong to bully me, and your brother is wrong, too. His contempt—"

"Let it be," he said softly.

"No, I won't!" Why did Crispin seem so resigned to Atticus's poor treatment? It was clear that his brother's disdain was an ancient production. How much responsibility did Atticus bear for what Crispin Burke had become? "Why do you put up with it? You would never take such treatment from anyone else—"

"I had another brother once."

He spoke so casually, it took a moment to untangle his meaning. "What changed him?" Perhaps the entire Burke family was prone to bizarre transformations.

"No, not Atticus. I mean I had another brother. Jonathan was his name."

Confused, she held her tongue. She had heard a great deal of talk about Mr. Burke over the years. In her uncle's stories, Atticus had featured regularly as the proverbial thorn in Burke's side. But nobody had ever mentioned a brother named Jonathan.

"I tell you this," he said, "because you seem to like my family. Apart from Atticus." His smile was brief but wry. "Isn't that so?"

"I do," she whispered. "Your parents and Charlotte are . . . lovely."

"Yes, well, now you've spotted the pattern, you may see how far it goes," he said. "Charlotte excepted, perhaps. She is too young for it to shadow her knowledge of me. But you will see it, the more time we spend with them, and I don't wish it to harm your opinion. For they like you very much as well, I think. And you miss your family," he said gently. "Your stories are so full of longing. I would be glad if my family could lessen that ache a little."

She had the feeling of finding herself on unsteady ground, where each step might cause her to lose her footing. She chose the cautious reply: "Thank you. That is kind to say."

He stared at her a moment before seeming to reach some decision. Holding out his hand, he said, "Come with me."

He led her through the door that connected their bedrooms, closing it behind him before urging her onward, into his dressing room.

An oil painting hung between the wardrobe and pier glass. It was the only decoration in the room, an unavoidable sight from every angle. It showed four children, two gangly boys caught on the edge of manhood, and a plump little girl holding the hand of a baby just learning to stand.

Jane's throat closed. The baby carried a rattle inset with a gleaming ruby cabochon—the gem from Mr. Burke's missing ring.

"He was the youngest," Crispin said. "Ten years younger than Atticus, seven years my junior. I think he took my parents quite by surprise. Naturally, what with being sent away to school, I didn't know him well. But on holidays, as he grew older, as he learned to walk and then to run, he became quite the devil. Harassing me at all hours. Escaping his nurse and begging me to play with him."

He spoke quite neutrally. But she already knew the story would not end well. When his hand brushed against hers, she took it.

His hand remained lax in hers, his gaze locked firmly on the painting. "I found him a nuisance, if you must know. Oh, entertaining, no doubt—he was easily amused; anything I did seemed novel and astounding to him. A drawing, a riddle, a story composed off the top of my head . . ." He drew an audible breath, and his hand at last tightened over hers. "He was, in that house-hold, perhaps the only person I could be guaranteed to please. Even Charlotte liked to mimic our parents, to make a game of rolling her eyes and scolding me to get to my work. She didn't mean it, of course. But . . ." His laugh was curt. "She was a damned good mimic. Still is, in fact. Or . . . was. I can't say if that has changed.

"At any rate, I tolerated him. And once he was four or five, I put him to work, carrying the pails and bait when I slipped off to the fishing pond on summer after-noons. His nurse was always hunting for him. It was quite amusing, how clever he got at escaping her. I used to encourage him . . ." His voice hoarsened; he paused to clear his throat. "Well. Yes, I would encourage him. I thought it a great prank. Only then we got caught sneaking away together, and I was scolded for it. The next time he slipped out, I sent him straight back again. I was managing to get into enough trouble on my own. But he was stubborn." He drew a hard breath. "Took after me that way, I suppose."

For a long moment, he said nothing else. She gripped his hand tightly, to let him know she was listening. His silence spoke as loudly as his words; the oncoming trag-edy weighted the very air.

"The next day," he said finally, "Jon found another way out of the nursery. He knew where to find me—down at the fishing pond. I never heard him arrive. I was napping on the dock; I woke and checked my line. I slipped back to the house before anyone could catch me bunking my studies. They found him three days later." He swallowed. "After they dragged the pond."

Breathing felt difficult. He did not weep, so she wept for him. The hot dampness of her own tears made her flinch.

He pulled away, his face a terrible blank mask. He thought she had flinched away from *him*.

"No," she said, and grasped his face, looking directly into his eyes. "You can't be blamed for that. You were— why, you were all of *twelve*, Crispin. It wasn't your fault."

"Nobody blamed me," he said softly. "Why would they? They expected no better of me. They blamed themselves. They blamed the nurse. But no, not me. Of course I didn't watch for him. Of course I fell asleep. I slept on while he drowned. That was simply my nature, you understand. Careless to a fault. Unable to keep my mind on anything—even my brother's safety."

She shook her head. "That's mad. You misunderstood them. Crispin, it was a terrible accident, but— tragedies happen, too often, God in heaven. Your family would never have—"

He wiped her tears away methodically, with long, firm strokes of his thumb. "Jane. I am going to disown the bill. Publicly, at the third reading."

Thrown by this abrupt segue, she stammered. "In— in the Commons? Giving a speech, do you mean? That would—why, it would create a furor—"

"Yes," he said. "It will need to be the speech of my life."

"But you won't even recognize your colleagues." Imagining it left her aghast. "The hecklers—you won't even know how to address them by name. Your amnesia will come out! And then they'll dismiss you as a lunatic. You'll be ruined."

"Then what, Jane? What other option remains?"

"Let Atticus speak to Culver—"

"You still doubt me," he said softly. "Just as my brother does. Very well. I'll surprise you both."

"That's not it!"

202   MEREDITH DURAN

"Then what?" He lifted an ironic brow. "Shall I abandon my ambition along with my memory? Is that what you want? Resign myself to the quiet life of an invalid?"

"No," she whispered. "But if you waited—"

"Time is up," he said harshly. "You married a politician. A man who would be prime minister. Now you'll find out if his skills extend beyond bullying and bribery. It should be interesting, no?"

Words came short. She could make no reply that would not seem . . . flimsy, rote. Instead, she put her arms around him and hugged herself to his body. His palm came against her back—his touch somehow mechanical, a bloodless acknowledgment of the embrace. He was tolerating it for her sake, allowing her to take comfort in the fact that she tried to comfort *him*.

At last, she drew away. "I'll help you," she said unsteadily. "With the speech. If you wish it."

"Yes." His face was unreadable, his smile perfunctory. "You should sleep," he said.

He did not invite her to stay.

As she returned to her room, she passed the little table by the window on which lay the volume of Debrett's.

Almost against her will, she picked up the book and opened to the entry for the Burkes.

Jonathan Michael Alexander Burke,
b. 1836, d. 1841.

She swallowed the knot in her throat. That ruby ring, made from the rattle of a boy who'd died too soon . . . The other Crispin had not worn it out of vanity.

He'd worn it as a dare to his family. *Go ahead, judge me.*

Or . . . he'd worn it as penance. A constant punishment to himself, doled out every second of his waking
hours.

Perhaps both were true. She could not decide which
was the more terrible.

She closed the book, but not before another tear had
slipped free to stain the page.

CHAPTER ELEVEN

*ℛ*ead me that last line again."

Jane rubbed her eyes. They had been at this for seven hours now—and twelve the day before it, and ten the day before *that*. If Crispin truly had lacked discipline as a child, then he had found it somewhere along the way. " 'Fear,' " she read aloud, " 'may serve countless useful aims. It may sharpen our wits when danger is upon us—' "

"No, after that." He made a quick circle of his hand. "Skip the virtues."

Ah yes. She moved her finger down the page. This was from last night, very late; her handwriting had begun to slip. " 'But when fear is causeless, it becomes an enemy. Fear cripples our minds and breeds delusions; it blinds us to the true nature of the world. It hamstrings reason, for the foundation of reason is fact, and fact alone. So I ask you, without fear, in full view of the facts—' "

"That's enough." He clawed a hand through his hair, then dropped onto the settee beside her. He was doing a fine job of disguising his nerves, but through the door that connected their apartments, she'd heard him pacing these last few nights. He was barely sleeping. "Bit dry, I fear."

It would certainly mark a change from his usual approach. "Your speeches, from what I've read, tend to fix at first on a single MP. You mock his logic, then enlarge on his faults until they extend to indict his allies."

He snorted. "Yes, I noticed that in the transcripts. What a charmer I am! But that approach won't work here. How can I call a man out if I can't remember what he looks like?"

"You won't need to," she said gently. "And you won't give anyone time to question you. Once you've finished speaking, you'll slip out straightaway—"

"Slip out." He shook his head. "That's another thing." He turned to her. "Imagine this: I try to leave, and find myself lost again. I wander the wrong way, make an idiot of myself."

Her pulse hitched. "I thought that problem had passed."

"It's improving by the day," he said. "But I was glad to have your escort into the dining room the other night. And if it happens on the floor of the Commons . . . the talk won't be of the bill."

This did pose a problem. "We'll find someone to guide you from your seat."

He offered her a faint smile. "Are there men in the Commons whom I can trust?"

She bit her lip. Many men claimed Crispin Burke as a friend. But she knew what "friendship" had meant to him. Trust was not a part of it.

Inspiration struck. "We'll procure you a cane," she said. "We'll say that the attack left you unsteady—that you'll need an escort to and from St. Stephen's Portico."

His brows lowered. "And make a show of infirmity?"

Her breath caught. She sat forward. "In fact, perhaps *that* is what the speech requires. You're right; it is very dry. And without the knowledge at your fingertips to identify those who will heckle you, to call them out by name—why, you have no choice: you must make yourself heckle-proof."

"I remember enough of politics to guess that pity will not protect me," he said wryly.

"No, not pity. Heroism!"

He sat back, lifting his brows. "Go on."

"This speech does not account for *why* you've changed your mind on the bill. Obviously, the truth will not serve; it might be used to call you unfit for your post."

"Ah." He tilted his head. "But if I made a point of emphasizing my physical injuries . . ."

"Precisely."

He rose and began to pace. "Yes. Of course. Of all people, *I* am the true authority in that room on the problem of crime. After all, I was savagely attacked—felled by a band of hooligans. But the experience, so near to death, has caused me to . . ."

"Awaken," she said.

He pivoted toward her. "Awaken. Exactly."

"And you saw, by the grievous state of poverty so evident on the bodies of the men who attacked you—"

"Ah yes, I remember it well," he said dryly. "Poor, desperate, hopeless men, whose eyes will forever haunt me. Who deserve punishment, certainly, but not without mercy. For was it not in part the misery of their circumstances, their desperate poverty, that drove them to attack me for what lay in my pockets?"

Jane clapped. "Hear, hear!"

"And what good can come of a bill that would guarantee the deepening of that misery? How could such a bill claim to *solve* the epidemic that poverty has helped to create?" He lunged for her fountain pen, then carried a page to his desk and began to scribble notes. "There's promise here," he said absently. "This is . . . good."

"Indeed. And every time someone jeers, you must return to this one fact: you nearly died. You survived."

"Right. As a good Christian, I cannot believe in destroying those who sinned against me." He looked up with a grin. "But as a politician, as a man who has survived the worst, I also want, more than any other man in that chamber, justice: the best kind of justice, which diminishes, rather than exacerbates, the dangers that Londoners face on the street."

"Oh, well put!"

He sent her another quick, flashing smile, and then, for a long minute, the only sound was the scratching of his fountain pen.

"Clever as hell," he said at last. He laid down his pen and came toward her. "I would say I had married you for your brain, but your other charms are too obvious."

She laughed. "To be married for one's brain would be a great compliment, I think."

"Then do accept it as one." His gaze dropped to her mouth. "One among many," he murmured as he leaned down.

Crispin felt her shy away. It was not so much a physical rejection as a shuttering of herself, which registered on an ineffable, intuitive level. A moment before, he had sensed her as a warm, willing, open, *affectionate* presence. Now, in his mind's eye, her presence had dissipated, leaving him alone. She had gone . . . blank.

It was not fair to feel frustrated.

Jane had risen; was watching him warily. "I'm sorry, Crispin, I—we have become friends, I feel, over these past days, and I don't think . . ."

It was a peculiarly demoralizing thing, to watch one's wife grope for reasons she did not wish him to touch her. Maddening, too, to try to fit those reasons to the facts: they had kissed several times, once by her own choosing. She had not seemed to dislike it. Quite the contrary.

She still looked poised to spring away. Like a deer gauging the intentions of a gunman. It became increasingly difficult to avoid the conclusion his brain had been pushing forward for days. On that extraordinary occasion when she had kissed him in the park, she had forgotten that other Crispin, the one she had intended to live apart from. But in the time since, she had disciplined herself not to forget again.

She still intended to leave him. She was not persuaded by his change.

He sat down on the sofa, deliberately filling his hands with the scribbled, scratched-out pages of composition. She was safe. His attention, most conspicuously, was focused elsewhere.

The floorboards creaked as she stepped toward him. He kept his eyes on the page. She wrote a fine copperplate script, very elegant. He turned the page. It was clear from the places in which her penmanship occasionally lurched, the loops loosening, where she had lost patience. Or felt fatigued. But she'd admitted to neither, although last night, as he'd caught her yawning, he asked three times if she wished to stop, to put the work aside and sleep. Defeating the bill was deeply important to her.

That, he saw suddenly, was the passion that animated her, that kept her close to him. He had mistaken it as something intimate and personal between them, the slow growth of a true attraction. But, no.

Ah, vanity.

"Crispin," she said, very low. "I wish . . . you would look at me. Talk to me. I didn't mean to . . ."

His pride winced at the potential completions of that sentence. Hurt him? God above, what a sorry figure he cut, sulking over a woman's rejection like some hapless suitor kept out on the porch.

"It's no matter," he said briskly. He stacked the pages and smiled at her. "I understand. It's an awkward situation."

"No, it *isn't*." She lifted her thumb to her mouth, caught herself chewing the nail, and snatched it away again, blushing. "It isn't awkward at all," she said raggedly. "I . . . that's the problem, you know."

No, he didn't know. He took a large breath. "Did I mistreat you?" And then, although surely it wasn't required, he specified: "Before."

"No!" Her denial was instant. But then she frowned and reconsidered it. "That is—well—you were . . . *different*."

No revelation in that. But if she wanted to discuss it, then they would discuss it, frankly, without euphemisms. "When I bedded you," he said evenly. "Did you enjoy it?"

Her blushes were marvelous. The original template,

surely, on which all other women's blushes had been modeled. She was not so fair as to turn red; the olive cast of her skin translated the sudden rush of blood in her face as a blooming pinkish rose.

The blush kept spreading. He watched it, fascinated. Down her throat. Across the delicate skin over her collarbones. How far did it continue? He would never know. The high neckline of her brown silk gown concealed it.

She sat down suddenly, heavily, as though some great weight had become, all at once, too onerous to be carried. "We never . . ." she said.

It took him a long, stupid moment to believe that fragment of truth. He could not believe, once granted the full force of godly and state approval, he had not immediately carried this woman to a bed. "Never," he repeated carefully, not wanting his disbelief to show. He had never, in his memory, been a lecher, but since he'd woken to this new world, half his waking thoughts had been of her—the sounds she would make, the way her skin would feel, what it must be like to cause her immense self-possession to tremble and splinter apart. All the little wonders he had forgotten. All the wonders he felt damned sure he would have laid claim to, the very moment the wedding was over.

"Never," she whispered. Her profile was to him. She sat beside him but faced straight ahead, like a fellow passenger on a train—perhaps a stranger, a lady intent, through her fixed attention elsewhere, on communicating to him that he must not take liberties or attempt to forge an acquaintance with the journey bound to end so soon.

Was it some peculiar sense of loyalty that guided

her? Did she keep herself away from him now, from allegiance to the man he had been? But she'd not been in love with that man. She'd all but said so herself. A marriage of convenience, she'd called it.

He'd been so certain that deeper feelings had driven *him*. But if he'd married her and neglected to bed her . . . he must be wrong.

That man was a damned fool. She owed nothing to that man.

And he, the man he was now, certainly would not be guided by the actions of a fool.

He touched her upper arm. Felt, in response, the slightest flinch that traveled through her flesh, translated through the warm silk of her sleeve. Still she did not look at him. He smoothed his thumb up her arm, to the top of her shoulder. That point where her skin emerged, naked to the world. How tense she was. Her muscles were locked, straining.

"This is fine news for you," she said breathlessly. "A marriage that hasn't been consummated . . . you could pursue an annulment, if you like."

He massaged the rigid muscle, feeling how it yielded, the smooth pliancy of her skin. "Is that what you wish?"

She did not reply.

He slipped his hand beneath the heavy mass of her low chignon, cupping the back of her neck, kneading it. After a moment, her head drooped; she made some faint noise in her throat, and then swallowed. Trying to swallow that noise away, but too late.

He had caused that noise. With his fingertips, he searched for the spot that had caused it, and massaged a little harder. She remained silent, her face hidden now from his study, but her shoulders loosened.

A body, he thought, was like a complex and complicated clock. Each one unique in its parts. Through study, one might discover the tricks of its mechanisms. Through trial and error, one might calibrate one's touches on the gears and learn to make the clock tick.

He drew his knuckles down her nape, along her spine. She shuddered.

"I don't think," he said very gently, "that an annulment would suit you, Mrs. Burke. After all, you married for a reason, did you not?"

Still stubbornly silent. He spread his hand across her back, feeling the thick discipline of her corset, sliding higher, searching for the point where the corset ended, finding it. He pressed his fingers hard into her and massaged the muscles that flanked her spine.

This groan, she could not swallow. But as soon as she'd made the sound, she leapt to her feet, turning in a flaring sweep of skirts. "I—we—"

He had never seen her panicked before. But her eyes looked wild. "You'll regret it," she blurted. "If we—if we make it unbreakable. If it can't be undone."

He rose, a predatory hunting instinct still guiding him. But she took a step backward, and he forced himself to halt.

"So many opinions to do with me," he said. "What of yourself, Jane?"

"When you remember," she said stubbornly, "you will want to be free of me. All of this"—she cast a hand out to indicate the speech, which, forgotten, had spilled from his lap and scattered across the carpet—"will not please you. You'll be livid, Crispin. And you will blame me for it. And you—" She squared her shoulders. "*I,*" she said with sharp precision, "will not want to be bound to you then."

He shook his head. "What do you imagine, Jane? That the memories will flood back and replace everything that has come afterward? Even once I do remember, I will also remember *this*. Every thought and feeling I have experienced since I woke. And I will tell you now"—he stepped toward her, to hell with her retreat—"that regret is the very last thing I will feel when I think of touching you."

Her lips visibly trembled. For a moment, she seemed to sway toward him; for a moment, he felt a leap of triumph: he had convinced her.

But then she shook her head and said, with a broken laugh, "You don't know Crispin Burke. But *I* do. And for my own sake, I won't trap him. Not even for you."

It was the most aggravating, infuriating statement. She conjured an imaginary man, a version of himself that did not currently exist, in order to rebuff him.

To hell with the bargain his former self had struck with her. He wanted none of her money. He only wanted *her*. "And what if I never remember?" he said, speaking very quietly lest he shout. "What then, Jane? How long will you let this phantom control us?"

She stared at him for a stricken moment, then turned and fled the room.

A newlywed bride was allowed to cling to her husband, to whisper into his ear. And so, amid the swarms of well-wishers in the Sibleys' ballroom, Jane kept close to Crispin, watching those who approached, murmuring their names to him when she knew them. When she did not, Crispin stepped forward, presenting her with a show of enthusiasm and then leaving them to introduce themselves, some of them—the most self-important, the elderly and titled—appearing quite flustered by this breach of etiquette.

The plan was sound. Nobody would leave the ballroom tonight wondering how Crispin had forgotten old friends. This was the plan they had agreed on two days ago, between sessions of drafting Crispin's speech, when their manner had still been easy and companionable, even conspiratorial, bound together by hard work and mutual admiration for a few fine turns of phrase.

Jane tried to recover that mood. As they strolled the floor—he could not dance tonight, not if he meant to show up to the Commons with a cane—she made pleasant remarks about the fineness of the orchestra and the beauty of his mother's decorations, drapes of black silk and garlands of white roses hanging from the sconces and chandeliers.

But his replies were perfunctory, polite but disinterested. She tried humor instead. The current fashions made the ballroom more crushed than necessary, the great belling of ladies' skirts turning the room into a maze. "Doorways will have to be widened," she said, "if this fashion continues."

He smiled. He patted her hand with the polite approval of a disinterested but dutiful uncle. He kept his eyes on the dance floor. Something was broken between them.

She followed his look. He was watching a young couple, a burnished golden pair who looked utterly delighted by their cleverness in finding each other. Jane did not recognize them; if they weren't married, then they were behaving very recklessly. It wasn't so much their animated laughter, the clear pleasure they took in holding each other, as it was the sinuous grace with which they waltzed. The gentleman swung the woman daringly wide; she tossed her head in glee, encouraging his recklessness. As he gathered her back to him, she stepped closer than necessary. Their bodies were communicating. A fine sight, very romantic. Jane felt ill-tempered, suddenly. They did not mean to flaunt themselves, of course.

I'm not at fault. She felt as petulant as a small child sent to the corner unjustly, blamed for someone else's wrongs. If anything, she had been more truthful with Crispin than wisdom recommended. He was right: she had married him for a reason. By admitting that the marriage could be undone, she had given him a weapon he could use to cast her back into the Masons' poisonous embrace. It felt tremendously unfair to be punished for that.

More frustrating yet: she knew he did not intend to punish her with his courtesy. He was treating her just as she'd instructed. He was not flirting with her, seducing her, or touching her save when necessary. He was behaving precisely as she'd asked.

And what if I never remember? he'd said. Slicing so neatly to the core of her churning unease.

The answer in mind was unspeakable, but also inarguable. If she felt certain he would never remember, she herself would never leave.

Mr. Gaultier had written with news of a court date. In thirteen days, a judge would force her uncle to hand over her money. Why not take those days as a gift? Why not cast caution to the wind and live, however briefly, in a dream?

Indeed, why stop there? The marriage certificate was flawless. No one else knew her secret. She was already halfway to forgetting the truth herself. Who would be harmed if she did?

Mrs. Crispin Burke. Forever.

She leaned into him. He glanced at her, no doubt surprised, but as their gazes met and held, he seemed to read her thoughts, for some minute transformation softened his features.

"Jane," he said, "I—"

"Burke." The man who stepped toward them moved as stiffly as a soldier presenting himself to his regimental line. "Wanted to congratulate you."

The man looked about forty, lean and handsome, his graying temples lending him a distinguished air. Jane did not recognize him, so she pressed Crispin's arm.

They had mastered the routine. "A pleasure seeing you here," Crispin said easily. "May I introduce my wife—"

"The Duke of Farnsworth," the man said to her with a brief bow. But she barely registered his courtesy; Crispin's sudden tension had distracted her, his forearm flexing violently in her grip. "My felicitations, ma'am," the duke was saying. "Might I borrow your husband for a moment?"

The words were courteous, the tone perfunctory. This was not a man accustomed to issuing requests.

But mere rudeness could not account for the distress radiating from Crispin.

She felt cold suddenly. He did not remember the last

five years. Why, then, should the sight of his lover's husband distress him? Unless . . .

"Of course," Crispin said, gently detaching himself from her grip. "Mrs. Burke, I will find you momentarily."

Was it wise to let him go? Farnsworth could not be a friend to him. The duke would leap on any weakness he detected.

But Jane could think of no excuse to prevent their private meeting. Stomach leaping, she watched them walk away together—two men whose reputations, combined, caused the crowd to hurriedly clear a path for them.

She pressed a fist to her belly as the truth became clear. If he remembered a cause to dislike Farnsworth . . .

Why, then his connection with the duchess must be older than five years. It had not been a simple affair, after all.

"Jane!" Charlotte swooped up, smiling. "At last, Crispin lets you out of his clutches."

"Yes," she said. "He . . . the Duke of Farnsworth wished to speak with him."

Charlotte wrinkled her nose. "I cannot like that man's wife. What a blessing that Crispin found you!"

Something in that statement niggled at her. "Crispin had . . . hopes for her?"

Charlotte blinked, making some quick reassessment of the situation. "I—well, she was quite the star, the season we debuted. All the young men were infatuated." But her smile now looked forced. "At any rate, she never took *him* seriously. She had aims for a coronet, that one, and no care whom she'd wed to secure it. Thank goodness for that! I always dreamed of a sister-in-law I could love." She leaned over to kiss Jane's cheek. "Now, won't you dance? My husband tires of a left-footed partner."

She felt sick. Why should she feel sick? She felt like a single great bruise, aching from some injury she did not recall. "I think . . . a moment's rest might do me good."

"Of course," Charlotte said. "Goodness, I hope it wasn't anything I said—it was all so long ago, Jane, and Crispin was a different man then."

Jane knew that better than anybody. "Of course. No, it's only the heat in here."

"Come," Charlotte said. "I'll show you to a quiet spot."

"Dined at the club today," Farnsworth began casually as he followed Crispin into the morning room. He shut the door with a sound thump. "Heard the most curious rumor. Seems you are persuading your confederates to drop their support for the bill."

Any man might resent his wife's former suitors. But this man's hostility was not casual, the product of impersonal circumstances. He watched Crispin with the bright, glinting aggression of an enemy. "No sewing circle," Crispin said, "could outdo a club for the gossip on offer."

"And yet so much of that gossip has a way of becoming news," Farnsworth drawled. "So tell me. Is it true? Have you disowned the bill?"

"If so, I can't see how it should concern you." Although at present, Farnsworth looked ripe to shift from *concern* into fury.

"We had a deal, you and I," the other man growled.

Crispin felt an astonished, somewhat black admiration for his former self. Nobody would have accused him of lacking brazen initiative. From mere gentlemen to dukes, nobody escaped his machinations. "Your vote is your own, Farnsworth. If it passes to the Lords, you'll make your own decision, with no comment from me."

The man looked to be wrestling with some inner demon. His lip curled back, exposing the topmost row of his teeth; he made a fist as he hissed out a breath. "I held my tongue for longer than any other man would have done. I thought—I told myself, fool that I was— that matters would take their own course. That my best chance lay in patience. A man such as you, who takes no act without calculating his own gain—I told myself that she would come to see it herself, given time."

She?

"But I was wrong." Farnsworth's voice dropped to a raw whisper. "It isn't *you* she sees, after all. It's . . . who you were, and who *she* was, back then. The dreams she had. A vision, a fantasy. How can a man compete with a fantasy? It changes, it reshapes itself to fit whatever need I have failed to meet on any given day."

A terrible premonition rolled through Crispin. He felt himself paralyzed, unable to speak, lest it be fulfilled.

"So I am done," Farnsworth said, sharper and stronger. "Done with waiting. Done with hoping that there remains a shred of decency in your twisted soul. I am taking her away, Burke. And if she so much as receives a *mention* of you from some passing acquaintance—"

The door flew open.

Laura stepped inside. She swept a contemptuous look over her husband, causing him to fall silent and flush.

"And how will you take me?" she snapped. "Will you

tie me up and drag me off in a cart? I carry your child, sir, but that does not make me your property."

"In fact," Farnsworth said coldly, "it does. Or so near to it as to make no difference."

She yanked the door shut, locking them all into this airless little salon. "The law has changed. *You* voted to make that change. A woman may divorce now, given proof of abuse and infidelity. I think I can supply both."

"Infidelity, I'll not argue." Farnsworth's words lashed like a whip. "But abuse? I challenge you, madam, to name one instance of it."

"I will have that, once you remove me from London. For I'll not go quietly. You will need to use force."

Farnsworth stood quivering, his fists white knuckled at his sides. And then, with an explosive cough, he stalked past her to the door—turning back there with a snarl. "Have it your way, madam. But the child in your belly will be a stranger to you. That, I guarantee."

The door slammed behind him.

Laura did not lose a beat. "Crispin," she cried, and came rushing toward him, stumbling once on her diaphanous silver skirt before throwing her arms around him. "My God—I was worried! Not one word from you, and I dared not write—he has been watching my post, looking for evidence against me!"

The smell of her was jarringly familiar—the same rosewater seasoned with musk that she had favored as a debutante, laughing at her mother's criticism that the scent was too heavy for a girl. As it crept up his nose, the world seemed to lurch around him.

He was in his parents' house, but it now counted as a blessing that this room held only one door. He knew without looking that he had lost his way again.

"Laura," he said, grabbing her arms, unlocking them from around his neck and guiding her forcefully apart from him. "What . . ."

A single tear had slipped free of her eyes. It carried with it a dark trace of whatever unguent she had used to darken her lashes. She looked . . . no older than in his memory, no less beautiful, though her face was rounder, her arms plump, and her waist thicker.

With child. Her husband's child.

By God—*was* it her husband's? He felt nauseated. How deep did his own rottenness go?

She saw the change in his face, mistook it for some emotion that wanted comfort from her. He stepped out of her reach, retreating another pace. There was no other way to interpret what had just passed here. She thought it her right to touch him. Her marriage had not ended their connection.

"The child." He made himself say it, though the words nearly choked him. "Whose is it?"

Her head tipped back, a reflexive puzzled gesture. "What—what do you mean? His, of course." Her mouth twisted. "Do you regret insisting on it now? I told you that you would!"

He clawed his hands through his hair. Her face was so familiar; he could not look on her without remembering . . .

A dark hallway. Her desperation. *Forgive me*, he'd told her. *Was I meant to place you above politics?* Thinking of Farnsworth as he said it.

The memory was so clear. But he could not place it. It had happened, though. He felt certain of that.

"We broke it off," he said slowly. "I . . . spoke with your husband." Thank God for that! This man he had been, he had possessed *some* ounce of decency.

"In exchange for Farnsworth's vote," she said bitterly. "But now you don't want it. Isn't that so? That is what Culver told him. He's been frothing ever since."

Crispin loosed a sharp breath. By God, but he was done with surprises. No silver lining existed in the man he had been. He'd been a bastard, finis.

"But . . ." She inched closer. "I don't—I felt sure you'd changed your mind! If you don't need his vote . . ." Her hand alighted on his wrist, trembling, damp. "There's nothing to keep us apart. I meant what I said, Crispin. It was a terrible mistake to marry him. And the divorce court, they say it favors the wife—"

"I am married."

Her eyes widened. He'd once lived for the sight of those eyes, so magnificently blue, like the hearts of violets. "I know that," she said. "But . . . haven't you heard me? These marriages, they can be dissolved now."

You could pursue an annulment, his wife had told him. Dear God, had Jane known of this? Had she been keeping this secret from him, this knowledge that he'd been entangled with Laura?

He felt light-headed. Laura kept crowding closer to him. He moved away again. "I have no desire to end my marriage," he said hoarsely.

She scoffed. "You can't claim to love her! The girl you called the brown goose? Why, she's the daughter of a *factory man*! If it's the money you need—"

"Enough."

She fell silent, but a strange creeping smile came over her mouth. "I do love it when you order me about."

He remembered suddenly his dream—that strange dream from weeks ago.

It had been true. The ugliness in her voice, the contempt in his own.

Christ! He started for the door, but she threw herself in front of him. "This is a punishment," she said eagerly. "I understand. I knew you hadn't forgiven me. Very well, I will wait for you. Punish me as long as you like! But I will be waiting, I vow it."

She had plastered herself against the door. "Step aside," he said.

"No. Not until you promise you will forgive me. Eventually, Crispin. A single mistake—years ago, and not even my own doing! Tell me you'll forgive me, and I'll let you out."

He contemplated lifting her bodily. But the prospect of touching her made him queasier yet. For those dark feelings he'd dreamed . . . they still lived inside him. Like a banked black fire, the embers barely glowing, he could feel them preparing to kindle anew.

They felt alien. He wanted nothing to do with such feelings.

She thought he was softening to her. Her own expression relaxed. "I was frightened," she said. "That was all. I had no idea Papa would lie about it. I know I should have guessed—he was so intent on making me a duchess! But I would never have allowed it. I promise you, no lie has ever given me such misery in all my life as that one."

He had no idea what she meant. "What lie?"

She looked startled. "Both of them," she said nervously. "But I never knew that Farnsworth told your father of it. How many times must I say so? If I'd known, I would have gone to Lord Sibley directly—I never would have let him believe such things of you."

There was a peculiar sensation in his belly. Like something was cracking apart. "But he believed it." Whatever it was.

"I didn't know!" She made a frustrated noise. "And when I found out, it was already too late. You said it yourself—what good would it have done to tell the truth, once the corps had rejected you?"

"My father believed you." This single fact fixated him. What had he believed? *Why* had he believed?

Her brows drew together. She had darkened them, too. A flake of black powder fell to her cheek. "Not me," she said. "Farnsworth! But—perhaps he didn't," she said hesitantly. "I—I only know what *you* told me. Have you found out differently? I never credited it myself. What father would think his son capable of molesting a lady? No matter what Farnsworth said!"

The pieces swam together. "Farnsworth caught us together," he said dully. "That was the cause."

Her mouth twisted. "He knew you weren't molesting me! He saw that we were standing two paces apart. We weren't even touching! But to catch me alone in a dark room with you—oh, his pride couldn't bear it. Sheer spite was what drove him. He's a monster, I tell you. And I won't stay with him!"

Farnsworth had caught them together. Laura's father had smoothed over the scandal by claiming that Crispin had secluded her by force.

Farnsworth was the reason that Crispin had not been selected for a diplomatic posting.

And Crispin's father—his *own father*—had chosen not to make inquiries because he *knew* why Crispin had not been selected. He knew the reason and chose to *believe* it.

He swallowed hard. This was an old, old injury. No matter that it felt as fresh as the slice of a blade. It was done. Over. Long ago. "Step. *Aside*," he said through his teeth.

Paling, she obeyed. He went into the hall, dragging the untainted air into his lungs: no roses, no musk, thank God.

"Crispin!" His wife stood at the end of the hallway. Whatever she saw in his face caused her to snatch up her skirts and hurry toward him.

But as Laura stepped out, she skidded to a stop. Her skirts swung wildly. "Oh—pardon me," she managed, and then turned on her heel.

Laura wiped her face with the back of her hand. "Do you see? Even *she* knows the truth. Nobody can come between us."

He did not acknowledge her by so much as a glance. "Jane," he called as he started after her.

Her pace quickened; she pretended not to hear him as she cut left, away from the ballroom.

To hell with this. She was his wife. She would not run away from him.

CHAPTER TWELVE

*S*he could not outrun Crispin, so she did not try.
But Jane could feel from the great heat in her
face that she did not look as composed as she might
hope. She felt gutted by betrayal.

Her skirts nearly tripped her as she stalked onward.
The hall was empty, not that she cared if that one lone
bit of good fortune held. She did not care if anybody
saw her, or what they thought. How dare he closet himself with his mistress? Here at a ball to celebrate his marriage to another woman?

She tried the first door she passed. The library. Fireplace dark, only the dim glow of gaslights to illuminate
the spines of books. The high ceiling of the balconied
gallery receded into shadows. She leaned against a bookcase, panting. He would come inside in a moment. He
had seen her duck in here. And then what would she say?

Damn you.

But no. He was not her husband. She had no right to
expect fidelity of him.

He *believed* himself her husband, though!

She wrapped her arms around herself, struggling to calm her breathing. The duchess was his mistress. She had known that since her uncle's ball. If Jane had interpreted Charlotte correctly, the duchess had also been Crispin's first love.

It had been no passing affair.

Pain twisted through her. She'd assumed Lady Farnsworth to be one of a dozen lovers that Crispin Burke kept on the line. But maybe there had only ever been one. In which case, Crispin had forgotten more than his own dark nature. He'd forgotten that he loved a woman.

The duchess must be astonished by his marriage. Jane knew how others saw her: tall and frizz-haired, unaccomplished and awkward. She could imagine Lady Farnsworth's incredulous demand: Of all women, *her*?

The door opened. Without looking, Jane spat, "Go back to her, then."

His voice was sharp: "*What?*"

Lady Farnsworth was stunning, a porcelain doll of miniature and perfect proportions. Immoral and faithless, too—a fine match for Mr. Burke. "Go back to her. There's no need to explain."

"No need, is there?" Crispin caught her by the arm, pulling her around to face him. His lips were white. "I am your *husband*. If you discover me closeted with another woman, there is every need to explain."

Had the duchess neglected to tell him of their affair? Was this delightful task to fall to *her*? "That woman is your—"

His palm covered her mouth, stopping the word.

He looked feverish, his dark eyes glittering. His hand burned against her lips. "Do not say it."

She stared. Her imagination had concocted a dozen visions as she hurried down the hallway. A passionate reunion of long-separated lovers. In fairy tales, a true lover's kiss awakened the slumbering victim. He would remember everything at once, and then—whispered confidences as their hands tracked down each other's bodies. *You are everything. She is nothing. Forget her.*

But the look on his face pierced her delusions. He looked gripped by some inner battle, his skin drawn tight over his cheekbones, his eyes haunted.

"Why?" he bit out. "Why would you tell me to go back to her? Do you even know what that means?"

His palm conveniently kept her from replying. She narrowed her eyes.

He recoiled. "You do know. You always knew, didn't you? You knew that she and I—" He gripped his temples as he turned away.

Through the walls came the distant lilt of the orchestra, the merry rhythm of a reel.

Her anger began to curdle. He was distressed. Not faithless, but deeply upset.

"So, then." His voice was so raw that it seemed a blessing she could not see his face. "Is that why you've rebuffed me? Is *that* what you think of me? That I would turn away from you, that I would spurn you for—God above, Jane, for someone else's *wife*?"

She felt accused by him. How unjust! Had they truly been married, what other conclusion would she have drawn from that little scene in the hallway? "I told you we married for convenience," she said stonily. "If you took that as license, who am I to blame you?"

He pivoted back. "You are my wife," he growled. "And whatever reason you had for wedding me, whatever man you thought you married, *I* am the man in front of you now. I am bloody sick of hearing about the other one—about what you thought of *him*, what *he* expected of you. Do you understand?" He stepped toward her. "*His* reasons," he gritted, "*his* feelings, mean nothing to me. Do you hear? I am not that man."

She swallowed. No, he wasn't that man. Everything in her yearned toward this man he had become.

But he might still change back.

He also might not.

And if he never changed back—then what was she to do in this moment? *Everything.* Her fingers curled into her palms, making tight, painful fists. How could she squander the chance to be with this man?

Sometimes she felt as though she had dreamed this man to life.

He narrowed his eyes. "I see the look on your face. Even now, you are thinking it. 'This isn't him. This isn't real.' What else can I say, Jane? Shall I break open my brain and let you inspect it, to make sure that the injury will last?"

There was violence in his voice, in his face. "No," she whispered. "I believe you." She *believed* him.

Oh, God save her. She could not bear to squander this chance.

"Good." A muscle flexed in his jaw. "Because here I am. I am real. I am here, standing in front of you. And

I am telling you—for the first time and the last—that if this won't serve, you *should* walk away. By God, do it. Do it *now*. Gaultier will win the lawsuit. Take all the money; to hell with the deal you claim that we struck. Or else an annulment—I will grant you one. And if it's your uncle you fear, I'll see you safely onto a ship, and give you half my accounts to see you safe. Yes," he said with a black smile when she failed to hide her surprise. "I've seen you poring over the shipping schedules. You wish to go? I'll book the ticket, carry your trunks to the quay myself.

"But if our connection means *anything* to you." He pushed out a ragged breath. "If you meant those tears you shed when I told you of Jonathan. If your laughter was real, and your smiles. If you feel, as I do, that you could wish for no better partner—in politics, as much as in life. If all of that is true, and not simply an act, a mask to cover your indifference—then tell me so now. Because I am finished with this stalemate. I will not endure a wife who tells me to go back to a mistress. I will not have a wife who refuses to *demand* explanations."

. The moment felt crystalline. Even the music had stopped. The glass beading that trimmed the sconces, which had been shivering from the stomps of the dancers, had fallen still.

He cursed. "So go," he said flatly, and turned away.

She watched her hand leap out to catch his arm. Quick as a striking snake, his own covered hers. His grip tightened to a degree shy of painful. But he did not look at her.

"Think carefully." His voice was threadbare. "After this, I am done with questions."

Fear cripples our minds and breeds delusions. They had penned that line together. But the Crispin before her . . . he was not a delusion. He was here, real, gripping her hand. He was a fact.

And a rational decision could only be made on facts, not fears. *The foundation of reason is fact, and fact alone.*

"Yes," she breathed. "I will stay."

He pulled free of her. Leaving! Confusion, panic, gripped her as he walked to the door.

He turned the key in the lock. When he turned back, his expression was calm and focused, his gaze intent.

The revelation felt like a flush of heat. No, he was not leaving.

Far from it.

He came straight into her, crowded her against the wall as he took her face in his hands. His mouth came down onto hers. With his lips, he opened her mouth, penetrating her without permission, tasting her thoroughly. She had already given permission. *Yes*, she had said. *Yes.*

She pulled his body harder into hers. His body listened; it improved on her idea. With his pelvis and chest, he pinned her solidly, a silent aggressive confidence that should have frightened her, but instead . . . undid something in her, loosened some knot that had held her rigid all night. Her knees loosened. She sagged, and his arm snaked around her, sparing her the bite of the bookshelf. He kissed his way down her chin and throat, licked her pulse and trailed lower. His hot exhalation burned her collarbone.

Her nose brushed his hair, untamed by pomade, disordered now, soft, smelling faintly of soap. He whispered something against her skin, some murmur she would pay dearly to hear better—

"Jane," he said, and lifted his head, his beautiful face alight. He cupped her cheek, studying her, a heavy-lidded look that made her blush. Through her corsetry, through the layers of cotton and silk and wool between them, the muscled force of his hips still pressed into her. The frank boldness of it made her breathless. She could feel the hard prod of his desire. It made her belly tighten, her lips part.

"Touch me," she said.

His gaze dropped to her lips, her throat, the swell of her breasts over the low-cut neckline. She felt exposed to him, but without shame. *Seen.* Her breasts felt tight, aching as he dipped his head to kiss the valley between them.

His clever hand skated down her body as he nuzzled her, his palm brushing her waist, then sliding lower yet. A firm, unhesitating touch, from a man who no longer doubted. She gasped as he palmed her hips, his grip closing on the fullness of her buttocks.

His liberties triggered a realization, wordless, delightful. So much of a body could be touched! She slipped her hands between them, returning the favor. He was taut, solid, densely muscled. So different. She felt beneath his waistcoat, gripped his lean sides. His belly contracted sharply as he sucked in a breath. Touch now wed with memory; she could feel the bands of muscle that she had seen in the bath and in her bed one morning, so long ago it seemed. Through the cloth, her thumb found the indentation of his navel.

"*Jane.*" An urgent, raw note in his voice. He kissed her again, even more deeply, so her head bumped back into the spines of books. His palm quickly cupped the crown of her head, an apology that did not interrupt or distract from the matter at hand.

Eyes closed, she let her hand slip farther. Past the placket of his trousers, until she found a tumescent swelling. He groaned into her mouth. Then his grip found her waist; he pulled her away from the wall and swung her over to a nearby sofa, laying her down before he knelt on the carpet beside her.

"If you still have doubts," he said hoarsely, "I am going to make you forget them now."

She did not know what he meant, only that the vow made her feel . . . luxurious, like a queen. Someone to be attended to, served and persuaded. He was watching her face so closely, his concentration lending him a severe, ascetic look. He was waiting, she realized, for her assent.

She stretched her arms over her head and gave him a smile that felt foreign and wild.

Since the moment he had woken from near-death in his parents' house, Crispin had felt like an adventurer robbed of sea legs. Revelations had come as unrelentingly as waves, and each new surprise had unbalanced him. No safety ropes but one: the woman who stretched out before him now, and gave him a smile of such unabashed invitation that it bypassed his brain and raised an animal instinct that felt raw and primeval.

His memories held no match for it. Youthful fumblings with flirts in Cambridge, uninhibited tavern girls, and one wise, jaded courtesan . . . He remembered the mechanics of seduction but not this driving, raw hunger, which felt desperate, driven, bottomless.

Ambition had always made him anxious. The prospect of failure was so clear. But as he leaned down to kiss her, fear was some distant myth. He would brook no failure now. He would stay here beside her as long as it took to realize his aim.

Her lips were soft and damp. *He* had made them so. She already wore his mark. There were more marks to leave. The night was young, the door locked, and he did not give a damn who might discover so.

He laid his hand on her shoulder, massaging lightly, and kissed her until he felt the tension ease from her. Until, with a soundless sigh that warmed his lips, she settled more deeply into the velvet cushions of the sofa. Only then did he allow himself to kiss his way down her smooth throat, his hand to slip down her bare arm so their fingers entangled.

There was a beast inside him. It strained at the leash, inflamed by her poreless, flawless skin. Perfume of lavender, and beneath it, traces of her natural scent, which she scrubbed away in her morning bath, such a deep injustice; he would keep her in bed for days, simply breathing her. Tracery of veins beneath the fragile skin of her chest, a map for his mouth, to be traced with his tongue.

Soft sounds, the rustle of silk as she stirred restlessly beneath him. He slipped his hands around her waist, found the buttons of her gown. Whence came this dexterity? For once, he felt a deep gratitude to his forgotten self, for having mastered the art of undressing a woman.

The ball gown molded to her like a second skin, but

the silk was soft, pliant; once released of its fastenings, it became a conspirator. With the flat of his palm pressed to her back, he raised her off the cushions—no, he did not wish her help. He kissed her again until she relaxed into his grip, then coaxed the shimmering silk down to her waist.

His fingers flexed. The beast had claws, bottomless hunger. Such a fragile slip of fabric separated them now. He took a sharp, hard breath. *Discipline.* The transparent lawn conspired with him, too. Her breasts were full, her nipples large and dark. He bent and took one in his mouth, tasting her through the fabric.

She made a mewling noise, and twisted in his arms. He closed his teeth gently around her, then used his tongue again. Yes, he could make her whimper. What other aspiration had ever been so sweetly rewarded? As he sucked her, he reached down her body, found the edge of the crushed crinoline, and gathered it slowly, collapsing it in handfuls.

Inch by inch. She tossed beneath him, her face flushed. Her chignon was tumbling down; curls sprang out around her, reaching for him, stroking his brow, brushes of encouragement. He closed his hand on a stockinged calf. Her flexing foot hit his shoulder. He caught it, held it there, kissed her ankle, tracked up to the hidden cove behind her knee.

She gasped. "Crispin—"

The name itself felt unfamiliar suddenly. He had been so concerned for so long about what he had forgotten, had guarded so jealously all that he still remembered. But in this moment, none of it meant anything. Only this: the feel of her, her submission to him, the faith that had guided her to lie down beneath him, to place trust in him, this beast who loomed over her with the intention to devour.

The stocking fastened above her knee, but the beast had clever teeth, and undid it in a moment. Beneath the lace cuffs of her drawers, her thigh felt plump, quivering; he pressed his mouth hard against it. He would provide its surety. He would be her balance.

Through the slit in her drawers, he palmed her.

"Ah!" She started to sit upright—fell back again. Their eyes met. Hers looked startled, luminously amazed. Then, deliberately, she let her head fall back onto the cushion. Her unwavering gaze spoke a silent but unequivocal permission.

He took another deep breath, another sharp grip on self-control.

Inch by inch. Still looking into her eyes, ferociously studying each twitch of her mouth, each moment when her lips parted and her lashes flickered wildly, he learned his way. His fingertips traced lightly, until her hips suddenly jerked.

There.

He stroked her, once, twice. Her eyes came open again, widened. "I don't—I don't think—"

He pressed harder, leaning forward to capture her mouth. "Don't think," he growled.

She writhed beneath him, then cried out, her thighs clamping around his hand. He swallowed her shallow gasps and kissed her more deeply yet. Consuming her.

Her hand found his hair. Clutching hard to hold his mouth to hers.

As if he would let her go.

At last, she sagged back, releasing him. His hand did not wish to move. He forced it back down her thigh, around her knee, which caught his attention; the warmth there, secret, reserved only for him. Her ankle, so trim and narrow; another secret, which he kissed once more. Then, very gently, he helped her upright, kissing his way across her chest and shoulder to her back. Her buttons had undergone a sea change, becoming troublesome; he fumbled with them. His hands were shaking.

He kissed his way back around her. Cupping her elbows, he helped her to stand. The cage crinoline fell into place—some voluptuary had designed it, surely, for the steel bands provocatively framed each erotic detail: the rip in Jane's stocking. The flushed skin of her thighs. The tender dimples in her knees.

But once her skirts fell over the hoops, she looked again the picture of decorum—save her hair. It spiraled wildly all around her.

He stooped to retrieve a discarded hairpin. When she reached for it, he caught her hand and kissed her palm.

An unsteady laugh came from her. Husky. It made his breath catch, his cock throb. He could not go into public in this state.

"I can't be seen like this," she whispered—her tone shy and pleased. She touched her hair. "Everyone will know."

The notion sparked some deep, primal gratification in him. Yes, let them see. He felt . . . exorcised, cleansed, light on his feet, omnipotent. Let them all see. This was his wife.

But she would not like that. He would spare her the gossip.

"Stay here," he said, "and I'll go fetch your cloak." It was hooded, and would conceal her.

As he started to turn away, he caught how she crossed her arms and shifted her weight, a flicker of uncertainty passing over her face.

No. None of that. He caught her by the waist and kissed her again soundly. "We'll go home," he murmured into her hair. "I can't share you any longer."

And after a moment, her arms came around him, and he felt the full, sweet weight of her against his body again. "Yes," she murmured. "I would like that tremendously."

What had she done? Jane would not allow herself to think on it. She was done with analyzing, plotting, calculating the cost. In the carriage, she leaned against Crispin and kept her mind carefully blank. She filled herself with the scent of him; she kept her nose in the thick disorder of his soft black hair. If this was a spell, then let it remain unbroken. She would not think ahead, either. Fearlessness had brought her here. It could carry her through the night.

But as the brougham pulled up outside Crispin's home, her spell fractured. Something was awry. All the windows were lit from top to bottom, and as they stepped out onto the curb, the front door opened to reveal Cusworth shifting his weight in the doorway like a dog straining at the leash.

She exchanged a look with Crispin, who took her arm and hurried her up the steps.

Inside, Cusworth launched into an explanation as the porter took their coats. "One of the maids heard a crash, sir. When she went to investigate, she interrupted a—a ruffian! He escaped out the window. It was only half an hour ago. I had a note dispatched to you, but I expect you were already en route. The entire household is in an uproar."

Crispin took her arm, drawing her behind his body as he looked beyond Cusworth to the stairs. "Has the rest of the house been searched?"

"Yes, yes," Cusworth said. "At once, sir. No other signs of disturbance save in your study."

"I'll take Mrs. Burke to her rooms, and join you there momentarily."

"No," Jane said. "I'll come with you."

"Your room bolts on all sides," Crispin said tightly. "And it's a sight too high for anyone to go leaping through windows—"

"I'll go with you," she said.

A muscle flexed in his jaw. "All right," he said at last. "But keep close."

They followed Cusworth down the hall. Inside the study, a window stood open, the curtains playing in the breeze. The drawers of the desk sat ajar. A dozen books lay scattered on the carpet.

Crispin stooped to retrieve something. A flower, which he showed to her. "A white bluebell," Jane said, startled. "Those are very rare."

"Do we keep these?" Crispin asked the butler.

"No, sir, we never have done. It must have been dropped by the intruder. I touched nothing, sir—I did not wish to disturb the scene, lest the police want to see it as it stands."

"Send for them," Crispin bit out. "You should have done so at—"

"Wait," Jane said. She had a very uneasy feeling. Why had the books been pulled out? And from only two shelves. The rest stood untouched. "Don't send for them just yet."

Whatever Crispin saw in her face caused a guarded look to come over his own. "Cusworth, give us a moment."

"Certainly, sir. I'll have one of the footmen run round to Bow Street—"

"Not yet," Crispin said. "Wait a moment. I'll come speak to you."

The door closed behind the butler. Jane, conscious of Crispin's probing look, walked over to the molested bookcase, taking care to step around the scattered books. Sixteen, twenty, twenty-two, thirty . . . She squinted at the other shelves, still full. It seemed likely that all the books from the emptied shelves were accounted for. Some of them were no doubt very valuable, but they had not been the intruder's aim.

"What are you thinking?" he asked from behind her.

"I'm not certain," she said slowly. "But . . ." How to put this delicately? "I would not call the police just yet. It is possible . . ."

"Your uncle," he said tersely, "will need to account for his whereabouts this evening."

He was a natural suspect, to be sure. But the ransacked desk . . . "Whoever was here tonight wished a look at your papers. I doubt my uncle would have required that. You worked together very closely."

But Burke had not trusted him, had he? He had asked Jane to spy on Mason—in one matter in particular.

She wheeled back, frowning at the desk. "You went through its contents," she said. "Didn't you? A few days ago."

He nodded. "I was looking for notes I might have

made on the bill. But I found nothing useful. Documents from three, four years ago. Correspondence and bills and whatnot. Nothing more recent." He grimaced. "I might have ransacked this place myself, in fact. I've no idea where I kept more recent files."

The intruder, too, had found nothing useful in the desk. And so he had turned to the bookshelf . . . ?

She pivoted back. The bare shelving showed the pattern in the plaster wall, the intermittent medallions. She tucked her hands beneath her arms. She felt quite cold suddenly.

Crispin noticed, perhaps. He crossed to close the window. The lock snapped into place with a brassy clink. Footsteps creaked; she heard him curse softly.

"Unlocked. All of them." He walked down the row of windows, fastening them one by one. "A moment, Jane. Cusworth needs to check all the others."

"Of course." She remained staring at the bookcase as he walked out.

Below the emptied shelves, a single book caught her attention. It sat at a slight angle apart from the others, as though someone had hooked it by the spine but not managed to tug it free.

She watched her hand move toward it, knock it out. Then the next, and the next. Spines thumping, cracking against the carpet.

One of the medallions looked different from the others. Raised a fraction higher. She laid her hand on it. Traced the scalloped patterning with her fingertips.

The medallion fell into her hand.

She recoiled, her heart drumming. The medallion had concealed a lever of some kind.

The door opened. Without thinking, she turned,

placing her body in front of the bookshelf, the medallion clutched behind her back.

"It seems the maid is in hysterics," Crispin said. "I should go speak to her. Calm her down, see if she has any information."

"Yes." Her voice came out hoarse. She cleared her throat. "I'll look through the books, see if there's anything to find."

"Indeed not," he said curtly. "I'm not letting you out of my sight until we—"

"Crispin." How cool she could sound! "You said it yourself: the windows were unlocked. Well, they're locked now. And I very much doubt a prowler, even a very stupid one, would come back the same night he was caught at his work."

"Fine logic," he said, equally cool. "But you will come with me anyway." He extended his arm.

Given a moment's clear thinking, she might have wondered at this panic inside her, this desperate need to get him out of the room before she pulled that lever. "I see. When I lay down on that sofa tonight, I did not know I had surrendered the right to make decisions for myself."

He recoiled as though she'd struck him. "Christ, Jane." And then his mouth tightened. "Apologies," he said stiffly. "But I—that is not, of course, what I meant. I only think of your safety."

She wanted to apologize too. But some demon, self-serving and vicious, had seized hold of her tongue. "Then I will thank you for letting me look around a bit more. I may only be a woman, but perhaps I can spot something useful."

He studied her a moment, looking troubled and . . .

hurt? But then he etched her a precise, cutting bow and walked out.

She swallowed. Waited a moment, her ears straining, to make sure he would not return.

And then she turned back and pulled the lever.

On a groan, the bookshelf swung inward.

The passage it made was narrow. Darkness was all she could see. But she knew what she would find inside. Crispin Burke's papers.

You will listen for a name, he'd told her. It felt so long ago. She had largely forgotten about that charge. Stupid, sloppy, unforgivable.

No. The truly unforgivable thing: she had no care for any of his papers but those that had been written in her hand. Those alone, she did not wish *this* Crispin to see.

Her skirts made it difficult to wedge herself through the passage. The darkness felt profoundly still and close, but the air was not stale. This was no ancient priest's hole, no abandoned secret passage. This space had been used too recently to smell like forgotten secrets.

But forgotten secrets were precisely what it contained.

She groped along the wall until she found the valve. The gas lamps made a peculiar *whomp*, then hissed to life.

Another desk in here, smaller, the chair drawn back at an odd angle—as if its occupant had only just shoved back his chair to rise.

She felt frozen as she stared at it. "Hello," she said very softly. *Hello, Mr. Burke. I have not seen you in some time.* His presence seemed to fill the room, cold and menacing.

This desk's drawers also stood ajar. As did those belonging to the three tall wooden chests that stood against the wall. The intruder had found this room as well. He had known to look for it somehow.

Perhaps it *had* been her uncle's man.

One of the chests had long and narrow drawers, the same type her father had kept to house plans of his factories. The other two had deeper, taller drawers, each of which was engraved with letters, sections of the alphabet.

She flew to the first one, sinking down to pull open the drawer marked *L–M*.

Inside, neat dividers further separated the files: *Mason, J.*

With trembling hands she pulled out the envelopes. Her handwriting, uncharacteristically sloppy. She had addressed these envelopes in a fever of resentment.

She slid shut the drawer and stood. Along the other wall hung a great map of the world, decorated with colored pins. A line of red pins arced out from Southampton, leading down the western coast of Africa, cutting across the bottom of the world to a point in the ocean. Nothing there. A spot close to the coast of Australia.

The name is Elland. That is all, Miss Mason. You see? Very simple.

But I have never heard my uncle mention a Mr. Elland. As I said, I fear I won't be of use.

Elland is not a man, Miss Mason. It is, I believe, the name of a penal colony. A very small one. Not much known. But your uncle knows it. Of that, I feel certain.

Temptation felt dark, a slick black poison coursing through her blood. *Step out. Shut the door. Replace the books. He does not need to know.*

But that map, those pins the color of blood, felt like a warning. A warning from the old Mr. Burke. *This is not a secret to keep.* She could almost hear his mocking voice. *A great passion, is it? A passion great enough to deceive and betray the man whom you claim to so value?*

What had happened tonight had been . . . unbearably sweet. She had allowed herself, at last, to believe.

But she had not given herself to him entirely. She might yet tell the truth. Endure his shock, his scorn and dawning contempt. And then emerge unscathed. Whole-bodied.

But not whole. Not any longer.

She was a coward. She did not want to see his face change as she confessed the whole of it.

She would not wait to see his face change.

She turned down the valve until the room sank into blackness, then inched back into the study. The detached medallion lay discarded on the carpet. She stepped over it, feeling the maw of the passage behind her like an open mouth spilling darkness into this brightly lit room. It seemed to unfurl tendrils of cold air that wrapped around her as she walked to the door.

He would come back and find the passage. He would push inside and make his discoveries. She would be waiting. Whatever came later, whatever look on his face when he finally rejoined her upstairs, she would endure it. She had that much courage.

But not enough to leave behind her letters. Those she carried with her as she mounted the stairs. They would make fine kindling.

*   *   *

The parlor maid, Mary, sat curled up by the kitchen fire, huddled in a great dark blanket, the other maids and a scullery girl fussing over her. As they caught sight of Crispin, they scattered like dandelion seeds in a wind, leaving Mary to hunch into herself as she warily watched him approach.

"I'm ever so sorry," she blurted. "I didn't mean to cause trouble—"

"It wasn't you who caused it," Crispin said. "But we hoped you might say, once again, what happened tonight."

Cusworth cleared his throat officiously. "Mary here—"

"The girl can speak for herself." Crispin knelt beside her, causing her to shrink back. "Another Mary?" he asked gently. "That makes four of you, which seems rather unlikely. How many Marys do I employ?"

The girl's laugh sounded forced and uneasy. "My real name is Katie."

"Katie," Crispin said. "A fine, lovely name. Tell me, Katie, what happened."

A hand crept out of the woolen folds, showing her white-knuckled grip. "I had just laid the fires in the bedrooms." She looked whey-faced, freckles livid on her cheeks and in the corners of her mouth. "As I came down the stairs, I heard a sound, a thump, from the study. I thought—why, something has fallen." Her russet brows knitted. "Don't reckon I gave any thought about *how* it would have fallen. But I walked over to check, and when I opened the door—" Her breath shook. "A man jumped out at me. Head to toe in black. I screamed, I did! Never had such a fear. I thought he would kill me—garrote me, just like they almost did you, sir!"

"Mr. Burke was not garroted," Cusworth put in sharply. As though his master's dignity relied on the correction of this small detail.

"Oh," the girl said, her gaze dipping to the spot where Crispin's cravat rose to conceal his throat. "Begging pardon, sir! The newspapers all said—"

"That's all right." Crispin took effort to keep his tone mild, encouraging. "Go on, Katie. What then?"

"Why . . . I shrank back, and he turned on his heel and bolted across the room. He jumped out through the window." She swallowed. "I thought he would be kilt. But when I rushed over to look, he was running away."

"You never saw his face?"

She shook her head forcefully. "He was wearing a dark cloth, all the way up to—" She touched the bridge of her nose.

"And he never spoke?"

"No, sir."

"Think carefully."

She hesitated. Her eyes widened. "Why . . . sir, I think he did. He spoke a curse when he saw me. I had forgotten."

"And how did he sound?"

She reddened. "Like . . . like quality, sir. A proper gentleman."

That boded ill. No common robbery, then. Crispin rose. "Thank you, Katie. You've been very helpful. Mr. Cusworth, Katie will require a few days to recover from this shock. I hope you will manage to keep the household running smoothly in her absence."

"Of course." Cusworth spoke tightly. "Sir, I do not wish to presume. But shall you send for the police now?"

It was tempting. But he thought of the look on his wife's face as she'd spied the destruction, her curious hostility that had seemed, to him, borne more of panic than of offense.

Until he understood that reaction, discretion might serve them better. "Later, perhaps. You'll have my instructions."

He turned on his heel to go find his wife.

CHAPTER THIRTEEN

$\mathcal{T}$he knocking was what finally ruptured his trance. When Crispin looked up from the pages, he had the sense that it had continued for quite some time, only now pervading his awareness. He rubbed his bleary eyes. "Yes?"

"Mr. Burke?" Cusworth's voice, nervous, high-pitched. "I am sorry to disturb you, sir, but a letter has come. Quite urgent, the man assured me."

He rose slowly, his joints feeling rusted. When he stepped out into the study, the morning light streaming onto the carpet came as a shock. He had gone looking for Jane, and instead found the bookshelf gaping open, the room inside . . .

He had been there all night.

His majordomo had a hard time holding his eye. The man kept glancing nervously at the opening through which Crispin had emerged. But he was too well trained to ask questions. "From your brother, sir," he said as he handed over the envelope.

The note was brief:

Caught a rumor after you left.
Third reading to begin and end today
They mean to push for a vote.

He crumpled the paper with a curse.

"Shall I—shall I summon the police, then, sir?"

Cusworth's voice seemed to come from a great distance. And then, all at once, the remark registered, and struck Crispin as funny.

He laughed. He saw from Cusworth's pinched expression how inappropriate that was. But he could not help himself. He sagged back against the wall, spines of books poking him, and laughed again. It was a great joke, wasn't it? "No," he managed. "No, I think not. That . . . will be all."

Cusworth's overhasty departure closed him into silence again, a silence in which his laughter seemed to linger, ugly and jagged, like broken panes of glass.

He found himself sliding down the bookshelf, accepting the bruising pain of the shelves, enjoying it in some strange way, until he sat on the carpet. A new view of the room. His staff still wanted discipline. He saw dust in the fringes of the Turkey carpet.

He'd fallen into a black trance inside that little room. Turning page after page, his own script winking up at him, smug and conspiratorial. *You wrote this. No need to look shocked.*

She'd said something to him after the dinner party. *Some would argue that corruption is required to prove effective.*

Perhaps so. Was it disappointing, somehow, to discover himself an ordinary criminal? He tested the theory, consulting his gut. Yes, he supposed he had a talent for

disappointed ambitions. There was no cause for pride in
the back-door dealings his own documents chronicled.
A novelist would have invented more dramatic sins than
his. He'd murdered nobody, from what he could tell, or
issued threats more alarming than social embarrassment
and the withdrawal of his political support. But he'd done
so in such cold, cutting, clever language. He had not
known he could sound so much like Atticus until today.

His wife had left that door open for him, then fled.
His amazement had, at first, been mixed with bafflement, concern. Why had she not come to find him, to
share her discovery?

But after reading only a few files, he'd understood.
She'd not had time, in his absence, to uncover much information from that room. So it logically followed that
she had already known what he'd find there. She had
done him a generous favor by not sticking nearby to
witness his own discovery of himself.

She had known not to summon the police, too. She
had guessed they might find the hidden room, and insist on looking through it themselves, only to uncover
the kind of information that no politician could survive
being learned by authorities whose discretion was not
guaranteed.

So many favors she'd done him. Above all, this: she
had clearly known exactly the kind of man he was. But
she had protected him from it as long as she was able.

Why had she married him, really?

His spine straightened. Alertness flooded through
him, sharpening his weary brain.

You don't know me, she had said. But he knew enough.
She had principles. She opposed this bill. She dreamed
of using her father's money to spread justice and hope.

She was not a woman who would have wed a man such as he, even in order to get her hands on a fortune. There were too many other men in the world to settle for one such as him.

And he . . . the man who had written all those letters . . . that was not a man who would have wed a woman of such principles—a woman who, by her own admission, did not know how to mince words.

Crispin cherished her for the same reasons that his other self would have scorned her.

He rose, his breath short, though he could not say why. These were not revelations of the kind to instill dread. What was done was done; he could not change the man he had been, and if anything, he should pray to God in thanks for having been so forcibly alienated from that other self, for having been gifted a woman whom he would never otherwise have deserved or known how to love.

But some premonition was on him, crushing and dark. He would not have wed her. She would not have wed him.

Why, then, had they done it?

She was lying to him. It, their marriage, had had nothing to do with convenience.

No document in that room spoke of her. No letters from her. No mention of her in any of his correspondence with her uncle. Crispin had found no journals, but one drawer of his desk had held several appointment books, each meeting of the last four years carefully chronicled by date. Her name had not appeared in those he'd scanned.

The confusion infuriated him. He was done with living in a murk, taking a step that seemed to lead out of darkness only to collide with something else he could not remember. He would have it out with her, today, now.

As he stepped forward, his boot caught the crumpled note, sent it shooting ahead of him, skittering across the rug.

The vote. Today.

He took a hard breath. Scrubbed his hands over his face and inhaled again, longer, more deeply.

Confrontation must wait. He needed to bathe, to shave and dress. To prepare himself for the speech of his life.

Jane slowly made her way up the narrow stone stairway, still clutching the order of admission that Crispin had left behind for her. She had heard him come upstairs this morning, but like a fool, an exhausted sleepless fool frozen by fear, she had not gone to him. She had sat on her bed and listened to his footsteps, straining for each remark he made to his new valet, muffled through the door that connected their apartments. And then she had heard the door open and close again, and his footsteps on the stairs.

A minute later, she had flown to the window to watch the brougham pull out from the curb, carrying him away.

Her stomach had dropped then. She'd felt sure she would be sick. He had obviously discovered all he needed to know about her. He was heading straight to a lawyer, she had no doubt of it.

But when a maid came by minutes later, she carried a note from him. Enclosed was an order instructing the guards at Westminster to admit her to the Ladies' Gal-

lery without delay, and two lines for her, handwritten
with evident haste:

> *The speech goes forward today.*
> *Will look for you.*

Jane had often heard the Ladies' Gallery referred to
by a rather more vulgar phrase, the Ladies' Cage. The
nickname made sense to her at last as the guard escorted
her into a box bounded by iron railings, and separated
from the room at large by an iron grille. As she sat, the
ladies in the front row, a group of handsome matrons in
middle age, turned to inspect her. Not recognizing her,
they returned to their conversation.

The cage stood above the Speakers' Gallery, from
which foreign dignitaries and distinguished guests
watched the proceedings. She spotted Atticus in the
front row there, leaning forward to converse with a
dark-haired, tanned gentleman of astonishing good
looks who himself sat in the backmost row of the
benches reserved for visiting peers. At the opposite end
of the wood-paneled hall stood a gilded throne, before
which the Speaker of the House stood, the party whips
arrayed at his sides. Along the left and right walls, in
three long lines of benches, sat the majority of the MPs,
cast in rainbow-hued light from the stained-glass windows behind them.

She did not see Crispin on the floor. But she knew,
from so many newspaper editorials mocking the indisci-
pline of the Commons, that the benches were unusually
full today. The third reading was under way, a young
man in a pale morning coat concluding his forceful dis-
avowal of the bill, to the clear boredom of most of the

assembly. "There is nothing new in what I have said today. I have said it all before—"

"Quite right," called a heckler from the benches of the Opposition.

"I admit it," the young man said tightly. "Yet while I have registered these objections three times now, sirs, I have yet to hear a credible reply. And so now, I must register my amazement and contempt as well. Good sense has deserted this assembly—"

Hisses rose, and then hoots. "No," the young man called stridently, "you will not silence me *that* way. Mr. Speaker, I demand to be heard."

"Order," intoned the Speaker in a bored, indifferent voice. As he sat back down, he scratched absently at his thick white wig. The day had dawned unseasonably warm, and half the MPs on the floor had discarded their silk hats and were slumped in their seats, fanning themselves with pamphlets that Jane recognized from her uncle's possessions—pages printed with the orders of the day.

Still, they had enough energy to mutter among themselves, and as the young man said, "Thank you," one of them called, "Finish it up, then, your mother's waiting."

The man flushed. "Is that how it goes? Very well, I have no intention of arguing with children. I am done." He flopped back onto his bench. The man to his right clapped his shoulder in sympathy, but he angrily shrugged away.

Jane's uncle now stood, waiting to be recognized. Throat tight, she leaned forward, glancing anxiously to the passage that opened onto the private arcade through which members entered. Last week, she and Crispin had

studied a map of Westminster together, in case the worst
happened and his escort abandoned him. Had he lost
his way? Why was he not here to lend support to the
bill's opponents?

"I will not take much of your time, sirs," her uncle
began, pausing to allow his cronies to rap the benches
in approval. "I think young Mr. Morris quite correct:
we have heard every objection several times, and found
none of them persuasive. From the speed by which this
bill has proceeded, and the fierce passion of those who
spared their time and effort to speak so eloquently in its
favor in committee, I think we have seen the noble use
of it. The people, our own constituents, our country-
men and friends, deserve better, I say, than to live in
fear. And those who would argue it"—he shot a forbid-
ding glance toward the opposite bench—"have failed
to account for why they rate the safety of law-abiding
citizens below the comforts of criminals."

More thumps and rousing cries of "Hear, hear!" Her
uncle had often let Crispin do the speech making for
him. But to Jane's great and unpleasant surprise, it was
not for want of talent on his part. Had she not known
the facts—and, moreover, the secret motive behind his
passion—she might have believed his sincerity.

"And so," he went on, "I propose that we waste no
more of this assembly's time on a matter that has already
been decided, not only by ourselves, but by the will of
the people. I move to close—"

"So soon?" Crispin's voice rang out as he walked onto
the floor. He had Lambert by his side. "It's only half
two, sir. Surely old age has not made you so feeble as to
require an afternoon nap."

A startled pause, then a wave of chuckles. Her uncle

glowered. "Mr. Burke. What a preposterous interruption. Mr. Speaker, are we to have no order here?"

But the Speaker's reply was swallowed up by a great gasp as Crispin crossed the floor, abandoning his erstwhile allies to take up a seat on the Government benches.

"What's this?" someone cried, and a great hubbub arose, causing the Speaker to heave himself upright.

"Mr. Mason," he said. "You will continue. Mr. Burke, should you wish to speak, you will be recognized in turn."

Her uncle spluttered. "I—I cede the floor," he spat, "on the condition that I be allowed to speak after him."

The Speaker shrugged. "Mr. Burke, you have the floor."

Crispin rose, walked a few paces to the center of the room. He looked over the Opposition, and a hiss went up. He was smiling faintly as he pivoted toward the gallery; when his eyes met Jane's, her breath caught, and suddenly she forgot the debate at hand, the great challenge before him.

What had he found in that secret room?

Her heart tripped. *Do you hate me now?* she asked with her eyes.

His smile told her nothing. It did not alter a fraction. But he looked at her a long moment, and she felt pinned, like a butterfly to a board.

"Anytime now," her uncle muttered, and Crispin turned to face his new allies, many of whom looked back at him incredulously, and bent together to confer, no doubt warning each other to beware of tricks.

"I address this good assembly," he began in a clear, carrying voice, "as one of its members, but also, perhaps more pertinently, as a recent victim of the very crimes which this bill purports to prevent. If anyone here has cause to fear that our penal system has failed us, that tolerance has become dangerous, that law and order are threatened—why, sirs, it is me. And if anyone doubts it, I will be glad to show you the cleft in my head, which I have been assured by my wife does not add to my charms."

A muted chuckle from one side, stony silence from the other.

"But I need not prove it, do I? For you all have no doubt followed the story in the newspapers. Perhaps marveled at the irony of it, too. For I authored this bill, and then, as if my own words had conjured them, a group of criminals felled me in my tracks. I will tell you, sirs, that they were never caught. They still roam the streets, a threat to us all. You may well imagine, then, that I have every cause to stand in support of this bill, not only because I wrote it, but because I then lived through the very experience which this bill promises to spare you."

Silence now. Her uncle was twitching in his seat, but even he would not disrupt an audience so obviously en-rapt. Crispin had not shared this version of the speech with Jane, but he had taken her advice to the letter: he was crafting a personal narrative rather than one based on facts and figures. Facts and figures could be ridiculed and shouted over. But a tragic narrative was far too in-teresting to ignore.

"Crime is a plague," he said gravely. "It is alarming enough when we imagine it locked away in those slums that we, the fortunate men of this assembly, never will visit. When it spills into our own streets, when it threat-ens our wives and children—why, then we feel doubly outraged. This is hypocrisy, of course, but I do not protest it. I dislike it, but it is only human. Meanwhile, to wish to take every measure to keep our loved ones safe—that is human, too, one of the most noble aspects of our nature. Those who have supported this bill are to be commended, then—not condemned. Their intentions are honorable." He fixed his eyes on her uncle and offered a sharp smile that undercut his words. "Even Mr. Mason's."

A jeer came from the Government benches, aimed at her uncle. An answering jeer rose from her uncle's men. The noise rose, threatening to drown out the speech.

"But as I lay dying," Crispin said loudly, and the shouts faded. "As I lay bleeding on the pavement, skull broken, I looked up for the light. I will admit it: I looked up with the hope of heaven, for I did not expect to survive. But instead of any light, what did I see? I saw the faces of darkness. The men who had murdered me—for I was dying, let us be clear—the men who murdered me wore the looks of hell on their faces. And that hell, sirs, was not wickedness alone, oh no. It was a wickedness fueled by hunger and want, fear and base desperation—"

"What ho!" cried her uncle. "Are we to weep for murderers?"

"—and I saw in that moment," Crispin said sharply, "the noose that would hang them, and I was *glad*."

Silence. Those on the Government benches now looked uncertain. Jane felt the same. This did not sound like a speech to defeat the bill.

"Yes," Crispin said more quietly. "I was savagely glad, God forgive me. It was not Christian, sirs—but I am no Christ, to forgive my murderers even as I lay dying. God save my soul, but what I wanted was vengeance. And had they been caught, sirs—I would have had it. For our system spares no sympathy for murderers, not even if hunger and misery drive them. We hang murderers in this country. And this bill does not dispute or change that. But what it does advocate, sirs, is that we should punish petty criminals with the same ferocity that this assembly decided not so long ago to reserve for those with blood on their hands."

Her uncle rose, calling an objection, but nobody looked at him. The full force of the floor's attention was locked on Crispin now, and he radiated gravity, sober confidence, forceful conviction. "Shall we go back, then?" he demanded. "Shall we reverse course, and punish all lawbreakers with equal harshness? Should I, lying on that pavement, bleeding to my death, have felt no worse than a man robbed of his cuff links? Should I have wished for my murderers to receive the same terms of imprisonment as a boy who stole bread? *Should I?* You tell me, gentlemen. You tell me, and I will counsel that man dying on the ground in blood-choked gasps. I will tell him, 'These men who laid you low, they deserve the same treatment as the boy who stole lace. That boy, let him rot alongside these men while they wait for the hangman. Let them whisper their evil lessons into his ear, when with a ticket-of-leave he might have returned to the discipline of his parents. Let them teach this boy their ways, so he might grow into a man just like them, who will put *other* men onto the pavement, bleeding to their deaths in the name of justice.' Yes, sirs? Shall I so counsel myself?"

He paused. He paused so long that Jane grew afraid he left too much opportunity for her uncle. But her uncle's jaw looked clenched too tightly to unhinge, and nobody else spoke.

"I withdraw my support of this bill," Crispin said—softly enough that his colleagues leaned forward in their benches to hear. "I withdraw it," he said, louder, "and I urge you to do the same." At full force: "I withdraw it, and I will answer any objection Mr. Mason might raise, with facts and statistics, if the Commons so desires. But I have shared the main reason already, don't you think? We have sufficient murderers in this country, enough to lay me low already. I will not have it on my head that I helped to create more of them."

Jane waited until the vote had been called. Sat trembling as the decision was pronounced. She could not see Crispin's face; he was angled toward the Speaker. But when the victory was declared, and the floor burst into a chaos of cries, jubilations and curses mixing together, she rose.

Atticus went bounding out into the throng, catching his brother by the shoulders, swinging him around into an embrace.

That was all she needed to see. She picked her way out of the gallery, down the hall, and out the door, knees trembling. Her emotions were too large for words. She felt as though she had run five miles and drunk a hundred cups of coffee, a dozen glasses of wine, and then been cast off a cliff.

We changed history today.

It should have been enough.

Yet that man on the floor, his strong golden voice, his restrained passion, his ferocious wit—watching him, she had ached with animal longing. Such a man. How could she bear losing him? But if losing him were the price of victory, how could she regret it? What would it make her to regret that loss in the face of a triumph that would save thousands of lives?

It would make her selfish, small-hearted. *Human.*

When the carriage came around, she could barely manage, with the help of the footman, to climb into it. As it turned onto the road, she stared unseeing out the window.

It took two hours for Crispin to return to the house. She sat in the morning room, stitching. She had not stitched in weeks. She had not required the numbness it delivered.

Her fingers now were reddened from the careless pricks of her needle. She could feel them, and the pain kept her steady, helped her keep grip on her composure, when Crispin at last came into the room.

His color was high, his smile wide. "Mason raised hell after you left. Like a bawling child. You should have stayed—it was a wonderful show."

So he'd looked for her afterward. That was something.

"Congratulations," she murmured. "It's an extraordinary victory."

His smile faltered. "One for which you're owed a great deal of the credit."

She smiled back—not persuasively, it seemed. She saw his mood dim to match her own, and felt anew the sting of her own selfishness, her petty cares.

"The speech was all yours," she said. "It was grand, Crispin."

He paused, then sat down across from her. "That was

not the speech I would have given, had you not shown me the way to go with it. We make a great, powerful pair, Jane."

The pause that settled felt curiously weighty. She sensed no animosity in it. He had not come home intending to accuse her, after all. Whatever he'd found in that secret room did not anger him.

But no part of her felt relieved. He had found *something* that had altered the very air between them. Otherwise he would have fetched her before going to Westminster.

The door opened. A footman wheeled in a cart, atop which rested a silver wine bucket, a bottle of champagne submerged in mounds of ice.

She glanced at Crispin and felt a little internal jolt as their gazes connected.

"I think you deserve," he said, "to share in this celebration."

So the guillotine would not drop just yet. He would keep hold of the rope for a while.

But she did not want to celebrate with a blade over her head. "I am not in the mood," she said quietly. "Why don't you go to your club? I'm certain there will be a hero's welcome for you."

"Those men had nothing to do with this victory." His face was calm, his gaze speaking. "This was our work, yours and mine. And so we'll drink to it together, too."

He rose, taking the bottle from the footman, dismissing him with a nod. His strong hands twisted once. With a sharp pop, the cork released; he let the foam spill into the wine bucket before pouring.

As he handed her a glass, the novelty registered. She had never before been invited to claim a political vic-

tory, to celebrate it as her own. She had never dreamed
of such a moment. But now that it was upon her, she
could not enjoy it, for her mind insisted on calculating
the cost.

Her parents had believed that politics might be a
virtuous art, practiced nobly, without compromises.
But maybe they had been naïve. Had they lived longer,
and had Papa amassed the kind of power that her uncle
enjoyed, they might have learned that idealism shaped
noble goals but rarely helped accomplish them. In the
political world, conspiracy and manipulation were not
sins but skills to be wielded.

Crispin had changed greatly. But as he faced her now,
smiling so calmly, revealing no sign of what he had discovered last night, he showed how much he retained of
Mr. Burke. He was the consummate tactician, his skills
superlative.

"To us," he said, holding out his champagne flute.
"To a partnership that proved victorious."

She tapped her glass against his. But her throat was so
tight that if she tried to swallow, she would choke. She
mimed sipping, and then lowered her glass, untouched.

"So," he said.

The house seemed very still around them, her breathing too loud. As though the pale upholstery, the silken
walls and thick rug, swallowed all noise save their
own. A singer onstage at the opera must feel this self-
conscious. The acoustics all designed to amplify her
alone, so that even the temptation to clear her throat
would seem risky.

She could not play this game. "You looked through
the room."

"I did," he said—readily, neutrally, with no show of

surprise. The subject had been broached, of course, as soon as he'd stepped inside. It had entered with him like a shadow.

"And?"

"And I thank you for discouraging me from sending for the police."

She looked down into her champagne. Bubbles rising, causing the liquid to seem to sparkle. This was a drink to mark a joyous occasion, not a reckoning.

She set the glass aside. "You must wonder how I knew what you would find."

He took another measured sip. His wedding ring gleamed in the lamplight. "No, in fact. It was quite clear, in retrospect, that you had taken my measure thoroughly. You had been doing me a kindness by failing to divulge the whole of it. But I did find myself wondering about you, Jane. All along, I'd imagined I was the mystery. But you are not a woman to wed the man whom I discovered in that room."

It was not a question. He did not try to make it one. He regarded her, his dark eyes opaque, his face in unstudied repose: the ascetic beauty of his brow, his glacial cheekbones, the sharp stark angle of his jaw. He was not trying to leash some inward emotion. He was perfectly calm, and she was . . . not.

How tired she was of feeling strung thin. Of feeling her heart hammer, lurched by every new twist. Of wanting him and then fearing him; of lying and then hoping, hoping with a sick, desperate feeling in her gut that he did not discover the whole of it. Lying awake yearning for him, and hating herself for doing so. For being so much more foolish, so much more girlish, than she had ever been as a girl.

"I have lied to you," she said.

He nodded once. Casual, unhurried. As though she had just told him, *I slept until ten o'clock,* or, *It looks likely to rain.*

It angered her. She was in a fever of misery. She had built the courage at last—to bare her own throat, to let him release the rope, so the blade finally cleaved her.

And he merely looked at her and drank again from his glass.

"Is this some technique of yours?" she asked. "Some art of interrogation you perfected on your enemies?"

He blinked. At last, she had startled him—but not badly enough, not as violently as she wanted. "So. We're enemies, then. I wasn't certain." He laid aside his champagne flute. "Perhaps this was my technique," he said. "I don't remember. I don't remember your enmity, either. I don't think I'll ever wish to recall that. I see no cause to try."

She thought of the map. Of the name he'd once asked her to listen for. Of the mysterious intruder. "All the papers you looked through. Did any of them mention Elland?"

"Elland? No, I don't believe so."

Then those were the files the intruder had come for.

"I know no one by that name," he added.

"It's not a man's name." She had made the same mistake. Mr. Burke had corrected her.

He nodded again. And asked nothing.

She clenched her fists in her lap. She had worked to bury her suspicions about Crispin's attackers. She had tried to focus only on her own goals. Her father's money. Her freedom.

But she did not have the blessing of amnesia to help

her forget. And worse . . . she could no longer think only of herself.

Even if her uncle had some miraculous change of heart and released her funds tomorrow—even if the money were in her hands by dusk—she would not go to the pier. She would not leave this house. She would not leave with the knowledge that Crispin might be in danger because of what she had hidden from him.

"I think I must explain it to you." She barely recognized her own voice. It scraped like steel against stone. "I think, perhaps, that the intruder wanted to know about Elland."

He looked at her directly. He *did* feel, after all. His face was alive with tension, his mouth taut.

"Yes," he said. "Ghosts do not lie down on their own. He will rise again, I am sure, and so will she. But not tonight."

He. For a moment, she'd thought he still misunderstood, that he was referring to Elland. Then he said *she*, and she realized he was referring to himself and to her. Their old selves. The ones they had been.

The breath left her on a long, slow wave. This reprieve—it was not part of her punishment. It was his gift to them both. He wanted it as much as she did.

"Then . . . what?" she asked in a whisper.

He rose, looking down at her.

"Give me a night," he said, "with my wife."

CHAPTER FOURTEEN

Could a truth emerge from lies? Like a lotus from mud, say. What existed between them was built on falsehood. Yet it had just changed the course of the nation. It had saved lives and prevented future misery. It was *great and powerful*. Yes, it was built on falsehood—but was it false?

Besides, weren't there other forms of honesty? Honesty too raw to be fitted into words? That was what she saw in Crispin's face as he held out his hand. That was what she gave him when she took it.

They climbed the stairs in a silence that seemed to change as they walked, softening, growing lush and anticipatory. A pillowy silence that promised a safe place to fall—but not to speak.

Jane said nothing, then, as Crispin led her into his bedroom, but each of her lesser senses, those that she neglected by habit, senses that had nothing to do with logic and abstraction and things that could not be touched—sight and hearing, smell and taste—they seemed to blossom and expand, revealing a new world to her.

The sunset light through the uncurtained window, illuminating motes of dust.

The gilded planes of his face as he stopped in the middle of the carpet and faced her.

The champagne that lingered on his breath, and beneath it, the musk of his skin.

The brush of his lips on hers, rough and slightly cracked. These lips had spoken much today, to great affect, but they moved over hers like a discovery: this, too, was their purpose. There was skill and fluency in the way he kissed her, for this was a language, too. Her body was learning it.

She kissed him back, not closing her eyes. Vision, more often used to look for reasons, for chances at escape, also had this talent: of beholding without evaluation or judgment. She saw a man, his own eyes closed, kissing her with an earnestness that, as his tongue came into her mouth, took on a desperate edge. Kissing her as though to consume her. As though taking her inside was the only way to keep her with him.

He was gripping her face, this beautiful man. She could be honest with him now, here, only. The future had no place for her honesty. The past was a lost cause. She took his hand and spoke in this new language, more real than any framed by words. She moved his palm to cover her breast, and let her kiss explain it.

He made a guttural noise in his throat, low and approving. His thumb stroked over the thin wool of her gown, making promises to what was concealed. She felt his other hand at her back, setting her free of all the small tokens of decency, which great factories in the north pressed into buttons, clasps and hooks that women fastened dutifully, knowing their place, knowing their role. Covered, bound, laced, wrapped, bundled away from the world like objects to be kept on a shelf. Put away from this kind of honesty and the revelations it might bring.

She bit his lower lip as a message: she did not require care. She drank his startled breath, then smiled into his mouth as he nipped her in reply. He used both hands now. Fabric parted, layers unfolded and peeled away. Strings snapped as her corset loosened. The air was so still, faintly fragranced by citrus and linseed. Clean. Tapes undone, crinoline falling, metal creaking into collapse. His palms gripped her waist, her hipbones, reminding her of her own solidity. Her feet felt so firmly planted, as though the world tilted to meet the soles of her feet, and nothing could unbalance her. His hands smoothed around her hips, a reverent touch, and then palmed the fullness of her buttocks, speaking to her of substance, of her own power as he made another animal noise.

Off came her chemise. The air greeted her, small cool touches, calling her back to nature's intention for her, never to have been rendered a stranger to the feel of the air on her skin. She took a long breath, lungs flexing, freed of constriction. He went to his knees, his fingers trembling over the ribbons that fastened her stockings. He drew them down inch by inch, his mouth tracing the skin he bared, his lips feeling for his success. With his large, warm hand he gripped her ankles, one by one, lifting each foot to slip her stockings free. And now came her drawers, his lips on her navel, her belly, which startled and contracted, so new to what it deserved—the honesty of the light and his reverent, fierce regard.

She stood naked before him, shaking with the force and amazement of it: the honesty of the body. A body undisguised, unprotected, not requiring protection. Her shoulders straightened; she felt taller, her neck longer, her spine straighter and more limber, as he slowly rose, beholding her in her fullness. She felt . . . at home in herself.

He was still clothed. It seemed a mistake, a sweet one, an oversight so clumsy and easily remedied that it stirred indulgence in her, a tender unrecognizable fondness. She stepped into him, the cool, crisp edges of his clothing another delicious shock against her nakedness. She felt the starched edges of his cravat, wilted now from the work he had done today. It had not only been words that had won the victory. Every fiber in his body, the athletic confidence in his long, fine-muscled limbs and the forcefulness of his dark eyes, had brought the world briefly to its knees in submission.

She fitted her fingers beneath his cravat, feeling the warmth of his throat, the slight roughness of his skin. The sharp jerk as he swallowed. Her fingers had their own wisdom; she watched them in fascination as they unwound the stock. They slid over his broad chest, which contracted as though by instruction, and then shoved the jacket off his shoulders, smoothing her palms over the bunching bulk of his upper arms. She squeezed, and then accepted his kiss against her ear, the hot flick of his tongue, the touch of his teeth, as tribute.

His waistcoat. As soft as the fur of a diligent cat. Her fingertips caught the subtle groove of the patterning, the shaded stripes of pearl and dove gray. They led her hands downward, to a button of winking gilt.

She flipped it open easily. Men's buttons were not designed as armor. They wanted to be loosened. Up, up, up her fingers trailed, the buttons yielding eagerly. He shrugged off the waistcoat, and his suspenders as well.

White shirt. Cut expertly, sewn with great care. She yanked it free of his trousers, the undervest as well. Slid her hands up the hot, muscled expanse of his abdomen. He was kissing her ear again, gripping her buttocks to pull her directly against him. Body to body. His hand brushed the side of her breast, his thumb lingering, reaching between them to find her nipple. As he touched it, she felt her skin contract, a pulse between her legs.

She unfastened the placket of his trousers and let them drop to the ground.

His hands offered help. She shoved them away. A new logic guided her. She sank to her knees as he had done. She unveiled him as he had done to her. His belly was tight, his navel a neat inward knot, underneath which a narrow trail of dark hair led downward, a path over segmented bands of muscle. She laid her lips to it. Far above, he made a restless noise, and his fingers threaded through her hair, dislodging pins, which scattered like pebbles past her shoulders.

The cool mass of her curls came down around her bare shoulders, causing her to shiver. Her own body, unrecognizable to herself. Native pleasure, so long denied.

His hips were narrow. She placed her thumb on the blunt point of his hipbone. Beneath it, a stark line of division, mirrored at the other hip, angling downward in a vee. She traced this angle, to the point where his penis rose, obscuring the path. Thick and heavy, impossibly soft skin. She learned it with her palm, taking guidance from the strained rhythm of his breathing, his sharp exhalation as her grip tightened. The skin, such an impossibly soft sheath for the unyielding hard length.

She slowly lowered her mouth. Kissed the very tip.

"Jane." He took her by the arms and raised her to her feet, kissing her feverishly as he walked her backward, then lifted her onto the bed. She lay back and he climbed over her, his hair in his face, dark ends ragged around his hot eyes. She pushed her fingers through his hair, took it in great handfuls to pull him down for a kiss. Then he broke away, licking and nibbling down her body. His mouth brought her alive, kiss by kiss, waking each spot which it touched. Her collarbone. The valley between her breasts. The straining points of her nipples, which, as he suckled them, seemed to draw on some tightening cord that ran deep through the core of her, through her belly to the place between her legs: quivering, empty, alive.

He placed his hand there. His hard palm closed over her, pushing and then rolling, concentrating and tightening everything in her, her hips thrusting against him. "Yes," she heard him growl, and he did it again, and a strange noise broke from her, urgent, pleading, encouraging. The bed creaked; he moved in one long, leonine stretch, and then his mouth was where his hand had been, his tongue . . . He licked into her, gripping her thighs and widening them when they forgot briefly that this was the truth, this was the honesty, that the other world and the before and after did not exist now. He held her to the vow she had not spoken but had made and that his body understood.

He held her open as he licked and sucked on her, and she threw her arms over her head and felt the wall pushing back and forcing her to it as well. Unyielding, forceful, his rough grip on her thighs, his adamant, driving mouth—

It came violently through her, the seizure. She cried out; she locked his head between her thighs and shuddered beneath him. His grip was gentle suddenly; he petted her to soothe her, kissing his way back to her, taking large, gentle bites of her fleshy hips, her rounded belly, his tongue tasting her nipples again, his lips finding her own.

She reached down to grasp him. The hard pulsing force of him. It fitted against her; it caused her private flesh to quiver again. Impossibly hard. She could not—

He seated himself inside her in one slow, steady push. No pain, but a slight burning, a stretch—he began to move. His hips gentle, his mouth languid on hers, his tongue stroking the same slow rhythm as his pelvis. Her body loosened. She opened her eyes, looked into his tight, focused face, traced with her thumb the fringe of his dark lashes, the tracery on his closed lids, so delicate. A breath flowed from her, and it filled every corner of the room. She was larger than this room. She held everything.

His hips made some subtle adjustment—her breath caught. His eyes came open, darkest blue, riveted on hers as though nothing else existed to be seen. He cupped her cheek, a whisper's touch. His hips moved again, and she gasped.

A slow smile. It twisted on his mouth—one moment like pain, and then, as she shuddered again, like triumph. So deep inside her—filled and overflowing.

She turned her head, moaning, and his arms tightened around her, crushing her to him, his own cry mixing with hers as she felt him join her in this pleasure that undid her sinews and left her complete.

Crispin woke slowly. It felt carnal, how voluptuously sleep clung to him, caressing and coaxing him to stay in the deep. His limbs felt loose, humming with the deep relaxation that followed extended exertion. His eyes opened.

Darkness showed through the curtains. He had no notion of the time. The light from the fire, softly crackling across the room, threw odd shadows across the top of the bed canopy. The embroidered figures, mounted huntsman returning to a castle, women in wimples awaiting them, seemed to come alive. The women held out flowers, fruits. The men raised their hands in greeting. A bugler called his tattoo.

Tasteless. Something embarrassing about acquiring a piece that had probably been stitched in some dark workshop by miserable children three years ago but pretended to be centuries old. Laura had never given thought to such considerations. She was so easily lured by the outward flourishes.

A sigh from his side. The mattress creaked as his wife turned toward him in her sleep, carrying a dark curl over the joint of his elbow. He stroked it very lightly, wonder purling through him again, cleansing him of dark thoughts.

The way she had felt beneath him . . .

The miraculous look on her face, the hunger in her touch . . .

This bed felt to him like hallowed ground now. He would have the canopy replaced. Jane deserved to sleep beneath some more innocent piece of fabric, untainted by pretensions or suffering.

He eased very slowly onto his elbow to study her. There was a childlike abandon in the scissored sprawl of her legs, the way she tucked her hands together so neatly beneath the pillow. Her full lips parted on each breath. Her cheeks flushed with slumber. The wild sprawl of her glorious hair.

Who would guess that this woman beside him had routed the Commons? What a secret to keep. A man might live his entire life in greedy contentment, knowing such a secret. Crispin had grown up aware of such possibilities, of marriages in which great men drew their strength and brilliance from the women at their side. But he had thought it a distant myth for himself.

She had tried to disown credit today. He understood the reason. She had done it as a kind of apology for all the things she had kept concealed.

But he did not want her apologies. He wanted her to own herself, brazenly and unabashedly. She had shown him only one part of herself in these last few weeks— an extraordinary part, tentative and earnest and kind despite her better judgment, clear thinking and funny, compassionate and full of wit. But she had closed away all the rougher, sharper angles. The grit, the steel mettle at her core, the defiant anger that had kept her safe for so many years. And he wished to see those as well. To show her, to prove to her, that those parts of her could be admired and loved, too.

He could lie here for hours, staring at her. Slowly,

slowly, he wrapped the curl around his hand. Gentleness, tender care, reverent praise—these were what she deserved. He had a great deal to make up for. In the rain, that night, when he had grabbed her—

His hand fisted.

She murmured in her sleep, reached up to scratch her head. He opened his hand, watched the curl escape from it. That was the only movement of which he felt capable. He held himself very still, waiting.

Her hand crept languidly back under the pillow. After a moment, she rolled to her other side, nestling deeper beneath the blankets.

He counted her breaths, waited until she had drawn a dozen or more. Then, with the greatest care he had ever granted any movement in his life, he slipped from the bed and stole across the carpet. Eased open the door and guided it closed again.

His house. He stood in the moonlight flooding through the skylight above, heart pounding, and stared out over the balconied walkway, seeing nothing of what lay below.

So. This was how it came back to him, then. Not in some flooding rush, but as the aftermath of such a flood. The river of Lethe, the waters of forgetting, subsiding as he slept, leaving him standing, with no sense of surprise, on the ground that had been concealed only hours before.

He stepped forward to grip the railing, though he did not feel unbalanced. Unknitted, disjointed—no. He knew who he was, how this body worked, how unthinkingly he could rely on it.

Elland. He had asked her to listen for him. Christ, he had not asked, he had blackmailed her into it. But

what had she discovered? There were deep waters
here still. He could not remember the attack that had
felled him, or what had led to it. He could remember
her at Marylebigh, her bastard cousin's savage enjoy-
ment in humiliating her, not even realizing how he
failed—her dignity unbreakable, her contempt quiet
and cutting. The dark beauty of her chignon so heavy
against her nape, the foulness of imagining her wed
to Archibald, who so maliciously squandered the only
opportunity he might ever have to know a woman
better than himself.

But his admiration had been calculative. Cold.
He'd had no interest in the complication of a woman
who could match his own wit, who might outthink
him, given the chance, whose presence would prove
exhausting for the same reason it proved enlivening.
He could not remember what came after that night,
when he had helped her back to the house in a driving rain.

His hand ached from gripping the rail too tightly.
He squeezed harder yet, until the bones in his hands
threatened to break. It felt like a drug in his system, a
drug and he the recovered addict, this black cast into
which his thoughts might so easily slip again. He understood his coldness. He knew why he had forced the kiss
on her that night in the countryside. He remembered
his own manufactured indifference to his family, who
had misjudged him once too often, abandoned him for
the final time. *No atonement will ever be possible. You
will always be the villain to them. So be it. Accept the
verdict,* he had thought. And also: *They think you useless.
Prove the opposite.*

But that cold, dark cast had been blinding. These

past weeks proved it. Half-dead, he had woken into his family's arms. And into the care of a woman who might so easily have spat in his face and walked away. This marriage . . . he felt deeply confused. How had it happened? And afterward, with his memory gone . . . Wives had walked away before. Nothing would have stopped her. But she had chosen to stay.

For her father's money. Of course. That was what she'd been waiting for. The signature from her uncle.

He pivoted toward the bedroom, feeling gutted.

What had happened in there tonight. The rapport between them. Their laughter. Their triumph. None of that had been feigned. And tonight . . . She had taken his hand and followed him to that bed. She had pulled the clothes from his body of her own will, and put her mouth to him.

To the man he had been. To the other Crispin, scrubbed clean of the sins of his past.

He ran a hand up his face. His throat felt raw, as though he'd been screaming.

Once she knew he remembered—how would he blame her for anything she did then? The contract forged in that bed today had not been for him. She had not consented to *him*, but to the other man.

He could be that other man to her. He could remain so. Could he not?

That was a better man by far. His regrets were ancient, not fresh. His sins accidental, not designed. He knew how to love the woman in that bed. He had a feel for it, a growing talent, a desire never to cease learning more.

Crispin exhaled. Yes. Why not? He could be a son again, to his parents whose concern and love were even stronger than their doubts. He could be a brother. Charlotte desired nothing more. And today, Atticus's embrace, his congratulations, had forged a new path as well.

Above all, he could be a husband to her. He could persuade her, even once her damned uncle signed the papers, that she belonged here. That New York had never been meant to claim her. That there could be freedom with him, too.

Only one flaw marred this plan. He remembered enough now to know that he was caught up in something very dark. Elland, the penal colony that did not exist, whose operators, their true identities frustratingly difficult to prove, had so handsomely funded Mason's campaigns—that mystery had sharp and long-reaching claws.

And today, in the Commons, he had dared them to aim for him.

He had pulled *her* into this mess. Had asked her to spy for him.

And then married her.

God above. She was no safer than he was.

He felt for the scar on his scalp and imagined her prone and lifeless on the pavement, bleeding out . . .

No, he could not regret remembering. He knew enough now to protect her truly. Even the crushing clarity of his regret felt tolerable, for it was *his* regret, not some stranger's that had been saddled to him unjustly. He had earned this dark weight. He knew its contours well. He knew how to carry it without letting it brush against her.

She never needed to know.

Some noise came from below. The sound of a settling foundation. Or of a prowler's careless footstep.

He made his way down the stairs. Naked—it made no matter. His body was a weapon that he remembered now how to use. He walked through every room twice. The windows were all locked. He stood alone in the darkness, listening.

CHAPTER FIFTEEN

*W*hen Jane woke, it was dawn. She sat up, alone in the bed, amazed she had slept so long—soundly, dreamlessly. Hot visions rolled through her mind. She heard a footstep at the door and braced herself for embarrassment. She had not been modest. She had not been a lady.

Crispin stepped inside, already dressed for the day, a tray in his hand. She clutched the sheets to cover her nakedness.

"I bring coffee," he said, "for the tradesman's daughter." When she laughed, he added, "Tea and chocolate are also on the way, but only if you insist, to my regret, on playing the lady." He sent a slow, suggestive smile to her as he laid the tray on the table. His lingering look down her body was hot, unmistakably admiring.

Modesty suddenly felt like an empty reflex. Her grip on the sheet loosened; she smiled back at him. "Are you so very thirsty?"

"Very," he said, coming to sit beside her on the

bed. His hand found her knee beneath the sheets. There was something possessive in the heavy drape of his palm. He pressed a kiss to her throat. "Hungry as well," he murmured against her skin. "You smell . . . edible."

Her laughter felt so easy. As though this was precisely how it was meant to be, nothing to marvel at. So familiar and right.

As though she were some other woman who had not lied to this man to his peril.

He sensed, perhaps, the sudden shift in her mood. He stood again. "So? Will you wait for tea, or may I tempt you now?"

The words were pleasant, but they felt emptied of suggestive undertones. His perceptiveness would never fail to amaze her. "Coffee, please. My brain feels furred. And . . . would you hand me my wrapper?"

"If I must," he said reluctantly. And as simply as that, she was smiling again.

Once the cups were poured, they took seats by the window that overlooked the small garden that ran along the eastern wall. He opened the window, allowing a fresh, cool, flower-scented breeze to drift over them. It seemed to carry away something else with it: her comfort and ease.

Having been honest with her body, she had hoped this other honesty might come easier. Instead, she felt she had gained something new, which now, like so many other things between them, stood to be lost.

"You asked me to spy for you," she said. There was no elegant way to begin this conversation.

His nonchalance, as he sipped from his cup, seemed a kindness to her. "Rather low of me."

"Yes," she said. "So it was." But she felt no animus for the man sitting across from her. He'd had nothing to do with it. "It wasn't you."

His hand hitched briefly as he laid down his cup, causing a few drops of coffee to splash into the saucer. "But it was," he said evenly. "This body, this brain. I won't ask to be forgiven for it."

"You did me a favor in return." Now she was defending the other man, for the sake of this one. But it was true. "My uncle had arranged a trap to force me into marriage with his son. You helped me to escape it."

He studied her. The rising light caught his face slantwise, illuminating the blueness of his eyes, painting in crystalline detail the curve of his mouth and the square angle of his jaw. "You once claimed not to mince words," he said. "A favor is something one does without repayment. You were backed into a corner, Jane. One which you should never have found yourself in. I think the better word for my assistance would be blackmail."

For a moment, she felt startled; he spoke as though he remembered it. But she supposed this man, guided by nobler principles, could neatly distill the injustice even from the scant details she'd provided.

She shrugged. "There was no one else to help me. So whatever it was, blackmail or a favor, it came in handy for me."

Those words were *not* kindness, she realized, but plain truth: had it not been for Mr. Burke, she might well have been bullied into submission.

No. She never would have submitted. But her uncle was a master of rationalization. Had he gained the advantage over her that night, guaranteeing that his guests would spread word of her supposed disgrace with Archibald . . . then she would have had no choice but to turn openly defiant. And defiance, the unsheathed force of will—that, he would not tolerate in a woman. She knew that from watching him with his wife. She knew that from her painful first months at Marylebigh. He would have persuaded himself then that the time for bullying was over, that no choice remained to him but force.

Crispin was waiting, his silence patient and watchful. She remembered suddenly a moment last night . . . the way he had used his keen perception as he'd touched her to study her face, gauge her reactions, adapt his movements to what she liked best.

Her face warmed. She looked down into her cup, cleared her throat, and rose to fetch more sugar.

When she came back to her seat, she said, "The main point is this: you asked me to listen for the name of Elland. It is not a man's name but the name of a penal colony."

"I see."

"But this penal colony doesn't officially exist."

Nothing else. He watched her as steadily and unblinkingly as a great cat.

She sighed. "I don't know the whole story of it. But from what you told me, it was never used for ordinary prisoners. It was opened decades ago, during the Luddite risings, to house insurgent leaders. The kind of men whose followers would deify them, call them martyrs, if they were hanged. It became a place to hide these men. To make them disappear, as if they had abandoned their people and their cause overnight."

"How democratic," he said flatly.

"Yes, well, you found some private intelligence that suggests it was decommissioned in the forties. But then . . ." She paused, trying to recall as precisely as possible the explanation that Mr. Burke had given her. She remembered too clearly the mild amusement he'd shown at her shock. "My uncle, you know, took over my father's seat in the Commons. But while he promised to carry out my father's plans, he quickly showed himself a liar. He knew he would not retain the seat in the next election, but he managed to endear himself to the right people, who invited him to stand for a different borough. That campaign did not begin promisingly. Then, of course, the peculiar miracle—well, of course you don't recall it. His opponent vanished. Ran away with a mistress, everybody said—he was last seen in the company of a very flamboyant woman. I think you were suspicious of my uncle's role—I'm sure you weren't alone in that. So you looked into it, probably hoping that it would yield information that would help you keep my uncle in line.

"Instead, somehow, you uncovered mention of Elland. You never told me how. But you started to hunt down that lead instead. Perhaps it was connected to my uncle's sudden extravagance? The ball, the new coach . . . He could not have embezzled so much from my trust without getting caught. It must have come from elsewhere. At any rate, you told me to report anything I heard of Elland."

She heard him release a long, measured breath. "And what did you hear?"

"Not much," she said. "Almost nothing, in fact, until one night . . . My uncle received a letter. You

asked me to copy it, but all it held was a single line—
'Elland in revolt'—and three names. I think . . ." It
sounded mad. "I think you suspected them to be men
imprisoned at Elland. Forgotten there for the last
twenty years."

He nodded slowly. "Do you remember the names?"

She remembered how frightened she had been, slipping into her uncle's bedroom to hunt for his keys. How
her hand had shaken so violently that she'd dropped
the key ring in the hall outside his study. No explosion
had ever sounded so loud as the clatter of that key ring
on the bare wooden floor. Nor had time ever dragged
so slowly, minutes turning into hours, than when she'd
unlocked his desk drawers, combing through them one
by one.

"I do remember the names," she said softly. Her
hand had been trembling so hard that she'd botched the
words, nearly spilled the inkpot. She'd had to recopy the
whole thing before it came out with clarity. "All three
of them," she said. They had burned through her brain
that night like a drumbeat, the terrible tattoo played at
an execution.

She had been so wild, so desperate, to escape from
that house. It had been shaping, all around her, into her
coffin.

The fierce grip of his hand on hers brought her back
to the present. He was leaning close, whispering her
name. "It's all right," he said. "You are safe now. Here
with me."

"Am I?" Her voice was unsteady. "Crispin, you
loathed me. You will do so again."

"I did *not* loathe you." A sharp, fierce denial. His
hand hooked through her hair, still heavy and loose

on her shoulders. He pulled her into him, kissed her deeply.

She relaxed in his grip. His mouth had magic in it. Sweet, languorous nectar, drugging her into ease.

But a drug wore off. She pulled away. "You don't understand," she said. "You don't *remember*. But once you do—"

"I will remember this," he said, and kissed her again, dragging her up and onto his lap. "This," he said hungrily, nosing through her hair, finding the sensitive spot beneath her ear, brushing his mouth against it until she shivered. "And this," he whispered, kissing his way down her throat. His hand slipped under her robe, palming her breast, his skin hot and rough against hers. "This," he said very low. "Do you think I won't?"

This argument could not be won. She did not *want* to win. She threaded her hands through his hair. "Take me back to bed."

Crispin's public resurrection in the Commons, and the explosive results of his speech, made two-inch headlines in the morning newspapers. As his wife lay beside him reading the florid accounts amid giggles ("'His eyes flashed like Caesar's as he strode the floor, the indignant flames of justice transfixing his peers'—Crispin, do flash your eyes at me!"), a great agitated knocking came at the door. It was the kind of knock that announced a crisis, something on fire, somebody shot. As Jane grabbed for her robe, Crispin strode naked to the door and opened it a crack.

"Sir." His majordomo looked too harried to remark on his master's dishabille. "There is a—a *line* of visitors, sir, coming and going. I told them you are not receiving, but they refuse to believe it."

"They?"

"Some of them claim to be your constituents, sir. Four or five colleagues—I have seated them all in the drawing room, where they are growling at each other. A passel of young men came to beg tickets of admission to the Strangers' Gallery—they seemed content to write their names on a list and come back tomorrow. But the others . . . I do wonder . . ." Cusworth's jaw ticked. "You might wish to hire a secretary, sir. It is very difficult to manage this business, and the household's besides."

"I'll be down momentarily," Crispin said, and pulled shut the door again.

Jane looked wide-eyed as she finished knotting her wrapper. "Will you manage?" she asked. "Cusworth will announce them by name, of course."

"I'll do my best." He gathered up the clothes he'd discarded in haste. "As for Elland, we'll pay a visit to the General Register tomorrow to look into the names you found in that letter. For now, will you join me downstairs? Until we've figured out the Elland business, I intend to go very cautiously—to listen a great deal, and say very little. But it would be very useful to have your observations on my colleagues."

She snorted. "I doubt *they* would like it. A woman, listening in?"

He grinned at her. "If they're here to damn me as a turncoat, their opinion can go hang. And if they've come to befriend me, then they're expecting and hoping to find a changed man—in which case, they can take what I offer, or nothing."

After a moment, color bloomed on her face, and she nodded.

Jane had found a new use for needlepoint. She sat in a handsome armchair in the corner window of Crispin's study, her skirts gracefully arranged in the blaze of morning light, the embroidery frame in her lap as Cusworth showed in supplicants.

To a man, they startled on spotting her. She had dressed to be noticed, in a cherry-red silk gown fringed dramatically in silver-threaded lace, a dress as bright and sparkling as her mood. The color was too vibrant for a pale English rose, of course. It made her olive complexion glow. When they stared, she smiled serenely.

Crispin, meanwhile, trained his regard on the newcomer, his brows slowly rising as the silence drew on. "Are you quite well?" he would finally ask. *No*, his remark silently implied, *there is nothing odd about the lady's presence.*

Then the newcomer flushed or fidgeted and took a seat opposite Crispin, trying his best to forget about the woman.

They all did a fine job of it in the end. Conservative or radical, liberal or independent, men were raised with the skill of overlooking a lady. Jane helped by sewing with conspicuous vigor, making a good show of being fascinated by the flash of her own needle. But her mind remained on the conversation across the room. She took note of every detail, to discuss with Crispin later.

Many of the old Peelites, now proudly parading as Liberals, were desperate to acquire Crispin's support.

Their leader, Prime Minister Palmerston, had done much in his time to make prisons more sanitary places, and so most of them came into the room assuming that Crispin was already won over. But while Palmerston's social policies were humane, his opposition to the extension of the electorate had never struck Jane as laudable. "I wonder," she said, after another old Peelite strode out, "if you might not remain independent, at least for this session. Lord Chad is very persuasive, but what will you gain by committing to the platform now? You'll have no voice of your own, only a trial period in which they'll expect you to fall in line in order to show what a loyal party member you'll make."

Crispin nodded, tapping his fountain pen thoughtfully. "On the other hand, an independent is a yipping dog. He may cause some annoyance, but he won't win anyone over."

"Small steps," she said gently. "And your barking yesterday changed minds, though you had no friends on the floor to support you."

As the door opened again, he laid down his pen and she turned hastily back to her embroidery.

Crispin's chair scraped—he had thrust himself out of his seat. She broke form and glanced up, and then dropped her needle.

"Well," said her uncle from the doorway as he looked between them. "Isn't this picturesque."

"Cusworth, you may show this man out," Crispin said, but her uncle lifted his hand.

"It won't take but a minute. And I do not come to quarrel."

Crispin glanced to her—silently asking her to make the decision. Her heart had moved into her throat. She swallowed it down. A snake was better kept in plain view. "A minute seems short," she said. "If you mean to grovel, I hope for an hour at least."

Uncle Philip narrowed his eyes. "You came out quite cheeky, didn't you, Jane? I thought we had stomped that tongue out of you. But you were cleverer than I'd hoped."

"You will address me alone," Crispin bit out, "or you will go."

"Oh, I don't think my niece wants for your protection." Philip's brown beard, trimmed with dandyish precision, did not disguise the smirk he gave Jane. "But very well. So long as she moves around to where I can see her."

Her laughter startled her—and Crispin, too, judging by his face. "It seems we think of each other in *precisely* the same way," she said. "I suppose one could call that an *understanding*, Uncle. A sympathy of minds."

But she laid aside her needlework and walked to Crispin's side. A twisted dark part of her—perhaps that part that made her blood kin to Philip Mason—was flattered that her uncle considered her a threat.

Crispin gave her his chair and stood beside her, one hip perched on the edge of the desk. "All right," he said curtly. "Speak and be gone."

But Mason would not be hurried. He sat back, lacing his hands over his belly, and considered them in turn. "I don't come to congratulate you. Any piece of showmanship can sway a crowd of monkeys, and this Commons, I fear, is a circus all around. But I think, going forward, we must set rules for our disagreements. There is a code even among thieves, is there not? I know a great deal about you, Burke. A great deal. And I will admit it—you know no less about me. So it would be wisest, for both our sakes, and for the sake of the country which we both serve, to move forward in good faith, ignoring what came before. Otherwise . . ." He shrugged. "We both end up skewered. That does no good to anyone."

"I see no objection to that," Crispin said.

That was not the answer Jane wanted from him. But perhaps he had no choice. He hadn't struck her as a man to fully trust her uncle even when they were working together. But this Crispin could not count on the discretion of the other one. He had no firsthand knowledge of whether his old entanglement with Mason had the power to undo him now.

"Very good. Then you will do two things to prove it," her uncle said briskly. "You will hand over the funds that you were holding for our party. They were never yours, as you well know. And you will drop any inquiries into Elland."

Jane's breath caught. She had never expected him to say that name aloud.

Crispin tipped his head. "In exchange, of course, for your signature on the documents required to release Jane's trust. Is that your proposal?"

Mason's mouth tightened. "Yes."

Crispin's smile looked cold and sharp. "I will release the party funds to you the moment my wife's rightful inheritance is in her possession. But Elland?" He shrugged. "Curiosity is a vice of mine. And that had nothing, I think, to do with politics."

Mason's palm slammed onto the table. "It has nothing to do with *you*! Yet you poked your nose in it anyway!"

"And our midnight prowler?" Crispin said. "Was that your nose, poking in from afar?"

Mason seemed to shrink in his seat. "Here?" he whispered. His glance darted wildly around the room. "When? What did he take?"

Unease prickled through Jane. She had never seen her uncle look frightened before.

"Damn you," Mason said, his voice lifting as he rose. "If you've ruined the both of us—!"

As he loomed, Jane's instinct was to recoil. She fought it, glaring. She would not let him make her cower.

Crispin's hand closed over her collarbone, massaging her. Her uncle's glance dropped to note this intimacy. His rage popped like a bubble; his shoulders sagged. "Too late," he said in disgust. "Too late, isn't it?" His lip curled. "I should have seen it coming: who better suited than a lowborn harridan and a highborn fool? But you will not enjoy your marital bed long, Burke. If you keep poking where you don't belong, then we're both dead men. And your lovely wife—well, dream tonight of the new fool she'll find to keep her entertained."

"I had no idea you thought so highly of me, Uncle." She did not disguise her malice. "Why, I sound like a regular black widow. But I assure you, any scheming you sense is aimed solely at you."

He laughed down at her. "You've no love for me, girl, but what of yourself? Bullets hit women as easily as men."

"Enough threats," Crispin drawled. "Out with you."

"Blast you. I'm not the one you should fear!"

"Then who?" Jane asked, rising too. "Go ahead, unburden yourself. Who is behind this mess to do with Elland?"

He stared at her, jaw working. "If I thought him an easy target, wouldn't I have had done with him?" He scoffed. "Fools, both of you. Playing about, with my throat on the block!" He stalked toward the door, then wheeled back. "Leave Elland alone," he said fiercely. "Forget you heard the name. Or we'll *all* end up in an early grave."

CHAPTER SIXTEEN

*T*he next morning dawned bright and clear, the air so balmy that Jane took her tea outside in the garden, beneath the trees coming into leaf. Then, before the house could fill with petitioners, she and Crispin set out for the General Register office. Over dinner the evening before, they had gone round and round, debating what to make of Mason's threats. "I would not take him seriously," Jane had said, "save that he looked so afraid."

But assuming he told any of the truth, following his suggestion—keeping their heads in the sand—seemed a very good way to ensure their vulnerability. And so: to Somerset House, on the trail of three names somehow associated with Elland.

Crispin was armed. Rubbing her eyes—they had not had much sleep, between their earnest discussion and . . . other matters—Jane watched him check his pistol before holstering it inside his coat.

Lightly she said, "You know how to use that, I hope."

He grinned at her. "If your uncle calls again, I'll demonstrate."

The brougham lurched into motion. "There will be hundreds of Thomas Clarks," she mused. "It will take hours to find the right one."

His mouth twitched as he looked up at her. "But Baggott Shufflebottom? If there's more than one of *those*, I'll eat my hat."

She gave a wry tug of her mouth. "Mr. Shufflebottom deserves our sympathy."

"Oh, agreed," he said easily. "If not for his name, then certainly for where he ended up."

That was a sobering thought. She glanced out the window at the gray street. The morning's brief sunshine had been swallowed by clouds. The gloom felt appropriate.

How long would it take to be transported to Australia? Shackled and chained. She could not imagine.

She could not imagine sailing at all, in fact. She had never set foot outside England. "Have you been overseas?" she asked. It was a great irony that she knew more of Mr. Burke than Crispin did, but so little of Crispin himself. "Not the Continent, I mean. But farther? India, say, or America?"

Crispin shook his head. "I had a great-uncle who worked for the East India Company in his youth. He used to promise to take me to Calcutta with him one day. His house was like nothing I'd ever seen—filled with strange and marvelous statues, carved wooden screens, fountains with flowing water, enclosed by great skylights . . . He told wonderful stories. I wanted nothing more than to grow up and travel the world as he had."

"Why didn't you?"

"I tried," he said after a moment. "Not civil service,

but the diplomatic corps. But you know they reformed the selection process back in the forties, instituted an exam. Suddenly it wasn't one's connections and breeding that mattered so much as one's brains."

"I don't think you lack for those," she said, "regardless of what you say."

"But discipline," he said with an easy smile, then shrugged. "I sat for it. The exam, I mean."

She pulled a face. "Oh. I'm sorry—"

"No. I passed." He smiled more faintly now. "I did quite well, in fact. Two years of cramming. I felt sure the German would be the end of me—I've no talent for languages. But somehow I ranked in the top ten percent."

"Then . . . why am I not addressing Ambassador Burke?"

He laughed. "I'd still be twenty years away from an ambassadorship. But as it turns out, I wasn't selected."

"Despite your marks? That seems odd."

She saw the hesitation come over him. "You know so many black things about me," he said slowly. "I dislike to contribute another one."

But he was mistaken. These pieces of his more distant past she was eager to collect. They were part of the larger puzzle, and her curiosity, her need to understand the man he had been so she could find some way to square it with the man he was now, felt like a fire in her. "I would like to know," she said. "I would like to understand you better, Crispin."

He looked troubled. "Would you? How much of it, Jane? All of it, or only the bookends?"

Bookends to the man he had forgotten. And yet . . . hadn't that man grown out of the boy who'd come before him, who dreamed of travel and diplomacy, and spent two years buried in his books in pursuit of a dream?

"Maybe they're all of a piece," she said quietly. Logically, it seemed true. And in her prayers as well. "So tell me. What happened?"

"I took a second in classics at Cambridge," he said. "By the skin of my teeth. I don't know why I chose to read classics—I never had an interest. Atticus had done so, I'm sure that's why. At any rate, I stayed on afterward. Spent most days in the library, cramming. By the second year, I felt certain of everything but the German. My parents wanted me in town for the season. To keep an eye on me, perhaps." His mouth crooked. "I was not, let us say, particularly well behaved on the nights I did not spend in the library. Word must have traveled. Anyway, they procured a German tutor to lure me south." Here he took a large breath, then lapsed into brief silence. "I'm not sure there's any point in remembering this."

She moved onto his bench, settling beside him, gathering up his hand. "Why? This isn't the part you forgot."

"It is the part I didn't understand," he said very quietly, "until the Duchess of Farnsworth explained it at the ball."

A sizzling little jolt ran through her. It felt red, venomous.

She was very careful to keep her grip steady over his. Not to let him see the jealousy brewing in her. "You were in love with her," she said. "Charlotte told me so."

His huff sounded like the first syllable of laughter. "Charlotte babbles. You must have noticed. She relies on her listeners to curate her words for good sense, and half the time it's a useless attempt, I tell you."

That wasn't a denial. "She said the duchess was the diamond of her season. That every gentleman admired her."

The tension eased from his face. He turned his hand in hers, threading their fingers together. She resented her glove for keeping his skin from hers. "You're a generous woman," he murmured. "Do you know that? You could coax a stone to speak, and make it feel clever besides."

She laughed. "You're hardly a stone. Although . . ." Her cheeks flamed. Was she truly about to say this? "You are capable of turning tremendously hard."

His guffaw rocked him back in his seat. The look on his face was delighted amazement. He lifted her hand, kissed her knuckles. "I will have to prove that anew," he said, "once we get home."

She ducked her head to hide her own smile. She felt at such liberty with him, and in turn, it opened glimpses into parts of herself she'd never guessed to exist. She was *bawdy*.

"What I feel for you," he said, low and rough, "is incomparable to anything that came before it. I hope you know that."

She swallowed. Her skirt, ashes-of-roses silk, glimmered in the patterning of light through the window. "Thank you."

It was not the right answer. But she could give no other. She felt the words sticking in her throat, wanting out; she would not listen to them. She had gone as far as she could. The future was real. No amount of pretending would prevent its arrival. She would keep what dignity she could in the meantime.

"The duchess," she prodded. "You—" She did not want to say it. "Fell in love with her."

She heard his long breath. "I offered for her."

That was worse. She wanted her hand back. She sat very stiffly. "Oh."

"And she accepted," he said. "And then, the next day, took it back. Her father intended her for Farnsworth."

"Married against her will." She did not want to feel pity for the woman! But she knew what it was like to feel forced.

"No, in fact not." He sounded thoughtful now, oddly detached. "I think she hadn't known Farnsworth might be within her reach. He's a standoffish man by nature—difficult to read. But once she realized she might wear a coronet, she scrambled to undo her promise to me."

"Crispin." With sympathy, she studied his face. But he looked unmoved, his bland smile entirely persuasive.

"Of course, I was devastated," he said. "But I wished her the best, through gritted teeth. I took the tatters of my pride back to Cambridge, where I sat for the exam. Then, when news came of my marks, it did a good deal to steady me. And then, I—" He abruptly closed his mouth. Cleared his throat. "And this is where my memory grows dark," he said with a shrug. "But I must have come back down to London. Found myself alone, in private, with Laura—I expect to share the news with her, that I had come in at the top of the rankings." A very slight smile. "I had my pride, after all. No doubt I thought to torment her with visions of the glamorous life I would lead in Paris or Washington—when in fact I probably would have been running errands in Kabul, but no matter. We

were alone, and we were interrupted by her father—
and Farnsworth."

"Oh dear."

"Quite. And from there . . ." His face darkened.
"Farnsworth stormed off. Not sparing a moment for
explanations. We had not been touching—but the
situation. A darkened room, privacy, standing so close
together. A man of pride, Farnsworth. With one look
he leapt to dark conclusions. Laura's father threw me
out, then concocted a lie: I had forced my attentions on
Laura, harassed and stalked her after she turned down
my suit. Farnsworth believed it—he never bothered to
ask Laura for the truth. He decided to punish me, to
teach me a lesson. He sabotaged my career, so the diplomatic corps did not take me. And . . . I believe he told
my father the same tale. My father—"

"He could not have believed it," she said, aghast.

"I can't know." He spoke very slowly, as though the
words took almost too much effort to push out. "But
he refused to intercede for me. He had several friends in
the corps. All I wanted to know was why I hadn't been
chosen. But he refused to ask. He told me I must make
my own way. And once I realized what had truly gone
wrong, the lie that Laura's father had spread—why, I
looked on my father's refusal in a new light. He thought
me deserving of the punishment."

They sat in silence for several long moments. The
wheels rumbled over cobblestones, the brougham jud-
dering and shaking, then passed onto smooth pavement
again, settling them back into their seats.

"Lord Sibley owes you a great apology." Not only for
his lack of faith, his betrayal of his fatherly duty to believe the best of his child, but also for this: for laying

the groundwork from which the politician had sprung. What had Mr. Burke's motto been? "Need no one, trust no one," she said softly. Betrayed by his beloved and his family—"I can see why you once believed in that wisdom."

On a deep breath, Crispin sat straighter, as though shrugging off the weight of old memories. "Well. There you have it anyway. Instead of traveling the world and cleaning up politicians' messes, I stayed here and made the messes myself. And you, Mrs. Burke? What aim did you have for yourself when you were young? I know you have a powerful desire to do good unto others, but what of yourself?"

He wanted to change the subject. She tried her best to cast off the gloom, this frustrated tenderness that bade her to hold him, and the aching resentment for all who'd done him injury. "I also wanted to travel," she said. "I had a dream of walking to the nearest quay and letting my destination be decided by the next departing ship."

"Dangerous," he said. "What if it took you to Liverpool?"

She burst into laughter. "Liverpool isn't so bad. My father had several factories there. The people were very kind."

"Fair enough," he said. "It was the journey you wanted, then, more than the destination?"

"I liked . . . the idea of possibility." She paused, puzzling it out. "Yes, I think the unboundedness of it—the unpredictability, the notion that anything, anywhere, might be possible. My parents were very good to me, Crispin. I had the same education they would have given a son. But I was still a girl. Their hopes for me, the happy tales they spun of my future—they always stopped at my great and glorious marriage. And I suppose I did not like the idea of my story ending at twenty-two, much less being so . . . predictable."

"It needn't be." The serious note in his voice brought her startled glance up to his. He touched her face very lightly. "Having a companion," he said, "is no bar to making the journey."

Her chest felt full suddenly. Whether the weight was hope or foreboding, she could not say. But it gripped her into perfect immobility as she gazed up at him.

It made the words so easy to speak. "You are incomparable, too, you know."

He kissed her as the carriage came to a halt.

"But this makes no sense," said Jane. They stood at a long counter in the north wing of Somerset House, behind which rose, as far as the eye could see, shelves of records, overseen by harassed clerks, which contained the birth and marriage and death records of every man, woman, and child in Britain in the last thirty years. "Shufflebottom got married."

"Did he?" Crispin looked up from his own ledger. She'd been right: four hundred Thomas Clarks and counting. "Good for old Shufflebottom. It takes a brave woman to bear that name."

"No, he got married *recently*." She shoved her ledger toward him, then grimaced as a nearby clerk hissed at her.

"Have a care with those," the clerk said. "Those are Her Majesty's own books."

"Let us hope Her Majesty is fond of dust," Jane muttered, and rubbed her nose again. She had been sneezing since her first step into the room.

Crispin bit back a smile and offered a grave nod, masculine and conspiratorial, to the clerk, who looked mollified and turned back to his business. "Married when?" he asked quietly.

Her finger guided him down the cramped lines of the page. "Six months ago," she whispered. "By a Reverend Cleminger of Agar Town, St. Pancras."

"Perhaps the bridegroom is the original Shufflebottom's son."

His wife shot him a speaking look. "Would *you* name your son after his father, if the name were Baggott Shufflebottom?"

He could not contain his snort. The clerk, in the corner of his vision, scowled.

"Agar Town," he said. "Well, that's one place to start. We'd spend the better part of a year tracking down all these Clarks."

"There's something else." She glanced into the gloomy depths of the record room. "Jebediah Smith. There were twenty-four of them. Most of them deceased. The others, born too recently, in the last ten years. Crispin, I don't think these names have anything to do with—" She dropped her voice. "Elland." She wrinkled her nose, widened her eyes at him in a mute look of desperation, then turned away to sneeze into her glove.

"Poor Jane," he said. "Come, let's get out of here, shall we? For the sake of your nose."

"Oh yes," she said gratefully. "Only I—" She glanced hesitantly toward the clerk. "There was one other thing I wished to look at. Shall I meet you outside?"

"I'm glad to wait."

But a furtive look had fallen over her; she shifted her weight and carefully closed the ledger. "No, it won't take but a moment. Do go send for the coach."

Yesterday, he might have bowed and walked away without hesitation. Yesterday, he'd been a better man. But he knew now a dark impulse to press her until she disclosed her intention. The effect of five years in which he'd practiced and perfected suspicion, and honed a talent for manipulation, held him rooted in place, battling himself as tension tightened her brow.

Don't ask me, her eyes pleaded.

But the goal was to keep her. In that dark hallway, discovering himself again, remembering himself, he'd also uncovered this singular desire. And each secret between them would make it more difficult to bind her to him.

He exhaled slowly. He was not ruled by his vices. This dark vein of possessive greed did not control him. "Of course," he said evenly, and turned on his heel, making his way into the dim light of a murky afternoon.

She emerged just as the coach was drawing up. "You seemed so certain about those names," she said as he helped her inside. Whatever information she had requested did not seem to have distracted her from the main point. "So certain they were somehow important."

"Even the devil is fallible, I suppose."

Her startled glance told him that he had failed to keep the darkness from his voice. "You . . . weren't the devil, Crispin."

Another way to cut through these lies would simply be to speak the truth. *I remember it all, Jane. Or most of it, all I need to understand exactly who I was.*

Who I am.

But in that last bit lay the catch, didn't it? *Who I am.* A rock beneath the water might appear seamless and plain, but in the light, it would reveal itself cut through by black veins. So, too, with him. He had not been cleansed by his period of forgetting, simply . . . disguised by it.

Instead, he might say: *Tell me why we truly married.*

But he could not ask that question, either. Perhaps he was afraid to know. Or maybe it did not matter. They *were* married. And he meant never to let her go.

Need no one, trust no one. Before the assault had addled him, he had believed this maxim. But now he understood differently. He needed her. Not to succeed at worldly aims, but to want to *live* in the world. To feel, on waking, that there was good reason to rise, and to smile, even, at what the day might hold. She had spoken of possibility, the precious sense of its wide scope. She was his sense of the possible. When he imagined the world without her, it calcified around him.

Need no one, trust no one. He wanted to trust her. He trusted her in every matter not to do with himself. But he'd not been a man deserving of trust. What hope that she would feel differently, that she would *trust* him when he said, *I remember—but I am different now, regardless*?

"We'll pay a visit to Agar Town," he said. "If Shufflebottom was married there, then the parish priest should be able to tell us something about him. At the least, it will settle the matter."

"Yes," she said. "I suppose so."

"The man I was." He had to let this go. His darker self knew it was futile. His darker self saw an easier way, in which he spoke the truth years from now, after she was so thoroughly bound to him that it could make no difference. A child in her lap, another standing beside her. A family and a life together, which she would have no choice but to honor. "Do you still look for him in me?"

Her expression softened, her puzzlement clearing away. Large, brilliant eyes, filled with compassion. "No," she said. "Of course not."

But the answer, which would have pleased him yesterday, sank like a knife into him now. "He was successful." He told himself to stop. But the words would come, despite him. "Celebrated. With every promise of going higher yet. He would not have been counted a poor match by anyone."

"By anyone who did not know him," she corrected instantly. She thought they were in a different argument; she was defending him against that man. "But I knew him, Crispin. And despite all you've forgotten, you are a better politician than he ever was. You proved that with your speech. You will continue to prove it. I have no doubt of you. The men yesterday—not Sutton, but Burghley and de Witt. They mean what they say. If you wish it, there is a place in their party for you. And perhaps you should take it, after all. You can still go very high, but this time, your efforts will be undertaken in partnership with honest men, for the greater good—not simply for personal glory."

"Perhaps that other man might have made the same choices." *Shut up.* "All he lacked was proper guidance. Your guidance, say."

Her hand fell away from him. "That man wanted no guidance," she said quietly.

What rebuttal could he offer? None. He looked out the window. They were nearing Agar Town.

"But I understand him better now," came her tentative voice at last. "I see . . . why he became what he was. Oh, I don't know . . . I don't think he would have changed." He felt her puzzled study of him. He had lost the ability to disguise his thoughts from her, it seemed. She sensed his mood. "I'm sorry," she whispered. "But I will say it: your mother was right. Great, miraculous good can come of evil."

And so the judgment was cast. He felt flayed by it. He locked his jaw tightly. It was her right to judge him. That did not mean it felt pleasant. "For a woman who argued so ardently for the ticket-of-leave system," he said, "you have a marvelous cynicism for the possibility of reform."

The bench creaked as she sat back. "Oh," she said very softly. She sounded wounded.

He felt the same. Like a desert had opened in his chest, barren and hopeless.

Agar Town barely deserved the name of a township, being a crowded collection of low huts and cottages growing organically around a ragged-edged road. In the yards, clotheslines held patched petticoats, and here and there, stinking sole skins left to dry in the weak sun. Their stench mingled with pungent notes of sewage and acrid smoke from some nearby manufactory.

Crispin had wanted her to wait in the coach, which stood parked tight against the terminus of the Great Northern Railway, but Jane refused. Her mother had never scrupled to take her along into the poorest and most miserable neighborhoods. Jane's only concern was that she came empty-handed, particularly when they discovered that the church in fact doubled as a school, and the reverend, sitting on a stool in the cramped entry, was handing out pairs of socks to a grubby line of children.

"And you, Mary?" the reverend called to a little girl in a tattered dress who crouched some distance away from the line, walking her doll across the floor. "Don't you want socks?"

"Don't need socks."

"Why is that?"

"I've quite enough of 'em."

"Oh?" The reverend laughed. "How many do you have?"

The girl looked up, scowling. "Why, the ones on my feet," she said, and Jane laughed, too, the sound catching the reverend's attention.

"Goodness!" The reverend rose. "Forgive me, madam, I didn't—" He paused. "Back again, are you?" This to Crispin, far less warmly. He dismissed the children with a wave. "Soup is waiting in the kitchen," he told them. They scrambled off amid cheers, Mary grabbing up her doll and leading the way.

Crispin cleared his throat. "I was here before?"

The reverend busied himself with neatening the basket of socks. He was a young, lanky man, with a gaunt face and a tightly disciplined air that lent his movements a jerky, almost violent quality as he straightened. "You didn't seem drunk," he said. "I can't imagine you've forgotten."

Judging by this cold welcome, Crispin had not impressed the reverend at their prior meeting. Jane stepped forward. "This is a church?" she asked. "And a school besides?"

The tight line of the reverend's shoulders eased a little. "Quite so," he said to her. "And also a soup kitchen for the local residents. A pint of broth for threepence, and gruel for a penny, and barley water and lemonade to encourage temperance."

"What a fine undertaking," she said. "I wonder if we might not support it."

His eyes narrowed as he looked over her wardrobe. She had dressed thoughtlessly this morning, in one of the ready-made gowns ordered in haste, and the silk and lace shone too finely for their surroundings. "If it's charity you offer, very well," he said. "But I have told the gentleman already that I have no interest in bribes."

"That's very good of you," she said with gentle care. "And a testament to your success here. When my family undertook the rebuilding of Palmer Corner, in Liverpool, we could not afford to distinguish between charity and bribes; every penny was welcome in that effort."

His jaw tightened; for a moment, she feared she had provoked him too sharply. And then, sitting back onto his stool, he laughed.

"Touché, madam. Pride does go before the fall. Your family directed that reform? I have read of it. That corner of Liverpool is now thriving, I hear."

She was stealing credit from her mother. But she would make good on it. "It was a long and difficult process," she said, "but the result made it well worthwhile. And it sounds as if your efforts go similarly. We found, in addition to a soup kitchen and a school, that a mother's society and a day nursery proved very useful.

The extra income, from allowing the women to work without worry for their little ones—"

"Precisely! And a workingman's institute as well. We are planning on it." Some clatter came from deeper inside the building, and the reverend cast a worried look in that direction before rising again. "I should like very much to talk with you at length, madam. We could learn a great deal from the example of Palmer's Corner. Do you have a card?"

"I'm afraid not, but my . . . husband does." She had never said that word before, and she felt a shifting of the very atmosphere, Crispin's subtle movement at her side. She pushed onward quickly, ignoring the strange pleasure of the word. "Please, do take it."

"Ah." The reverend looked skeptically at Crispin but accepted the card. Something in it caused him to smile unkindly. "You neglected to give your name when last you called."

Crispin clearly had not been courteous.

"I wasn't the man I am now," Crispin said evenly.

"Well. I—" A crash came from the distance, followed by shrieks, causing the reverend to sigh. "As you see, I'm rather busy. But . . ." He cleared his throat and looked at Jane. "If there is something I may do for you, Mrs. Burke?"

"We were looking for a man whom you recently married," she said. "A Mr. Baggott Shufflebottom."

His brows rose. "Do you truly not remember?" he asked Crispin. "Very well, just as I said before: you came too late. Mr. Shufflebottom was buried a month after his wedding."

Ice curled through Jane's stomach. "How did he die, may I ask?"

The reverend shook his head. "Mrs. Burke, this is Agar Town. A drunkard can find a thousand ways to meet his maker. I believe he drowned in a cesspool, but as I told your husband before, his widow may know more of it. You will find her at the end of the road, in the cottage with the red door."

For all the ramshackle appearance of the hunched cottages to right and left, handsome lamplights flanked the road, and a new smooth pavement led them quickly toward Mrs. Shufflebottom's house. Jane noted these to Crispin. "These must be the reverend's improvements. I think I *will* meet with him; would you mind it?"

"Of course not." That was the truth, but inwardly Crispin still wrestled with himself. Perhaps her only mistake was to condemn the man he had been while sparing the man he was. They had stepped into the misery of that scene in the school—bony children queuing for socks like priceless gems—and he had inwardly grimaced. She had turned immediately, briskly, to plans for improvement.

They had both been raised in a sheltered world. But in his parents' circles, noblesse oblige meant showering coins down from a distance. Jane, on the other hand, had been raised to see herself as part of a whole. To put her hands to work as well as her purse.

Hers, he saw, was the better way. It would be difficult, after working alongside the poor, to forget them in the halls of power. Impossible, too, to think of politics as a game, rather than the machinery through which real lives could be saved or squandered.

"This must be it," Jane said, drawing up. The cottage

was freshly whitewashed, a fine bright role model for its sagging jaundiced neighbors, but one side had begun to buckle, weakened by rot.

The door bore a curious mark on it, a crooked X as on a treasure map. It stood open, allowing a wedge of light to illuminate the broken wood flooring and the patches of bare earth that rose through it. When Crispin knocked, splinters of wood flaked free.

"'Oo is it? Come in, then."

They ducked through the doorway into a dim, damp room strongly scented by a roasting chicken that a woman stood turning on a spit over the fire. She glanced up at them, and the tartan shawl fell from her brow, revealing lank blond hair and a smile that bloomed and faded in a moment.

"I knew you wasn't dead," she said. "Cats and snakes 'ave got nine lives. Well, and I'm glad they didn't kill you. But you'll need to get out."

Jane took his arm, understanding it a moment before he did. "It was here?" she asked. "That he was attacked?"

The woman wiped her brow with the edge of her shawl. "What? You don't recall?"

"I was found outside Clerkenwell station," Crispin said slowly. It was a half hour's walk, which he'd been in no condition to make.

"Aye, we moved you there—my brother and I." The woman—Mrs. Shufflebottom, he supposed—sighed heavily. "I felt right poorly for not calling the police. I 'ope you believe it. But they would've fingered me for it. There's no justice for us in Agar Town. And I figured somebody would find you, once't the next train came in."

"Who was it?" Jane asked. "Who attacked him?"

Mrs. Shufflebottom cast a hunted look toward the lane outside. "Never 'ad their names," she said. "But they knew you was coming. One took me at knife-point—if I'd screamed 'e would've cut me. And I saved your life," she added aggressively. "Afterward, I did. And we even dumped the body."

"The *body*?" said Jane, and he took a deep breath, feeling—whether through thickly buried layers of forgetting or through instinct—that he would not like this next news.

"Aye, you 'ad a gun," the woman said to Crispin. "Got off only the single shot, but by luck it found its way."

He felt Jane's horrified look. But he kept his eyes trained on the widow. "Where is the body?" This was no time to recoil, to indulge finer sentiments. The corpse might hold clues.

"Long gone," Mrs. Shufflebottom said flatly. "My brother keeps pigs."

Jane made a muffled noise and walked out into the fresh air. The widow looked after her with an odd, sour smile. "Must be nice," she muttered. "Must be nice indeed."

He forced himself to stay focused. He would contemplate later what it felt like to have another man's blood on his hands. "You must have got a better look at that one. When you disposed of him."

"I did my best not to," she said bluntly. "But 'e wasn't a gentleman. Built like a dockhand—that's what my brother guessed. Now, the one who put the knife to my throat, that was a proper nob. Smooth palms, never knew a day's labor. So there you 'ave it. That's all I got, and if you want to thank me, you'll leave."

Jane came back inside. "Has anyone come back to trouble you since then?"

"No, but there's nothing to keep 'em from doing so, I reckon. Doing me the way they did your bloke here, and Baggie."

"But—then why have you stayed here?" Jane sounded aghast. "If they—if they killed your husband, as you say—"

The woman exploded. "Where'm I to go, princess? My entire family is with me, ain't they? Brothers and sisters and my ma besides, all living down the road. No, you'll not talk with them," she added sharply when Jane looked out the door. "Leave them out of this if you've got any decency."

Crispin reached into his jacket. "Fifty pounds," he said. A handsome year's salary for a clerk. "That should pay for all of you, I would think, if you wish to go."

The woman's jaw dropped. Then she crept forward, reaching hesitantly, fingering the edge of the note. "Didn't know they came so large." She glanced up at him, wide-eyed, and he felt a curious twist in his chest.

Yes, this was what it meant not to condescend from above. One looked into a person's face, and saw what had been done to them. In another life, this woman would have been cosseted and adored. She had strong cheekbones and pale clear eyes. In silk and lace, she would have been celebrated as a beauty.

"Take it," he said quietly. "But tell me this: how did your husband catch these men's attention? Why did they kill him?"

She gathered up the bill to her breast, breathing hard as she stared at him. "They told me never to say. That 'twould be my death to speak of it."

"Bravery can't be purchased," Jane said softly. "You must decide on your own if you wish to tell us."

Crispin bit back a protest. But Jane read it in his face, and gave him an adamant look. "It is *her* life," she said. "It does not come so cheap as ten thousand pounds, much less fifty. Which, I might add, you may keep regardless, madam."

"Kind," the widow said faintly. "But—no, I want to be done of it. It's been a curse on us." She dropped to her knees, rapping her knuckles on the floorboards until the sound turned hollow. Then, using her fingernails, she clawed up the edge of the board.

The sheet of paper she extracted was dank and smeared with dirt. Crispin unfolded it, revealing a clumsy jumble of lines.

"Baggie should've never sold the ring," the woman said, hushed. "Fancy piece, solid gold. Got a fine price, but it wasn't worth what it brought to us. I 'ad a fancy gown for my wedding, and a dead 'usband a month later."

"This is a drawing of a ring?" He wanted to be clear.

"The sign on it. That's right."

"And where did your husband get it?" Jane asked.

The woman's mouth twisted. "On the transport ship." She turned to spit into the fire. "Transported for what? Oh, 'e'd stolen, 'e'd thieved. But 'e never meant to strike that bobby."

"When was this?" Jane whispered.

"Three years ago." The widow's lips trembled. "Imagine that, three years . . ." She took a hard breath and continued. "Well, the point: they brought another man to take 'is place. Threw Baggie off the ship. But before it, the man slipped over the ring. Baggie fell right into the drink, barely knowing 'ow to swim. A miracle, 'e

called it—washed to shore, swapped out for a stranger."
A tear spilled, tracking through the soot on her cheek.
"A miracle, ha! Maybe 'e'd still be drawing breath if
they'd kept 'im a prisoner."

They did not speak until they were in the coach again.
Even then, the silence felt unbreakable, a great boulder
between them. Perhaps neither of them wanted to say it.

But at last, Jane held out her hand for the drawing,
to look it over once more. "This is heraldry," she said.
"A family crest."

"Yes."

"It was a signet ring."

He nodded once, his troubled gaze fixed firmly out
the window. "Jane," he said. His neutral tone was the
product, she sensed, of great inner discipline. "I want
you to go on holiday. To France, or New York. You
wanted to travel. This is your chance."

She laid down the soiled drawing. "You think my
uncle is right. That we aren't safe."

At last, he looked at her. His face was bleak. "I think
a signet ring generally denotes a man of some power. I
think a man of power does not find himself forcibly impressed, transported to a penal colony said not to exist,
unless his enemies have resources at their disposal that
they would not hesitate to aim more broadly."

A tremor passed through her. "So we'll find them before they find us," she said softly.

"With what clues?" He raked a hand through his
hair. "This was as far as the trail led. Besides . . . you
cannot help me in this."

"But I have done. I just did." She was angry suddenly.

After so much, he would discount her? "Don't condescend to me. This won't be a contest of brute force. We are using our wits, and mine haven't failed you yet."

His smile was bitter. "I cannot say what kind of contest it might yet become."

"Then hire guards. Show me how to use a gun. But I won't . . ." She hesitated, suddenly confused. Was escape not her plan all along? "I won't run away *from* this," she said slowly. "That wasn't what I dreamed of. That isn't . . . freedom."

"There are many degrees of freedom." His glance fell to the paper. "I expect one doesn't realize that until all of them are stripped away."

Here, at last, was the question that had weighted the silence. "Whose family does this belong to?" she whispered.

He shrugged. "The College of Arms will know."

At Whitehall, an hour later, the clerk took his time studying the sheet. But at last, his brow cleared, and with a triumphant smile he handed back the paper. Wiping his fingertips clean with a handkerchief, he said, "The Devaliant family. I have no doubt of it."

"I feel sure I've heard that name," Jane said to Crispin as they made their way back outside. "But long ago."

"Your uncle stopped having cause to mention it," Crispin said. "William Devaliant was once quite active in the House of Lords. But he grew fed up with the corruption. He married, I believe, and then he went traveling."

"Traveling?" She blinked. "It's been three years, Mrs. Shufflebottom said. What of his wife? She never reported his disappearance?"

"If so, it never reached my ears. And I imagine such news would have caught my attention."

"Crispin. Do you mean that *nobody* is looking for him?"

"As far as I can tell," he said, "no one on earth knows that the Earl of Lockwood is missing."

CHAPTER SEVENTEEN

*T*he Duke of Auburn lifted his glass of whisky to the light. He appeared lost in admiration. "A very fine year," he said. "A day is not complete without a taste, I think. Are you certain you won't have one?"

Crispin wanted his wits about him for this conversation. Auburn was legendarily deadly, a survivor of a massacre, which had broken something inside him. Sitting in this small library across from him felt akin to being caged with a panther. "No, thank you."

"Ah. Well, allow me to refresh my own."

Auburn rose, a tall, black-haired, broad-shouldered man whose green eyes made a startling contrast to the golden hue of his skin. His leanness, the athletic ease with which he moved, belied his apparent devotion to liquor. He was toying with Crispin—not for the first time, either. The duke was a powerful voice in the House of Lords, and had made a game, over the last few years, of frustrating bills that Crispin put forward with Mason.

Crispin could remember his own former animosity

for the man—a deep-seated irritation at Auburn's righteous, idealistic speeches; his fondness for lost causes; his inability to compromise. But Crispin had guarded his opinion closely, for only fools underestimated the duke. Crispin had witnessed it countless times: when heckled by opponents, Auburn returned setdowns masked in cool, exquisite courtesy, so that it took his enemies several minutes to realize they had been sliced to the gut.

But Crispin was no longer an enemy. Auburn knew this. Had he not realized so—had he misinterpreted the news of Crispin's about-face in the Commons—why, then Crispin would never have made it past the front door, much less been shown to this dark oaken library where Auburn had sat reading the newspaper.

"So," the duke said, returning to the maroon leather couch. They were both of an unusual height, and other men would have taken pains to sit tall, lest Crispin manage to look down his nose. Auburn, however, leaned back in his chair, crossing an ankle over his knee, unconcerned for the subtler strains of intimidation. "I was unaware," he said, "of your friendship with Lockwood."

Crispin had barely known the man. "I would not call us friends."

A sudden smile, which showed a hint of teeth. "Nor would he, of that I feel sure. However, as one who does enjoy his long-standing friendship, I assure you that his absence is not unusual."

"Three years now," Crispin said.

Auburn shrugged. "He was fed up with England."

"And is it like him to go so long without a word?"

Auburn laid his glass down. "Letters often go astray. Perhaps he wrote to me in India. You may recall there was something of a *disturbance* there recently. Why, your confederate Mr. Mason made quite a fuss over how to quell it. He favored bloodshed, I recall, and—what was his word? Oh yes." Auburn's lip curled. "A 'cleansing.'"

"I did not stand with him in that debate," Crispin said flatly. Even in his darkest hours, he'd had some standards. Mason had been pandering to popular sentiment, furious when Crispin had crossed him on the floor.

"I didn't take you for naïve," Auburn said. "We are judged by our friends, Mr. Burke."

Crispin's patience thinned. "I did not come here to be judged by you," he said bluntly. "But if you must do so, then judge me as you would Lockwood, for I am acting as a friend to him now. The man is not *traveling*. He was kidnapped and thrown onto a prison hulk bound for Australia."

Auburn blinked. Tipped his head. And then laughed, a low musical sound that held an edge of mockery. "What a marvelous imagination, Burke! You missed your true calling. The stage would have—"

"This is his crest, is it not?" Crispin shoved forward a copy he'd made of the drawing. "It was found in a hovel in Agar Town, in the possession of a widow whose husband was sentenced to transportation, but who was set free at the last moment when a stranger was put in his place. The stranger was wearing a ring with this design. Three years ago, Auburn."

With one fingertip, Auburn drew the paper close. A muscle leapt in his jaw. "This is a damned poor joke."

"I agree," Crispin said. "Whoever did this tried to

have me killed, and I much prefer my head in one piece."

"A drawing." Auburn flicked it back toward him. "This is your proof? Give me pen and paper, and I'll draw a man in the moon."

"There is more. I went by the docks this morning, and then to the Royal Exchange. The company that operated the transport ship no longer exists. The only record of its ownership traces to a privately held corporation, controlled through a trust. You have friends in the Home Office, Auburn—men who know how to prod and pry and chip away at secrets. I want to know who owned that company."

Auburn stared. The nearby fire caught his irises oddly, calling out gold striations within the green. The stare of a predator, unimpressed. "Dirty work," he said. "Now that Mason won't do it, you look for another way."

Crispin battled to keep his temper. "It is an implausible and ludicrous story. Do you not think I could have concocted a more credible tale? I gambled on your long friendship with Lockwood. But I am not disinterested myself. My wife will not be safe until I handle this."

"Nor will you, of course." Auburn spoke in a dry, ironic tone. "Don't forget that." But he picked up the paper again, studying it with a frown. "This is ridiculous," he said at last, mouth twisting as he cast it down. "I've no idea what scheme you're on—"

Enough. Crispin stood. "Every other transport in 1857 was granted to a single company under contract with the Crown," he bit out. "But their warehouses burned in May of that year. A single transport was given

to this company that has since become a ghost. Look
into that, and then decide how far you can trust me.
Good day, Auburn."

The morning room smelled like a hothouse. Every hour
brought more flowers, vase upon vase of chrysanthe-
mums, roses, hyacinth, and heliotrope. Each of these
was addressed to Mrs. Crispin Burke, sent by women
whose surnames Jane only knew from her uncle's contemptuous ranting. By breaking with his former cronies, Crispin had unwittingly invited the rest of the
Commons to lobby for his support. His wife would be
lobbied as well.

Jane sat on a stiff, overstuffed brocade settee, which
offered no comfort. She was staring at the piles of paper
on the table before her. On the left lay all the invitations
that had arrived in the post. On the right were a dozen
calling cards left by the wives and daughters of politicians.

And between these two piles lay a single sheet of
paper that the clerk had copied out with laborious
care.

The door stood closed. Crispin had gone out before
she'd woken. They had shared the same bed, last night,
but had touched only by accident. He was livid with her
for refusing to go abroad.

In the coach yesterday, en route to Agar Town, she
had misspoken somehow when condemning his former
self.

No, she had not misspoken. But he had taken her
judgment poorly. She had felt him withdrawing from
her, shuttering himself, retreating into a silence that the

smile on his mouth had cast as courteous, only his eyes telling the truth. She had hurt him.

She hadn't understood how. A day's reflection had not clarified her puzzlement. She worried every day, increasingly panicked, about the many ways she might hurt him. The possibilities crushed her as she ransacked her brain for some way out of this mess. A great mortal blow she could deliver him, if she told the whole truth. But she had comforted herself with the notion that he would be too enraged to be hurt. That the magnitude of her lie, once unveiled, would kill the affection between them.

Affection. That was too pale, too casual. She would not think the word that better fitted.

But the thought that somewhere in this great city, men had conspired to kill him . . . that they might try again . . . It made her wild with rage and fear combined. It was not their *right*. He was *hers*.

But he wasn't.

On a breath, she unfolded the sheet.

The clerk had not been surprised by her request. But he had probably wondered why she flushed, why her hands twisted together on the countertop as she spoke. Her heartbeat had counted out the moments it took him to disappear into the stacks. The sharp lurch in her chest had marked his return, the folder beneath his arm seeming ominous as an omen.

He'd unwrapped the twine with practiced efficiency. Drawn out the record. "All in order," he'd said briskly.

Yes. She was married in every way that mattered to the government. The archbishop's skills had indeed been flawless. This paper was the proof.

She smoothed her hands over the certificate. It was

freshly written, but no less official than the original. It bore the stamp, the clerk's signature, the seals of authority.

This marriage was real in all eyes save God's.

A tap came at the door. She startled, then hastily folded up the record and slipped it under the invitations. Cusworth stepped inside. "Mr. Gaultier, madam."

She rose, but the solicitor waved her back to her seat as he approached, wreathed in smiles, his round cheeks and bald skull shining. "I come with very good news," he said as he sat opposite her. No sense of drama, Mr. Gaultier. He produced the document without a flourish. "Your uncle had a change of heart, it seems. He provided his signature with no instruction from the court." On some less dignified man, his sudden, crooked smile might have resembled a smirk. "I cannot say with any certainty that this decision relates to his dinner with a certain judge at his club yesterday. But I do wonder if he might have been informed that his suit held no merit, and would result in a humiliating defeat—the second, I believe, that your husband would have delivered him recently. At any rate, here is a record of the transfer of funds. Your father may rest easy now, madam."

She looked at the document but did not take it in hand. The timing was too coincidental. She felt the weight of divine judgment pressing down from above. *Here is everything you wanted. At what cost will you accept it?*

Mr. Gaultier frowned. "Do you not wish to inspect it?"

"I trust everything is in order."

He nodded. "Two accounts, as the will specified. The other, I will deliver to your husband. But this one is solely accessible to you." He paused. "You might note the sum. Your father was most generous, madam. It represents a precise division of the total estate."

She could spot the number from here. An enormous fortune, hers alone.

"And a list of the stocks and bonds also so reserved." Mr. Gaultier added another sheet to the first.

"Thank you." What else was there to say?

"I thought these would be cheerful tidings," he said, his puzzlement showing.

"Oh, they are." How leaden she sounded.

He studied her a moment longer, his eyes sharp behind the winking lenses of his spectacles. "Mrs. Burke . . ." He made a thoughtful *hmm*. "I don't suppose you've read the newspapers this week?"

"Oh yes." She felt on surer ground suddenly. She would be glad to speak of Crispin's victory.

"It's a pity and a shame," said Mr. Gaultier, "that the journalists must look for notoriety where none is deserved. I think any Christian must feel for Mrs. Hewitt."

She blinked. "I beg your pardon? I'm afraid I don't follow."

"Ah. Perhaps you haven't followed the story. Well, I hate to speak of it, for it's a very sad tale. Mrs. Hewitt is an heiress, not quite so great a one as yourself, but she brought substantial properties into her marriage. Only too late, she discovered that her husband was not the man whom she had believed him to be. The courts, you know, have come to recognize the injustice of marital cruelties. Why, they prove quite generous. I believe Mrs. Hewitt has been granted full restitution of her moneys along with her divorce."

"How . . . marvelous," she said faintly.

Mr. Gaultier held her eyes. "It's a matter of having credible witnesses, you see. Gentlemen of good standing to testify to the indignities a wife has suffered, and the firmness of her moral character besides." He rose abruptly. "I am, as I have said, always at your service, Mrs. Burke. In memory of your father, I hope you will never hesitate to call on me, no matter the need." His color was rising as she stared at him. He swept her a deep bow and then showed himself out.

She sat for a long, frozen moment as his footsteps retreated. And then a strange laugh scraped out of her.

You weren't the devil, she'd told Crispin. She'd been right. For between the two of them, who found herself presented with a devil's bargain? Mr. Gaultier had just shown her the only options remaining.

First, to exploit the gullibility of the law and divorce Crispin, thereby keeping her money and her freedom.

Second, to tell him the truth and perhaps have her money sent straight back to her uncle. For what man, gulled into a marriage, would insist on remaining in it?

And the final option . . . to lie to him forever, and live as his wife.

Forever his wife. That phrase worked a spell on her. For a long minute, she stared unseeing at the sunlit room, lost in a fantasy that felt drugging, hypnotic. A happy-ever-after, so close within her reach.

But the fantasy would be based on a lie.

With her uncle, she had gladly been a liar. But with Crispin, forever?

She laid her palm over her belly, as though to press away the nausea that boiled there. *Bravery can't be purchased*, she'd told Mrs. Shufflebottom. So where, then, should one look for it?

            *   *   *

Crispin returned home barely in time to dress for dinner. He listened for Jane through the door connecting their rooms; he had left word with Cusworth to tell her of the evening's engagement. But when he knocked on the door to her apartment, she did not answer. He stepped inside and found it empty.

Unease prickled through him. The dressing table lay bare, save for a comb and a mirror. The small tea table by the window gleamed emptily in the fading light. The counterpane was unwrinkled, the air somehow stale. It had the look of a room abandoned, awaiting a new occupant.

He made his way downstairs goaded by a nameless panic—then stopped on the first flight. She was standing in the entry hall below, wrapped to her throat in a thick woolen cloak that seemed too heavy for the weather.

"There you are." His good cheer felt false, stilted. Matters between them had been strained since she stubbornly refused to remove herself to safety. She seemed offended, of all things, as though he doubted her ability to help him. It was infuriating. He would not apologize for ranking her safety more important than her assistance. "I looked for you in your room," he said.

She lifted her face, her wide eyes catching the light, glowing amber, unreadable. "Cusworth said we were due at your parents' house at eight. I've already sent for the carriage."

He took the remainder of the steps slowly, gathering impressions. The hem of her cloak revealed skirts of a dull gray. She held herself arrow straight, her expression impassive as she watched his approach. Holding on to the discomfort between them, which she might have let pass so easily.

He groped for an apology. But it was impossible to shape one. He had said nothing unkind to her yesterday. He had merely been . . . distant. And his pride balked at apologizing for his failure to be forever charming.

Instead, he offered his arm. She took it, walking outside with him into the cool of oncoming night. He had never realized how much could be communicated through touch, how much trust and warmth could travel through a hand simply laid over one's arm. But he felt the loss of it now. She held herself away from him. The space between their bodies felt vast.

The drive was brief. He wrestled with himself as the first street passed, and then the next. The side lamp swinging out the window brought her face into sharp clarity, then cast it back into shadow. Her jaw was squared. She resembled a victim mounting the block. He wondered if she had powdered her face, though it had never been her wont. She looked so pale.

"You're upset," he said. But she radiated a degree of distress too large to be explained by their recent disagreement.

"Not at all," she said coolly.

"Then something has happened to affect you."

"Many things have happened."

A more infuriatingly unrevealing reply he could not imagine. He bit his tongue and sat back. Their first proper quarrel as a married couple! He would take it as a chance to prove his patience to her. She would divest herself of her complaint in her own time.

"Mr. Gaultier paid a call today."

"Did he?" He sounded too eager, too grateful. He saw himself like a punished puppy, gladly bounding from the corner to lap up this token of forgiveness. His voice stiffened. "What brought him?"

"My uncle signed the papers. The funds have been transferred." She was studying the view, sitting very tall on her bench, her long neck bare and graceful. "I left the documents in your rooms."

He hadn't noticed them. "That's good news," he said cautiously.

The look she gave him then closed his throat. It was charged, fraught—entirely at odds with the smooth, blank composure of her brow and mouth. "Yes. So it is."

The carriage halted. He did not want to bring this mood inside with them. "Jane. I don't know what ails you. But for . . ." This favor felt very difficult to ask. "For my sake," he said, "please let us put on a happy face for my family."

The door started to open. He waved off the footman and waited.

She was studying him, her gaze moving slowly over his face. "You care what they think," she said very softly.

He felt . . . flayed, somehow, by the observation. Humiliated, as though it were an embarrassment to value his family's opinions of him.

For a very long time, he had pretended not to care. He had worked, in fact, to spite them, giving them no room to surprise him with their disapproval. He'd invited condemnation.

But no longer. It was a fool's game that yielded no victor. "I would like," he said on a deep breath, "to begin again with them."

She seemed to turn paler, which a moment ago he

would not have thought possible. "I didn't know . . ." She moistened her lips. "Did *you* arrange this dinner?"

"Yes. I had hoped . . ." He shrugged. "The opportunity is ripe."

"Opportunity?"

"To make amends," he said quietly.

"Amends." She seemed to think this over. "With your family."

"Yes. After the speech . . ." He caught himself before he shrugged again.

"Of course. Your speech, where you"—her mouth twisted—"*proved* yourself."

"Precisely."

She flinched. He didn't understand the cause. He reached for her, but she was gathering herself, rising and bending for the door, which swung open.

Charlotte was waiting for them in the front hall. The porter took Jane's cloak, uncovering a dull gray gown that no doubt made *him* flinch. He recognized it. He would not have thought it reparable after the abuse it had taken during her slog to the Cross Keys tavern on that night that he was not meant to remember. His glance dropped down her body, finding the stains only because he knew where to look for them.

This choice had been deliberate on her part—a private statement she did not expect him to understand. Nor did he understand it, even though he had more facts at his disposal than she could guess. When he met her eyes again, she was frowning at him.

He offered her a blinding smile.

She blinked, then returned it full force, a smile of such dazzling falsehood that even he, who knew it for a lie, felt himself dizzied. She was a beautiful woman when she chose to be. When she threw back her shoulders and lifted her chin and put her wide, rosy mouth and her enormous eyes to use, it made no difference that the gown she wore looked fit only for a maid.

"Charlotte," she said warmly, and took his sister into an embrace. Heads close together, they walked on toward the drawing room, leaving Crispin to dog after them, his gut tight and foreboding thick in his throat.

The rest of the family was already assembled, glasses of sherry in their hands. Very unusual. As Crispin stepped inside, Atticus pressed one upon him; his mother handed a glass to Jane. And then they all raised their tumblers.

"Well done," said his father.

"A sound routing," said Charlotte's husband. "No other subject at the club this week than Mason's face."

"Nor should there be," Atticus said jovially. "Man was apoplectic."

And then, amid laughter and congratulations, they all drank to him.

It was a peculiar thing, to suddenly find oneself thrust into the very scenario that one had dreamed of for years. To find his hand enfolded in his father's, in a stiff but sincere handshake. To be embraced by his mother and told in a whisper, "We are so proud of you, dear." To be clapped on the back by his brother-in-law, and receive Atticus's gruff, warm nod.

He looked for his wife and discovered her watching from a short remove, one arm crossed almost protectively over her body, the other lifting her sherry to her lips for a long, contemplative sip.

The color had come back into her cheeks. She looked flushed.

She looked furious.

She lowered her glass. "What a warm welcome we receive tonight," she said in a foreign, cutting voice.

The others turned—her mother with a frown, Charlotte still beaming.

"But of course," Charlotte said. "Do you know, it used to be a family tradition to have supper together every Sunday."

"So many traditions that the Burkes keep," Jane said flatly. "And Crispin, being a gentleman, endures them. But I will not. I am afraid, Lady Sibley, that I will wear out my welcome now. I see that this family has made such a habit of judging Mr. Burke that it sees no harm in praising him on that rare occasion when he pleases you. But I was raised differently, in a family that considered love to go hand in hand with loyalty, and did not portion out either of those qualities depending on whether they felt it deserved, any given Sunday."

His mother had made a noise of bewilderment and drew close to his father. His father, in turn, glowered at him. *Take her in hand*, that look said. *Control your wife.*

But Jane's gaze, which had swept the room, now found his. And he felt gripped by it. He did not control her. He would not wish to do so.

"My husband appears to have forgiven you," she said, staring at him. "Why, he thinks to forge a reconciliation."

"Forgiven us?" Lady Sibley gasped. "For what?"

"Young woman," his father bit out. "You are clearly unwell. If you—"

"Forgiven you," Jane said, "for any number of things. For having made him the scapegoat for a terrible acci-

dent. For having placed on him the burden of a haunting, so the rest of you would be spared. For becoming
the figure who allowed you to warp grief into accusation. For having discounted him, doubted him, and
abandoned him. And now, you congratulate him? You
cheer him for showing himself other than he once was?
What he *was*, what he *became*, was no less your doing
than his. You don't cheer because he's proved himself.
You cheer because he grew into an honorable man despite all the injuries you did to him. You cheer for the
alleviation of your guilt."

Her glass clicked against the marble top of the side-
board. She bowed deeply.

"I bid you good night," she said, and swept from the
room.

"Crispin, what in God's name—"

He ran after her. Caught her by the door as she
waited for the startled porter to fetch back her cloak.
"Jane. What—"

She turned to him. Tears glistened on her cheeks.
"Go back there. Make them grovel for you."

"What on earth?" He caught her by both wrists when
she tried to pull away. "Grovel? Jane—"

"All right, perhaps that's not what *you* want," she said
angrily. "It's only a story to you, not a memory. But it's
what he deserves, Crispin. If he deserves anything, it's
an apology—from your father, and the rest of them besides. Go take it for his sake."

For *his* sake.

Shock loosened his grip. She was speaking of the man
she thought he'd forgotten. Fighting on *that* man's behalf.

The foreboding, the shock, the crushing pressure

of the unsaid—it had weighed on him all day, but it collapsed now, subsumed by a great dawning hope. "I am coming with you," he said as she shrugged into her cloak.

"No." She yanked the cloak closed at her throat. "Listen carefully: if you care for me, you will go back in there. You want a fresh start? Then settle the old accounts." Something bleak moved over her face, flattening her mouth. "Then come home," she said dully. "I will be waiting. There are accounts to settle there, too."

CHAPTER EIGHTEEN

*I*n Jane's childhood, her father had liked to lie
with her on the balcony at night, showing her
the constellations. She had pretended to see the ani-
mals and figures he described; she had memorized
their names for his approval. But it hadn't been until
after his death, when she'd moved to the remoteness of
Marylebigh, that she finally understood how ancient
peoples saw pictures in the stars. At Marylebigh, even
on a moonless night, it was never truly dark. Countless stars glimmered and streaked overhead. By the pale
broad light of the Milky Way, one could make her way
through midnight fields.

In London, the stars offered no help. They had
abandoned the city, retreating behind a sky made half
of clouds and half of smoke. A great city wheezing out
its congestion. At Marylebigh, she had imagined this
would be the place where she could finally draw a full
and free breath, but she'd been wrong.

There must be a place. How she had hungered once to
find it. *Possibility*, she'd told Crispin; that had been what

drove her. But standing here on this cramped balcony, she could no longer locate her wonder or hope. The glamour of distant places, the lure of perfect freedom— she felt numb to them. If she did manage to find herself aboard a ship sailing for the sunset, she feared she would carry this numbness with her, or worse. She could no longer dream of a voyage without him at her side. Even if he was good enough to provide her a chance of escape, she would no longer be running to freedom. She would simply be leaving him behind.

"Here you are."

She inched to one side so Crispin could step out to join her. An hour had not passed since her return. Had her outburst been in vain, then? She would not regret it, either way. It had hurt her to speak harshly to people who had been nothing but kind to her. But their kindness had become an unbearable hypocrisy, the more unjust for all the times they had denied it to him.

He seemed content to stand beside her, breathing the night air. Spring was fully upon them now, all the flowers in bloom. But their novelty had worn off. She could no longer smell them. "So?" she asked at last.

"So." His hand found hers. She did not have the will to pull away. Not yet, at least. "You're a fearsome woman in a temper."

"I take after my mother that way."

"I would have liked to know her."

The darkness above offered no features to admire. So she stared fixedly into the darkness below, the square terraced garden where the kitchen staff grew herbs. "She was clever, and witty, and a great collector of jokes. She was my father's fiercest champion; he had not been raised to expect greatness of himself. He would have remained a businessman, I think, had it not been for her. All her charities—she did not take them as lightly as a lady should. She wept for the people she couldn't help. And she railed at the injustice of it. And she infected him with her passion, and gradually she persuaded him to do what she couldn't."

He lifted her hand. She felt his mouth in the dark, warm against her knuckles. "So the blood runs true."

She drew a ragged breath. "My mother never lied, though."

He turned toward her. She could not make out his face, only the silhouette of him. But perhaps he saw better in the dark. He hooked a curl away from her cheek, the movement unbearably tender. "Shall we go inside?" he asked. "Or shall we settle it here?"

"In the dark," she said roughly, "would be easier."

"But you've never taken the easy way." The faint sound that escaped him sounded like a laugh. "The scene you left behind . . . the clamor they made. The confusion, the protests . . . and then my sister speaking out. 'Well, she is right,' she said. 'And if you all won't admit to it, then Richard and I will walk out, too.'"

Her breath caught. Bless Charlotte. "And then?"

"And then . . . tears from my mother. My father tried to steady her, but she wouldn't have it. She turned on him as you had turned on her. The very same tone, in fact. Telling him that they had much to account for. And then . . ." A kiss on her brow now. "Apologies, Jane."

"Oh." Her eyes closed. "That is . . . good. But not enough."

"A start," he murmured. "Exactly what I wanted. I didn't know, until I heard my father admit to his failings, to . . . apologize for not having routed Farnsworth . . . how much I needed to hear it."

Her last chance. No additional harm could be done, surely. She put her arms around him and hugged him tightly.

He embraced her in turn, pulling her so hard against him that her breath wheezed. *Harder*, she thought. *Crush me, imprint me with you.*

But then he eased back. "Come inside with me now."

Nerves jumped in her stomach. She stepped inside her bedroom quickly, walking ahead of him, pacing to the bed, bending to reach under the mattress.

"Here," she said as she turned, holding out the marriage certificate.

"Is this what you wanted from the General Register?"

"Yes." *Say it.* "It's fake."

His brows lifted as he took it. He glanced from the sheet back to her. "Indeed? A forger for a clerk?" His tone balanced carefully between humor and puzzlement. "He didn't look the type."

"The forger was the late archbishop whose demise Mr. Gaultier informed us of. He drew up the marriage record. You never proposed to me, Crispin. We were never truly wed."

He took a breath as though to speak, then blinked and sat down. She locked her hands together at her mouth, ground her knuckles into her lips, and braced herself through pain.

They stared at each other.

"Well," he said at length. "This, I hadn't guessed."

His next pause seemed to last forever. She could not move, could not breathe.

He lifted the certificate, tilting it toward the light of a nearby sconce. "Remarkable," he murmured. "I didn't know he was quite so good as that."

Confusion weltered through her. "He?" She had imagined this moment so often. Had anticipated his disbelief and then his rage. Had rehearsed her own defenses. But it was not going to plan. She stumbled over her next words. "He, the archbishop?"

"I doubt anyone else could have managed it." How dry he sounded!

"You—you knew that he made false marriage lines? Five years ago, you knew?"

His gaze concentrated on her with a hawklike sharpness. "Better to ask what I knew even yesterday. The woman you are, Jane—you never would have married the man I was. And that man—he would never have married you."

Concise truth, coolly spoken. It smarted regardless. She should feel grateful that he remained so calm. Instead, tears pricked her eyes. "I might have married you," she said dully as she sank onto the bed. "To escape my uncle, I might have done anything."

"Balderdash." He leaned back in his chair, kicking his feet out and crossing them at the ankles. The casual posture, his conspicuous ease, felt grotesque, somehow mocking. "Since you began this conversation so truthfully, you may as well see it through the same way. Let me guess how it went: you heard that I'd been attacked and was not expected to live. You saw the chance to solve your problem: you would marry a dead man."

"You cannot be so calm," she whispered.

He flashed her a horrible grin. "Oh, I'm not calm. If you could take the measure of my pulse right now, you'd send for a doctor. But—bloody hell, Jane, what is there to do?" His laughter sounded wild. "The archbishop is dead and the government calls you my wife. Who's to disprove it now?"

She recognized the cutting edge in his voice. It belonged to Mr. Burke. "*You* can disprove it."

"Oh, yes, a fine idea. After managing to hide the injury to my brain, I will have it announced in three-inch headlines."

She was angry now. "Is that all? It's a scandal you fear? A divorce will be scandal enough! And Mr. Gaultier will ensure that *you* look the guilty party—"

He rose with such sudden, athletic force that she shrank back on the bed. Seeing her recoil, he twisted his mouth.

"It is not the scandal," he said darkly, "that concerns me. It is your continued need for a villain. If it can't be me—why then, it must be you. You didn't tell me this news hoping I might understand your deception. You don't want my understanding, or my forgiveness, either. No, you were hoping for my anger. That . . ." He paused, clawing a hand through his hair. "Why, *that* is why you had it out with my family tonight. Your final tribute, before I shoved you off. Oh, you wouldn't leave when I wanted you safe—that would be too messy. You wanted a clean break, and *me* to cause it." He swore. "*Divorce*, Jane? Have you already hired Gaultier to file the suit?"

"No," she cried, and then, with a forced false laugh, "Listen to your nonsense! To divorce, we would first have to marry. And the moment you recover your memory—"

"Oh, to hell with that." He came prowling toward

her with a look that should have alarmed her but sank hooks into her belly and tugged. "You should be grateful to that man. The man you think I was—the man you fear I'll become again—was *precisely* the man you needed."

She threw herself to her feet. "You don't—"

"Do you imagine that forgeries are sold on the open market, easy to buy as eggs? Or that you would have found some boy in a ballroom able to outwit your uncle? You needed me. *Him*."

She swung around the bed, putting the mattress between them. "What of it? He was—"

"You exploited him, Jane, as much as he did you. What makes you so afraid? That *he* will return? Or that you might realize you're more like him than your conscience can bear? If he was a villain, what were you?"

She opened her mouth. But the wind felt knocked from her.

He gripped the bedpost, staring at her. "Oh, you had good cause to dislike him," he said with terrible patience. "But this loathing you claim to feel for him? It grows tedious. It grows *suspect*. It's useful to you, somehow. It makes a salve for your conscience, a justification for having gulled him. But no matter the reason, you *used* him. He wanted power. You wanted freedom. Both of you did whatever it took."

She shook her head. "I—that's not—"

"And as for me," he said forcefully, "the man before you now—you want to see me as the innocent victim, the very opposite of *him*. But you're wrong. He and I are one and the same. That is the *other* truth you don't wish to admit. That is why you keep insisting that all will change once I remember. Because if it doesn't, Jane—then you'll be forced to see that there is far less difference between him and me than you want to believe."

Her cheeks were stinging. She had braced for his rage, but this was worse. This offered no punishment, and no chance of atonement, either. He laid her bare to herself, in a few devastating words.

"Here is something else. Neither of us, he or I"—he offered her a brief, unpleasant smile—"has any intention of divorcing you. Or of accusing you of fraud. Or of mistreating you, abandoning you, or whatever your fearful brain has fancied. You, Jane, are the wife I want. And a fine thing." He crushed the paper and tossed it onto the carpet. "For the law says you are the wife I have."

She kicked the paper. "You are full of talk!" she screamed. "But talk all you like—*I know you!* And yes, you were a villain—but a villain I owe *this* much: to be free of me, once you remember!"

He seized her wrist and yanked her against him. "I remember."

Her heart was drumming. She could barely hear through the rush of blood. "Wh-what?"

"You heard what I said." His thumb stroked forcefully over her cheek, angled her face toward his. "You're simply amazed that I haven't sprouted scales and horns to announce it." He gripped her chin. "Look at me. Men can change. Especially when fate intervenes and gives them a reason to do it. I am the man I am, in this moment, because of you. Not because of a head injury. And not . . ." His jaw flexed. "Not because I can't remember otherwise. I remember it all, Jane. Barring the days before the attack."

"What—how—" Her mouth had come unhinged from her brain. "*When?*"

"Three nights ago. When I woke beside you."

And he had not told her!

Her vision contracted. He had remembered, and said nothing of it. He had sat across from her and asked her to explain Elland to him. Then, in the coach, he had asked her to look kindly on that other man he had been—

That man who was *him*.

She recoiled. He grabbed hold of her again. "Listen to me," he said sharply, but she shoved him, broke free.

"What a great joke you made of me!" Her voice felt like an animal twisting from her throat. So much for respect. So much for trust! "Asking me if you might not have *improved* in time—" No wonder her answer had wounded him!

A pulse beat in his temple. "It was a fair question. Although I disliked the reply intensely."

She stared at him, some great tumult of emotion quaking through her, making her tremble. His face was still beautiful, unchanged by his recovery. But those lips could cut now, for they had remembered their old smiles. His mouth could turn brutal. She remembered that first, awful kiss.

"Need no one, trust no one," she whispered. "That's who you are. You are toying with me. You'll grow sick of me soon."

His expression turned stony. "You admired that advice. You followed it yourself."

She flinched. "We are nothing alike."

"Liar," he said. "Or is it cowardice?"

"Oh yes, I'm a liar indeed!" She swallowed. "Both of

us, liars. No trust at all. What a fine basis for marriage!"

He reached for her, but she shied away. His jaw tightened. "There is trust here," he said. "I trust you."

She scoffed. If he truly trusted her, he would have told her instantly when he remembered. Only one fact would have made her believe he was truly changed. "Did you remember everything before you disowned your bill in the Commons? No!"

"I remembered," he said fiercely, "before you sat in on my meetings to offer political counsel. I remembered when I arranged for the dinner with my family tonight. Had I *not* remembered, Jane, would those acts have meant more? They would only have proved something about who I was *not*. Instead, they show you who I am, now and here."

"What a pair we make," she whispered. Lies upon lies. "I—" She could not think clearly with him in the room. "I am going." She needed time to think. "I need to be—" Elsewhere. *Safe*.

But from whom? The conspiracy shadowing this man? Or the man himself?

"I have to go," she said.

His hands had made fists. But he said neutrally, "Of course. Charlotte, I am sure, would be glad to host you."

CHAPTER NINETEEN

$\mathcal{C}$harlotte proved remarkably tolerant of being interrupted at half past ten by two people whose icy silence seemed to frost her foyer. She was glad to host Jane for the night; it would be delightful, in fact. She showed Jane to a handsome bedroom done up in yellow silk, rang for hot milk and more pillows, and then pretended to leave before turning back at the door.

"I hope you don't mind my asking. Is everything all right between you and Crispin?"

Jane had settled onto a pale settee by the window with a book. "The speech in the Commons set off a furor," she said. "It's become a perfect madhouse over there, what with all the constituents and hangers-on and the reporters . . . I hope my presence here doesn't pose an inconvenience to you."

Charlotte sank down beside her in a draft of warm air and spiced perfume. Her smile was soft, her regard inquisitive and curious. "You're family, Jane. And whether you believe it or not, our parents did raise us with a great loyalty to family. I don't know how Crispin became the scapegoat for so long, but I do know we're in great debt to you for forcing us to see it squarely."

"I doubt Lord and Lady Sibley feel so grateful for it." She had wrecked her chance to have a family again, one that reminded her of her own.

"Oh no!" Charlotte squeezed her hand. "They do feel grateful to you. If they were staying in town, you'd know it by tomorrow, from their very own mouths. But they mean to go to Chestleigh for a few days." She cleared her throat. "That is where it happened, you know. And where Jonathan is buried."

Her miserable anger shifted, now all for Crispin instead of herself. "So once again, they place a ghost above their living son."

"I think they go to lay that ghost to rest," Charlotte said after a moment. "You didn't stay, you didn't see their faces . . . Things will be different now between them and Crispin."

"That decision isn't entirely theirs. Crispin was on the heels of victory, feeling generous." But he was a man who never forgot a word spoken to him, much less a slight. Her uncle had always said so. Crispin Burke had mastered the art of a grudge. He'd lost faith in her uncle after the parliamentary debates about the uprising; thereafter, she saw now, it had only been a waiting game, as Mr. Burke looked for a way to declaw him. Elland had been his weapon.

Crispin Burke did not forget or forgive. It wasn't in his nature. That he'd lied to her about remembering was the proof of it.

Eventually, like his triumph in the Commons, his passion for her would wear off as well. And then he would come to dwell on the wrong she had done him. It would appear in a new light to him—the original sin that explained his growing discontent with her. He would begin to look for a way to punish her for it. It would not take any secret as dark as Elland, either. Somewhere along the way, she had lost her defenses against him. He would crush her so easily.

He would stop asking her counsel on politics.

He would stop caring what she dreamed about.

He would lose patience with her ambitions.

But she would be destroyed long beforehand. All it would take was his first show of contempt.

"Your brother won't forget their old treatment," she said.

"What a cynic you are," Charlotte murmured.

Mr. Burke had said something similar once. Jane had discounted his remark. But maybe he'd been right.

"I have seen very few happy endings in this world." Not the world of her parents, but of polite society, of power.

So leave it. Board a ship, find another place to belong. That was the solution. Why was she hesitating? Why was she here, rather than at a hotel?

She could go now. She had the means to stay anywhere she liked. The Carlyle, even. But as she gathered herself—slowly, her muscles feeling rusted—Charlotte made a soft, exasperated sound and stood.

"Sometimes I wonder if you know my brother."

Jane gaped. "Sometimes I wonder if *you* do."

Charlotte's jaw squared. "Only since I was born, Mrs. Burke."

Jane felt obscurely stung. "And through the last five years? Did you know him on the nights he came to visit my uncle, to lay plots in the parlor at Marylebigh? Or were those five years before his . . . change . . . simply an aberration, to be discounted entirely now that he once again suits your tastes?"

"How you talk about him sometimes! As though you loathed him!"

They stared at each other, Charlotte clearly waiting for a denial. But Jane felt too stubborn to offer one.

"I knew him then, too," Charlotte said at last, forcefully. "I knew him when my first fiancé jilted me, almost at the altar. He was the only one who didn't ask what *I* had done to cause it. He said, 'I'll handle the bastard, if you like.' He said, 'There's no cause to go hiding in the countryside. Come stay with me if you don't wish to go to Chestleigh.' He said, 'Why should the whispers even touch you? Hold your head high, Lottie, so high that you no longer notice the jackals sniping below.' He has always been a brother to me, Jane—the brother I turned to when I needed help, when I needed comfort, when I needed *courage*. Do you think I was *glad* to see him so changed? Confused and not himself? I mourned for him. But I *was* glad to see him happy after so long. I thought *you* were the cause for that. That alone was the silver lining, but it was more than enough for me. All I've ever wanted was someone to be as good to him as he has been to me."

No speech could have been more expertly designed to shame her. Worse, Jane could not disbelieve it. Everything Charlotte said matched the man she had come to know in recent weeks.

But not the man who had lied to her. "I am not that woman," Jane said softly. Why, she was not even the woman whom her parents had raised her to become.

Crispin was right: she was as much a liar as he. Why should *he* trust her?

But for some reason, he did.

"Perhaps you aren't that woman." Charlotte paused, making a cool, thoughtful study of her. "Or perhaps, despite your brave words to my parents, you've forgotten what love and loyalty look like. They aren't sacraments, Jane, for only God is perfect, only God deserves our love without judgment. Men—women—we make mistakes. We judge those we love. But we keep loving them anyway, because we know that mistakes can be repaired, and that tomorrow, our love will be deserved again. It only takes faith—or loyalty, as you called it. Those *are* what tie a family together, through thick and thin. And they tie a husband and wife together, too. There is no happy ending, you're right—not in the singular. But in a marriage, there might be countless happy endings and even more sweet beginnings, if loyalty and love are what guide you."

Jane felt tears prick her eyes. She ducked her head, but Charlotte sank down and embraced her, so generous even in her frustration.

But then, Charlotte imagined her to be family. She was offering loyalty and love, regardless of whether or not they were deserved.

"Why are you crying?" Charlotte asked very softly as she rubbed Jane's back.

Jane took a deep breath. Was her imagination failing her, or did Charlotte wear the same perfume that her mother had favored?

Perhaps every person on this earth was haunted by something, but the haunting did not always have to be a curse.

"I feel . . ." Her voice broke. *I feel my mother here.* No doubt this was a speech her mother would have given, had she survived.

Her parents had loved each other deeply and intensely. But Charlotte was right: they had been human, too. Jane could remember their disagreements, their sharp looks and quarreling nights. And she could remember just as clearly their forgiveness, their fondness, their tenderness, as together they found a path back toward each other.

"I'm sorry," Charlotte said as she eased away. "I shouldn't have said such things. I didn't mean to upset you. Or . . . perhaps I did," she confessed with a sheepish laugh. "Only I see you and Crispin together, and I hope so much that . . ." She wiped Jane's cheeks, her face solemn. "I hope for both of you to be happy."

Jane kissed her cheek. "Thank you." Her voice was ragged. "No woman could wish for a better sister, Charlotte."

Blushing, Charlotte rose. "Well, you say so now. But you will mean it once you've tried my cook's morning chocolate."

They both laughed, an effortful but kind sound. And then Charlotte stepped back. "I'll let you sleep," she said. "I hope you dream sweetly, Jane."

Crispin rapped the knocker again, his impatience mounting, fueled by anxiety. If Charlotte's servants were such laggards, then he could not trust them in any regard. But if he hired guards to stand watch outside this house, Jane would no doubt misinterpret it as an enemy surveillance. She had made clear that when she looked at him now, she saw only the man he'd once been.

To hell with it. He would hire guards and let her stew.

The morning sun was hot on his back. He rapped with his fist now. At last, the door swung open. He pushed past Charlotte's butler and found his sister hurrying into the hall.

"Is she still here?" he asked.

"Of course," said Charlotte, giving him a wondering look. "Where else should she be?" Her mouth tightened. "Well, aside from your house, of course—"

"It's good that she's here." He'd had a visitor before noon. Auburn had made inquiries. He was persuaded. "Where is she?"

"In the library." Charlotte turned in that direction, but he was already striding ahead; this was his sister's house, he would not stand on ceremony.

Jane was sitting at the middle of the large table that filled the center of the library, a magnifying glass in one hand, a fountain pen in the other. He locked the door; she did not seem to hear. Charlotte's husband had a hobby of designing buildings; the table had been crafted to hold three unrolled blueprints side by side. The entirety of its broad, flat surface was covered in newspapers. Great stacks of them sat piled in the chairs on either side of her. She was taking notes as she moved the magnifying glass down the page.

She did not look up until he stood opposite her. Even then, her absorbed expression barely flickered. "I had these ordered from the office of the *Times*," she said, as though continuing an ongoing conversation. "This business . . . Crispin, I don't think Lockwood and Clark and Smith are the end of it. I know warehouses burn with regularity, but it's not simply that—every year, some disaster has befallen the fleet in such a way that another company was forced to provide a substitute vessel. It only happens once or twice in every year, but the timing always aligns with a shipment of prisoners. The trick is, it's never the same company . . ."

"I know." He sat down across from her. "A dozen or more corporations, each of them registered to a ghost. Jane, I did not want you looking into this. Tell me you didn't fetch these records yourself."

She waved aside this question. "This ghost," she said briskly. "Have you made inquiries at the Exchange? If any of these companies were publicly traded—"

"They weren't." He saw how she wanted it to go between them, impersonal and businesslike. Well, for the moment, he would play along. "I met again with Auburn this morning. The man behind those companies, all of them, is Patrick Burton." He paused. "Burton's wife reported his disappearance to the police the morning after my attack."

"Oh," she whispered. A softness flickered over her face. After a moment, she reached for his hand, but he withdrew it. Her pity was not what he wanted.

"I don't remember killing the man," he said flatly. "It won't keep me awake at night."

An awkward silence followed. She pulled her hand out of sight, into her lap, and looked down.

He blew out a breath. "The point is this: Burton worked as a dockhand for the Bastland Shipping Corporation. But not regularly, and not well. He was let go after several warnings. His employer said he seemed to show no care for his living, but always had a spare coin for a drink, which he spread very freely. 'A bad influence on the others,' the man called him. So where did the money come from?"

She shook her head. "A dockhand would not have had the means to organize this kind of plot."

"Precisely. Burton's widow told the police that her husband had fallen on hard times. That before they married, he'd been in the employ of a great man."

"Who is?" she whispered.

"Not your uncle."

Her reaction was curious. She sighed, her disappointment plain. "Oh, well."

He smiled despite himself. "Bloodthirsty, aren't you?"

She went pale. And then, haltingly, she said, "Yes. I am. I can be. You were right, last night. I'm no saint. I am . . . flawed."

He took a sharp breath, restraining every predatory instinct that wished to leap on that small admission, to exploit it and turn it to his advantage. He would not manipulate her. Honesty would have to serve. "I do not want a saint, Jane. I want you. All of you. Your flaws as much as your virtues."

She bowed her head. She had combed her hair into a viciously tight chignon. He fisted his hand against the urge to fix that atrocity, to pluck out all her pins.

"A less flawed woman," he said, "would be married to your cousin by now."

"I know," she said, very low. "And had you been a less flawed man, I might have had to marry him, regardless. I am . . . indebted to your flaws, Crispin."

He loosed a slow breath, willing her to look at him.

She cleared her throat. "Well. It would have been easier if it were my uncle behind this plot. Neater." She glanced up. "Who was it, then?"

Very well, he could bide his time. He would not push her just yet. "When your uncle lost your father's old seat, he was invited to campaign for a different district—by one Daniel Marlowe."

"The inventor?"

He hesitated. "You know him?"

She grimaced. "He made the most horrible toys for Archibald."

"He also made a fortune with inventions for the military—first in field technologies like the chronometer, then, more recently, smokeless powders and weapons. The Crimean War solidified his fortune. But in the aftermath, if you recall, Britain was weary of war. Aggressive expansionism lost favor. And so, in your uncle, Marlowe spotted a natural ally; Mason has never hesitated to propose the military as the solution to every problem."

"My uncle's opponent in that campaign was said to have run off with a lover," Jane said softly.

"Yes. More damning yet is the fact that our itinerant dockhand once worked on Marlowe's yachts. So there is the connection."

"That's enough, then," she said. "To have Marlowe arrested. Surely, with the proof—"

"Burton is dead," Crispin said. "The evidence is circumstantial at best. More to the point, we have no way to know who else Marlowe disappeared. As you say, he's been at this for some time. He would have no cause to confess anything."

"So . . . what?"

"So Auburn and I mean to make him talk."

She looked troubled. "How?"

He stared at her. "I think you know how."

"Don't underestimate him. If my own uncle was afraid—"

"He keeps a townhouse on Park Lane, pretensions to civility. It won't require storming a castle." He allowed himself a smirk. "No matter what he calls it."

"I don't know," she said slowly. "Surely this is what the police are for. Even if the evidence is only circumstantial—"

"Is this concern?" He paused deliberately. "For the villain, Jane?"

She recoiled. "That's unfair."

"You really must make up your mind," he said. "One moment fearing me—the next fearing *for* me. Which is it to be?"

"I never feared you."

"Sorry. Loathed me."

"I didn't loathe you."

"Did the amnesia prove catching? Or are you inventing a new history?"

"Stop it."

"No, I'm quite curious. You clearly felt unsafe sharing a roof with me. What was the cause, if not fear or hatred?"

"Confusion," she whispered.

A dark, calculating pleasure ran through him. Yes, that was what he wanted to hear. But he kept his voice pleasant, bland. "Ah. Confusion, is it? Perhaps I can help with that."

"No, I don't think you can." She hesitated. "The confusion is . . . all in me, Crispin."

"Yes, that I know." He was not confused at all. He wanted her. He wanted to keep her. He had said so. "My own mind is clear. That makes me a fine teacher in this matter." He rose, and she flinched backward, her hands locking on the arms of her chairs. "Unless you mean to run away from me again?" he asked lightly. "I thought you weren't afraid."

"I'm not," she said tightly. "But I don't know what you can teach me."

He stepped around the table toward her. "No student ever does until she's shown."

Some part of her was not surprised. Some part of her had noticed the click of the lock as he'd stepped inside, and had been waiting to discover what he intended to do with their privacy.

A very large part of her, in fact, wished only to be persuaded. No, more than that: *decided for.*

He set her against the wall very gently. Held her there, studying her, his fingers flexed on her upper arms, as though straining to break free of the inner restraint that disciplined them. He was not hiding his intentions now; had he not told her that he'd remembered, she would have known it with one glance. She recognized the calculating look he wore as he studied her.

She lifted her chin and stared back at him. "This won't help," she said. "This is a lesson I already know." Their bodies, together, made a kind of sense that bypassed logic. But it offered no answers to her doubts.

"You don't look afraid," he murmured. "So you spoke the truth about that, at least."

"I am done lying to you." But there was a breathless note in her voice that made her wonder. The closeness of his body against hers, the warmth of it, was speaking to her. Drawing her skin tight. She could say she did not want this. But that *would* be a lie.

"So there is some small measure of trust," he said. "And will you trust me in this?" He leaned forward, and as his hair brushed her cheek her eyes closed of their own volition. So lightly he kissed her ear. "Yes?" he asked, very low.

She bit her lip. She would not answer him. Trust had nothing to do with this—the sudden hollowness in her stomach as he nuzzled the tender spot hidden beneath her ear, the feathery brush of his mouth down her neck. This was need, not trust. He had already taught her about hunger, she had learned that lesson thoroughly. Had she ever denied it?

But when his hand slipped over her breast, she moaned.

"Do you trust me to do this?" he whispered, his clever fingers sliding beneath her neckline. Dipping inside to find her nipple, which he thumbed lightly, almost casually, toying with her as his mouth came back to her ear.

She screwed her eyes shut more tightly. Some stubbornness like a knot drew taut in her chest. It felt like resentment for him—for pushing the question on her like this. And resentment for herself—because she could break away in a moment, and she didn't want to.

"So quiet." His voice was husky, hypnotic. "Could it be you don't wish to argue?" His hand smoothed down her body, over her hips; she felt cool air on her ankles as he began to lift her skirts. So few of them to lift: she had not expected company. She was not armed against him.

Perhaps she had expected him, after all.

His hand slipped around the back of her thigh.

Palmed between her legs. She shuddered, her knees giving way.

He caught her by the waist. His mouth came into her hair; she felt his deep breath. "And you trust me to hold you."

"Yes." The admission slipped from her. It was only the truth. But she felt its effect on him; the almost imperceptible pause, the coiled tension releasing.

"Well, then," he whispered. "That's a start."

He lifted her. She fought the urge to open her eyes, to look out for where he carried her. Yes, here was trust: she knew she would land softly.

A solid surface—the crackle of newspaper as he laid her back onto the table. Cold air on her calves. He hooked his hands behind her knees, urging them apart, then stepped between her thighs, coming hard against her. Her body answered, arching into his, finding anchor against the hard solid length of him as he bent down over her and opened her mouth with his lips.

She would not push him away. The revelation, inevitable, snapped some leash inside her. She wrapped her arms around him and dragged him against her, crushing his lips, devouring his mouth.

It was never she in danger of leaving. That was the real lie, the one she had continued to tell herself. It was he who would go—if not today, then eventually. Did he not see that? There was nothing to hold him but this.

This was enough, though, was it not?

What *would* be enough, if not this?

Love does not last. Life steals it away. Had she not learned that when her parents died?

The thought startled her. It awoke some animal desperation. Her hands made claws, raking down his back. Closed over the bunching muscled power of his buttocks. She could hold him right now, force him harder against her.

He growled into her mouth, nipped at her, licked her. When he started to ease away—to move down her body—she felt panicked. She pulled him back to her and reached between their bodies, fumbling for him. He would not go anywhere *now*.

He caught her hands, his kiss gentling. Flavored perhaps by puzzlement. He drew back from her, and no, she did not recognize his face at all now; she had never seen this man clearly before, save in her dreams. It was a face worth risking everything for—even bottomless, soul-eating grief. His dark beauty took her breath away. Hard, sharp bones, a mouth so much softer than it looked. This was the face in her old dreams, before she'd had cause to long for him. Beauty's terrible power, she'd decided, but that wasn't right. The miracle of intuition: her dreams had found him worthy.

Worth any risk.

"Do you trust me?" he asked very softly.

Faith did not require reasons at every moment of the day. Faith was a great leap, regardless of the possible cost.

"I trust you," she said.

He loosed a long breath and then bowed his head. Watching his own thumb trace her lips. Grave, sober mien. A man beholding a charge that he intended to keep.

He leaned down to kiss her mouth. A strange, solemn kiss, less passionate than ceremonial. But then she moved against him, and he made a noise in his throat, and she put her tongue in his mouth and he came against her below, hot bare flesh, and she twisted her hips and he pushed inside her.

Nothing careful, nothing measured or calculated. Raw, fierce force. She met him stroke for stroke, her fingers digging into his back, using his strength to lift herself against him, no space between their bodies.

Neither of them cried out. The silence felt charged by pleasure, pulsing with it. Afterward, they held each other, skin against skin, breathing together.

"Tonight," he said at long last, as his palm ghosted delicately over her hair, her shoulder, her waist, "after all of this is done, you'll come home with me."

"Home with you," she whispered. It felt hopeful, like a prayer.

"Castle." Jane sat straight. Something about a castle.

"What's that?" Charlotte looked up from pouring the tea. She'd been in a marvelous cheeky mood all afternoon, as though she knew precisely what had happened in her library. Crispin had told her that he would be back for Jane in the evening, and Charlotte had made a game for the last few hours of guessing how he'd won her back. "I saw no flowers. Hmm . . . no new jewelry, either . . . However did he persuade you?"

But while it was a delightful feeling to be teased like a sister, Jane's own blissful mood had slowly eroded as the hours drew onward. Something was niggling at her . . . something that Crispin had said before . . .

"Is there a castle," she asked now, accepting the teacup and then laying it distractedly aside, "on Park Lane?"

"Goodness, no." Charlotte's head tipped. "Whyever would you ask?"

What had Crispin said, exactly? *It won't require storming a castle . . .*

A common expression. Why did it stick in her brain like a burr?

"Is the tea too bitter?" Charlotte asked. "I fear I let it steep too long."

"Oh no. I'm sure it's fine." Jane retrieved her cup. It was only natural that she would feel uneasy. Crispin was going to confront a man capable of organizing a long-lived and very dangerous plot. A man, moreover, who had arranged to have Crispin killed.

But he had assured her again, before leaving, that he was well prepared. The Duke of Auburn had battle experience. They were both going armed. And Marlowe would not expect trouble. Nor was his evil the kind to go to work in broad daylight, in plain view, against enemies who recognized him for what he was.

Jane glanced at the clock. The men had no special plan to surprise Marlowe. They intended to visit at the normal calling hour. A duke and an MP would not be turned away.

It was half four. They might be in Marlowe's house already. Which was not a castle—*no matter what he calls it*, Crispin had said.

"Is there a house," Jane said, "that is called a castle? On Park Lane, I mean."

"Goodness." Charlotte laughed. "Among the newer residents? Perhaps so. Who knows what names they give their houses? Do you know, a friend told me of a stockbroker who calls his cottage in Hampton a *manor*. It isn't far from *that* to a castle, I expect."

The tea was bitter, in fact. Jane could not swallow it. She abandoned her cup. "I'm thinking of a"—*particular gentleman called Marlowe*, she almost said, but stopped herself. Crispin had not wanted her involved; he would not thank her for bringing his sister into it, either.

"Go on," Charlotte said, but Jane shook her head.

"I think—I'll go for a walk." She had to channel this dreadful energy somehow. "Will you join me?"

Charlotte cast a squinting glance toward the window. "I'm afraid it looks likely to rain."

"That's all right, I could use the fresh air."

Charlotte studied her for a thoughtful moment. "All right," she said. "Let me just go fetch my pattens. I have a talent for stepping into every puddle."

The door closed behind Charlotte. Stepping . . . castles . . .

Her uncle. Some remark, a long time ago, tossed off to Aunt Mary as Jane stood nearby, invisible, ignored, wholly discounted as always. *A castle, he calls it, no doubt for Udolpho. A proper dungeon, I tell you. Step in the wrong spot, and—* Here he'd drawn a hand across his throat.

How Gothic, Aunt Mary had murmured. *I hope you'll take care.*

Oh, I make sure to watch my step, I promise you.

Her heart hammered. Gothic, indeed. Ridiculous, in fact. A booby-trapped house?

Charlotte came back into the room, breathless, her pattens in hand. "Oh, do you need a pair? I'm sure I can find another—"

"No, no." She felt sure she was making a mistake, that she would end up looking a fool. But on the chance that she was right— "Actually, I have a favor to ask of you. A very peculiar one. Will you come with me to visit my uncle?"

"Your uncle! But I thought—you aren't friends, Jane. Crispin made that clear. I don't think he'd want—"

"That's why I need your help." She took Charlotte's arm, steered her into the hall. "If you're there, he'll behave himself. But I really must speak to him."

"But what a marvelous story," said Daniel Marlowe. Auburn had tendered his card to the butler, who had gone away only for a minute before dispatching a footman to usher them down a hallway done up in gilt and mirroring, into a drawing room that looked modeled after the receiving rooms at Versailles. Amid the ormolu and enamel and silver-and-gold brocade, Marlowe reclined on a chair whose clawed legs boosted him a foot higher than his own height would warrant. A small footstool prevented the indignity of dangling feet. It was all but a throne, and was flanked on either side by tall vases filled with white bluebells.

The servants wore those same flowers pinned to their lapels. It seemed that Marlowe, or one of his men, had been Crispin's nocturnal intruder, the night of the ball.

"Which fantasist may I thank for this amusing invention?" Marlowe asked. "Have you hired Dickens, your grace, to keep you entertained?"

"I thought it a strange tale myself." Auburn had not succumbed to the luxurious invitation of the high-backed settee, but despite his straight posture, he gave every sign of being at ease—save that his tea remained untouched.

So did Crispin's. Unlike Auburn, he did not bother to hold the cup. He wanted his hands free, even though they were two against one in this room. That a man like Marlowe had not found an excuse to bring one of his burly footmen inside with him seemed significant: either a sign of his arrogance, or—the possibility Crispin did not prefer—proof of some hidden surety of his own safety.

"Well, then?" Marlowe tapped his lip with one manicured finger. He was younger than Crispin had expected, a florid blond man in his forties, not beefy so much as solidly, thickly built. His suit looked peculiarly old-fashioned, the sheen of the fabric, the ornate gold embroidery on his waistcoat, suggestive of the lost glamours of eighteenth-century court. "Am I to understand that somehow you were *persuaded* by this tale? Surely, if you had any proof, we would not be having this discussion. But I can't think why you might have called, if all you mean to do is launch accusations." He offered a slight smile. "Not that I am displeased to receive you. I had longed for such august company, of course. But I fear I know my station. A man of humble birth cannot expect to have a duke come calling"—his glance flicked speakingly to Crispin, as though to confirm that, yes, the other visitor did not merit acknowledgment—"without a cause."

"The cause is simple," Auburn said. "We propose a bargain. In exchange for your liberty—"

"Oh no." Marlowe lifted one beringed hand, multiple diamonds flashing in the light from the broad stained-glass window behind him. "If we are to *bargain*, then I should much rather hear it from a man who understands the cost of things. Mr. Burke, you've held your tongue longer than I thought possible. But your expression, sir, is far easier to read than once it was. Are we enemies now, sir? With you, I had hoped to dream of friendship. But it seems our common connection no longer appeals to you. Come now, sir, find your courage; you represent democracy as your profession, you should not let a peer of the realm speak for you."

In fact, Crispin had been making use of the distraction afforded by Auburn to assess the room around them, for something about it struck him as odd. Every surface not crowded with priceless objets d'art winked with mirrors, gilt and brass, and heavy furniture arranged almost haphazardly, like obstacles. These were not decorations, but camouflage. But to what purpose?

"The bargain is simple," he said. "You give us the names of the men whom you have spirited away. You ensure their safe return. And in exchange, you will not be tried." It was a bitter offer. But Marlowe had covered his tracks too neatly. And the lives that hung in the balance might not last the time it would take to uncover the evidence that the law required. For the sakes of Marlowe's victims, justice could wait—or it could find Marlowe in the dark.

"How humane," Marlowe murmured. "But you've miscalculated. If this story of yours held any truth in it, then I would not be the villain, only the villains' tool. The peasant whom great men hire to dispose of each other. And if there are *so* many victims, as you say— why, then there must be just as many villains to match them, men who paid for these disappearances you speak of. Even in a fictional tale, that would not be me. *I* would only be the one who made it possible."

"To hell with this," said Auburn. His fury was cold, murderous; after all, one of these victims was not merely a name to him but a friend.

But when he moved to withdraw his weapon, Crispin

saw the look of startled pleasure that warmed Marlowe's sallow face, and said, "Hold," very softly.

He sensed Auburn's challenging look, but kept his eyes locked on Marlowe. That chair—the arms so broad, the stacked feet—

"The snobbery and condescension of the ruling class," Marlowe said, "bores me very much. I would rest easy knowing you have no true proof, but then, that would require me to believe that justice goes unperverted by influence." His smile twisted. "And as you claim, I myself am proof to the contrary." His rings glimmered as he laid down his hand.

The air hissed. A great swinging ax fell out of the wall, slowing to a stop mere inches from Auburn's nose.

Crispin swore. "Now you have a quandary," Marlowe drawled. "If I say that this meeting is concluded, that I am doing you the favor of forgiving you for your baseless accusations, then of course you'll wish to leave. And the door, of course, stands behind you, some ten paces away. But will you make it there? That is the question. Ah—" His cold eyes fixed on Crispin's hand, which was creeping for his own firearm. "I would not do that, Mr. Burke. We are civilized men. Let us settle it with our wits, this question of your survival."

To hell with it. He met Auburn's eyes, then pulled his weapon.

His chair shuddered under him, tilting. The gun barked, and plaster rained down from the molding over Marlowe's head.

Crispin recovered his balance just in time to catch the creak from above. He threw himself flat, and two knives whizzed over him, landing with a solid thunk in the opposite wall.

Auburn was crouched close to the ground, studying the walls. "Marvelous work," he said flatly. "Not the original design, I'll warrant."

"No, indeed not. The engineer who made this room was one of the first to find his way to Elland." Marlowe smiled gently. "Will you keep crouching like a dog, your grace?"

Auburn lunged, and a wall of blades sprang up between him and Marlowe, singing as they ground to a halt.

Crispin dived for his gun, chambered the next round.

"You may try it," Marlowe said sharply, "but imagine what you'll lose. You'll never know the names of those men, Mr. Burke. For there is no list to find. I made sure of that. And there is no Elland, either. Not where you imagine it to be." He laughed. "What, did you imagine me so stupid to keep the same location chosen by the government? You'll never find it without me."

"So be it," Crispin said, but Auburn made a noise.

"Wait." The duke hissed out a breath. "Burke, he's right. Without him, we may never find—"

"And the men who paid me for my services?" Marlowe shrugged. "Their names—do they not matter, either?"

The door flew open. Crispin pivoted. Mason filled the doorway, sighting down the barrel of a rifle. Auburn cried out—

Too late. A shot blasted through the room. Blood blossomed between Marlowe's eyes. He sagged, then slumped off his throne, toppling onto the barricade of upthrust blades, his eyes glazed.

Blood spattered the floor.

"What in God's name have you done?" Auburn's voice, like death.

Mason lowered the gun. Jane crowded up behind him, her eyes huge and fixed.

"Saved your lives," Mason said, his color high. "You're very welcome, your grace."

"Saved your own neck," Auburn said savagely. "How much did you pay this bastard to fix your problems for you?"

Mason's jaw squared. "All right, then try to find your own damned way out of this room, now that it's armed." He turned, but Jane caught him by the arm.

"You promised," she said hoarsely. "We have a deal. Help them out, step by step, *now*."

Sighing, he turned back. "It's very simple," he said curtly. "Look to the mirrors on either side of the wall. Step only in the patches they reflect, or else you'll be gutted."

CHAPTER TWENTY

Crispin did not take her home that night after all. A man had been killed; the authorities could not be kept out of it now. But a woman could be spared the notoriety that might follow. Jane was bundled back to Charlotte's, left to wait as Crispin and Auburn and her uncle wielded their various degrees of authority to persuade, bully, and intimidate the police into accepting the story they offered.

The story was true, of course. But unbelievable, all the same.

Charlotte understood most of it now. She had listened in horror to Jane and Mason's rapid deliberations. Later, much later, when Crispin had finally walked Jane out of Marlowe's house, returning her to Charlotte, who sat waiting white-faced in the carriage—only then, at last, did Charlotte finally ask what must have been only one of a thousand questions burning through her mind.

"Are you all right, Jane?" she had asked.

And for the first time in memory, Jane had started to cry. *Truly* cry—loud, noisy sobs into Charlotte's shoulder as the carriage rolled forward.

What was she crying for? She could not explain it to Charlotte, much less herself. For family, perhaps, which would always put their concern for her over their curiosity, thinking of her first. Or for fear, perhaps—as she and Mason had forced their way inside Marlowe's house, she had known what she was risking by bringing him there. He had never guessed that Crispin and Auburn would be able to puzzle out who Marlowe was. His fear of Marlowe had been promptly overshadowed by his fear of what Marlowe might tell them. She had known that she was not asking for his help in saving Crispin as much as she was asking him to put an end to Marlowe's threat.

Perhaps she wept for horror, then—she'd had a hand in a man's death, and that was a weighty and grave thing indeed, though she would have done no differently if given a chance to repeat this terrible day.

And maybe her tears were also owed to exhaustion. As Charlotte helped her inside, up the stairs and into bed, she felt suddenly so weary. It seemed these last weeks had been one endless sprint, dodging from one surprise only to encounter another, each more baffling, the first and original mystery birthing a dozen more, and meanwhile, herself more and more a stranger. Her wants, her desires, becoming clear evidence that she had never known herself at all.

She did not want to run. She did not want freedom. She wanted to be here, a true sister to Charlotte, waiting in this bed for her husband to come home.

She slept, long and deeply. And when her eyes opened again, to the clock chiming three, the blackness at the windows proved the day was over.

A dark shape moved at her side, sat slowly on the bed. "You're awake," Crispin said, his voice rough.

She moved over for him without thinking. His exhaustion was all she heard. But he did not lie down next to her. His hand found hers atop the counterpane. He was reaching for her. Lifting her hand to his mouth.

She had not known she expected his anger until she felt the expectation dissolve under the great balm of her relief.

"I didn't know what else to do," she said. "After you left—you mentioned a castle—I realized that Marlowe was no ordinary man. That my uncle had spoken once of that house—"

"I know." He sounded peaceful. "Mason explained it. He explained, too, what you offered him in exchange for his help."

"He might have come anyway." She made herself say it. "I knew he would see an opportunity for himself. He was too frightened of Marlowe to approach him single-handedly. But I knew he would kill him, Crispin, if given the chance."

He made no reply. But he was still holding her hand to his lips, and she felt the force of his long exhalation.

"It wasn't that I didn't trust you," she said. "Only . . . I could not afford to risk you."

"Ah." Now he kissed her fingers again, then lowered them to the counterpane, his thumb setting up a slow, gentle stroke over her knuckles. "For that alone," he said quietly, "I would thank your uncle. I am glad to hear that, Jane. I cannot tell you how much."

Another pause. She did not feel awkward, precisely, but there was some absence between them, of a natural rhythm, of rapport. It unsettled her, despite the reassurance in his words. She sat up, wishing she could see him in the darkness. "What happened, after I left?"

"What you might have predicted," he said. "The sight of that room, all those blades unsheathed, gave the inspector a story to dine on for months. He sent for his supervisor then, who did not wish to let us search the rest of the house. I expect they feared another trick room, and a dead duke and a dead MP besides. Harder to finesse that for the press, after all. And Mason kept making dire predictions of trapdoors and the like— afraid of what we'd find, no doubt. But as it turns out, Marlowe told the truth. He'd covered his tracks very neatly. Not a scrap of paper in that house to prove the story was true. I suppose we should be grateful for all the blades—otherwise, it would have looked like we murdered him for no cause."

"Then . . . there is no hope for Lockwood. And the others."

He sighed. "Auburn has put a search into motion. It will take a week for the instructions to reach Australia—Marlowe said that his Elland was not the same as the government's. We'll find out soon enough. If he was telling the truth . . ." He paused. "It's a very large place. Elland will be the proverbial needle in the haystack."

"But the letter, Crispin. Do you remember? The letter said the place was in revolt."

"I'm not sure that's a comfort," he said at length. "Revolts tend to get crushed."

"We'll help with the search." She took hold of his

arm. "Half my fortune still leaves a good deal for private investigators, for a fleet of ships to go looking—"

"Jane." His laughter was soft. "Do you really think I mean to let you honor your promise to Mason? He'll not have your money. Nor will he harm a hair on your head, no matter how great his debts. Not on a cold day in hell."

"But . . . I promised him."

"So you did." His mouth found hers in the dark. "Let me be your villain," he whispered.

Pleasure rippled through her. Her very scalp seemed to relax, her cheeks to warm as she kissed him back. But then, after a moment, he eased back from her. "I said I would take you home. Shall we go?"

"Now? So late? Charlotte will wonder—"

"Let her wonder," he said. "It is far too late, Jane. There is something I should have shown you long before now. Will you come see it?"

Outside, a light rain was falling. In the light of the streetlamps, the raindrops glittered and the puddles winked. Jane sat close to Crispin, warm and drowsy beneath the lap blanket he'd tucked around her after drawing her against his chest. Home, he'd said to the coachman.

"We're still not married," she said softly.

"One problem at a time," he said, and kissed her temple. Then, when they drew to a stop, he lifted her and carried her up the short walkway into the house.

He carried her straight through the entry hall, a

bleary-eyed Cusworth looking on with a valiant effort at impassivity. She did not even feel embarrassed. She put her arms around Crispin's shoulders, feeling strangely childlike. Feeling . . . safe.

She expected him to ascend the stairs. Instead, he carried her into the study, where he set her down on the leather sofa. "Just a moment," he said as he turned up the gaslights. Then he knocked three books from the shelves and pulled the hidden lever.

She sat up, clutching the lap blanket around her. The shelf creaked open, an unsettling sound, the sound of bones grinding together. Old skeletons best left buried. Crispin disappeared inside the secret room, and she swallowed the urge to call him back. To tell him that whatever he had found, he did not need to show it to her. Let the past go. That was the only way to move forward.

When he stepped back out, he held a cloth-bound bundle. She spoke before he could open it.

"Don't," she said. "Whatever it is—everything in that room is finished now."

He set the bundle on the carpet before her, then knelt in front of it. "That isn't how it works," he said gently. "If we turn our backs on everything that came before, on the people we were, then they will haunt us, Jane. Honesty is the way forward."

She hesitated. "I *have* been honest with you. You know all of it now. And you—"

"Honesty is my aim here." Still kneeling before her, he laid his hand over hers. "All of the things you want for yourself—the chance to change the world, to do good with the blessings that life has offered you—I also want those same things for myself. But for that very reason, I *can't* give up on what we found in that room. Do you understand?" He paused, his gaze searching. "I am done with the tactics of intimidation—the bribery, the bullying, the corruption. But I will not disown the ambitions, Jane. After all, the ability to do good depends on the *power* to do good. And I still mean to pursue that power."

She swallowed. "You . . . still want the prime ministership."

"Yes," he said steadily. "But not for the sake of power itself. Rather, for the chance to *use* that power for good. To ensure, as you once said, that the machine of progress does not crush those most desperate for its boons. And I would rely on you"—his grip tightened—"to keep my eyes fixed on those who need our help the most."

Our help. He painted a riveting picture. But power . . . "Power corrupts," she whispered. "And you are a man . . . you *were* a man . . ." *Who could not resist its temptations.*

"It's all right," he said with a wry smile. "Speak your doubts. Honesty also means acknowledging whence we came—and understanding it, too."

She cleared her throat, suddenly anxious to have her fears quelled, even if only by empty words. "But you have changed. And so have I. Haven't we? That's the only reason we're here together. The reason I . . ." Her throat closed. *Say it. Don't be cowardly.* "I love you, Crispin." His gaze darkened, his mouth softening, but she continued quickly, before he could interrupt her. "And I want to stay with you. I want to be your wife. I

believe you; I believe that you're different, that you will
be incorruptible now."

"Do you really?"

"Yes!"

His laugh made a gentle mockery of her. He lifted
her hand to his mouth and kissed it. "If only you were
so naïve. But I think you have a few small doubts left,
darling."

She yanked her hand free, suddenly furious. Why
could he not simply accept her word? "I said I believe
you. I'm done with the past!" She wanted so desperately
to be done with it!

"But you aren't done," he said evenly. "Nor am I—
not until we, both of us, can look at it together and
see the same thing. I could tell you now that I love you
as well . . ."

Could tell her? A terrible pain pinched in her chest.
"*Could* tell me?"

She had not meant to squawk. She clapped a hand
over her mouth, eyes wide, and he laughed. He laughed!

"Yes, well, I do," he said, and retrieved her hand,
playing with her fingers. "But when I say I love you,
Jane, that isn't a sign of how I've changed. It isn't a mark
of some radical break from the man I once was. If it
were, how could you ever trust anything that I say to
you now? A man cannot alter his very nature. But he
can awaken to a better aspect of himself. That is what I
mean for you to understand."

She could not let go of his hand. She gripped it
fiercely, desperately. Enough of the man he'd been! She
wanted to hear more from the man before her. "Say it
again," she demanded. "That you . . . love me."

"Repeatedly," he said. "Very soon. But first, do have a look at this."

He opened the canvas and unfurled the object within.

It was her needlepoint.

Amazement rolled through her. "It . . ." The needle-point was half-burned, the colors sooty and dull. But the fire hadn't destroyed more than half of it. There stood her uncle, trampling on his poorest constituents. And there, at his elbow, was Crispin as the devil, his horns emerging distinctly from the smoke of hellfire behind him.

"How on earth," she whispered, "did you get this?"

"I took it from the fireplace that same night," he said. "After I saw you safely into the house through the garden. I walked in the front door and went to the drawing room to retrieve it."

"And you saved it," she said.

"And I saved it."

"But . . . why?"

"Because I couldn't let it burn," he said. "It was worth coveting. It was clever and sharp and devastating, all the things that you pretended not to be. But I was already well on the road to being devastated by you." He leaned in to kiss her. "Even then," he murmured. "No great break, Miss Mason. Even that night, I was on the road to loving you already. And on the road to being a better man as well, for the sake of deserving you."

His mouth, for a long moment, took all her attention. He came onto the couch with her, and she climbed into his lap, dazed and flush with the miracle, with the proof that faith should not require, but that an imperfect woman might need, regardless.

And she had it. She closed her eyes, but the sight of the burned embroidery remained with her. She smelled smoke as she kissed him. Not sulfur, but the sweet promise of warmth on cold nights, a fire in the hearth, and his arms around her.

At last, her lungs protested, and she eased back, gasping. "Miss Mason, indeed. I don't care what the government says—"

"Yes, that's the last task on my list." Crispin kissed her nose. "Will you marry me, Jane?"

It was two months later, a week after the close of Parliament, that the cable reached them. The telegram had been received in Gibraltar and then misplaced by a porter who apologized repeatedly, breathlessly, to Crispin, his face reddening by the syllable. He had glanced over Crispin's shoulder just once, and now was doing a manful job of pretending never to have noticed Jane sitting on the cabin balcony. The suite was a spacious maze of five rooms, certainly large enough for two, but it was registered only to Mr. Burke. Besides, had it been the size of a palace, the porter still would have been shocked to find a woman in it—much less Miss Mason, who had her own equally handsome suite on the floor above!

"Thank you," Crispin said, pressing a coin into the boy's hand and gently extracting the cable from it. "I was also hoping for a word from the captain. I had put in a special request . . ."

"Oh, yes, sir!" The boy snapped to attention. "He relays his congratulations, sir, and expects to meet you . . ." The boy trailed off, his eyes rounding; boldly now he looked at Jane again, and began to grin. "He hopes to see you at the bow at a quarter to four, sir."

"Very good," Crispin said. "That's worth another coin, I think."

The boy beamed, clutching his bounty to his chest and bowing low as he backed out of the doorway.

Jane came inside, and Crispin paused to admire her before breaking open the envelope. The brisk sea breeze was the only lady's maid she needed. It had teased the curls free of her chignon, arranging them in a wild halo around her newly freckled face. Her cheeks glowed. "News?" she asked.

"Overdue news," he said. "The cable was sent two days ago."

She came to his side to read over his shoulder, gasping once. "But that's . . ."

"A miracle," he said softly. The telegram was from Auburn. "Or . . . God forbid, false hope."

Jane took the cable from him, sitting down and smoothing it out on the surface of the cane table. "Singapore," she said. "Then Calcutta. Lockwood would be making his way west."

"Making his way home." He sat down beside her. "Assuming that it is Lockwood, and not an impostor."

"But to take out a line of credit at a bank, someone would need to vouch for him," Jane said. "Someone who knows him."

He nodded. "Plenty of Englishmen in both those cities."

"The timing, though . . ." She paused. "Or—" Their eyes met. "'Elland in revolt,'" she quoted softly. "Perhaps it makes sense."

"The mutiny succeeded."

But her flush of pleasure faded into a troubled frown. "What a strange journey it must be. If it really *is* Lockwood. Escaped after so long . . . plunged back into the world . . . So alone."

"I never knew the man," Crispin said with a shrug. "But I've heard tales of him. He has the devil's own charm, they say. So he won't be alone for long."

"But three years a prisoner." She bit her lip. "A man might survive that. But his charm . . . I think not."

For the first time in months, the silence between them felt heavy and fraught. Crispin knew where her thoughts had gone, for his followed exactly. Three years unjustly imprisoned—who could say what Lockwood had become?

If his westward route was any indication, England would soon find out.

Crispin and Jane would not be there to greet him, however. Crispin had fulfilled his parliamentary duties; had spent the spring working with Jane to build a new coalition of support in the Commons. He had also spent long evenings with his family, Jane coming to know them almost better than he did, for no jagged history lay between them requiring careful maneuvering and slow amends. And the nights . . . ah, the nights. He had not wasted those, either.

He gently took the telegram from her. The open door to the bedroom called like an invitation. But while the sky behind her was a bright, cloudless blue, it was well into the afternoon now, closing hard on a quarter to four.

This afternoon had been long in coming. The captain

of a British vessel had every authority to marry British subjects, and no cause or call to consult the General Register to make sure the couple was not already husband and wife in the eyes of the law.

But this solemn mood was not what they would carry with them to meet the captain.

"Are you pleased," he said, "with the destination?"

Jane smiled at him. "You cheated and consulted the schedules before we went to the docks. Didn't you?"

"Such suspicion," he murmured. She was right, but not even on his deathbed would he admit it. "One might think you didn't trust your husband."

"Well, that would be foolish," she said just as softly.

"Then it's fate you suspect? My betrothed is a cynic."

Laughter tugged at her lips. "What an ingrate that would make me," she said, "when fate brought me to you."

He could not watch her fight laughter without wanting to coax it free. Every effort she took to restrain herself, to temper her opinions and watch her words, seemed now like an unbearable provocation to him. Freedom in all regards: that was what he desired for her. He nipped her ear, and her laughter finally spilled out. He put his face into her hair and breathed in deeply of lavender and the salt of the sea.

"We should go," he murmured. "The captain will be waiting."

"Oh—my hair," she said, her hand fluttering up to feel what the wind had wrought. "I'll just go dress—"

"You'll go exactly as you are." He caught her hand to draw her to her feet. "You'll set a new trend in hairstyles, and tell everyone in New York that this is how London beauties prefer it."

She grinned up at him. "I don't think that will convince anybody. But very well. Let the captain be scandalized. So long as that doesn't keep him from marrying us."

"What's a marriage at sea without a little scandal?" As she ducked and protested, he pulled the rest of her pins free. She was laughing again as he led her out the door.

Explore the history of desire with bestselling
historical romance from Pocket Books!

More *sizzling* historical romance from Pocket Books!

Pick up or download your copies today!

XOXOAfterDark.com